Praise for Susan

"Is it possible that you are a born writer? There is ample evidence. Don't stop." - DICK CAVETT

"You're a beautiful and brainy young woman in the 60s, desperately seeking Mr. Right, but tragically picking a series of Mr. Wrongs, clawing your way up the ladder in a hot Manhattan ad agency from secretary to copywriter so you can afford a shrink to help you figure out why you can only love guys who reject you and reject guys who love you. You're Ali Abrams and you're the protagonist of *Water Baby,* a poignantly funny new novel by Susan Israelson, and people are going to be frantically turning the pages to find out what happens to you." - DAN GREENBURG

"Susan Israelson's *Water Baby* is a splash of a debut -- a buoyant personal story in which the reader can be happily immersed. Dive in!" - NICOLAS DELBANCO

ALSO BY SUSAN ISRAELSON

Lovesick, the Marilyn Syndrome
The Marilyn Syndrome
with Elizabeth Macavoy, Ph.D.

Water Baby

Water Baby

A NOVEL

Susan Israelson

ISBN: 0999004301
ISBN 13: 9780999004302
Library of Congress Control Number: 2017908220
Susan Israelson, East Hampton, NY

To Dad, fishing in heaven

"Amo ergo sum."
I love therefore I am.

— Miguel de Unamuno, *Niebla*

Prologue

I dove deeper into the sapphire sea, eyes wide open, caressed by the soft, sensual water. Safe. The ocean was my soul mate, best friend. Home. We were one.

I stroked till I touched the sandy bottom, exhaled an ocean breath of bubbles, shimmied and scissor kicked to the surface. I swam towards the horizon, did a front dolphin, floated on my back with water thoughts the while.

I started to swim in Mother's belly. A natural. Pulling a stuck drawer disrupted. Her water bag broke and out I tumbled feet first, a month too soon – the first and last time I was either early or underweight.

Didn't dare get back in till I was four, when I started to swim in the bay, calmer, more predictable than the ocean. The water tasted funny. Fishy.

I remembered the big race from the bay dock when I was twelve. Backstroke. I won a gold medal that shone on my flat chest but still lost -- no glory, respect or appreciation. Mother criticized, I hadn't swum in a straight-line wasted time. Dad was indifferent, talking politics with the Mayor ignoring me.

Lakes felt odd, harder to float. The one at camp where I learned the rest of the strokes and how to high dive had a gunky, muddy bottom. In high school, the smell of chlorine in the pool invaded my nose, eyes, forced me to wear goggles while doing laps and laps and laps on the swimming team. At college came water ballet and synchronized swimming.

I did better in the sea, could fly. Free. Never wanted to get out.

1

Sapphire Eyes

"If we miss the boat, goddammit, it's your fault," warned Dad as he floored the pedal of his prized '55 Buick convertible to 70 in the slow zone known as a speed trap. It was the final stretch of the race to make the 5:10 Ocean Beach ferry, the schedule like Moses' Law; we were going to make it. Period. No matter what. If the police stopped us, Dad was ticket-proof, magistrate's shield nesting cozily under his driver's license. Nervous, jerky -- worse, dangerous, inveterate lane-shifter without signals, light-jumper, tailgater, he was the worst driver in the world. I held my breath, shut my eyes crossed my fingers. Guilty.

As we blew through Bay Shore, Maple Avenue's mansions blurred by on the way to the Great South Bay. We took the last turn on two wheels as the valiant Century, a beauty -- black and chrome, red leather interiors, four portholes, white walls -- galloped full throttle to the finish line. We skidded to an abrupt halt at the Ocean Beach ferry, a dock full of frenzy.

Laden-down parents trying to keep track of their children, pets and belongings, converged in a last ditch attempt to board. We unloaded bags and cartons, counted, stowed them in a frantic pace, found a parking space. A miracle. I thanked Buddha, Mohammed, Zeus, Christ, Allah and Jehovah; I'd just finished a course in comparative religion at Smith. As the engines began to rev we sprinted the 200 feet back and made it -- the usual, an anxious journey.

Mea culpa. Over-packing had done it. And indecision. I'd taxied home to 88st Street and Park from Dad's office, Madison at 43rd, plenty of time for a round trip. I'd throw a few things into a suitcase, get the car from the garage then pick Dad up back in Midtown. All I really needed for the weekend was a bathing suit for day and an "in case" outfit for night; so far, no big plans. The trouble started when I couldn't make up my mind which "in case" things to take. I wanted to wear white to show off my tan, legal after Decoration Day weekend, according to Mother, the fashion maven. Could I get into the white linen Bermudas? I'd gained a few pounds during finals a few weeks ago, needed to go on yet another diet. Why wasn't I naturally thin? The white shirt had a spot. I'd bring it anyway, Mother, "the white glove," could get anything out with some magical potion that included a Q-tip and ammonia. Or was it Clorox? If she ever tired of being a housewife, she could go into the laundry business. Not even the yellow of age on white dared elude her potent formulations.

Was a Shetland cardigan warm enough for nights that always got cold? Beige or red? The black letter sweater or Dartmouth green? I broke out into the cold sweat accompanying decision-making desperate, I'd take everything. Everything wouldn't fit into one bag; I now needed two. I began to beat myself up, had enough clothes for two summers, let alone two days -- was hopelessly late. There'd be hell to pay. Dad would be mad, I mean angry, sorry, Mother, dogs are mad, people, angry. Anxiety made me hungry. I dove into our ice box, inspected for chocolate, struck out, settled on Oreos from the bread box that I scarfed down, minutes ticking away, upset. I loved Dad yet had done it again. Indecision plus lateness equals angst and guilt, the constant equation of my 20 years.

He was furious. Nervousness ran in the family, his side. Waiting made it worse. An hour's worth of silence filled the car with devastating noise. Would or wouldn't we make it, a noose hanging over my head. Dad was driving out to the island to escape the pressures of his overworked week. Oh God, I'd created more.

I'd just finished my own harrowing first week as receptionist-switchboard operator-typist at Dad's labor law firm. He represented teachers, elevator operators, window-washers, buttonholers, gravediggers and the Rockettes; mediator and arbitrator in New York, a judge in Ocean Beach. I'd been bored-depressed-humiliated. How could someone so smart be stuck with a job for which a moron was overqualified? Simple. No one else would hire me, since I was off to Paris in July as a summer exchange student -- a last ditch attempt to *parler Français.* I needed to make spending money not wanting to get stuck in the world's greatest shopping mecca without enough *argent.* The Big Fact was that Dad was tight.

I'd started French as a freshman. I was lazy and bored by endless repetition, didn't study; my good ear and accent did not make up for bad grammar. Who could spell or write it? *Impossible,* much harder than Spanish, which I read, wrote and spoke like Dad, *gracias* to his Argentine mother, Georgiana. She'd traveled from Buenos Aires to Boston at 15, 16, 17 or 18 -- notorious for lying about her age, for an arranged marriage to grandfather Isaac from Riga. They'd settled in Brooklyn, had five children, four girls then finally a boy.

Grandpa, a pharmacist, died when Dad was eight, well remembered -- a good guy. Georgiana on the other hand had a bad rep, or rap. Fortyish, give or take, when widowed, restless, a firebrand and a man-eater, still a beauty, the chase was on. She passed off her older daughters as younger sisters and preyed on my poor aunt's boyfriends and husbands, an abortionist in tow. No love lost there. Surrounded and outnumbered by women, Dad never said a word. He hid his feelings. Mother detested Georgiana, to put it mildly. 'She dyed her hair.' the crime. Years later I'd write the headline, "I'll never go gray," as a copywriter for Clairol. Glad you never did, Grandma.

Georgiana passed when I was two. The date of her demise was engraved on her tombstone but no date of birth. Her vanity, selfishness, hot temperament, and cold heart would set the stage for my life. A direct descendent of damage.

I learned clock-watching the first day on the job and during the next four waged war against the red and yellow spaghetti switchboard. Witchboard. Dad's trusted secretary Gloria, ever ready for dictation with spiral steno pad in hand, sharpened yellow Eberhard Faber #1 over her ear, tried to teach me. I couldn't get the hang of it, mystified, my mechanical gene M.I.A. When a call came in you were supposed to take a piece of yellow or red spaghetti out of one hole, plug it into another, pull a switch, remember where it came from, and at the same time keep track of the other wires, holes and lights. Which was which? Charlie Chaplin stuck in the middle of machinery in *Modern Times* came to mind. I sabotaged fifty percent of all incoming and outgoing calls, cut everyone off, created surprise conference calls.

My typing was worse, the old two finger hunt-and-peck system a disaster. Then, too, the subject matter was stultifying, legalese in briefs that were too long: The party of the first part heretofore, thereafter and in the hereafter shall be known as the lingo jingo party, etc. etc. I did nothing right or on time. A boss's daughter, I wouldn't get fired. Nepotism Saves. Just one week of skyscraper suffocation trapped in a sweltering city learning skills I resented turned me into a blasphemous idiot, oh God, a telephone operator *@i/)**&?T$*@rX! *Mierda. Merde.* Shit. Smithie Strikes Out.

Dad kibitzed with Jack, his fishing crony, laughing, a different person from the one in the car, relaxed at last. Charming. Handsome. A Cary Grant look-alike. Dad I'm sorry, you don't deserve it, I thought, the guilt building.

I worked my way to the open bow of the crowded, covered boat to get some fresh air, ran a gamut of "Hello," "How's college?" and "Look how thin you are." True. I'd been tubby, but two months in Mexico City at 17, after graduation, living with a Spanish family, their maids, and amoebas, and doing the Aztec two-step had done it. I could've drawn a map of every bathroom in the city by the time I was through dropping twenty pounds, which I'd kept off more or less. I'd stopped growing at fifteen, having reached the respectable height of 5'6." Everyone had known me since I was a little girl, our family old timers on the island.

Mother, as a teenager at the Cape heard that Fire Island had a beautiful, white sandy beach perfect for sunbathing. Dad remembered going fishing with his father as a boy to catch bluefish, a ferry ride across from Patchogue. Blues were bad news -- dark, oily scavengers that ate up all the good white fish like striped bass. There was a bounty on their heads, a half-cent each, a little money, a big fight.

At first they'd rented a fisherman's shack in Ocean Beach on the cheap, $200 for three months. There was no heat, light or electricity, an icebox, gas stove, kerosene lamps and a weathered wood wagon for transportation. It was called 'Sea Shells.' Houses on the island were known by their names: 'The Gildered Cage' -- The Gilder family; 'Just Wright' or 'All Wrong' depending, Buck Wright, head of the lifeguards; 'Gloca Nora', Abbot and Nora Copland; 'Witt's End', the Witts and so on, all part of the island's charm. Dad worked in town during the week, came out weekends. They managed, pioneers separated from progress and reality.

My first Fire Island memory was going to get ice with Dad down at the dock. I watched a half-naked man with massive muscles wallop an ice mountain, saw off a huge cube, pick it up with pincers and plant it on our wagon, fascinated by his physique. This primordial sexual glimmer was ineluctably imprinted into my two-and-a-half-year-old psyche. The mammoth muscle man-with-the-gong slowly striking the brass cymbal twice, featured trademark of J. Arthur Rank films later furthered my musclemania. When I landed a job doing publicity for Arnold Schwarzenegger in the film *Pumping Iron,* I was agog, looked but never touched -- he *was* my client.

After the Japanese attacked Pearl Harbor, fearful that Fire Island was too dangerous or vulnerable we went to Loch Arbour, a New Jersey beach near the amusement park in Deal. We returned in the summer of '45 after we'd won the war and it was safe.

The many unfamiliar faces on the ferry had to be "groupers," not the fish, a new word. Groupers, n. a large group of unrelated people that get together to rent shares for the summer. They were mostly "garmentos," n. B and Ts, (Bridge and Tunnel) workers in the garment center, 39th and Broadway. They were unwelcome in Ocean Beach, a family community. Watch out, there goes the neighborhood.

I put my head into the wind to smell the languid fishiness of the Great South Bay and purge myself of the worst week of my life. Hyperbole helps. We puttered in the harbor along the maze-like canals that led to the Great South Bay, past the Point O' Woods ferry, the Saltaire ferry, a sign proclaiming "Fresh Killies" -- tiny fish used for chumming, and Gil Clarke's, the best seafood restaurant in Bay Shore. If only I hadn't been late, we would've had time to stop for a half-dozen clams on the half shell. I pictured Gil, an enormous man, big fingers delicately shucking small

Cherrystones with a surgeon's slice, all the while exchanging fish stories. I could've killed for an oversized piece of chocolate cream pie.

The Margaret was one of Captain Robinson's fleet of prohibition rumrunners converted to ferry service, sleek, fast, dark green wood, 60 feet stem to stern. The engine roared as we left the harbor, entered the bay and shifted to full speed. A clear day, I could see land seven miles across, the exclamation point to the west was the black and white striped Fire Island lighthouse; the fat dot in the middle was the Ocean Beach water tower. On a foggy day it seemed like you were traveling to nowhere.

The bay bustled with traffic as ferries en route to Fair Harbor, Saltaire or Kismet at the western end vied for channel space. A hundred fishing hopefuls, one-man outboards, big charters, fifty lines out, clustered. Seagulls circled and squawked over the lucky ones, gobbling up castaways. I watched fascinated as clammers stood on their odd flat boats, making scissor motions with their rakes, loosening and scooping up invisible Little Necks, Cherrystones and Quahogs stuck in the mud at the bottom. An occasional sailboat arched its sails. The boat rode so low in the water I could put my hand out and touch the bay. I tasted it. Salty.

We zigzagged through snippets of uninhabited islands all the way to the western tip before doubling back, impatient at our progress -- not fast enough, gigantic waste of time. If the Great South Bay had been deeper than a foot outside the channel, we could have gone straight across to Ocean Beach in twenty minutes.

I spotted a big wave coming at us from the wake of the Point O' Woods ferry we were racing, no love lost between the two communities; they had a locked, iron chain fence, no Jews allowed. I turned to escape the wave but no such luck. Soaked. I hoped that nobody had noticed. I looked up to check right into a pair of staring, sparkling eyes. Sapphires, July ocean color, they belonged to the most handsome man I'd ever seen, thick blonde hair and a slightly shy attitude as if he was embarrassed for me, or was I projecting? The bottom dropped out of my stomach. Awestruck I turned away, unable to deal with direct eye contact, unsteady. When I looked back he was gone. Had I imagined him? A mirage? As we neared Ocean Beach I prayed he'd appear again. He didn't. I looked around wildly to no avail as I moved back to join Dad. We docked, only fifty miles from New York -- it felt like fifty thousand.

"Wagon, wagon who needs a wagon?" cried the assembled village kids hawking their transportation service -- the *modus operandi* of the carless community. How else could you transport groceries, baggage and small children?

"Wagon ma'am?" Oh God I was a 'ma'am'.

Mother waited with ours. I'd painted it black with our last name Abrams, in white, the outline of a fish in blue, a sometime artist, painting stones and shells -- so far. She couldn't whistle, trilled a family call. "Brrrrrt." She looked like an Indian, as did we all. Short, good figure, the olive skin that ran in the family, sun worship the only religion we'd ever practice. Mother was stylish, dressing 'right' very important, on full-time fashion patrol. A serious shopper, bargains her thing, she'd cut her teeth in her teens at Filene's Basement in Boston. Today she was dressed à la Fire Island, barefoot -- no one wore shoes, black bathing suit, white pleated Guayabero jacket, Mexican straw hat, emblems of her ongoing affair with the sun. Mother and Dad vacationed in Key West, Cuba, Acapulco, the Caribbean, leaving Billy and me behind -- out in the cold.

She had many skills, mothering not one of them. To her it was a daily chore -- nurturing unnatural. Our relationship was rocky, adversarial. I was afraid of her. She: Tough with a capital T, stern, a no nonsense New Englander. Me: soft, out of focus, up and down, emotional, daydreamer -- procrastinator. I was always doing something wrong *i.e.*, not her way. She was Dad's mouthpiece, the house disciplinarian in charge of manners and morals with total control -- Dad too busy for everyday family matters. The troubles we'd had since I'd been home were the usual, 'Why do you sleep so late? You're going to sleep your life away.' They all got up early. But I, the odd one out, knew that the best part of the day was the night. The other Problem with a capital P was that I was a messaholic living in a house of neatniks; not to mention that she was a meanie, out to get me, a big chip implanted on her small shoulder.

Mother took on a no prisoners, Marine drill sergeant voice threatening, "Why can't you keep your room neat? What man will marry you if he looks in your drawers, even worse, your closet? Can't you keep it straight?" No, I couldn't.

I wondered if she ever got bored, out at the island just with Billy -- sixteen, running around getting into trouble with his gang, not much company. No. Mother was independent no surprise that Emerson's "Self-Reliance" was her all-time favorite. She and other married, 'week widows', whose husbands stayed in town Sunday night till Friday afternoon, went to quaint Cherry Grove, six miles east by beach taxi, danced with 'the boys', who weren't allowed to dance together. Though most of the communities were heterosexual, Fire Island was infamous for the homosexuals in the Grove and Fire Island Pines.

"Hi." Mother kissed Dad on the lips, gave me the loud smack in the ear, 'the deafener.' "You're a mess, what happened to your hair?" as always quick to criticize.

"Soaked by a wave," on the defensive my back up, no hug, spirits down.

"How was your week, Mike?"

"Fine. Just fine." Dad cut Mother short, didn't like bringing the office home.

"How was yours?" She turned to me.

"Great." I hoped I sounded excited.

"Tell me about the switchboard?" A loaded question, had Dad told her?

"I haven't quite got the hang of it yet, but I will. Hope you don't mind, I'm going to run ahead so I can get a swim in before dinner." Had to escape the inquisition.

"Go along now." Her highness granted me permission.

I kicked off my high heels the prisons of my always too wide for a B shoe width -- they didn't make fashionable shoes for C or D feet, and unfastened my stockings. Unfettered and unbound, I wondered how the Chinese women of yore ever made it through life. I passed Dana Wallace Photographer, the chronicler of Ocean Beach's youth -- every family had a black and white picture taken by him of their kids posed on the dunes. I turned right on Ocean Breeze, passed De Pisa, a dress shop on our corner, waved to Hertzl the owner, petted Beauregard, his ever mournful, bloodshot-eyed Bassett hound moored outside.

The fresh scrub pine perfume became saltier as I neared our home, '*Sans Souci*' (without worry), no puns with Abrams. There at last, a barn-red Monopoly hotel suspended on stilts surrounded by sand, three houses away from the ocean -- by Ocean Beach standards private. They'd bought it for eleven grand in '50 after five years of rentals, Dad's practice doing better. I raced up the ramp, knelt and scrambled for the key under the second board. Mother had taken to locking it lately, her logic irrefutable, 'Why should we trust those groupers? We don't know them or where they come from." Times were changing, not to my liking.

I tossed off my serious secretary uniform -- crisp white shirt and straight black skirt, wiggled out of the girdle that sustained my stockings, pulled on a bathing suit, and grabbed a beach towel. I raced down the wooden ramp, up the sidewalk and wooden stairs to the landing. Two minutes. The wide white beach stretched to infinity; high dunes crowned by stubborn beach grass; glistening poison ivy patches punctuated with plump red beach plums, a picture postcard from paradise. I inhaled the strong salt sea air free from car fumes intoxicated by its purity.

"Hello beach. Hello ocean. My friends I'm back." The sea, sparkling magnet, beckoned, the water shimmered, the sand opalescent, bathed in six o'clock light -- magic hour. I stood over the crest of the dune poised in reverence... reverie. "Shall I write thee an ode, oh, Atlantic? I'm indentured to thee for the peace of mind thou bringest, need thee for calm, clarity, thy daughter besmirched by a week of hurry, mistakes, deadlines, lateness and guilt. Purify me."

"Come in. Come in. Come play with me. Hurry up. What are you waiting for?"

I climbed down the stairs, felt the cool grains of sand tickle my feet, stooped over, touched the ocean with my fingers, anointed face, temples and back of my neck. It felt chilly but not freezing... a big difference. I never tired of my satin sea -- it kept changing, inconsistent unable to make up its mind. Just like me. No sameness or patterns, many moods: one day, sapphire blue with angry whitecaps; the next turquoise, tranquil. My ocean caressed me when it was calm, challenged me when it was rough. I never knew what to expect, never bored, loved being in and under.

A wave arched, curled, broke, the translucent blue transformed instantly into soft downy foam licked my feet, lapped around them and receded. What makes waves? It was a question I'd considered for twenty years. The moon, of course. I pictured the man in the moon, puffed golden cheeks blowing water into a wave. After it crested and crashed, he inhaled mightily drawing it back in. I looked up at the sky and found the white day moon. "Ocean breathing must be tiring. No wonder you're so pale."

The next wave started to break too close, going to get wet. "Oh, no. Not till I'm used to you." I raced backwards to escape. An old hand at 'waiting and wading,' my method of getting in allowed me to stay much longer than showoffs who ran, took a splashy dive followed by the invariable big scream, the inevitable hasty retreat. My feet sank into the wet sand and disappeared. Hundreds of tiny holes popped open. I dug into one. Nobody home. Two sandpipers scurried by leaving V tracks behind them. A ship crawled across the horizon. The water didn't seem so cold anymore.

"Here I come, ready or not." I spotted the perfect wave and dove under the curl, tucking my feet up so that no part could catch me. I felt it crash over my head, surfaced. Another was ready to break. Instead of ducking I swam to the top of the crest suspended in mid air for an instant before I dropped back in the water. It felt like flying. I spotted a rider and raced to get in position.

"Go!"

I started kicking with all my might just as the wave began to arch, then had a second of fear. "Is my timing right? Am I going to get creamed? Do I have it? Yes? No? Yeeesss!" Its force propelled me forward, on top of the water and the world, thrilled. I washed up on the beach, laughed, thought again about the man from the ferry and his ocean eyes.

I was late for seven o'clock dinner. Billy was early; I was slow to his fast, opposites. The skinny runt had filled out, become, I had to admit, handsome. He'd had a growth spurt last year, claimed he was six feet, exaggerating as usual. You'd have thought he was Samson the way he fussed with his hair

-- an Elvis pompadour, Billy a big fan. This summer he was a lifeguard in Seaview, the next community east. He boasted constantly that he was king of the beach. He'd started off in the world a crybaby and had progressed to a pest. Our sibling rivalry was intense. We competed over everything -- friends: the vote was out; tennis, now he was bigger, stronger I'd lose; grades: I was winning, an A student, had gotten into Smith, one of the Seven Sisters, all-women equivalent of the Ivy League despite their Jewish quota. Billy bolted his food down in three gobbles and sat twitching until Dad excused him from the table.

Time to drop the bomb.

"I'm meeting Becker and we're going 'downtown'." I stopped breathing, anticipating Mother's cross-examination.

"Where?"

"Bayview."

"That new bar, just the two of you without dates? How's it going to look? Nice girls don't do that, people will think you're cruising." she snarled. Dad didn't say a word as usual.

"Mother, I hate to remind you but I'm 20, on my way to Paris alone. I was alone in Mexico City three summers ago, alone at Harvard Summer School two summers ago, alone in San Francisco last summer." Translation: I'm still a 'nice girl'. Meaning virgin if you ask me, which I know you're dying to do but won't. A silent generation, we never talked about anything important. "If you can trust me when I'm away, you should trust me here. "Didn't hear you ask Billy where he's going, what time he's coming home." I took a breath, "Becker's parents are letting *her* go."

I rested my case.

Dad allowed Mother to do the inquisition before taking over reluctantly, "All right. You don't have to argue it into the ground. Be home by eleven. No later." The judge handed down his decision. "I'm sorry about today." stuck in my throat.

I walked from the dining room through our barn-like living room, thirty by twenty feet, two-story high cathedral ceiling. We bought the house furnished, an interior designer had 'done it', unheard of at the beach. A giant fruit-filled tree painted on the bay wall grew out of a pink spattered floor -- our Jackson Pollack. Two chartreuse seven-foot couches, chartreuse reading chair, giant coffee grinder with red wheels, pair of blue and white striped ceramic beer kegs made into lamps, butcher's block table completed the eclectic mix. Mother collected early American antiques, her contributions -- pine hutch, dry sink, Boston rocker.

Next to the fireplace where Dad char-grilled perfect medium-rare sirloins, was an old organ, a relic from the Protestant Church down the street. It didn't exactly work. If you sat down, pulled out all the stops, put your feet on the worn carpeted pedals, pumped as hard as you could at the same time pushing your knees out as far as they would go to activate the side bellows, you might make music. Mother, who had perfect pitch, had quit the Boston Conservatory when they tried to change her voice from alto to soprano. She played and sang show tunes on a good day. On a bad one, Billy's improvisations sounded like Boris Karloff horror movie background music. I couldn't play or read music; the piano teacher quit on me when I was twelve for insubordination. I talked back. And never practiced.

'Sans Souci' was perfect for entertaining. Friends dropped by anytime without advance notice, one of the favored Fire Island customs -- welcome relief from Manhattan's formality. A warm, inviting, open house, Mother and Dad were an attractive, popular couple -- we, the perfect family, at least on the outside.

I shut the door of my cramped eight by ten bedroom, three quarters taken up by a queen-size spool bed. Dammit! Only ten minutes to get ready and the third drawer was stuck again, heat made it swell. After five minutes of prayer, swearing, cajoling, even resorting to "open sesame," I got it. Neither the rumpled mess nor my bags held a revelation. Instead I decided to cope with my fine Eastern European hair, curly from humidity. I took my brush in hand, and for the millionth time wished I had straight hair. I did the next best thing and wrapped it, a Brazilian trick I'd learned from a hairdresser -- they had the same problem. You combed your hair sideways, around and around your head till it was all tucked in, smooth, quickly tied a scarf as tight as possible to keep it in place. The longer you kept it wrapped, the straighter it turned out.

I had straight A's in WASP 101 after three years at a ninety-percent white Anglo-Saxon Protestant college. I dressed and acted the part, having had a head start. Mother had programmed me from birth to be Boston Brahminesque, talk with a broad "A", insisting I say awnt, not ant for aunt, to-mah-to for tomato. I cultivated manners, shaking hands when I met someone, helping the person next to me take off their sweater or coat. I practiced never raising my voice, God forbid shouting, showing emotion or using my hands to talk. I adopted the dress code: Shetland sweater, scarab bracelet, circle pin, and raccoon coat -- mine cost twenty-five dollars second hand and weighed twenty-five pounds. WASPs ruled. I was a Christmas Jew.

What most would call an anomaly began when a Hasidic Jew teacher in high school Latin class in Brooklyn rapped Dad's hands with a ruler at fifteen for not being able to decline *qui quae quod*. After that, Dad declined Judaism. When the subject of how to raise us kids came up Dad stuck to his guns. No religion, his children were going to celebrate Christmas. Mother, raised Reform and confirmed at Temple Israel in Boston, was okay with presents, an excuse to shop. When it came to a tree, Mother drew the line. Dad negotiated a compromise, his forte. I imagined their conversation.

"Jews don't have trees. My father didn't let us have one," the only Jewish family in Everett, Mass. "I won't allow it."

"This won't be Christian."

"What do you mean, Mike?"

"We won't have lights, angels, crèches, crosses, anything store-bought.

"How will we decorate?"

"That's up to you," the ball in her court.

"We can make cut outs from red oilcloth, string cranberries and popcorn, put the *mezuzah* on top." Mother was into it, resourceful, must have secretly wanted one as a child. And so it came to pass: we believed in Santa Claus, hung up stockings on the 24th day of December, exchanged Christmas presents on the 25th under our creative, Chanukah bush.

In spite of Anne Frank and the six million Jews that died in the Holocaust, I was ashamed of our name, and even more ashamed that I was ashamed. Why couldn't it have been Adams? Changing Abrams to Adams would've been so easy. Dad blew a gasket when I broached the subject during Christmas vacation freshman year.

"Abrams was good enough for my father and good enough for me."

"But Dad, Abrams is so ethnic." When I met a Harvard Porcellian, Princeton Ivy or Cottage, Yale Fence Club (pronounced Fawnce Club), it was like saying my name was Ali Jew. I wanted to blend in. Being Jewish was not kosher in the Ivy League.

"Might I suggest if you want to change your name so badly you do it by getting married," the only goal of a girl once she graduated.

I sighed into the antique mirror over my dresser that didn't reflect: beautiful, blind, wondered why men called me sexy -- hung up on that word. I saw myself as smart. They seemed mutually exclusive. The past Spring I'd gone to Yale for the weekend to watch my date Kent -- WASPs had that kind of first name, play rugby. I was crazy about the scrum, which sounded like a dirty word, meant dropping the ball in the middle of players who were arranged in a circle with their arms around each other, straining to kick it out to their teammates while holding their positions. I fantasized I was the ball surrounded by nine gorgeous guys.

Kent took me back to his dorm room after the game and made a pass, told me I reminded him of a sexy black cat.

"What do you mean, sexy?"

"Can't you see?" No, I couldn't.

'Sexy' haunted me. Why would anyone call a virgin, sexy? I was voluptuous, Size C, 35-24-35, hourglass, between sizes 8 and 10, my life changing when I grew boobs at 15. Guys called me *zaftig*. Built. Two years of orthodontia had corrected my overbite, but the gap had come back -- coincidently like Chaucer's bawdy Wife of Bath, Alisoun, my namesake. I identified with Marilyn Monroe, wondered what it would be like to have every man in America lust after me. When men talked about her it was dirty -- hubba hubbas, va va vooms, wolf whistles. Elvis the Pelvis was her male counterpart, the king to her queen. I went to see him in *Love Me Tender* at the Brattle Theatre in Cambridge, at Harvard summer school two years ago, above it all. I came out a convert, couldn't take my eyes off his skintight satin jumpsuit, crotch, hip gyrations, crooked, sexy smile -- even I used that word attracted and repelled, confusing. Marilyn and Elvis both vulgar idols, what was this country coming to?

I settled on white, tight sleeveless tucked into double-knit Jamaicas, in between short shorts and Bermudas. Gung ho, Josephine College, I dressed Ivy even on Fire Island known for dressing down -- sweatshirts, dungarees, tees. I brushed out my hair, the straight-as-a-board pageboy safe as long as I didn't sweat.

I waltzed into the living room upbeat, on my way to a caper, a dancer -- ballet lessons, on my toes, knew the steps to everything -- like swimming on land. Mother was curled up in the chartreuse window seat, absorbed in *Exodus* by Uris. Michener's *Hawaii* topped a column of books stacked on the table. She belonged to the Book of the Month Club. An avid reader, she'd get to them all. Dad tended to like books on politics or history. Billy couldn't sit still long enough. I was done with my heavy Russian stage having devoured all of Dostoyevsky, now on an existential kick, Jean Paul Sartre and Albert Camus front and center, Unamuno and Ortega y Gasset on the sidelines.

"How do I look?" I couldn't tell, the only full-length mirror in their bedroom, knew I was setting myself up, she only gave rejections, forget 'good', 'gorgeous', 'great.' Still hoping.

"Isn't your shirt a little tight? Have you gained weight again?" I pulled the tails out. She barely nodded okay, "Be home on time." I'd passed inspection, no approbation one-second late hell to pay. A bucket of cold water splashed over my head.

I called Becker, her last name. No one *ever* called her Myrna. "Ready? I'm leaving this second. Meet you in front of the Protestant Church. Don't be late."

As usual, she was. A Vassar grad, her name, like her straight nose and the freckles she fussed about could go either way, Jew or German. She went German, a closet Jew. This was the first of three strikes against her from Mother, who hated Becker, hissed her name and called her a snake. The second: she lived on the West Side. To an Upper East Sider this was not as bad as Brooklyn but not good. Third, she talked back to Mother, who expected to be obeyed by everyone.

It didn't help that I was always saying 'Becker's doing this' or 'Becker's doing that.'

"What happened? I've been waiting almost a half hour. My precious minutes are ticking away."

"Relax, Ali." She'd never apologize. I didn't really like her, nasty, a snapdragon -- not the flower, but needed a comrade-in-arms very reluctant to do things alone. Becker filled the bill. I always had girlfriend problems and problem girlfriends. Allergic to Home Ec. chitchat, I wanted to talk about anything else, a man's woman.

I raved about the man from the ferry.

"Blonde?" Becker knew me.

"Natch."

"Ivy?"

"Not sure," I fudged. He'd been wearing white shoes and a golf shirt, very California, wasn't an Ivy Leaguer, didn't want to admit it.

"Rich?"

"How do I know?" Couldn't have cared less. Becker was interested only in WASPs with impeccable social credentials, trust funds -- old money. She'd have given anything to be a deb and come out, embarrassed she'd been on scholarship. I kept her secrets. Becker's revenge for the cross she bore, so to speak, was going to clubs where no Jew had ever been allowed, attending social register balls.

Becker stuck to her guns. "You can always tell."

"I only saw him for a second."

"He'll turn up." It was a small town.

"Do you believe in love at first sight?" Starry eyed.

"Here we go again." Becker was a reluctant witness to my serial infatuations.

We reached the end of the walk, arriving 'downtown'. The village that ran along the bay was not much to look at, ramshackle, everyone barefoot -- the pavement spotless. We stopped at a foot high cement stoop that ran parallel to the Village Green in front of John and Anne's Ice Cream Parlor, the nerve center of Ocean Beach. It was there that everyone sat down to watch everyone else go by. Bayview, our target, was opposite. Becker started off.

"Don't you think it's too early?" I'd lost my nerve.

"You're such a straight arrow."

"I don't want to look like a loser. If we go in alone, everyone's going to think we're unpopular and no one asked us out." Mother's words had come back to haunt me. "I feel funny without a date."

"You've been to a bar alone before."

I remembered Rahar's, the famed hangout. "That was Northampton during the week with a bunch of girls, this is the weekend and we don't have dates."

"Stop harping on that. It's because we're picky and have outgrown the lifeguards."

"I'm afraid we'll bump into somebody we know and die from embarrassment."

"Would you rather get an ice cream cone and sit on the stoop with the other babies? This was *your idea*." She walked off.

'Babies' the operative word, plus 'your idea.' She had me. What would Marilyn do? I stood tall, pulled my shoulders back smiled, played her in *How to Marry a Millionaire,* caught -- sashayed up. The beef trust at the door, six and a half solid feet, blocked our entry.

"Holy shit, a bouncer," I was taken aback, prayed my resolve wouldn't dissolve.

"Do you have reservations?" El Morocco it was not.

"Of course we do. We're old friends of Tommy Kohler's." Becker gave him a snow job, me a wink. Smooth operator.

"Names?"

"Becker and Abrams. Do you want to call Tommy, he knows us..." Her intonation caustic, the implied threat, it would cost the bruiser's head if he made a mistake. I let her do the dirty work.

"Pass." He stood aside. We entered Bayview up a ramp, jammed with a strictly Seventh Avenue crowd.

Surrounded by garmentos, "I don't see a soul I know." Becker pushed to the bar.

"Check out the diction," a cacophony of des, dems and doses. "The Bronx? No thonx!" Ogden Nash's rhyme came to mind. She ordered a J & B on the rocks.

"Make it two." I'd acquired a taste for scotch by Thanksgiving freshman year, to Dad's dismay, 'I'm not paying all this money for you to learn how to drink.' He didn't have to worry. I was a cheap date drunk on one drink.

"How old are you, kid?" The bartender glared.

Stuck with a baby face, the drinking age eighteen "Twenty."

"Prove it."

"I don't carry around my driver's license. Everyone knows me."

"I ain't seen you before and I'm the only one that counts."

"I swear." I lit a cigarette like Bacall -- a well-practiced move, smoking illegally since 12, legally since 18, blew it into his face as if I were cool, prayed the sweat on my brow wouldn't betray me.

"Ask Tommy. The boss knows us." Becker's tough tongue lashed out.

"I ain't got the time, kid."

"What's going on?" Tommy Kohler appeared, 18, fresh faced, we'd grown up with him. "They're legal, Joe. Sorry, girls, it's his first night. The new village cops are on my back watching." Tommy had bought Kohler's, a dump that catered to the small year-round population of Ocean Beach, from his father, remodeled, transformed. From the look of things, he'd struck gold. Our drinks were on the house. "Catch the singer yet?"

"We hear him, can't see him." I'd been aware of the strains of a seductive voice, a pink cloud drifting over and softening the tough crowd, "I like New York in June..."

"What's with the bouncer," asked Becker.

"Big Lou? We need him, we'd be mobbed otherwise." He led us to the new back room, four deep around the piano, the backyard, the Great South Bay. I peeked through the crowd. Oh God, the sapphires. Shocked, my stomach turned over. Again.

"Becker!"

"Do you have to give me an elbow in the ribs to get my attention?"

"That's him playing."

"Who?"

"The guy from the boat."

"Hunka hunka!"

"Told you. We've got to figure out a way for me to meet him."

"You and every other woman in the room."

I threaded my way through the competition to the inner circle. My high hopes lowered as he got up to leave, "Taking a short break, folks. Back in ten." He slipped away.

What was I going to do? Wait. I'd stand there forever if I had to.

"Hi, girls. Can I buy you a drink?" It was Sean. Peroxide blonde hair, Irish eyes and wit, late twenties. A lifeguard on weekends, Smartee double-knit sportswear salesman during the week, Sean was responsible for activating and accelerating the growing-up process of every attractive young teenage girl in Ocean Beach. Not lecherous, rather devilish, corrupting another way of putting it. We were too old for him to hit on.

"No dates tonight?" typical Sean barb.

"We're checking out Tommy's new addition."

"Are you referring to the new back room, or lover boy?"

"Do you know him?" I gasped.

Becker gave me a kick, whispered, "Be cool, Ali."

"Oh, you *did* notice him," sarcasm oozed from every pore. "The bad news is he's got a girlfriend, if you don't mind a beautiful, model with a perfect ass and non-stop legs as competition. Jean's famous."

Sean pointed to a stunning, older woman with blonde hair, in shorts, great legs, wouldn't you know. "What's the good news?"

"He's cuter than Hot Lips. Your taste seems to be improving with age." Sean never stopped teasing me about a crush I'd had at thirteen on a lifeguard with big lips, trumpet player. People at the beach had memories like elephants. Do something once in your life and no one ever forgot about it -- worse they constantly reminded you.

"What else?" Hoping for more info. Any crumb.

"Want me to hand him to you on a silver platter? Find out for yourself."

A challenge was a challenge, not that I needed one. I positioned myself directly in front. He *had* to look at me. A hush fell over the room as he sat down at the piano after the longest break in history. Drop dead gorgeous. "Does anyone have a request?"

As the blues accosted me, my stomach somersaulted. I took a deep breath, now or never, "Do you know "My Funny Valentine?""

He cocked his head, smiled, "My funny valentine..." His voice curled around the lyrics, caressed as he crooned, I wanted to kiss him more than anything else in the world. Cupid's arrow had struck, a direct hit, smitten, I'll be your funny valentine forever. I would.

"Thank you." was all I could muster. Better than nothing.

He turned to answer another request. Jean stared me down. I averted her eyes, looked at my watch. 11:20, trouble.

I whispered to Becker, "Got to go. Coming?" Why would she?

"I'm going to stay for the rest of the set." I bolted out of Bayview.

Dad waited in the easy chair facing the front door. His perturbed look said it all. Late again. Thirty-nine minutes. To hell with the consequences, I was crazy about a pair of sapphires.

2

My Funny Valentine

My room was like an oven the next morning. It had to be a scorcher. I donned my new orange wool bathing suit, daring -- the back down to my waist, itchy but a big improvement over my boned latex squeeze suits. I put my hair into bunches, stuck a comb by my left thigh, grabbed my Mexican raffia beach bag, filled it: white bathing cap layered with lace scallops, no strap; bottle of Johnson's Baby Oil, pink -- maximum tanning strength, had added four drops of iodine last weekend; *The Stranger* by Camus -- the quintessential existential first line mind boggling, "Today Mother died, or was it yesterday?" No yesterday or tomorrow only today. I checked my Chesterfields, one left, would have to bum from Becker, she'd give me a hard time, like Mother, her things were her things. I draped a matching orange and white striped beach towel in front accidentally on purpose to hide my thighs. Ready.

I spotted Sean's telltale platinum hair, prone on a white sheet, tanning alongside his friend Jordan, nice guy. We'd never connected. He should've been my type, blonde, turquoise eyes, somehow wasn't. Sean and Jordan weren't ostracized like other groupers, their volleyball too good. They rented the first prefab house on Cottage Walk, 'Under the Water Tower', from Mother's friend, artist Lester Gaba. He was famous for creating Cynthia, Saks Fifth Avenue's first modern mannequin in the thirties. Stylish and very realistic, Lester had taken her everywhere dressed to kill. Cynthia had become a national craze after she was featured on the cover of *Life* magazine. Having invented modern window display, he was now the *éminence grise.*

"Still got stars in your eyes." Sean was on my case.

"What are you talking about?" I tried to stay calm. Exposed.

"You mean you've already forgotten about 'him'? Would you play "My Funny Valentine?" He imitated me.

"Give me a break!" I walked over to the girls, our beach encampment right next to the volleyball court for the one o'clock game. Becker, Kate and I, the three musketeers, had stuck together since the summer of '51. Kate went to Radcliffe, a tad chunky, always on a diet like me. She squeezed lemon into her wet light brown hair to bleach it naturally. She called the result strawberry blonde. Sean's peroxide platinum, she opined, was 'much too obvious'. A Jewish proboscis, which she complained about constantly, intervened between Kate and beauty. We discussed the pros and cons of a nose job many times - Mother referred to them as 'bobs', delighted I didn't need one. Most of the Jewish girls we knew who'd tried, had been nosed out by Jewish plastic surgeons creating pert Protestant noses, although perfect in the abstract, lost in the translation. Too much of a risk, Kate kept her schnoz and defended herself from the world with biting sarcasm, her Bette Davis *All About Eve* delivery flawless, 'Fasten your seat belts, this is going to be a bumpy night.'

Becker sat in a blue beach chair, nose covered in zinc oxide anti-freckle cream as she worked on Saturday's *New York Times* crossword puzzle, the hardest one, in ink, not for the faint of heart. We competed over who'd finish first. She usually won.

"What did I miss, Becker?"

She put it down, unhappy, an interruption. "We stayed for a few more songs. Sean took me for a night cap at Goldie's."

"That's it?"

"She hangs around his neck like a wet rag." Becker extracted a Pall Mall from a long red pack, lit it.

"Did you get his name at least?" I lit up too, my last one.

"I forgot. Don't ask Sean or you'll never hear the end of it."

"I've already heard the beginning."

"For your edification, Kate, Ali's crazy about the new singer at Bayview. He's gorgeous, older, comes with an attached blonde, model girlfriend. Hopeless."

"*Dum spiro spero,* nothing's hopeless," I protested, resenting Becker's negative review.

Kate turned over, handed me the Coppertone to grease her back, "Can't you pick someone you can get? Time's running out." Apparently I couldn't.

As seniors, the pressure was on to find Mr. Right, graduate with a MRS degree, settle down have kids. By now, most of the girls in my class were engaged or 'pinned' -- engaged to be engaged, sporting fraternity pins proudly over their left breasts. (You put your right thumb at the bottom of your throat, spread your fingers, where your pinky landed was the right place.) I'd gone through lots of guys, 'majoring in men', or 'boy crazy', as Mother put it, witness to the quantity. June, freshman year, one telephone per dorm floor, the central Smith switchboard operator opined I'd received the most calls of any girl on campus. All I remembered was being lonely.

Relationships didn't last. I'd meet an attractive guy become infatuated start to date. If he got too interested, I panicked, went on a faultfinding expedition, wouldn't answer his phone calls or see him again. I couldn't tell him why, I didn't know. Then there were those who rejected *me.* They'd disappear after three dates if I didn't put out. I *had* to be a virgin when I got married.

"You haven't heard him sing." I went on about his phrasing and timbre, loved the sound of his voice. Nick was a star. I could feel it.

"I'm sure he's the first and second coming, but haven't you heard? Gentlemen prefer blondes."

I started to coo, "Diamonds Are a Girl's Best Friend", Carol Channing style, "I'm just a little girl..." Kate chimed in and we sang the entire *Gentlemen Prefer Blondes* score. Marilyn. Jayne Mansfield. Doris Day. Dinah Shore. A blonde takeover, what to do? Be a brainy brunette.

"Going for a swim." I walked past the lifeguard stand, put my toes in the water. Brrr. Chilly on such a hot day, no justice in the world. I began cold-water entry. Finally in, I did a lap to warm up, swam parallel to the shore between the two red flags on the lifeguard's watch. I floated on my back letting the currents move me at will, at one with the water, at peace with the world. I lifted my head up for a second to check where I was. Never mind where I was, there *he* was at the water's edge, short plaid trunks, 5' 10" athletic body, thick blond hair I wanted to put my fingers through. Gentlewomen prefer blondes.

I watched him dive -- not bad at all, relieved he was a jock. It mattered. The girls at college labeled jocks 'low brow'. I didn't care, one myself. I'd started swimming lessons at five in the bay, a water baby. I'd raced at the annual swim meets, backstroke and crawl, won gold; learned sidestroke, breaststroke and diving, earned more medals at Camp Pinecliffe. I 'lettered' at Fieldston, a private, co-ed prep school on 'the hill' in Riverdale, the tony Northwest corner of the Bronx. Four large orange felt 'F's' for being on varsities -- hockey, tennis, captain of the swimming team and a cheerleader. Since Smith had no swimming varsity, I'd done the next best thing, become a "Lifeguard", member of the elite water ballet and synchronized swim team, a big deal.

I maneuvered closer riding the waves, discreetly drifting towards him. In his sightline I performed my complete repertoire imagining I was Esther Williams: back dolphins, surface dives, fancy strokes. I never once looked in his direction, hoping he'd spot me. Suddenly there was a perfect rider. I turned to take it. He *was* watching. We both ducked the wave. He surfaced and swam a few strokes towards me. The sapphires matched the color of the water.

"Hey baby, want me to sing 'My Funny Valentine?'"

He remembered. My stomach flip-flopped. Say something clever. Anything. "Yes. I mean can you sing in the sea?"

"Sure. *A cappella.*" He began it. I was struck dumb as we treaded water.

"You must be a native. You swim like one, have the kind of tan you don't get from spending too much time in the city. You look like an Indian. What's your name? Don't tell me, it's Pocahontas."

"Ali Abrams."

He cocked his head, "Abrams. Sounds familiar. A lot of Abrams out here?"

"Just us."

"I got a fine of fifteen bucks plus a lecture from a Judge Abrams for not separating the glass from the garbage last weekend." We ducked another wave. "Related to you?"

"My father." Oh dear, bad start.

"I've been on my best garbage behavior since. Promise."

"What's *your* name?" I managed to get it out.

"Nick Rose."

"Rose is a beautiful name. 'A rose is a rose is a rose'." Gertrude Stein came to mind.

"Was a Rosenthal, I shortened it for the stage. Catchier. So… how old are you Ali?"

Another wave gave me a second to calculate. Twenty-four? Terrible liar, he'd never believe me. Stick with something close to true.

"Twenty two." I crossed my fingers. "How old are *you*?"

He paused for a second.

"Twenty nine." Both lying, in his thirties for sure, "What do you do, Ali?" We swam closer to shore so we could touch bottom.

"Working in New York this summer." I prayed he wouldn't ask more about my job, didn't bring up Smith, wished he'd kiss me. "Loved hearing you last night. First time I've been to the new Bayview."

"I've got this gig weekends to pick up some extra scratch while I break into recording." Musician slang a special language I'd first heard at Jimmy Ryan's on West 52nd, listening to Dixieland when I was thirteen. The establishment had 'an arrangement' with the cops -- they let in minors. "Oh when the saints come marching in…"

"Have I heard any of your songs?"

"'Happy Times'?" I'd heard it on the radio, started to sing it. "That's right, baby." I loved how he called me that. "You have a good ear." Thrilled. He could tell.

A throaty alto, I could sing the melody, knew the lyrics to every show, the Gershwins, Rodgers and Hart or Hammerstein, Lerner and Loewe my gods. We went to Broadway often, birthdays, celebrations, whenever a good one came on the boards. Dad used a scalper, Jack Schneider, who he cursed, saying he'd been Schneidered, instead of $6.95 per ticket, $15. We'd just seen *Gypsy*, $60 for four. Highway robbery worth every cent.

"I've just released a new single."

"Oh, yes?" Impressed. "What's it called?"

"'Heaven Sent'. They picked me to record over Tony Bennett."

"Wow." Nick *was* a star sent from heaven. I wanted to stay forever, but my body betrayed me, fingertips like prunes, June's frigid water to blame. I started to shiver. "Have to get out, got a chill, s-s-sorry."

He hugged me. I couldn't stop shaking. "Wish I could warm you up." That made two of us. We rode the next wave in. "I run my dog on the beach after five when it's legal. I've never seen such a small town with so many big laws. Your father must be a hard working man."

I shrugged, defensive about Dad. What could I say?

"Maybe I'll see you later, pretty girl. Love that smile." Music to my ears.

Mrs. Nick Rose. Okay, he had a thorn, like the rose in *The Little Prince.* I'd have to get rid of that girlfriend. I imagined a little plane like the ones that flew by on crowded days, a banner behind, "GIVE JEAN THE HOOK"; a huge skyhook hoisted her into the sky, out of my life. I dreamed, walking back to the beach blanket.

"Well, well, well." Kate put down *Doctor Zhivago.* "Look what we have here, a space cadet. It was broad daylight the last time we checked. Earth calling Mars, Earth calling Mars, come in please." I toweled off afraid to break the spell. "What's up?" Kate wouldn't let go.

"I met Nick Rose in the water."

Becker looked up, "The singer?" She put down the crossword. "Details please." I held back. There was something private about Nick, mysterious. I had the feeling if he knew he was being discussed he would be none too happy. I'd always been public with my life -- everyone knew everything. Not today.

"He's too old for you," insisted Kate. When we saw older men -- they were always bald with younger women -- they were always tall, we talked behind their backs. *Those girls,* we whispered, were in it for the money. "Remember your last experience with an older man?" Kate would. A disaster. Edward was Dad's best friend's son. At twenty-one he'd been a senior at college, while I was seventeen, a high school senior. He didn't know what to do with a virgin, fearful Dad was watching him like a hawk. He was right.

"I don't like threesomes," he'd said. Who did? We'd danced close to Sammy Davis Jr., "And This Is My Beloved" from *Kismet* at Maguire's on the bay, so romantic, went to the beach to make out. He kissed me, got hot, wanted to pet. I panicked. Fed up, he insisted we leave the beach. The more he wanted to go, the more I wanted to stay. Frustrated, he turned nasty, 'You're acting cheap'. Edward left me for Carol, who, people said 'went down'.

Miserable for weeks afterward, I'd played "The Man That Got Away" from *A Star is Born* over and over, singing along with Judy Garland: "The night is bitter… all because of the man that got away." Rejected over sex -- rather, not sex, the elephant in the living room, my virginity -- so important we couldn't talk about it. The proverbial question: what's so holy about a hymen? Awful word. According to prevailing theories mine was probably broken from horseback riding anyway.

It was certainly not physical fear that kept me from 'doing it'. If it hurt, I'd have read up on the subject. By accident one day when I was eleven I'd found a brown-paper covered book in Mother's New York bedroom cupboard. Pornography. Shocked by the contents and Mother, I got over it fast dove into her stash, reading the new ones before she passed them along, unaware of my secret membership in her underground network. Smuggled in from Paris, they had soft moss green covers, Olympia Press.

Page eighty-seven in *Lady Chatterley's Lover* was dog-eared where Mellors makes love to Constance, puts flowers all over her private parts which they name, tells her how beautiful she is down there. Every time I read it I got excited. On the other hand, *Tess of the d'Urbervilles*'s death hung like a dark cloud over my libido, tainted merchandise her life ruined just because she'd 'done it'. I *had* to be a virgin when I got married. If not, there would be dreadful consequences.

Then again maybe I should get it over with and just not tell anyone. On my wedding night, which I fantasized about almost as often as my wedding, I'd get some red paste and place a few drops discreetly on my white bridal sheets to fool my husband. I'd read about that Oriental trick in one of mother's books. What if Dad found out? He'd kill me. I'd be damned, roast in hell for eternity, according to James Joyce's definition in *Portrait of an Artist as a Young Man,* a bird came to an enormous beach once every million years, took away one grain of sand. When all the sand was gone, that was one second of eternity. I couldn't take that chance, one hell of a long time.

I wondered how one of those big things -- Becker called it a cock, could fit inside me. The Tampax instructions, as close as I'd ever come to anatomy lessons, left a lot to be desired. So too did *Growing Up and Liking It*, a pamphlet put out by Kotex. Why was everyone so silent about sex? Something wrong?

The girls continued to weigh the pros and cons of older men. I watched the ocean continuum as waves curled over, splashed into white bubbling foam, my thoughts on Nick Rose.

"Hey Ali. Let's see what the crowd's about." Meggy passing by gestured for me to get up, interrupting my reveries. A sweetheart, Meggy's father had been Mayor of Ocean Beach, Dad the elected Trustee -- Disraeli to his Gladstone. A wall of well-greased people, skin tones ranging from rare to well done, congregated fifty feet away, moved slowly right then left like an ocean organism. Meggy and I rushed over. In the center of the crowd stood a man, fishing pole arched in two. It was Dad with a big one. He had two loves, Mother first, fishing, a close second, his way of unwinding from the pressures of work he referred to as 'the aggravation.'

The assemblage oohed and aahed, enthralled at the sea duel. I left Meggy at the fringe, worked my way to the center kept a respectful distance. Speculation was high as to what kind of fish was on the line.

"Must be a shark, look how the rod is bent."

"See how it's fighting, gotta be a blue."

"Could be a striper."

God, I was proud. My dad was the best fisherman on the beach. I loved him from afar, easier than in everyday life, since it had always been difficult, all right, impossible, to talk to him, his shyness a curtain dropped between us. There were scores of people he 'took care of', helped, straightened out, got jobs or apartments for; hundreds who depended on him for advice or counsel; hero for the masses, he made sure millions of working men got a break but never talked to me. I missed having a father.

Since I'd been home, I seemed to be doing something wrong every other minute. Dad complained to Mother, she to me, the chain of command. Yesterday's lateness had filtered down this morning. 'Your father's employing you and sending you to Paris; the least thing you can do is to be on time.' I talked back, 'No one could have made it, not enough time, too much traffic', starting another in a series of running battles in our 'cold war', a mushroom cloud hovering over our relationship, the lines drawn in the sand. And I knew I was wrong, blamed it on what I called the 'Imp of the Perverse' from Edgar Allen Poe's story of the same name, a self-destructive impulse that tempted one to do things "merely because we feel we should not."

My interactions with Dad had changed at fifteen after I'd finally grown boobs. The perfect Daddy I worshiped, who'd helped me solve math problems, took me fishing, turned out to be the biggest prude in town, a watchdog, no necking or petting allowed. He'd thrown my boyfriend, Jeff, out of the house after he'd found us kissing on the couch, slammed the door in his face. Other mortifying incidents followed. I wouldn't have been surprised if he'd make me wear a chastity belt. Daddy's good little girl chafed at the bit, angry at his double standards -- he laughed at Billy's girl-chasing episodes, yet kept me in curfews. What would he think if I told him I was smitten with an older man who sang at a grouper bar and I was dying to have sex with?

The battle nearly over, Dad had the star drag on, reeled in the exhausted fish. Out of nowhere, a man grabbed the line. It snapped. The pole sprang back upright, Dad's face fell, contorted in anguish, "What the hell did you do that for?" He'd never mention it again. The crowd dispersed. Something inside me snapped as well.

I waited for Nick perched on my aerie, the weather-beaten bench on the platform at the end of our block, jutting out and over the dune covered with stubborn beach grass, tough enough to trap sand in its roots. I pulled a strand, tensed it with my fingers and blew. The snow fences were piled high with seaweed and driftwood. An emphatic sign read "No Walking on the Dunes". Big penalties if you didn't comply. The shrill sound of fifteen silver whistles, a scrum plus some, signaled five o'clock, the end of the lifeguards' vigil. The circle of red trunks and bronze bodies disbanded. They dragged the lookout chair towards the dunes and overturned it.

I loved this time of day best, the sun's rays warm without punishment, light glowing with such clarity that beach, sea and sky seemed struck with gold like the fairy tale kingdoms of my childhood imagination. I watched the last of the sun-drenched bathers gather up their belongings, give blankets a good shake, leave. Don't you know you're missing the best time of day? I faced west, looking and longing for Nick and a dog, worried. '*Maybe* I'll see you later,' the words played again and again.

I sighed relieved as I spied them, specks, five blocks away. Eagle eyes. I raced down the steps to the beach, strolled slowly towards them, gave an award-winning performance as a beachcomber, made it look as if I were meeting him by accident. I picked up a white clamshell inspected it, a hole, not a keeper, found a flat grey stone tossed it. It skipped three times.

"Good shot pretty girl. Meet my dog, Rosencrantz."

The dog whose paw I shook was an extremely large enthusiastic German Shepherd, obviously the light of Nick's life. "How do you do Rosencrantz. Is he named for the character in *Hamlet*?" I remembered Rosencrantz and Guildenstern.

"My name plus my ex-wife's maiden name. It was Cranston." Bad news, people didn't get divorced. I'd have to keep this from Becker and Kate.

"How clever." Rosencrantz didn't look too much like the kind of dog you cuddled. "A retriever?" I was careful not to ask if he was a killer.

"Try him."

I picked up a piece of wood, heaved it as far as 1 could. Rosencrantz loped down the beach, returned, same piece between his teeth. I tried to get it away from him.

"He's growling."

"You have to play games with him and pretend you don't want it."

"You're right I don't."

"As soon as he sees you're not going to take it, he'll let you have it, then you can throw it again."

"What a treat." I hoped to sound enthusiastic, Rosencrantz obviously the love of his life.

"Hey, why don't you join us?" Old khaki army blanket, portable radio in residence, "I'm listening to hear if they play 'Heaven Sent,' the song I told you about." He kept changing stations. We heard a few bars of "Mack the Knife", Bobby Darin's new swinging version of the old song from *The Three Penny Opera*; a chorus of "Poison Ivy!" by the Coasters, perfect for Fire Island where it flourished; the last seconds of "Love Potion #9," something I'd already drunk.

Nick gave up. "Let's take a swim if that's a bathing suit."

"It's a leotard." I'd tried on two other suits with horrendous built-in bras. My black leotard had long sleeves and a scoop neck. I wore it without underwear, pushed up the sleeves, somewhere between show off and prude. We waited to get used to the water.

He took my hand. "Ready?" We dove under the wave. He kept up with me easily, not bad for an older man. We stroked back to shore so we could touch bottom. We treaded water, just his head visible, the sapphires sparkling. I was so attracted I almost couldn't bear it, hypnotized.

"Come to me," he beckoned. I exercised my last ounce of control, swam slowly to him. He put his arms around my shoulders pulled me close, his whole body pressed against mine. Chest against breasts, groin against groin.

"Let me kiss you, Valentine." Our lips touched, I shut my eyes. My first sea kiss, salty, sexy. He forced my mouth open with his tongue, gently explored. I kissed him back, my skin prickling, started to breathe harder. He began to caress my shoulders and back with increased ardor, turned me around, kissed the nape of my neck, put his hands under my leotard touched my breasts. I rode a roller coaster of sensations and chills. He turned me around pressed his body into mine, slid me up and down, took my hand and put it under his suit. Hard. I felt shy and inexperienced. What should I do now? Before I had time to figure it out, he pulled my leotard aside, put his fingers inside.

I gasped, "Don't!" He pulled back, arms still circling me, sapphires staring. "I mean don't stop." What did I mean?

"Easy, baby." He let me go. I didn't feel easy at all. Hot in the cold water, I vibrated with an unfamiliar ache. "What say we swim in before I take you in the water. The last one to the beach is a rotten egg." We missed the rider, took the next wave in, landing half in, half out of the water. "What's wrong? You were so startled when I touched you."

"I was a little surprised." Shocked more like it.

"Me, too. I usually don't make a pass like that but I'm very attracted to you. You're so sexy." He said the "S" word. Coming from him it sounded good. I thanked heaven I was tanned so he couldn't see me blush. The waves washed in gently, receded, no undertow.

"I don't feel like this every day, either." Never as a matter of fact.

"Valentine, how old did you say you were again?" He cupped my face in his hand.

What had I said? Time for the truth, "Almost twenty one."

Long pause. "Are you a virgin?"

"Why do you ask?" Avoid an answer with a question, lawyer's daughter.

"You are, aren't you? I should have known. Just great Nick, a virgin, under twenty-one, jailbait, and her father's the judge. Batting a thousand."

I should have said he was older, had a girlfriend and was divorced. Didn't have the nerve. A wave washed over us. Very *From Here to Eternity*, we kissed again.

"I haven't known a virgin in so long that I can't remember what to do." He corrected himself, "What not to do."

"You sound like I've got the plague."

"I can't cope with this black thing."

"Leotard."

"It's driving me crazy whatever it is, looks like you're naked with a second skin. Can't keep my hands off you," he touched my breasts, nipples at attention. "See what I mean?"

I looked into his eyes hypnotized. '*La vida es sueño y sueños sueños son*'. Life is a dream and dreams are dreams, Calderon de la Barca -- funny time to be thinking of a 17th century Spanish playwright. Please don't let this moment ever end. I'm afraid it's only a dream. I heard people talking, laughter, buried my head into Nick's smooth chest to hide. If I couldn't see them, they couldn't see me. "Are they gone?"

"Yes."

"Don't ever be ashamed of something beautiful, Valentine." The spell broken, we stood up. "Let's go back to the blanket."

He dried me off with his towel. Even that sent a wave of shivers through me. How could he be so confident, in control, while I felt like a jellyfish? I touched his face. Yes, he was real. He turned the radio back on. Rosencrantz materialized, sat down on the blanket between us.

"Hey, Rosie. Good boy. Did you think your master had forgotten you? What time do you think it is?' Pinks and fuchsias gathered forces behind the water tower, a dazzling sunset.

"Around seven," I could tell by the light.

"Got to go." Was that blonde waiting? Becker would've asked. Not me -- afraid to make waves.

"Okay." It wasn't. "Let me help you with your blanket." We each picked up two corners shook the sand out folded it. Rosie barked the while.

"Goodbye, baby." I shut my eyes, kissed him as if I was never going to see him again, a distinct possibility. I dreamwalked home.

"Becker called." Mother was crocheting a colorful three by three inch square, multiplied by a hundred, an afghan throw some day. She'd been working on it for years, Madame Defarge. "Your father's in mourning for the lost fish; Billy's in the bathroom combing his hair. You have five minutes to get ready for the party." She pulled a red ball from her wicker basket, unwound a 12-inch woolen thread, and deftly captured it with her crochet hook. "Something wrong?"

"No." I came down to earth, noticed her old-fashioned bathing costume: a dress over bloomers, yards of bold pink and yellow stripes, an oversized matching bow in her hair, black tights, heels. How did they swim in all that fabric? It must have weighed a ton. At least they got away without showing their thighs. "Great outfit, Mother."

She would have none of it. Flattery would get me nowhere. "Why are you idling? Get going."

I'd forgotten that tonight was the big Brooks party. Jimmy owned Brooks Costume Company. They designed costumes for most of the musicals on Broadway and the Ringling Brothers Barnum & Bailey Circus. Tonight was a By-the-Sea circa 1900 gala. Jimmy had arranged for bathing costumes, alas, none for Billy and I. I loved to dress up. I'd been Snap of 'Snap, Crackle and Pop' from the Rice Crispies box at six in the annual Ocean Beach Baby Parade. The next year I'd won second prize, an Indian. I looked the part -- high cheekbones, braids and bronze. My theory about my genetic forbears was that a Volga Tatar had raped a Jewish woman in Kadan, Mother's parent's home, before they'd come to America. Mother didn't cotton to it. 'Possible, not probable' as Miss Rosenthal, my algebra teacher would say, her family had been the intellectuals and writers of the town, that's all she knew.

I rushed into the shower next to the bathroom with identical barn-red louvered doors and turned on the water. I waited for it to warm up. And waited. None left.

"Couldn't you have saved me some hot water?" Billy could hear me through the wall.

"You were so late I thought you were going to skip the party."

"You know damn well it's a command performance. Can't you think of anyone but yourself? Still trying to impress that married woman or are you pining over that Swedish mother's helper this week?" After the shortest cold shower, I got out and toweled off.

"Look who's talking. I hear you're mooning over an older singer who's got a girlfriend."

"You shut up now. Do you hear me?" Billy's best friend, Becker's brother, must have overheard her talking to me about Nick, and squealed. No secrets on this lousy island. I waited shivering outside the bathroom for Billy to finish his endless toilette.

"Are you still combing that greasy, disgusting hair? It's not going to make any difference. The girls always know a twerp when they see one. Hurry up or I'll be late." No answer. The same hateful interchange had been going on for years, the likelihood of truce, slim. When we were away we bragged about how great the other was, together we fought. I was furious. Dynamite? Hand grenade? How could I blow him out of there? I locked him in.

"A very special love, da da da da da da..." Billy started to sing the theme from the movie, *Marjorie Morningstar.* His voice flat, he sang too loud as if that would make up for it. Was I Marjorie Morningstar? I'd loved the book, seen the movie with Natalie Wood and Gene Kelly. She was a nice Jewish girl from the West Side who falls in love with an older singer at a summer camp in the Catskills. I was from the East Side, Fire Island was far from summer camp, but the parallels were there, the fine points arguable. The bastard had me.

"Shut up!"

"A very special love..." He started over again changed the tune, added a refrain, "She's in love with a singer, she's in love with a singer."

I heard him try to open the door. "Unlock it, Marjorie."

"Is Elvis ready to leave the room?

"Open it."

"That's what you get for being so vain."

"Singer. Singer. She's in love with a singer." His taunts louder I unlatched the door, watched the pompadour dart out and slam into his room. In the bathroom finally, I wrapped my hair, put on makeup, stared in the mirror, shut my eyes saw the sapphires. Magnets. I could barely breathe. How was I going to get back to Bayview?

"Are you almost ready, *dear*," she sneered. Translation: This is your last warning.

"Five minutes." I dashed to my bedroom, the horrors of clothes decision waiting. Something white. What? The phone rang. Mother answered.

"It's Becker," she cursed. "Don't stay on too long or you'll be late," that tough voice commanded me.

"Yes Mother."

"I'm stuck going to the Brooks' party with the family. What are you doing?"

"Got a date with Johnny. We're going to Goldie's."

I hesitated for a moment. How desperate was I? Very. Couldn't walk in alone. "Do you think Johnny would mind if I horned in?

Long silence. "All right." Becker, who had been counting on a private date, accepted grudgingly.

"Still on the phone?" Mother's second warning.

"See you at Goldie's." I threw on a white tube top over white capris.

"And awaaay we go!" Billy crossed his foot, opened it out, his hands swung from left to right, imitating Jackie Gleason's signature intonation and move from *The Honeymooners.*

The sultry summer night embraced us, the walks lit by a canopy of stars, a sliver of blue cheese. Like all thin-skinned Ocean Beach houses on top of each other, only a sidewalk of separation, when the lights were on at night even with drawn blinds, you could tell who was home and what they were doing -- if you were nosy. Who wasn't?

We entered the open gate to Seaview, the adjacent community to the east. Our hosts had recently emigrated, worried about a grouper takeover in Ocean Beach. I blamed Woolcott Gibbs, the drama critic of *The New Yorker* magazine whose house was on the beach near Wilmot. He'd written some short stories about Fire Island that ran in *The New Yorker,* which became a hit Broadway play called *Season in the Sun* in '50. People came out curious about wagons, bare feet, sex, booze our beautiful beach, and stayed. An invasion of writers, songwriters, directors and movie actors had transformed the laconic simplicity of a community that had never changed into *the* most fashionable watering hole in the United States... if not the world. Groupers and garmentos, Mother referred to them as 'the element', had followed in their famous bare footsteps, out in force at Bayview bedecked in gold lamé, glitz and the unthinkable, heels.

Seaview was exclusive. Affluent. Attractive. Bigger houses. More land. No fisherman shacks. Restrictions against Jews had been lifted recently, now our people could 'get in'. Of course they wanted to go to a place that didn't want them to belong. Right Groucho?

We turned toward the ocean on B Street, heard the party before we saw it, clinking, tinkling sounds, piano music, laughter, caught a glimpse of flickering paper lanterns, a crowded back deck. We arrived at '*Casa Bianca*.'

"Welcome, you beautiful Abrams. Hello, Princess," Jimmy's nickname a carryover from a party years ago when I'd arrived in one of Mother's horrendous upsweep hair concoctions, choker round my neck, he'd dubbed me, Princess. Everyone kissed everyone as if they hadn't seen each other in years, not days, even hours. Jimmy and wife Bianca, his costume designer, in vintage bathing costumes -- his, black and white stripes, hers yellow and white, dazzled us with their greetings. Jimmy, tall, elegant, a shock of white hair, twinkling blue eyes, theatrical in his moves, made grand gestures, an impresario. I was careful to keep a substantial distance between us to avoid his penchant for pinching women's fannies.

Bianca had cat glasses with rhinestones, a coffee cup voice, "Darling, come say hello to Gerry and Gloria." She took my arm and maneuvered me through the crowd, dropped me off at her daughter's feet so to speak and kept going.

"Look at you, Ali, all grown up and gorgeous." Geraldine Brooks was a pocket Venus in pink and white stripes, Broadway actress and minor Hollywood film star. I remembered watching her bead her eyelashes when I was ten, the exciting Saturday afternoon she invited me backstage to her dressing room while she made up for a Broadway matinee. She placed a small amount of black beading in a mini pan, heated it over a hot plate until it was molten applied a tad with the flat end of an orange stick, coating each lash separately. After two hours a tiny bead hung on each tip. Her eyes looked enormous, better results than false eyelashes especially for the camera. She was right, I hadn't seen her in a long time. She would later marry writer Budd Schulberg and die young.

"What's new?" What wasn't?

"I'm going to Paris for the summer." All of a sudden it sounded like a very bad idea. "I see all your movies. Love them."

"You're too kind. Gloria, look who's here. Little Ali Abrams, only she's not so little anymore, a beauty." Gloria was also an actress, her costume, light blue and white.

"My, my, the bee's knees." As if I wasn't there.

"A director friend of mine is casting for his movie. You might fit the bill. Would you take a screen test?"

"Maybe." Caught off guard, I hastily excused myself, found it hard to take compliments, brushed it away, rushed to the bar, ordered a scotch, content to watch from the sidelines for once, a party usually my favorite thing in life, tonight I pined.

I pictured myself in a lace wedding dress walking down the aisle with Dad in a morning suit. "Here Comes the Bride" had faded, Nick by my side. "Allison Abrams, will you take Nick Rose to be your lawfully wedded husband?"

"I do.'

He placed the ring on my finger, lifted my veil, ready for his kiss.

"I'll have a vodka and tonic." It was Jordan, Sean's friend. A surprise, I didn't expect to see him at this private party. He gave me a dimpled grin.

Long and lean, Jordan wore clothes well. His faded blue denim work shirt brought out the twinkling turquoise of his eyes, tight white jeans, really tight, bubblegum pink cotton knit sweater tied around his neck, gave him a Newport or Edgartown look. He'd slicked back his fine blond hair. Stunning. Had he crashed? Parties were closed to newcomers *i.e.* people who didn't have years of island tenure, exceptions made for weekend guests only. Maybe he was not as much an outsider as I thought.

He'd read my mind. "Gerry invited me tonight. She's friendly with my sister in L.A."

"Let's blow this pop stand. Can I buy you a drink 'downtown'?"

"You've just said the magic words. I'd love to. But you're going to have to clear it with my parents... ask their permission. Let's find Mother."

"I have nothing too much against parents."

We followed her guttural laugh, bellowing from the little piano that made the round of parties on a wagon. "Mother, I'd like you to meet an old" as in safe, "friend of mine, Jordan Kaplan."

"How do you do Mrs. Abrams, I'm an admirer of your beautiful daughter. Listen Mrs. A., you don't mind if I steal Ali and take her 'downtown', do you?"

She gave Jordan the eye, didn't like him, he hadn't buttered her up, "You'll have to ask her father. Better put that drink down, Ali." That voice, again. Didn't she ever go off duty?

Mother, a veteran partygoer, adroitly wound her way in and out of the clusters of threes, fours, fives, each a dynamic organism, till the nucleus divided to form a new pattern with the same patter.

Dad was involved in yet another Very Serious Discussion about the dunes, up to his neck in politics and policies. A nor'easter, as devastating for an east-west island as a hurricane, had wreaked havoc last fall and stolen all the sand from the dunes. Now the village had to rebuild. Our safety depended on it, Long Island's too. Fire Island was a barrier beach. No one could ever forget the Hurricane of '38, when the ocean and bay met in Cherry Grove -- the specter that hung over us, erosion the eternal threat. Often they bulldozed sand. One time they'd laid five expensive, cement groins that sank. This year's solution was pumping sand from the bottom of the bay through enormous pipes laid across the quarter mile width of the island to the ocean beach.

"It cost the village $30,000. Those clams, crabs and seaweed are freebies."

"But it stinks, Mike." He was right, the beach smelled like a garbage pail.

"That's the unfortunate part of the process. We have to look at pumping sand as a prophylactic measure and take the bad with the good."

"Excuse me dear, could I interrupt you for a minute?" Only Mother had the balls to interrupt Dad. "I'd like you to meet Jordan Kaplan." She remembered names. Mother, the only one in the family who could; Dad had memory lapses when it came to saying hello. He'd mumble, "What's the name of that guy? I know him." By this time we'd hustled to the other side of the street to escape, thus avoiding direct confrontation. "He wants to take her out for the evening."

"How do you do, Mr. Abrams, your daughter's in great hands, I promise."

"Please see she's home by twelve" Jordan had passed muster. Twelve?" It was Saturday night. Why, Dad? Why?

"Say good night and thank you to Bianca and Jimmy." As if I wouldn't. I knew my social P's and Q's.

"Mother!" We left in the middle of a chorus of "Bali Hai" from *South Pacific.*

"Night, Princess," Jimmy winked.

Jordan and I walked down the wooden ramp into the night. "Where would you like to go, Princess? You don't mind if I call you that? As you know, we have a fabulous array of nightspots to visit.

"Let's go to Goldie's. We can join Becker and Johnny."

"Your wish is my command." He put his arm around me, ostensibly to protect me. A starry, starry night, the Milky Way stretched across the sky, shooting stars streaked, sizzled, dazzled. Romantic except he wasn't Nick. I knew nothing about Jordan, peppered him with questions.

He was twenty-five from L.A. His father, a Jewish film producer, had married a model, a Philadelphia mainline WASP, who, with her husband's help, had been an actress till their children were born. He'd prepped at Andover, majored in English at Harvard, and though he loved films, wasn't 'cut out to be cut throat'. He'd come to New York, landed a job at Random House, assistant to famed editor Jason Epstein, a literary coup. Now a full editor, his career thriving, had a few short stories published, was working on a novel, volunteered for politics on the side -- a devout Democrat. I was impressed. Very.

His sister, a costume designer, had become friendly with Gerry Brooks on a film, entrusted her with the care of her younger brother when he came to New York. Gerry invited him out for the weekend. Jordan made a beeline to the volleyball game, he'd played on the beach at Malibu, met Sean who was looking for a roommate in love with Fire Island. I complimented him on how attractive he looked. His answer, "Think Yiddish, dress British." We arrived 'downtown'. He was funny, easy to talk to, smart. I enjoyed our conversation.

Goldie's, perched on the bay had replaced Sis Norris as the in spot this season. He'd taken pains with the decoration, fresh white paint, a Joe Palooka mural dedicated 'to Goldie with love from Ham Fisher', Joe's creator, on the back wall. Lester Gaba's painting of a luscious red watermelon slice on a blue and white checked tablecloth on the other. Lights from the mainland glittered like diamonds in the distance, a reminder we were on an island. Goldie and his partner Wayne Saunders were in the middle of a set, twin pianos at raked angles. Goldie nodded approval of Jordan. He might look but never touch.

Becker and Johnny, at a small table in the middle of the overcrowded room, waved us over. Donald 'Red' Ward, Goldie's headwaiter, recently of Sis Norris, pranced, balancing a tray with drinks.

"Hello, precious. Hi, Jordan. Well, well, well, what a gorgeous couple." Wrong. We weren't. We'd just had one conversation. I hadn't thought about Nick for a half an hour. Turquoise was warmer than sapphire, a better color. Why hadn't I met Jordan first?

"How are you tonight, Red?"

"Perfect as usual. There's almost enough room for you to join Becker and Johnny if you don't mind sharing a chair."

I refused to sit on Jordan's lap, so we both sort of sat, literally half assed. Jordan ordered drinks. Becker looked relieved I wasn't alone. I felt a rib nudge. "Catch that!"

I looked over to see Red nuzzling Barbara's' neck. No. Couldn't be. He was from Brooklyn, son of an Irish cop, her family, the Gardiners, famous writers, island royalty. Another Smithie, the last time I'd seen her was an awkward bump-into on the quad all suited up in the right uniform: a Shetland sweater, Bermuda shorts, long socks. She was in dungarees and a grey sweatshirt -- Fire Island casual.

"I hear they're having a thing." Becker filled us in.

"Why him? She could have anyone." Didn't make sense, I was sure he wasn't straight.

"She can have me." Jordan admired the beauty. I felt a jealous pang, more interested in him now that he showed interest in Barbara.

"What am I chopped liver?"

"Get serious. You're starry-eyed. We've been together for hours and you haven't noticed me yet." I had. "I may have to give up and take you to see 'him'. At least I can admire Jean's ass."

"Let's go; it's uncomfortable here." Becker and Johnny whispered and giggled together, oblivious to us. The rest of the room sang along with Goldie, "It's delightful… it's de-lovely..." We waited until the applause was over, tried to sneak out without Goldie noticing.

"Goodnight you lovebirds." Didn't.

We walked through town until we were in front of Bayview. "Let's go in the back, we can avoid the traffic jam and the bouncer."

"Fine Princess, lead the way." Past the Post Office to the rear of Bayview, through the sand, we entered the back door. Nick was surrounded. I panicked. What should I do? What if he ignored me?

"I'd love another drink, Jordan."

"Ladies don't have another drink; they have *a* drink." Always taking care of me.

"I'd like *a* Dewar's." Jordan disappeared into the crowd. I slid into the shadows, my heart beating like a schoolgirl's with her first crush. Mine had been Steven Klaidman in kindergarten. We'd played together, girlfriend and boyfriend, until Mrs. Fuller's second grade class when Phil Moss started flirting with me. Greener grass, I left Steven for Phil. Steven was devastated, cried. His mom kept calling Mother to reunite us, to no avail. The moment I told Phil I was all his, he left me. Steven didn't want me back. I suffered for my mistake, ostracized, alone -- a bad girl -- I'd dumped nice Steven.

I liked Jordan. Nick had a girlfriend. If I were smart, I'd quit while I was ahead. I wasn't smart.

"Your drink, Princess. Have you been hiding this whole time or have you made progress?" He seemed to have a crush on me yet was advising me about Nick. Why was he helping me like this? Rescue mission? I didn't get it.

"Yes, no and thanks. I need this." I didn't, was getting drunk. Jordan maneuvered us through the crowd so we could see Nick. I gasped.

"What's the matter?"

"Nothing."

"You look upset. Chill."

As he whispered those instructions in my ear Nick turned our way, registered us, smiled. Jordan went to the men's room. Nick broke into "My Funny Valentine". I smothered my first impulse to throw my arms around his neck. What would Marilyn do? A sex kitten crawl into his lap was much too forward. Bacall would wink, inhale her cigarette, blow some smoke into his face. I couldn't do the wink part well and was out of cigarettes. A Marlene Dietrich elbow lean on the piano? Should I blow him a kiss? I smiled and sang along. The song ended the set.

"How are you doing tonight, pretty girl? I loved our swim. Nice fellow, Jordan." Before I could answer or assure him that Jordan was just a friend he slid out. I watched Jean disengage from the crowd and follow him into the darkness.

"I told you that Jean has a beautiful ass." Jordan was back, hadn't missed a beat.

"Is that all you can say?"

"He looks interested, but so does she, and she's not going to let him out of her sight. Let's go Princess; it's getting past your bedtime and your father's waiting. If we come home any later, he'll shoot me."

"Les just have one more drink."

"I have a better idea. Let's go to the beach and neck. Now you're drunk I can make a pass at you. You didn't know this, but I'm a certified sex maniac."

"There's only one problem. There are three of you and I want to stay for another set."

"That's two problems, if I'm correct. Now listen to Uncle Jordan. Don't stay. Subtlety and mystery are a lady's greatest assets."

"Jordan, now there are four. I feel dizzy."

"That settles it. We're going. Grab onto my arm and let's make our third back door exit of the night."

The bed spun faster and faster. Around and around and around we go, where it stops nobody knows. I tried every trick in my repertoire to stop the whirly birds but nothing worked except the old finger down the throat. Disgusting.

The Anvil Chorus was playing in my head the next morning in time with rain tattooing the roof. A black cloud had snuck in during the night. Retribution. Not only did I have to endure Japanese water torture, I had no chance of seeing Nick, even if he ran Rosencrantz in the rain, I wouldn't know when -- couldn't sit on the beach waiting all day. Rain, rain, go away little Ali wants to play. I couldn't call him, clueless where he lived, summer rentals unlisted. Women weren't supposed to call men. Why shouldn't I be able to call? Why did they have all the power? Unfair. I wanted to change the rules.

'Hello Nick, how'd you like to go out tonight? I know this adorable little French place Le Veau d'Or on 60th, if you don't feel like a cozy candlelit dinner how about a movie? We could have a hamburger at P. J. Clarke's after. Freddy, who guards the back room, is a friend so we can always get a table. Of course you can dress casual. See you at seven.'

I knew Jordan would call and Nick wouldn't – he hadn't asked me for my number. I had to sing the siren's song, charm him away from Jean and see him again come hell or high water.

3

Humpty Dumpty

Sunday on the beach two weeks later, I talked to the girls, the burning topic, Paris. From the second I spied the sapphires I'd regretted having to go. How could I leave Nick? All I'd do would be miss him, worry he'd forget about me. Out of sight. Out of mind. Becker and Kate, my Greek chorus, weighed in incredulous I was even thinking about not going. Was I crazy? They'd give their right and left arms to live in Paris for two months all expenses paid.

Kate's dream was to live on the Left Bank, have *un café*, sit next to Sartre at *Deux Magots* in Saint-Germain-des-Prés, existential expat heaven.

On Becker's European jaunt last summer, she'd fallen in love with Serge, a Frenchman, couldn't wait to return, thought I was a flaming idiot forsaking Paris for an older man who wasn't available. 'Dumb,' she'd sneered. The more they tried to convince me to go, the more the Imp pushed back, 'no matter how great Paris was, Nick was better.'

I was afraid to discuss it with Mother, knew her view -- Paris was 'it', the epicenter of the fashion and shopping universe. French fashion ruled and we followed. She would've loved to live there. If she couldn't, I should.

I made the major decision Monday. Always did Very Important Things like start a diet the first day of the week. The Imp on center court won. I'd stay. I told Dad at the office, figured it would slip by. No such luck. He didn't want me lounging around with nothing to do; I'd have to keep working till the end of summer. Perfect Pyrrhic victory, I'd won but lost, would be under Dad's thumb, during the week, both parents on the weekend. Stuck in hell, *No Exit,* speaking of Sartre.

We bobbed up and down beyond the breaking point, tantalizing each other, Nick and I in the ocean, at it again.

"I'm going to catch a rider and cool off." He interrupted a long, hot kiss.

"How can you stop just like that?" Maybe he didn't really want me; my confidence not my long suit, under the best of circumstances, at an all-time low. I'd made no progress in our relationship if you could call seeing him a total of five weekends for a few stolen moments in the water, watching him sing while his girlfriend watched me, a relationship. Jordan was very much around to fill in the gaps. I felt empty.

"I'm not taking your cherry in the water." Nick was defiant.

"How do you know you wouldn't like it?" Between the devil and the deep blue sea, coming on when he said no, backing off when he got too close. He took a rider. I swam in. We walked towards his blanket.

"That's not the point. You're afraid of His Worship," the proper way to address a judge in the Commonwealth, he said in jest, "and so am I. If he finds out I'm fooling around with his daughter he'll probably punch me in the Adam's apple so I can't sing again, break both my hands so I can't play and send me to The Pines for a tea dance wearing a tight bathing suit and no jock strap." Nick laughed at his joke.

"Don't say things like that." Defensive. "He may be a prude but he's not a barbarian. Everyone loves him. You would too if you got to know him." Why not introduce Nick to the family. Overdue, lots of flack on the home front, they'd heard about him thanks to Billy, had always met my boyfriends -- couldn't call him that, before.

Mother was asking questions, "Why haven't you brought that singer over?" 'He has a girlfriend' wasn't such a hot answer, neither was 'he doesn't have time'.

Carpe diem Marilyn, "Why don't you and Rosie come over and meet my parents?" I tried to make it sound casual, seductive. As if it would be fun. Wrong.

Caught off guard at first he smiled, a setting of tiny wrinkles appeared around the sapphires, "Is that an invitation?"

"How about six tomorrow?" I held my breath, wished we were in the water so I could swim away, clueless how he was going to react -- so much at stake.

"Okay. But if something goes wrong with your dad, don't be surprised if I run like hell. I've got a lot of coward running through my veins and I don't mean Noel."

On a roll, "What about Jean?" Heart pounding. Thump. Thump. Thump. Atlas shrugged his shoulders. I let it go. At least I'd asked.

As I wended my way home, I searched for sea glass scattered among seaweed, crab carcasses and shells for Mother's collection, apothecary jars of blue, green, amber and clear on the ledge of our kitchen window. 'You're afraid.' Nick surprised me by being incisive -- he was right. More likely I was transparent, my heart on my sleeve, its usual position. I *was* afraid, caught between lust and fear of losing my virginity when we were together, miserable when I wasn't with him. Minutes of happiness were intercepted by hours of loneliness. Obsessed, possessed, I'd thought about nothing else, knew no more about him now than when we'd met. An impenetrable mystery, never knew what he was thinking, he had the power to cloud my mind like "The Shadow", Lamont Cranston alias Nick Rose.

And Jean still hovered over the Chagall sky.

I spied a piece of blue glass, the color of a milk of magnesia bottle, stooped to pick it up. It was oval, symmetrical, the edges sea smooth, same shade as his eyes, even nature in cahoots. I climbed the steps to our street, skulked into the house.

"Well, if it isn't Georgiana." My grandmother, mother's detested mother-in-law, known as a drama queen, her favorite put down. Mother sat crocheting, a critical mass.

"A very precious love, is all I want..." Billy at the organ, hummed a few bars, then said, "Hi Marjorie." He was a past master at getting my goat. I'd contemplated murder on several occasions but no death seemed horrible enough.

"Quit it." I rushed into my room, slammed the door.

Through the wall I overheard Mother ask, "What's that song you're singing?"

"It's the theme song from *Marjorie Morningstar.* Doesn't Ali remind you of Marjorie in love with the older singer, Noel Airman?" She'd read it, seen the movie, faithful to their friend, Herman Wouk, the author, who had a home in Seaview.

I'd had it, rushed back into the living room. "If you don't shut up you little twerp, I'm going to strangle you. You're the vilest, lowest creep in the world. I wish you were dead."

"Quit it you two. Billy, stop teasing Ali about that singer we've never met." Dripping with sarcasm.

"I've invited him over for a drink tomorrow." I blurted it out.

Mother took less than a second to respond, "Fine. What shall we serve?" Style without substance, she didn't care about my feelings, just wanted to check him out.

"You don't have to do anything, he's just stopping by for a few minutes around six. No big deal." It was huge. "I told him he could bring his dog." I continued in a whisper, "Could you make sure Billy's not around?"

"He has a right to be here it's his home, too."

"I'm going to tell Nick not to come."

"Don't get argumentative. Billy will behave properly, I'm sure." I wasn't.

"Promise not to let him out of his cage if he doesn't have his clothes on." Billy had the annoying habit of opening the door to meet my dates in his jockeys, anything to mortify me.

"Don't worry so much, that singer is only another man." Easy for her to say, for her, he was.

I avoided Bayview that night, fearful Nick might change his mind. If he couldn't see me, he couldn't cancel. What if he hadn't taken my invitation seriously? How was his memory? Was he reliable? I didn't know the answers. Why I didn't know them, a better question. I worried myself into insomnia. When I finally got up the next morning, everyone was gone. There was a note next to my coffee cup, 'Went to town to do errands. X Mother.' She was shopping for hors d'oeuvres, hard to believe the 'X' on the note. A kiss? Definitely no 'O', she never hugged.

I slid into my white bathing suit, grabbed a red and white striped beach towel walked to the volleyball court. The guys had lined up to see who'd play on which side, two eight man teams, no rotation, the measure of the man if he was chosen in the first few picks. A dead serious business, not a democracy, outsiders never made it into the game unless they were ringers. No personality secrets left after a game, twenty-one points, the Book of Revelations. Was there life after volleyball or was volleyball life?

I sat down to root for Jordan, a gifted player and a good sport. Why didn't I love him?

"Anyone home?" Nick was outside the screen door.

"Coming." I brushed my hair one last time, rushed out of my room, white Bermudas and man's shirt tied at the waist.

Dad was on the couch next to the radio fiddling with his fishing reel, faded navy *chemise* La Coste, patched Madras Bermudas, listening to 'them bums', his *ex* Brooklyn Dodgers battle it out against the enemy of the day. Their defection to Los Angeles two years ago was unforgivable, a blasphemy. Brooklyn-born Dad had gone into a depression, as had the whole borough.

Mother had gone all out -- a platter of Italian and French cheese, crackers, celery, carrots and radishes that she'd cut into little flowers, a bunch of fresh white daisies. She looked crisp. The pest's pompadour was in place.

"You've got the right house, Nick." I raced to get to the screen door before Mother, lost.

"Hi, I'm Mrs. Abrams. Please come in." She didn't offer her first name like she did with everyone else -- going to keep the interview formal. Nick stayed outside.

"Nick Rose, Mrs. Abrams. I've brought my dog, Rosencrantz. Do you mind if he comes in, he's very well behaved, or should I tie him up outside?"

Mother took a long hard look at Nick, then Rosencrantz. "Put him on the back deck."

Dad rose from his chair walked to the door, pronounced, "Bring him in, he looks like a fine dog." Enter Nick and Rosencrantz on a leash.

"How do you do sir.", they shook hands. Nick led Rosie to the back of the room, took off the leash, "Down." He lay on the spattered floor. Dad motioned Nick to sit down on the couch in front of the hors d' oeuvres. "Can I make you a drink?" Dad moved to the bar, the pine dry sink.

"Yes sir. Make it a vodka and tonic, low on the vodka. I don't mix drinking with work." Nice, Nick, nice. Dad handed Nick his drink, sat down in his chartreuse armchair across from the couch.

"This is Ali's brother, Billy," Mother continued the formalities. The pompadour shook hands, sat to his right, I on the left. Not too close. She passed radishes, cut a runny piece of Bel Paese, spread it over a Carr's cracker offered it to Nick with a cocktail napkin.

"Thanks." He ate it. "Delicious."

"You the new singer at Bayview?" Billy knew he was.

"Yes. Weekends."

Mother sat down opposite him. Pinned. "What do you do during the week?" The second degree arrived.

"Same thing. Sing and play. Some record dates."

"Where do you live?" Billy was the grand inquisitor.

"Ocean Road. A bungalow by the bay." For once I thanked him albeit silently. "Hey, boy, come here and meet these folks." Rosencrantz obeyed. Everyone shook paws with him. I gave him a hug, he licked -- slobbered me.

"Does Rosencrantz need a drink?" Dad loved animals.

"Some water would be great." Mother poured a bowl and put it on the floor, Rosencrantz lapped it up.

Billy polished off the herring. "Does he know any tricks?"

"Just a few of them. Sit, Rosencrantz. Beg, Rosencrantz." Rosencrantz complied.

"Does he know any others?"

"Up, Rosencrantz." He reared on his hind legs, his sizable paws rested on Nick's shoulders. "Down, boy. Good dog."

"You look familiar. Have I seen you before?" It was Dad's turn.

"My secret is out, sir. You found me guilty Memorial Day weekend of not separating the glass from the trash in the garbage, fined me fifteen bucks which I paid on the spot. It was my first time here, honestly didn't know about the garbage separation law, Judge Abrams." Nick was contrite.

"I hope you won't do that again." Great, Mother just what he needed another reprimand.

"No, it was an expensive lesson."

"The problem is our incinerator. It's too old and delicate to process glass."

"Yes, I remember, you told me when you fined me."

"How much does Tommy Kohler pay you a weekend?" Cheeky bastard. Bad manners. You never discussed money. Billy cornered Mother's cheese market.

"Interested in singing?" Nick deflected the curve ball.

"He's a monotone." I emphasized.

"Have you noticed our organ? It's an antique. Billy gets music out of it, even so." Mother would defend the brat no matter what.

"I can tell it played beautifully, once. They don't make them like that anymore. Bach probably composed on something similar."

"How do *you* know so much about classical music?" Now, Mother's turn in the inquisition.

"I studied it at school."

"Where?"

"Juilliard." Nick was batting a thousand.

"Mrs. Abrams is very musical, too. She plays the piano and sings." Dad was proud.

"I'm very rusty; was serious about it once."

"What kind of songs do you sing?" Billy was curious.

"Pop. Ever hear 'Happy Times'?"

"Sure. Dum de. Dum de. Dum de da da da da." The pest started to hum off key.

"Would you do me a favor, Nick?" Dad interrupted with authority.

"What can I do for you, sir?"

"Can we take Rosie over to see my friend?"

"Who?" Mother was curious.

"Harold."

"But Dad, he's afraid of dogs." I was concerned.

"Rosencrantz is gentle as you can see," Nick reassured.

Our neighbor Harold Berger lived two houses away, almost on the beach. Tall, Harold Lloyd glasses, quizzical expression in his big brown eyes, his two passions, the money he was going to inherit when his wife's extremely rich mother from Dallas died, and nutty inventions like ice creamless ice cream. He introduced himself, as Harold soon-to-be-rich Berger, appeared evenings in a crisp navy blazer, ascot, white pants and shoes, everyone else barefoot. When complimented on how wealthy he looked, he'd reply, "I'm practicing."

Dad had something up his sleeve.

We walked over to the Bergers, knocked at the door. Dad held Rosencrantz on the leash, told us to keep quiet.

"Harold? Harold? Anyone home?"

"Who's there?"

"Mike and the family. I want you to meet someone."

"Be right there."

Harold came to the screen door in all his English gentleman glory, opened it, took one look at Rosencrantz, started to scream. "Help. Help. It's a wild dog. Call the police. Call the fire department. He looks like he's going to kill me." With his shouting and everyone's laughter, Rosencrantz started to bark. "See what I mean? I'm never going to make it to be rich. I'll die poor. Please get that monster away from me, Mike."

"Calm down Har, he won't hurt you, he's a nice dog. Come here and pet him. I promise he won't bite."

"He's a killer. I can tell. Why he's as big as a house. He hates me."

"No he doesn't. His name is Rosencrantz. This is his master, Nick Rose."

"I don't like the way your dog's looking at me."

"I promise you he's all right," avowed Nick.

"Why don't you hold him?" Dad transferred the leash to his hand. Har, say up."

"Up."

On command Rosencrantz reared, put his paws on Harold's chest.

"Oh my God he's attacking me in cold blood."

This time he was close to going over the edge, Nick sensed it, cried, "Down, Rosencrantz; heel. Good dog."

Harold ran into his house, slammed the screen door. "I don't mean to be rude but I'll stay inside until you get that wild dog away from here."

We said our goodbyes. No time for post mortems, Mother and Dad's active social schedule included a cocktail then dinner party. "I've left supper for you and Billy warming on the stove. All you have to do is serve it. Be sure to clean up afterwards." She ignored Nick. They rushed off.

On the way back to our house Nick, Billy and Rosie walked ahead. I overheard Billy say, "Don't worry about my Mother, she's jealous of Ally because she's beautiful, it's not personal." Couldn't believe my ears. Billy was standing up for me.

"She sure is a pretty girl."

Billy rushed up the ramp. Nick whispered, "It's getting late, have to go. Coming to Bayview tonight?"

"Maybe," shocked at my answer, I wasn't rushing down there so fast, didn't want to go through the pain of watching Nick while Jean give me dirty looks.

Billy inhaled his food. "Is there dessert fatso?" Any good feelings I had down the drain.

"Yes, birdbrain, Huckleberry pie." We'd picked the wild huckleberries. Billy intimidated me with his constant taunts about my 'enormous girth', which set off my insecurity -- no one loved a fatty. I wouldn't eat my portion. He'd wheedled me out of mine. I fell for it every time. In two seconds, two pieces of pie and Billy disappeared. Still finishing the main course when the phone rang, Billy answered, yelled from the living room. "A man for you, fatso." He started singing "A Very Special Love". Was it Nick? My heart started to pound.

"Hello. Oh, hi." Just Jordan. "The Pines? Dancing? Great idea. Love to. Where shall I meet you? Fifteen minutes, yes, I'll be on time." Relieved, an alternative to 'downtown'.

Our chariot, a red and white jeep, the White Cap taxi, waited on the beach at the foot of Evergreen Walk, headlights on, motor running, Becker and Jordan inside. Jordan jumped out, a gentleman, "Hi, Princess. Got on your dancing shoes?"

"My dancing feet."

"Here comes Johnny." Becker's boyfriend arrived. "Let's go."

We drove eastwards on the beach following the tracks other taxis had carved out of the soft sand, navigated by headlights, half moon and starlight. We arrived half an hour later at the Pines, exhilarated by the balmy night. The Pines was the newest and by far the most dramatic of all the island communities. Elegant, breathtaking, it was *the* summer place for New York's most successful homosexuals. A Cecil Beaton stage, poison ivy tamed wide, symmetrical boardwalks, tall pines that hid private villas and lives with their fine green needles, rough brown cones. Funny signs read 'Trespassers *will* be violated'; 'Oedipus Wrecks'.

The lights were dim, the music romantic as we entered the Boatel on the bay. Jordan held me close as we danced a fox trot. He smelled of bay rum cologne, looked adorable in a navy blue and white striped French fisherman's shirt and tight jeans. The music changed to a lindy. Glenn Miller, he knew all the steps. We danced well together, a perfect partner, worked up a sweat, "Pennsylvania 6 5 0 0 0." The joint was jumping with the most gorgeous men I'd ever seen coupled off. "*Volare, oh, oh, cantare, oh, oh, oh, oh*", last summer's hit, a sing along. Jordan took my hand, led me to the deck overlooking the picturesque marina. Pleasure yachts and sailboats bobbed as we snuggled under the stars, his kisses surrogates for Nick's. He aroused me yet couldn't make me forget the sapphires four miles away.

Tap, tap, tap. Tap, tap, tap. I burrowed further under my giant pillow.

"Good morning." Mother opened my door.

"Go away. I'm sleeping."

"It's breakfast time."

"Please, please let me alone." Let me stay unconscious buried in feathers.

"Breakfast is on the table."

Waking up early put me in a bad mood. "I don't care."

"Your father insists you join us." A command. Pulling rank early.

"Give me a few minutes."

"Late night 'downtown'?"

"No, I went dancing at the Pines."

"Who went?"

"Why don't you come right out and ask if I was with Nick instead of giving me loaded questions?" I paused for effect. "A bunch of us." I stayed vague.

"Hurry up, the eggs will get cold." Mother left. She had a point. Nothing was worse than cold eggs except thinking about them.

"I'm coming." I pulled on the itchy orange bathing suit, wrapped on an orange and white flowered pareu, present from Tahiti via Martinique, where Mother and Dad had vacationed, without us, of course.

"Good morning." Dad was all dressed up, long pants, seersucker jacket, well buffed loafers, the official outfit for his day to hold court. Billy was off to lifeguard duty.

"Morning Dad." Mother had set the dining room table for Sunday brunch starring a platter of lox with lemon slices and capers, a wicker basket with plain, onion and everything bagels cut in halves ready to be toasted or not; cream cheese with chives, sliced onions, tomatoes, scrambled eggs and bacon, home fries. Perfect.

"Your father and I want to talk to you.", the scary voice.

"Now or after I've had a cup of coffee?"

"Before. Your father has to leave for court."

"What's up? I was home by 12:48 last night."

"It's about that man you brought over to the house yesterday."

Oh, oh, 'that man', trouble. "His name is Nick Rose. Remember?" Of course she did.

"We've heard terrible things about him."

"You're kidding." By the look on her face, she wasn't.

"He's a dope addict." She didn't mince words.

"What? You're out of your mind. That's the craziest thing I've ever heard." I couldn't believe my ears.

"Not only that, he's an alcoholic."

I cracked, started screaming. "You're lying. Dope addict? Alcoholic? Lies. Boldfaced lies."

"Don't you dare raise your voice to your mother." Dad reprimanded me.

"That's what we've heard. We aren't spending all this money to give you the best education for you to get involved with a degenerate."

"Degenerate? Get serious."

She was. "Your father doesn't want you to see *him* again. It's forbidden. He's off limits." She said 'him' as if he had the plague. "That's final. No point discussing it. People are talking about how you're chasing him." Oh my God. In shock, was I dreaming? A nightmare? It wasn't I was wide awake.

I didn't know what to overreact to first.

"What do you mean, people? Those dried up old hags you call friends? Lies. Lies. Liars. I can't believe you're listening to beach bullshit."

"Enough. I'm warning you to stop screaming at the breakfast table. Did you hear me?" Dad's sternest voice, I'd expect something like that from Mother but not my perfect Dad known for honesty. In the same one second that Lucifer got tossed out of heaven and went to hell, His Worship fell from grace and off his pedestal, crashed, our relationship smashed, my heart broken into a million pieces. 'Humpty Dumpty had a great fall… All the king's horses couldn't get Humpty Dumpty back together again.' Tears trickled down my cheeks.

I mumbled, "Yes, Dad," looked down at my plate, surreptitiously wiped my eyes, ran from the table, grabbed a shirt from my room slammed out of the house, tears streaming, Niagara Falls, distraught, destroyed.

'Alcoholic.' 'Dope addict.' Liars. 'You can't see him again'. What was I going to do? I cried my way down the walk. Why were they so desperate to stop my romance? That was a laugh -- one-sided love affair. I was doing the pursuing. Alcoholic? I'd never seen him finish one drink. Drug addict? No way. A few jazz musicians were drug addicts, Billie Holiday and Charlie Parker he was not. I would've known. How do you tell when someone's a junkie? Could he be one? I had a second of doubt as I visualized his arms. No tracks. Forgive me Nick.

I wandered down the walk distraught. What gossipmonger had slandered him last night? Maybe they'd made it up themselves. What was wrong with him? A singer? Older? Not Ivy League. Maybe. Couldn't say anything against Juilliard. Most likely didn't know about his ex-wife. Maybe Jean. Too good looking? Did Dad sense my virginity was at stake? Something out of a bad Victorian novel, I didn't know whom to blame first, what to do, stunned, my world crumbling. Destroyed. I couldn't see the man I loved because Mother and Dad believed lies or lied. Greek tragedy. I was mixing metaphors attempting to comprehend the worst moment of my life.

An iron curtain, wall of hate slammed down between them and me. Mother would much later admit it was the worst mistake they ever made. To say the least.

'Stop seeing him'. They had another thing coming. I'd run away. A quick tabulation of my assets came to the two hundred and fifty dollars cash I'd saved for Paris. Not enough. I couldn't drop out, not finishing college out of the question for a Jewish girl. You finished or were nothing -- my son the doctor, my son the lawyer, my daughter the what? My daughter who's going to marry a doctor or lawyer or other Ivy League graduate, 'We're not paying all this money to send you to college for you to fall in love with a dope addict.' I felt nauseous, desperate to see Nick. The bottom had dropped out of my life, stranding me in a leaky raft alone on the high seas.

Nick where are you? I walked down Ocean Road between Midway and the bay hoping to figure out where his house was; he'd said something about a bungalow. I crept along looking for the right one. All the houses were bungalows -- I needed a sign. Almost to the bay, I heard it -- that horrible hyena laugh, spied Jean lounging on a small back deck in a bikini. She would have one. I'd seen pictures of French girls wearing them on the Riviera in the fashion magazines, but never seen the real thing. Where was he? Nick. Nick. Come out. I have to talk to you. I heard him singing and playing the piano inside. Practicing. What would I say if he saw me? Pardon me, I was just passing by and wondered if I could borrow a cup of sugar even though I don't know how to cook and I'm half a mile from home.

I buzzed in front of the house like an insect. How could I get rid of Jean and that disgustingly perfect body? If I were a mosquito or a bee I'd sting her, she'd have to go into town to get something for the bite and I could talk to Nick alone.

As I hovered desperately trying to come up with a plot, a couple passed by and said hello. I pretended I was picking something -- no huckleberry bushes, just beach plums still green. I rehearsed answers in case they caught me, 'I was visiting a friend who lives up the block, and had a sudden diarrhea attack, could I use the john?' Gross. I resorted to mental telepathy, Nick I'm outside, please come out, shut my eyes whispered his name three times. I heard a chair creak, the door slam, ran as fast as I could into town and didn't stop until I turned the bend. My heart pounded as I entered the deserted village. It was a broiler and everyone was on the beach. I scurried past Dad's office in the Community House that served as a courthouse, prayed he wouldn't look out the window and see me, snuck into John and Anne's Ice Cream Parlor.

A few customers sat at the window tables, drinking coffee, eating, reading the funnies. The red white and blue Wurlitzer jukebox played "How High the Moon", Les Paul and Mary Ford '51, they never changed the music. I sat down on a cracked red leather swivel chair at the counter, watched Anne, a plain, hardworking local, take a swatter and go after an enormous fly. Whack. She got it. My secret fantasy as a child was her job -- behind the counter able to eat unlimited amounts of ice cream in a sea of hot fudge.

"Hi, Ali. What are you doing in town on a hot day like this?"

"I had an urge for an ice cream cone, Anne."

I felt like a banana split, black and white milk shake, hot fudge sundae, two scoops of chocolate ice cream followed or preceded by an egg salad sandwich on toast with mayo and a slice of tomato, a rare cheeseburger and a slice of apple pie à la mode. I wasn't hungry. I controlled myself, ordered almost a ladylike portion. "I'll have a double scoop of ice cream on a sugar cone."

"What kind?"

"Chocolate. And... do you have banana?"

“Sorry, Ali, just fresh peach today.” She’d already put a perfect orb on the cone, rinsed the scooper waited for my direction hands poised over the round ice cream bins. The pressure was on. Oh God, did I want coffee or peach? ‘Do I dare to eat a peach?’

“And a scoop of...” I wondered whether the aerodynamics of the cone could sustain a triple-decker, “…coffee.”

“Sprinkles or brown derby?”

“Brown derby, please.” There was more chocolate.

“Here you go, that’ll be twelve cents.”

“I’ve left home without money Anne, could you possibly charge it?”

“Sure, Ali, but please remind your father the bill for May is past due.”

“Thanks. Sorry. I’ll tell him.”

I walked out into the sunlight, consumed the cone in three minutes without tasting it needed more. Should I go into Phillips, the competitive parlor right across the street? No, didn’t have credit there and it smelled bad. I walked a block, the intoxicating aroma of freshly baked donuts wafted out onto the street at WalAnnes. Old Captain Pastorfield sat on the bench in front, a village fixture.

I remembered him telling stories while sitting at his bare feet, all the other kids assembled. It didn’t seem to matter that no one could remember what boat he’d been captain of or if he’d been a captain at all -- found out later he hadn’t, Jerry Pastorfield looked and played the part so well. A few strands of pure white hair escaped from the authentic Captain’s hat pushed back on his head. The pipe he lit, relit permanently poised in his mouth punctuated his thoughts. His white beard stubble looked like grains of sand on his wrinkled face, hard edge lines cut from years of squinting at the sea, the sun, we supposed, as we listened to him spin yarns about the old days at Fire Island, enthralled.

"Tell us about the Indians, Captain Pastorfield."

"Injuns? You're talking 'bout the Unkechaugs. They used to paddle their canoes here from the mainland looking for shells for wampum. Only clamshells mind you, and just the little biddy purple spot in the middle. They called us Sewanaka, the isle of the shells. Too bad shells aren't money no more... we'd all be rich today." He cackled.

"What about the pirates?"

"They'd sail across to the island and build big bonfires on the beach. Passing ships got fooled, came in and dropped anchor thinking they'd reached the mainland. Then the pirates dressed up in their eye patches, put on their swords, attacked and stole all their money and jewels. It's cause of them blasted fires that Fire Island got its name." Others might disagree, a clerical error, substituting an "R" for a "V", Five Islands had become Fire Island. Not nearly as romantic.

"Tell us about the great hurricane, Captain, please, please."

"Hurricane of '38? Big blow all right, worst of the century, ocean and bay come together, right here where you're sitting the water was this high." The line he drew with his gnarled hands was way over our heads. "There weren't no place to be safe 'cept up a tall tree and we don't have none of them around here." He cackled, lit his pipe took some interminable puffs, continued. "Hundreds of folks lost their houses. Tidal waves swallowed them up or they got blown out to sea like they were made of matchsticks. Fred Wallace found the top of his house floating in the bay, never did find the bottom. Madge Lawrence's best wicker couch or so she said, wound up on my back deck. Course I gave it back to her, in due time that is. Some blow all right, just 'bout destroyed the island."

By this time I was scared. "Captain Pastorfield, is another big hurricane ever going to blow us away?"

"Don't you worry your head, girl. Fire Island's lasted this long, it's going to last least till you get all grown up."

The smell of fresh baked donuts hovered, tantalizing me as I entered WalAnnes. Wally, the owner, august and benign, reigning donut king, stood behind his horseshoe counter, "Hi, Ali, what'll it be today?"

"I'll have four donuts for my family." They were all for me. "Is it all right if I charge them? I'll pay you next weekend. I seem to have walked out of the house without cash."

"Sure. With or without sugar?"

"With." I watched Wally vigorously sprinkle white confectionary sugar out of his enormous shaker over the brown donuts, wrap them individually with wax paper, place them carefully in a white paper bag. Precious cargo. "Thanks, Wally."

I doubled back to the other side of the village green past Bayview, avoiding John and Anne's. By the time I reached Kline's, I'd wolfed down all four. I bypassed the array of sports equipment, games, postcards, sneakers, Frisbees, Day-Glo hula hoops and headed straight to the new frozen custard machine.

"Hi, Bob." Bob Kline, the owner, tall drink of water, black hair, glasses.

"What can I do for you, Ali?"

"I'd like to try one of your new frozen custards. Do you recommend chocolate or vanilla?"

"We've been having a run on the vanilla, so there's none left. The chocolate's not bad."

"I'll have one."

He pressed the lever of the machine and a flat stream of light chocolate semi-frozen liquid oozed out. He made a forward and backward zigzag motion over the squat non-sugar cone as a chocolate Christmas tree grew out of the base. He shut off the machine with his other hand, wiped off the spout -- I was dying to do it myself. "That'll be ten cents, please."

"Sorry, Bob, I've just come from the beach... could you charge it to our account?

"Fine, but please remind your Dad he's overdo on his bill. I'm sure it's just an oversight on his part." It wasn't. Dad never paid bills on time, to the embarrassment of the entire family. Mother had to constantly nag him to do it.

I finished the frozen custard in half a block and righteously tossed the cone into the trashcan -- I wouldn't eat just anything. I should've bought Mounds or Baby Ruth – somehow, still room in my stomach.

Where had the road to overeating begun? Mother admitted I'd been so small due to my premature feet first entry into the world -- four and a half pounds, she'd nursed me for a year to fatten me up, a chubby baby with pinchable cheeks, more attractive than a scrawny one. As she overfed me I grew to be pleasingly plump, later called *zaftig*. Mother sent mixed messages, 'Have a nice apple or a nice glass of milk", *nice* a permanent adjective, 'Stop eating fattening things.' No fairness in life or metabolism, Billy could devour three boxes of Malomars, get skinnier. A sweet tooth restricted, I raided the refrigerator at night tempted by forbidden fruit -- ice cream and pastries – never liked fruit. I mastered the art of skimming off the top of a new carton of ice cream so no one would notice anything was gone; would cut an irregular portion of pie, steal the insides from under the crust of the next piece; crumble up two chocolate chip cookies, leave half.

I wondered if the fear of getting caught made the whole operation exciting. It certainly wasn't the taste of the food; because I always gobbled so fast for fear of being discovered, I didn't enjoy it. Resigned to a fat/thin life yoyo, figured I lost and gained at least thirty pounds a year. Hell, I could gain five pounds in an hour, which I was proceeding to now do.

I stared at the gelatinous blueberry pies in the window of the Blue Bake Shop. No, had to draw the line somewhere. I wondered whether to have an encore at John and Anne's, could get a hot fudge sundae with fresh peach. The shame of seeing Anne and charging twice in ten minutes stopped me. She might be out to lunch, peeked into the window -- no such luck, had to go to Cleggs. I never liked shopping there, smelled sour, the food unappetizing, like the hors d'oeuvres served at a WASP cocktail party -- sparse and bland. If only I could have a brownie from Greenberg's bakery in New York

-- when you bit into the chocolate it oozed... moist, rich, slightly underdone. Geographically impossible by fifty miles -- shame.

I rushed to the cookie department, settled on Nabisco chocolate chips, Oreos, a Hostess Ring Ding, Funny Bones, grabbed a container of chocolate milk. I waited in line, charged it, ran out before they realized that Dad hadn't paid. I carried my stash in a brown paper bag, walked behind Cleggs, sat on the back steps of the Community House, scarfed it down as I watched kids play on the jungle gym swing, swim in the bay. Life was so much simpler when I'd been a little girl.

Recriminations rolled in, replacing food fever as I waddled to the beach, my stomach sticking out and beginning to ache from the five pounds I'd put on in fifty minutes. How could I have overeaten that much? Sunshiny, hot, not a cloud in the sky, the perfect summer day, everything wrong, the beach crowded, feeling empty with a filled stomach. I avoided the girls, Becker's head buried in the Sunday Times Crossword Puzzle, pen in hand. I knew better than to disturb her, probably hung over, bitchy, couldn't talk to her about Mother and Dad because she didn't understand why it mattered what they'd said in the first place. She didn't have to listen to her parents. Becker's mother, in her own world, couldn't have cared less; her father, a salesman, on the road, left the family to fend for themselves. Becker suspected a girlfriend. She used her home to sleep in, answered to no one, got away with murder. Not a sympathetic ear. Kate would say, 'I told you so.' Jordan was playing volleyball.

I waded in the brownish, choppy August ocean -- too warm, tiny pieces of transparent jellyfish everywhere, on a par with insects in the disgusting zone. Nature was in cahoots against me, not worth it to go in. I re-ran the moment of untruth. 'Dope addict.' 'Alcoholic.' Forbidden to see the man I loved who lived with someone else by liars, my parents. If that wasn't grounds for suicide my newly acquired five pounds was. I'd leave a note behind to punish the liars, 'Dear Mother and Dad, I've decided to kill myself rather than deal with your dishonest and unfair decision not to let me see Nick again.' They'd be sorry. I was a chicken.

"Missed you last night, Valentine." Nick surprised me.

"I bet." Hung my head.

"Hey what's this all about? Where's that beautiful smile? Baby, what's the matter?" He put his arms around me, "Your parents seem like good people. I didn't mean for Rosie to scare Harold. Your father's idea... I just went along with it." The last straw, Nick complimenting me on what nice parents I had. Those bastards. Tears of self-pity appeared out of nowhere.

"Please don't cry. You'll get those beautiful eyes bloodshot. Tell me, what's the matter?" I stared down at the water. He tilted my face towards him.

"I can't."

"Why not?"

"Because you'll never see me again."

"Ridiculous."

"Promise?" He put his hands over his heart, "No matter what I tell you?"

"You're getting married to Jordan?"

"Why would you think that?"

"I've seen him around you. The guy's in love."

"That's ridiculous. We're just friends. All I talk to him about is you." As I blurted it out my cheeks went hot.

Nick grinned, "What's the problem?"

"My parents." I closed my eyes, "They've forbidden me to see you again."

He put his hands on his hips, surprised, "How old are you?"

"I told you, almost twenty-one. That's not the reason. They think you're a… I just can't."

"Baby, let's get something straight. You're the most beautiful Indian princess I know and nothing can change that."

"They said you're an alcoholic and a dope addict."

Now he laughed. "That's the funniest thing I've ever heard. You know I don't drink. Dope addict? That's really nuts. Do you believe them?" He cocked his head.

"No, of course not." I bit my tongue as I thought about my one-second thought crime.

"I wonder where they got that one. They must think all musicians are dope addicts. I swear I'm clean." The sapphires stared straight into my eyes.

"I believe you."

"Tell you what. I'll meet you in town this week. We'll have a drink. I'll be at P. J. Moriarty's 6:30 on Wednesday." He gave me a brisk kiss on the cheek and quickly walked away. Wild horses couldn't stop me.

The traffic was stalled. The cabby had a lot to say about it in between grunts of approval as the Giants pulled ahead full blast over the radio. He would be a Giants fan.

"It's not the heat, it's the humidity, lady."

It was both, 99 degrees in the shade. My white shirtwaist stuck to me, enormous rings of perspiration under my arms, I could just picture the middle of my back. Worse, my hair was curling. What should I do? Get out of the cab? I could walk faster, either that or be late. I paid the fare, tipped him in spite of his unfortunate baseball persuasion -- even a Yankee fan was better. I trudged up Third Avenue, my feet killing me, the high heels, size 8 B should have been an 8 1/2 C. Third Avenue was its usual shambles -- they'd been taking down the El forever. I felt like I was in the middle of the ending of *Duel in the Sun* when in heat not unlike today's Jennifer Jones and Gregory Peck shoot one another, crawl into each other's arms. If I ever loved a man that much, I'd crawl to him too. Today I was hobbling.

I checked my watch at 61st Street and Third in front of P. J. Moriarty's. Ten minutes early. A quick look in my compact revealed I had a major hair repair job on my hands. I pushed the heavy door open, channeled Marilyn again. The room was dark, woody, masculine. The long bar on the left was filled with businessmen holding highballs, their elbows crooked in relief. No Nick. I looked again to make sure.

"Excuse me, sir could you tell me where the ladies room is?" Somehow sir wasn't the right way to address the bartender.

"Over there, lady, take a right." 'Twas the Irish lilt of the old country.

I wrapped my hair in the blessed air-conditioning, emerged five minutes later, straight hair, knot of panic in my stomach. What if he was there? What if he wasn't? Still no Nick, I'd have to wait. How? Where? Put one foot up like the other men? Sit down at a table? As I was pondering my dilemma, a man at the bar got up, offered me his seat. "A pretty lady like you shouldn't have to stand."

"Thank you." I sat down.

"What'll it be, miss?" The bartender confronted me.

"I hope you don't mind, I'm waiting for someone." If I ordered, should I pay or wait? What if Nick didn't show? The bar book of etiquette not my long suit.

"Mind if I buy you a drink?" the man who'd given me his seat, square jaw, seersucker suit, loosened tie, Wall Streeter, mid-twenties. Attractive. My native New Yorker training took over: do not under any circumstances talk to a stranger.

"No thanks."

"Thought you might like some liquid refreshment."

I was dying for a drink. "No thanks." Eyes glued to the floor, as cold as possible. He kept persisting. Perhaps I should let him. Why would anyone want to buy someone who was waiting for someone else a drink? What would I owe him if I did?

"Sure I can't tempt you?"

"Is this gentleman bothering you?"

My belated champion had parked his white charger at the curb. "No, he's been very polite, even gave me his seat."

Nick nodded at the man, "Thank you. Sorry I'm late, my recording session ran over." He kissed me on the cheek, "Why don't we grab a table." God he was gorgeous. I thanked Mr. Squarejaw. We sat at a cozy table against the wall. Nick excused himself. A minute later, "... a gift from the Gods, you're heaven sent." His song was on the jukebox, no wonder he'd picked this place. The sensuous sound softened the masculine room. I thought about sex in the water. The song ended. "Nick, please let's hear it again. So beautiful."

"Here's a quarter. G 6."

A waiter materialized. "What'll it be?

"Tom Collins, please." I'd rehearsed my answer.

"You, Mr. Rose?" Nick must be a regular.

"Give me a vodka and tonic, lots of lime, Jimmy." He put three fingers up to the right side of his forehead like a boy scout, "On my honor, I promise I won't turn into an alcoholic."

"That's not funny. I hate my parents, haven't talked to them since Sunday."

"We're here, aren't we? If ever I have a daughter, I'll want to protect her, too." I fantasized how ours would look. She wouldn't have his eyes or hair, blonde and blue eyes recessive traits, too bad.

A toy train I hadn't noticed high above the bar gave it's 'all aboard' warning. Seven cars made the rounds of the room as the engine blew smoke. What's the conductor's name? I couldn't think of a thing to say, tongue tied, dumb struck, awed, awkward, wished I were in the water -- all I had to do was float. Were we going to dinner? I was hungry. He had all the answers. Unfair. Uncle.

"Shall we cut out?"

"Sure." Unsure. Fasten your seat belts…

"Check, please, waiter." Mr. Squarejaw winked at me as we made our way out into the liquid heat.

"You don't mind walking a bit, do you?"

"I love to walk." Liar. Slow, in pain, it took every ounce of my diminished energy to keep up with his brisk pace and not give into the beginnings of big blisters. Feet don't leave me now. We took a right on 61th, a tree-lined row of brownstones, elegant oasis in the middle of asphalt. That's what got me about New York. Every time I got disgusted, there was something to regenerate my enthusiasm, the constant of the city its unpredictability.

"Beautiful block."

"Glad you like it. Here's where I live."

We stopped at a grey brownstone on the south side near Park, spiral stairs led to the first floor lit by a lamplight. "Would you like to come up for a drink?"

Yes, no. Yes, no. At least he hadn't said *voulez vous couchez avec moi ce soir*? Or asked me to see his etchings, the standard come on line. Did I? A fear pang hit me in the stomach. You asked for it, kid. Was I ready? "Yes." I'd think about later... later. I was curious to see what a bachelor pad looked like; other boyfriends still lived with their parents. We walked up three excruciating flights. Nick unlocked a door in the rear. Rosie's tail wagged to beat the band. A Steinway piano dominated the room, more like a music studio, piles of sheet music, silver machines, white walls, rubber plant, framed photographs of Nick with celebrities.

"Shall we take Rosie for a walk?"

"Do you mind if I stay? My feet are swollen from the heat." And heels.

"Relax, I'll make you a drink."

"Point me in the direction of the booze and glasses. I'll bartend."

"See you in five."

I furtively inspected for signs of Jean Hyena, looked quickly at his pics. No trace. Nick and Rosie returned I handed him his drink. In seconds he was at his record player – stereo, a contraption with a turntable separated from speakers, Mother would call it a Victrola. First we heard "Heaven Sent", then "Happy Times".

He sat down at the piano. "How'd you like to hear the new song I'm recording? Here baby. Next to me." He patted the right side of the bench. "Turn the pages." Nick sang just for me, no crowd or Jean to compete with. I'd died and gone to heaven.

Ten minutes later the performance over, Nick kissed me, "Come, baby." He led me into a tiny bedroom with an enormous brown corduroy king size bed. He caressed, undressed me slowly. Down to his boxers, he deftly removed my bra, kissed my breasts. Gooseflesh. He took my hand put it on him. Hard. As I stroked him he became softer and softer. Was I doing it wrong? Oh God, what should I do?

"I can't go through with this, Valentine." Too fat, he didn't like my body. Something was wrong with my breasts, my thighs. “It’s not what you think.” He should only know what I was thinking. “I’m worried about your father. He’ll kill me if I take your cherry, you’re underage; he is the law. And I don’t think you’re ready.”

“Why not?” Caught myself before I said, ‘I love you.’

“Come here, pretty girl. Don’t turn away. It doesn’t mean I don’t like you or think you’re beautiful, because I do. It’s your father.” As he kissed me, I pictured Dad surf casting on the beach. Kill joy.

4

The Look of Love

It was the summer of my discontent. Manhattan was a hot box, my life a Shakespearean tragedy. Stuck in a stifling, airless canyon, smothered by high-rise buildings that hid the sky, struggling at work, everything wrong. I'd given up Paris for Nick, now mid-August and hadn't seen him since the July fiasco, my life a record stuck on the same track going nowhere. Hoisted by my own petard.

Nick hadn't called. How could he? *They* might answer the phone. I thought about calling him like every other second, snuck out to find him on the beach, couldn't, didn't dare to go to Bayview, eyes everywhere.

I reviewed our date for the millionth time with a mean case of the 'what ifs', 'shouldas 'wouldas' 'couldas' and 'whys'. He didn't want to be unfaithful to Jean and blamed it on Dad the latest scenario. I'd never know.

Jordan was around town courting me, tried to make me feel better. Couldn't.

There'd been another disaster. Geraldine Brooks, true to her offer at the 'By the Sea' party, called to set up a screen test for me with Peter, her director friend. Flattered and excited -- me, a movie star, why not? I called Jordan for help; he knew about film. I thought I'd wear white, my signature color. Jordan suggested black.

"It's more slimming," he said. "The camera puts on ten pounds."

I asked him over that night for what he called, 'wardrobe'. Dad was at a meeting, Mother at the beach. I hurried home after work to clean up my room.

Jordan arrived, dimpled smile, always on time. I gave him the grand tour of our eight-room apartment. He loved the early American pine antiques, cousin Dick Kamm's bronze bust of Mozart, the grand piano in the living room opened as if in a concert hall, the round pine lazy Susan table in the dining room, the chessboard set up in the foyer over black-and-white square checkerboard tiles. I steered him to my bedroom. The windows overlooked Park Avenue.

"What's with the blue?" he asked. "It's not you." I shrugged it off -- Mother's favorite color.

In spite of the fact that she always said no man would marry me if he ever saw my closet, I let Jordan look. He opened the door of the walk-in, but my clothes were crammed so tight, he couldn't move the hangers. I never threw anything out, a permanent source of annoyance to Mother, who cleaned out her closets religiously. He took an armful of clothes on hangers and laid them on the bed. He nixed everything -- too young, boring, bad fit, wrong color forget plaid or print.

"Don't you have anything black?

"I have a leotard." It was the 'second skin' I'd swum in with Nick.

"What about your mother's clothes?"

"Oh, no, she's tiny, size 6. Nothing of hers would fit. Plus, she never lets me borrow anything. Her stuff is sacred."

Sherlock Holmes on the case, he found a dress at the back of the closet I'd forgotten. Mother had brought it from Paris in April, her Vuitton bags laden with 'the latest' clothes. With the dollar so strong, she'd gone to town, torn out the French labels, sewn in American ones -- the four B's: Bonwit's, Bergdorf's, Bendel's, Bloomingdale's plus SFA. In case customs looked, they were her old clothes. Mother didn't like American designers -- Dior, Balenciaga and Chanel, they were not. The only exception was Claire McCardell, who'd died last year. Only 53, a tragedy -- she'd created the first "American Look", casual women's sportswear mass-produced, affordable and stylish.

I happened to be home for the weekend. As she unpacked, Mother gave me a present she'd had made for me by a chic young designer she'd discovered on the Left Bank named Louis Feraud. It was a black wool sleeveless sheath with a discreet V-neck in front and daring back -- no back -- open to the waist, where a black satin bow sat. I'd never worn it. Where would I? A sophisticated cocktail dress was not right for the beer-infested fraternity parties I frequented. I'd buried it deep in the closet and never thought about it again till now.

"Oo-la-la! What do we have here?"

"It's not me," I told him. "Too risqué."

"Try it on. The part could be for an older woman. Or a sophisticate." He left the room. I pulled it over my head. It stuck on top of my boobs. I tried to pull it down. No go. Distraught, I stepped into it, tried to pull it up. It wouldn't go over my hips. Too small. More like Mother's size 6, not my 10. I changed into a print number, knew it was no good. Jordan didn't approve, "too busy."

"Where's the black dress?" I pointed to the floor. He picked it up. "What's the matter with this?"

"It doesn't fit."

"I thought you said your mother had it made for you. Just this spring, right?"

I didn't know what to say. I hadn't gained weight. Odd. Jordan looked at the seams.

"Looks like Monsieur Feraud left lots of room," he said. "My sister's seamstress will take care of it."

True to his word, Jordan saved the day. I made a beeline to New York's best lingerie department, Saks Intimate Apparel, bought a special bra -- the straps went straight down, hooked into my underpants.

The big day dawned. I had my hair done at lunch. Pierre persuaded me to *essayer* -- try -- an up do for my low back dress. I splurged, even had my nails done, *Cherries in the Snow,* Revlon.

Jordan insisted on coming along, supportive as always. He picked me up at Dad's office, looked snappy -- white linen double-breasted jacket, white shirt with a wing collar and black bow tie. I changed in the ladies room, added the final touch, Mother's faux diamond earrings with pearl teardrops. She'd never know. Jordan was agog, showered me with compliments, "Princess you look like a star!"

We took a Checker cab. The studio was somewhere in the very far west 40s. Dicey neighborhood. I was glad Jordan was along. I gave my name, a man with a clipboard checked me in, handed me a mimeographed one page script. My character's name was Lana, "Learn all her lines," he intoned. On the right side of the long black room, fifteen women were scattered on the steps of a staircase, all holding the same page. I climbed up, teetered on a rung, talked to the ingénue below me. An actress – she had an agent, said it was a casting call for the lead in a feature film. Lead? I panicked, they were pros, I was an amateur who'd never memorized anything but poetry. Nor acted. Three poems came to mind: "I think that I will never see…" "Trees", by Joyce Kilmer; "Let us go then you and I…" "The Love Song of J. Alfred Prufrock", T.S. Eliot; "*Córdoba. Lejana y sola.*" "*Canción del Jinete*", Federico García Lorca.

Gerry Brooks materialized, motioned for me to come down. I was thrilled to see her; she must have made a special trip. She took me in hand to a small room where she made me up, the works: pancake makeup, eyeliner, mascara -- no beading, not enough time, rouge, red lipstick which I never wore, made my full lips bigger. She told me not to worry about a thing.

"You look the part. Peter will love you!" Peter was the director.

I went back to the stairs. Jordan sat on the side, taking it all in. When he saw me he made a two-thumbs-up sign. I looked at the words on the page, said them softly out loud, praying I'd remember. My turn came too soon. The clipboard man explained I had to do three things: walk down a runway, say my lines with an actor, kiss Jordan -- Peter had okayed him.

"Take one."

I teetered onto the runway in my new high heels and froze -- pure unadulterated stage fright. One foot went out then the other in lockstep, my arms, stiff, like Frankenstein, I barely made it down the runway.

Peter said, "Try it again. Take two." The Zombie walk redux. He gave me a third chance. Same result. Disaster. I wanted to push an eject button, disappear out of there. S.O.S. The ship was sinking. Time to say my lines. I was positioned next to an actor. The director's assistant slated it. Peter called, "Action."

John or Jim or whatever his name was, said, "I was thinking about you, Lana." My cue. What was I supposed to say? I'd just read it.

I turned to him in desperation, "I don't remember."

Peter cried, "Cut." A man rushed over, showed me the page with my lines. I looked at them in terror. The Imp of the Perverse assured me no way I could do it. I smiled weakly. We got back in place.

"I was thinking about you." The big blank. No third chance.

Time for the screen kiss with Jordan, they set us up, lit it. We kissed passionately for three 'takes'. I pretended he was Nick. Easy.

Peter said, "Your kiss was good. Next." He looked at Gerry, shook his head. No way. "Sorry."

I'd let everyone down, and myself. Blown it. What a revoltin' development this was. Shamed. Not that I had big time star aspirations -- only a week. All I had to do was walk, talk all I could do was kiss. Three pathetic lines. Major memory lapse.

Jordan tried to console me. "Princess, where's your favorite place in the world? You look like a million bucks. Let's show you off."

We took a cab to the Rainbow Room on the 65st floor of Rockefeller Center. I'd been there before for special nights, family celebrations, after proms. We got in -- happy to have us, their regulars out of town -- no one who was anyone was in New York in August. Breathtaking. Magical. Sophisticated. Art deco. Big band orchestra live, revolving dance floor, wraparound views of the glittering skyline, the Hudson, the Statue of Liberty. It defined elegance and romance right out of a Fred Astaire, Ginger Rogers movie. We dined, danced and drank champagne. I was never more humiliated in a more beautiful place. Dad's favorite story came to mind. A man goes into a cheese store, tries the Limburger, the smelliest -- like B.O. A tiny piece lands on the end of his nose. For the rest of the day the whole world smelled bad. Did it ever.

Jordan tried to make me feel better, "Not everyone is cut out to act." He could say that again. "I heard what happened to my mother. Cattle calls like that and rejections wore her down. She took it personally, became depressed lost her self-esteem. You need thick skin and a big ego. You have neither."

The AFGO? (Another Fucking Growth Opportunity): Next time I'd get the script ahead wear 'walkable' shoes if I wanted to be a movie star. Vote still out.

Jordan asked me to the Fireman's Ball that Saturday. I accepted wished he were Nick.

The screen door opened and closed with a bang. On the island, people walked in just like that. "Anyone home?"

"Hi Jordan. If you're looking for Ali, she's late as usual. If you're lucky, it'll only be fifteen minutes." Billy was nasty.

I called through the walls of my bedroom, "I'll be out in a tenth of a second. Ignore Billy and anything he says."

"Now children, I came to pick up my date, not referee a squabble." A slight edge to his voice, he was embarrassed.

That did it. I came out in a white off-the-shoulders dress hoping to save my dramatic entrance. Jordan did the wolf whistle. "You look gorgeous."

"Don't tell her that, she'll believe you."

"She does. You happen to have a great looking sister."

"She's fat."

"He's a horrible twerp and I hate him so can we please leave now so that I don't have to listen to his horrible comments one more second… unless you'd like a drink. I'm sorry, Jordan. Would you?"

"Whatever you say, Princess." That dimple smile.

"Let's go." We were going to gamble and dance at the Fireman's Ball determined to have a good time with him tonight. Nothing could rain on my parade.

The village green, a grassy rectangle, was transformed into an outdoor gambling casino for the night. Caramel canvas covered the top, back and sides of twenty booths. Most were wide enough for seven people to stand in front, the ones with wheels of fortune or craps tables, double. The prizes were on display in the rear. The top shelves held the coveted stuffed animals while less interesting plastic pink piggy banks sat on the bottom. The booths manned by Fire Department volunteers and lifeguards, the proceeds would go to the Fire Department. In Ocean Beach, where all the houses were made of wood, maintenance of the two shiny red fire engines that lived side by side in the firehouse on Midway and Bayberry was a serious business. In action, they took up the entire walk.

A fire was announced by loud-enough-for-everyone-to-hear blares in a sequence that could be translated by looking at yellow charts posted in every house. Four then three would be our corner. Volunteers rushed to the firehouse, the rest of the town to the fire. Usually it turned out to be a false alarm and turned into a social gathering. No one remembered a house burning down, but the specter of fire was ever present, which is why Jordan and I were going to the Fireman's Ball more than willing to pay the steep fifteen dollars per ticket. The Ball was always sold out.

We reconnoitered, inspected the booths for a combination of lucky feel, the game and the prizes. I looked for the biggest stuffed animals, Jordan the best action. After our stroll, we agreed on our first stop. Sean's head peeked out from a poncho, ten feet away. Jordan cheerfully paid fifty cents for each of us. We soaked our giant sponges in soapy water, all the while eying our target, a sitting duck, soon to be a dead pigeon.

I threw first, nicked Sean on his ear. "Rats, I missed."

"Have no fear, milady, I'll make up for it." Jordan threw a perfect pitch, bull's eye. Splat. It was worth every penny to watch Sean, not a good loser, swallow all expletives and smile.

"So long, sucker."

"I'll get you back."

"I know."

We walked to the crowded crap table. Jordan immediately got into the game. I waited politely until he finished his turn rolling, but soon lost interest. I didn't understand the myriad complications of the come line or how to bet it. Craps. Bad name, anyway.

"Right back, going to check out the Wheel of Fortune." An innocent enough proposal. Nick was a heartbeat away I had to see him, the chances of getting caught minimal. Out of Jordan's sight, I rushed in through the front door of Bayview. The bar almost empty, I made my way easily to the back. Jean was standing her usual two inches away from his head. Shit. There were ten faithful listening. I needed some kind of tactic. Go Marilyn. I sashayed over. He was playing the introduction to a song, smiled, nodded hello. I could feel Jean staring me down, beginning to laugh the hyena. I co-opted her move, whispered into his ear the way I'd seen her do all summer.

"I've got to talk to you. Important." He nodded. "Will you meet me in the back after the set for a second?" He nodded again. I walked out the front door, doubled around to the back and waited.

"You look so pretty tonight, Valentine. Come let me kiss you but only if you missed me," he teased. I nodded suddenly shy. He pulled me close, gave me a body hug and kissed me.

"Stop."

"What is it?" He released me.

I shut my eyes, "I want to see you again before I go back to college." He looked surprised. I was being forward, putting him on the spot.

"You can always reach me at Famous Music. Got to go." His goodbye kiss sent shivers up and down, set me on fire. I stared into the sapphires memorizing them. "Be a good girl and keep smiling."

He turned abruptly. I wandered back into the crowded night. 'Be a good girl.' He should have said, "Be a bad girl." All of a sudden I remembered Jordan. Poor Jordan. If only I could love him. It was the millionth time I'd thought the same subjunctive thought. My favorite Spanish professor, Mrs. Whitmore remarked that 'if', *si* in Spanish, 'was the most useless word in Spanish, English or any other language.' If I were twenty-one, if I was blonde and thin, if Nick loved me...

I found Jordan. "Been looking all over for you."

"I've been right here, Princess. Shut your eyes. Now open them." I stared into brownness, reached out and touched furriness -- a big teddy bear.

"Oh, Jordan!" I started to cry.

"Princess, this is supposed to make you happy. Hey Teddy, tell your new mistress to laugh." Crying turned into bawling. "What's the matter?"

How could I tell him I was guilt-ridden about his gift, wished Nick had given Teddy to me or that I'd just said goodbye to him perhaps, forever. I rallied.

"Tears of joy. I always wanted a teddy bear and never thought that someone would win one for me. I'm going to take him back to school with me. Whenever I see him, I'll think of you." I threw my arms around Jordan.

"I should give you a bear more often. Let's take him to the Fireman's Ball unless they charge extra admission."

Teddy was a hit, had to turn down three dance invitations. Jordan walked us home. I endured his goodnight kiss beat myself up for not being more responsive, wondered again why he liked me.

I avoided Sunday brunch to minimize exposure to "the hostiles" -- how I positioned "them" in an extremely awkward truce in our cold war -- came back from the beach hungry. Mother was in the dining room setting up the table for a party, putting out platters, cobalt blue cocktail napkins and paper plates -- too many people for china.

Dad rushed in wearing the big smile that accompanied two stripers and a blue, dashed into the kitchen, put them in the sink, ran the cold water, got out his tools, a knife and a scaler.

"What's happening?"

"Don't you read the papers," snapped Mother. "Robert Moses is trying to convert Fire Island into a four-lane highway. That's all everyone's been talking about. Your father's having a meeting here to see if we can stop him." She placed four stacks of blue plastic glasses on the table, a really big gathering.

"Are you kidding?"

"As you know we have a major erosion problem." As Dad gutted and scaled the fish, in the kitchen, he warmed up for the meeting with me as his sounding board. "The community of Ocean Beach hasn't got enough money to fix it, and the safety of our homes is at stake." He explained that Moses' solution was to make Fire Island into a four-lane highway. Moses would get New York State money to build a bridge at the western tip -- from Fire Island to Jones Beach, another bridge at the eastern end of the island to the mainland -- connect them with a highway. This way he'd have another state park with easy access for the masses by car, and get credit for saving us from erosion.

"What about the houses?"

"He wants to raze them all."

"How? That's undemocratic. They're private property."

"What does he care? Our expensive homes are expendable for the many -- his 'people'."

I imagined our house bulldozed, erased -- a tar top in its place, "Can we stop him?"

"All the communities are going to have to band together..."

"Your father's already started working on some congressmen and senators." Mother interrupted.

"Let me finish." Annoyed. "If we get all the Fire Island communities to come together as a coalition, we can go to the federal government and petition them to make Fire Island part of the National Seashore. Then it will be their responsibility to protect us from erosion."

"And Robert Moses."

"Right."

"Holy shit."

"Don't swear." Mother hated it, Dad and I both big time blasphemers.

"Does Moses have a chance, Dad?"

"Your father will take care of it." He always did. "Bring a date tonight. I don't want you to look like you're alone."

"I'll ask Jordan."

"Too old," she said. Five years. No big deal. He hadn't cozied up to her when they met so she hadn't cottoned to him. Mother never changed her mind.

I pressed my case pulled the trump card, "He's a Harvard grad." She nodded -- it was barely okay.

A napkin slipped to the floor by my foot. Mother bent over to pick it up. Out of nowhere, came the horrible voice, "Am I seeing right? Your toenails don't match your fingernails." As she stood up I looked down at my toes, Revlon *Platinum,* my fingernails still *Cherries in the Snow.* "How can you be so stupid? You have no fashion sense at all, stupid, stupid girl." She was getting worked up over nothing. "How could I have such a dumb daughter?" The fashion police in a rage, a criminal, my mismatch rocked her. If she had a gun she'd shoot me. I couldn't fix it. I only had *Platinum* polish, and wasn't about to ruin my perfect $2 manicure, still no chips. She should have said, 'Nice nails. Great color.' Instead she was throwing a tantrum, ragging, raging. I started to shake, her wrath so scary that I dropped the white platter I was carrying to the table. She went nuts.

"Now look what you've done. Broken my platter, you clumsy girl."

"I'm sorry, Mother." I started to pick up the pieces.

"No, let me do it, you can't do anything right." She went to the kitchen got a white paper towel, dustpan and brush, pushed me away, went to work. I surveyed the damage, near tears. I couldn't glue it back together, thanked God it wasn't an antique.

Dad to the rescue, "Don't you need some things from Cleggs?" He knew how to deflect her outbursts by creating an errand.

She snapped, "Yes. Two more boxes of Carr's crackers, four bottles of ginger ale, two bottles of quinine water, a bag of ice, two lemons, a bunch of parsley. Write it down or you'll forget it."

"Yes, Mother," for once happy to walk the half-mile 'downtown'.

I called Jordan. He'd be thrilled to come.

Three hours later, seventy-five local dignitaries and concerned citizens jammed the deck overflowing into the house. Moses' name was spoken as if he were Hitler, an enemy of the people. Someone brought a sign, "Go down, Moses." The theme of the speeches was unity. It was evident that the future of Fire Island was in jeopardy. Dad was in the center, a quiet yet powerful presence and riveting speaker: the mover that got things done.

When the speech was over, Jordan wanted to talk to Dad. I went with him.

"Sir, I've been working for Senator John Kennedy. I'd like to see him President. What are your views?" Jordan was so interesting. Harvard grads stuck together.

"I think he's a good man. People are afraid of a Catholic president. He's going to have to overcome their fears and distance himself from the church."

Dad disengaged politely, as someone else required his attention. Jordan stood tall.

We went to the back of the overcrowded deck. Jordan asked, "Will you vote for Kennedy?"

"Of course. I'll be twenty-one just in time. He's the cutest Democrat I've ever seen."

"That's going to get him elected."

I wanted to talk to Dad but there was no opening. Instead I focused on Jordan whose immense charm worked on everyone except Mother. I steered Jordan away from her and tried not to think about Nick.

"Get up." Mother shouted.

"Go away. Leave me alone."

She pinched my arm, "Wake up."

"Ouch."

"It's 5:30. Better get dressed quickly," she said, urgency in her voice. "Jordan is on the way over."

"What?"

"There's a hurricane... the house isn't safe. The rain's coming from the bay side, Billy's room's flooding, too."

I heard it. The wind was screeching, the ocean roaring, rain pummeled the roof and windows. "Holy shit. How could I have slept through all this noise?"

"Don't swear. Hurry."

Panic propelled me out of bed onto a soaked straw rug that made squishy noises as I touched it. "Everything's wet. What should I wear?" Mother was my fashion arbiter even in a hurricane, a relationship we both accepted: for me it beat indecision; for her she kept control. She pulled clothes out of half stuck drawers.

"Here's your nice red turtleneck and sweatshirt. Put on your clean dungarees", she emphasized the word 'clean', "and the red checked woodsman's shirt over it. Don't dawdle."

I attacked my clothes, started to worry. Our house wasn't safe. A glorified single-ply cottage on stilts perched on the sand like an ostrich. We were vulnerable, exposed, an Achilles' heel. Fire Island for that matter was the wrong -- hell, worst place to be in a hurricane. How could we be having one without warning? If there was even the most remote possibility of danger, the Weather Bureau was supposed to alert us and send the Coast Guard to evacuate. They didn't take chances because, as everyone knew, the Hurricane of '38 had caught them unawares.

One hundred twenty mile per hour winds at high tide and tidal waves had devastated the island as the Atlantic breached the dunes, surged over the quarter mile width of the island embracing her daughter, the Great South Bay. Two thirds of the island's houses had disappeared, half the remaining ones damaged, all the boardwalks downed, four hundred people stranded, four died. I'd seen the curled pictures, yellowed clippings that Dad kept in the top drawer of his dresser. More than twenty years ago but still vivid, everyone had a horror story.

I rolled my dungarees up to my knees, touched my gold figa, a Brazilian black magic good luck charm -- a left fist with index finger crossed over the thumb I wore around my neck to protect me in case of disaster which this might just be. I charged into the living room. Billy ran from one window to another, pressing his nose against the panes, trying to see into a night as black as beach tar. It sounded like the waves were breaking right under us.

"How come they didn't evacuate us? Is it high tide? Are we at risk?"

"I don't know." Reassurance was not part of Mother's emotional vocabulary.

We heard pounding on the front door. Billy yanked but had trouble opening it. Jordan blew in. Rain followed his entry before we could push the door shut, a two-man operation. I was relieved to see him, Billy a loose cannon, Mother scary. Jordan had a clothesline, always prepared. We followed his instructions, lashed ourselves together and cautiously cracked the back door. Easier than the front, it blasted open. As in a fairy tale, I imagined there was a giant outside with inflated cheeks and big blue lips huffing and puffing.

We forced our way into the blackness. The power of the wind took my breath away. We held onto the ramp railing for dear life, inched our way down: Jordan first, then Mother, me, finally skinny Billy. Four paper dolls on a string, our destination the Altsculer's basement where we'd hopefully be safe, two long blocks away along the ocean walk. The rain beating on my cheeks felt like hundreds of little lashes, blinding. My hair escaped from the hood, whipping my face. The wind slapped, stung.

We'd advance a yard then get pushed back or sideways. Jordan led us, fearless leader, strong, positive, determined to keep moving until we got there. Mother was stalwart, Billy in heaven, the adventure of his life. I was trembling, terrified by the ominous ocean's thunder.

"Hear me roar, I'm coming. I'll gobble up the dunes for breakfast."

Any moment we'd see a tidal wave, and that would be that. I couldn't see a damn thing. We tried to make the left turn that would take us towards the Altschulers, but the wind had a mind of its own. Inflated cheeks and big blue lips, "I'm going to blow you away. Turn away from me? Ho ho ho. No no no."

We tried to get around the corner again and again. Impossible. Jordan changed our strategy. We'd do it in stages. After a few failures, he got around, sat down. He pulled Mother. They hauled me. Beef on the hoof. Better go on a diet. I made it, sat down with them. We all pulled Billy. He crawled, sat down. Four crumpled paper dolls.

Jordan shouted something. His words flew into the wind. He pointed ahead. We knelt then pulled each other up, the wind sideswiping us. Head down. Keep going. Advance. Retreat. Advance. Were the dunes high enough to protect us? Would they hold? Were we going to die? The sound of the wind was eerie, unearthly, the heavens crying. Old Captain Pastorfield's stories about the Hurricane of '38 popped into my head. 'Is another hurricane ever going to come and drown us, Captain?'

'Don't worry your head, girl, Fire Island's lasted this long, it's going to last least till you get all grown up.' Twenty was pretty old. Did he really only mean 'till'? Was he a soothsayer? Tiresias? For the first and only time in my life I hoped I wasn't all grown up. I checked the dunes again now silhouetted with putrid grey light. They looked low and worn out. I prayed to them. Please hang on, keep the ocean back, save us. I was doing an awful lot of praying for an avowed atheist, existentialist or was I an agnostic? Under the circumstances I'd become a believer. Please God let us live. Please God let us live.

The Altschuler house loomed on our left through sheets of rain. We'd have to make another turn and go headlong against the wind, the entrance to the basement fifteen feet away. The wind's force battered us as we came around the corner. Suddenly skinny Billy was blown into the iron chain fence surrounding their land, taking us with him. All four of us tumbled together into a patch of poison ivy, held onto the fence, recovered.

"Everyone okay?" Jordan shouted. He grabbed Mother's hand who took mine, motioned for me to do the same thing with Billy. We'd be each other's ballast. Four stubborn paper dolls. We couldn't stand up so we crawled. Would I ever see the sun again? Keep going, Jordan an engine pulling three cars, the little locomotive that could. We reached the wagon ramp, slid down, knocked at the basement door. Fat Albert, their neighbor and fellow storm refugee pulled us inside, four paper dolls on a string and three oranges. Hallelujah. Amen.

Ernest, the Altschuler's black, totally bald, butler cut the clothesline and helped us peel off our wet outerwear then handed us a basket of beach towels, as we huddled together like four Indians, still connected. I looked around the pine-paneled basement, high windows on three walls for ventilation. No view. A stairway led up to the first floor. Still pretty scary, our safe haven not so safe, we were below sea level for God's sake. I wished that Dad were here, we needed him. Did everyone else realize how serious this was? Seasoned Fire Islanders, of course they did.

After a few minutes I stopped shivering, felt warm again if not relaxed. Mother sipped the coffee Maria, our erstwhile hostess, insisted on. It was Maria's second hurricane. She'd been trapped up a pole in Saltaire, the big sailing community a few miles west, in the Hurricane of '38, while the Atlantic Ocean and the Great South Bay got to know each other on a first name basis beneath her. Maria, Spanish, devout Catholic, ex Ziegfield show girl, like Mother's other friends, sat in the corner saying her rosary. I asked myself for the fortieth time how Mother could be so cool. Nothing ruffled her except my 'bad taste' in nail polish. I tried to forgive her for lying about Nick but couldn't.

I was frightened in spite of Jordan's efforts to calm me down. Would the dunes hold? They were weak because people had built on them, destroying the stubborn dune grass infrastructure that held the sand and our safety in its roots. If we died it was their fault, hubris -- excessive pride in having a dune house. What would be the retribution? I pictured a tidal wave bursting through the windows. I'd tread water while waiting to be rescued, save anyone who couldn't swim with a cross-chest carry. Death by hurricane and I hadn't yet made love. Hell, I'd die a virgin!

I paced the room stopping at the three silver candy dishes, the platter of cheese and crackers, peanuts, then back to the chocolates again, at least they were well stocked. If I kept on eating like this and the water came I'd sink.

As Jordan put his arm around me, Mother got up in distaste. She made her way to the piano. We gathered around her, finally something to do. She started on the Rogers and Hart songs she remembered by heart. "Bewitched, bothered… am I." When I joined in, her voice broke. "Sorry." She got back on key, continued to the end. She'd wanted to be on Broadway, singing and dancing. Her father had forbidden it: no daughter of his was going on stage. Instead, she was stuck being a housewife and mother.

Mrs. Goldman took a turn on the piano next. She was squat, overweight, her house diagonally across. Her short, plump fingers shook as she played gloomy choruses of "Molly Malone" from the *Great Folk Songs Book*. "Now her ghost wheels her barrow through streets long and narrow crying cockles and mussels alive alive oh." A dirge. How appropriate.

Billy and I played Chopsticks.

Fat Albert, far from a comedian, droned on through his repertoire of epitome jokes. "The epitome of conceit is a fly floating down the river on its back with a hard on saying, 'Open the drawbridge'." Fifi, Maria's spoiled, decidedly unattractive daughter with affectations that she was, announced, "I'm going to play my last year's piano recital." We'd heard it before. Dreadful. I looked at Billy, rolled my eyes. He nodded back. She got stuck at the same place three times in a row, started over -- a captive audience is a captive audience, finally gave up.

Ernest brought more trays of food: a precooked ham, left-over roast beef, peanut butter and jelly sandwiches, tuna fish salad, milk, cookies, cakes, donuts, fruit, cokes and more coffee. He'd emptied out the icebox. With the power out it was all going to spoil, anyway. "Brunch is served." He started to cry. "Eat well y'all, this may be our last meal." At least we'd die well fed. And all the time we heard the wind crying, the rain pounding the panes.

Jordan had an inspired idea. "Let's list our favorite movies."

I went first. "*Gone with the Wind, The Wizard of Oz, Casablanca, A Star is Born,*" Garland, my anthem, "The Man That Got Away", "and *Some Like it Hot.*" I'd waited an hour in line to see the first showing in Northampton. "What a movie!" I pronounced. "I loved Marilyn as Sugar." I whispered to Jordan, "You have to be a smart cookie to play a dumb blonde." He laughed and gave me a knowing hug. Strong, capable smart Jordan.

Staying on *Some Like it Hot*, Jordan did Tony Curtis imitating Cary Grant, put his hand in front of an imaginary navy blue double-breasted blazer and vamped, "Judy Judy Judy." "That flick has the best last line ever, Jack Lemmon tells Joe E. Brown that he can't marry him because he's a man. He replies that nobody is perfect. We roared. "My number one favorite is *Citizen Kane*, Orson Welles is brilliant, a genius."

Billy's turn, "First on my list is *Marjorie Morningstar*." He looked to see if the zinger had registered. It had, then he blurted, "Just kidding. *On the Waterfront*, Brando." He did his version of Budd Schulberg's lines, 'Coulda been a contender… '

We applauded. Mother was up. "*The King and I*, almost as good as Broadway. Yul Brynner was brilliant in both versions, Deborah Kerr is no Gertrude Lawrence." Mother had seen the original. "I loved *An American in Paris* and *Singing in the Rain*." a Gene Kelly fan. Billy interrupted, whispered, "Would everyone please be quiet for a minute? I think the wind is dying down." Was it true? Were we safe? Jordan opened the door a peep. We listened as one. Who has seen the wind? Who hears it?

"I'll go outside and see." Fat Albert ventured out the door in the moment of heroism he'd always remember. He returned, declared the crisis over. In a flash, Billy was out. Jordan and I followed. The light was shocking, brilliant as if the hurricane had given birth to a second sun, the sky electric blue. Little white clouds scuttled across when the wind came back up in gusts. Except for a few downed pine branches, rain puddles, an occasional displaced shingle, it was as if nothing had happened. I took a deep breath, relieved from the hours of worry, a miracle to be alive. An 'X' on our door, the lord had passed us over. *Dayenu.* Amen.

Jordan, Billy and I raced up the steps to the wooden platform that led to the beach to see the ocean. Surrealistic, it went nowhere, the snow fences and steps down to the beach washed away. Black and green bilious, mountainous waves streaked with angry brown foam came from all directions, crashed against each other in chaos. The ocean was having an epileptic fit, the waves shook violently, foaming at the mouth, retching. The water came to the base of the dune below us. Mother climbed up. I approached her. She shrugged me away, not big on displays of affection, had never hugged us, why should now be different. But Jordan put his arms around me. A wave of terror broke through my body -- the after shock of the hurricane made me shake. Such a skinny island, miraculously, our stubborn, sandy, thirty-one mile thread didn't snap, sink, or float away. What if? What if? What if? It was the epitome of conceit that the exhausted dunes had withstood the hurricane. Hard to believe that my beautiful ocean could be so ugly, would it ever be the same again? Would I?

We found out later we'd been lucky, saved only because the wind had come off the bay. Had it come off the ocean...

The Weather Bureau never issued an apology.

I thanked my new best friend, God.

The day after the hurricane, the bay settled down, Mother and Billy went back to town to shop for school. He'd grown out of everything.

The hurricane bonded Jordan and me. I invited him, Becker and Johnny over to celebrate -- they'd weathered the storm, too. We'd been working on the bottle of J & B Jordan brought, laughing, dancing. In the wee hours, Becker slurred her words, sloshed, "Johnny and I are going to sleep. We're tired." They weaved to my bedroom. Some nerve. I supposed she really was too drunk to go home.

After one last slow dance, "You're getting to be a habit.." from Sinatra's, *Songs for Swingin' Lovers,* Jordan and I wound up on Mother and Dad's bed.

"You know how much I want you, Princess." He started to undress me.

"Quit it, Jordan. Stop it." He covered my protests with his mouth, kissed me.

"Shhh. The others will hear," the walls were paper-thin.

I started to think about 'the others'. Were they doing it? No. Becker was a good girl like me, wasn't she? They'd been going together for a long time. Two years. Johnny thought they were going steady and was proudly faithful. She wasn't; cheated on him with other guys. If they were sleeping together, Becker hadn't told me, not that I expected a radio announcement, just her confidence, like a best friend. If the situations were reversed, would I tell her? Yes and no. Yes, because I had trouble keeping secrets. No, because there was something about her I couldn't trust.

Jordan made another advance. I pushed his hand away. Should I get it over with, let him be the first?

"I love you, Princess."

The kiss of death. Enter The Imp of the Perverse, that dastardly voice in my head, 'Don't do it with Jordan. He's not Nick. You don't love him.' Click. A light switch went off.

"No!" He wasn't listening, down to his jockeys, pinned my wrists with one hand while he tried to pull off my underpants, all that remained of my modesty, with the other. I struggled to get my hands free so I could pull them back on. "Let me go. Let me go." I wrenched away, hit my head on something hard -- the antique brass curlicue headboard. "Ouch!" I saw stars, started to cry.

"Princess, what happened?" Jordan put on the lamp, "Oh, my God! You're bleeding. My poor baby, I'm sorry. I'm sorry." He was totally devastated.

I started to round up my clothes in tears, pulled them on, frantic, not knowing what to worry about first, another aborted chance at losing my virginity, my head or my parent's besmirched bed. Jordan dressed quickly.

Johnny knocked on the door, concerned. "Everything all right?"

"Come in."

"Where's Becker?"

"Sleeping. What's the matter?" Jordan held a bloody handkerchief to my head. Johnny rushed out to wake up Becker who was out cold. I could hear her snoring. Jordan walked me to the bathroom. "Come on, Princess, sit down on the john and lean your head forward." He put cold water on my head, dabbed at the cut with damp Kleenex.

Becker finally stumbled into the tiny bathroom. This better be good. She looked at me, "Oh. Oh." It was bad.

It felt like we were in the middle of the overcrowded cabin in the Marx Brothers' *A Night at the Opera*. "Please give us some space," roared Jordan. They backed out. "Now let me have a good look at your head."

I had a terrible headache, hangover and fear of sex anxiety attack, all rolled into one. "Let me see, unless it's so bad I'll faint."

"A strong girl like you? It's a small wound."

I looked into the medicine cabinet mirror where I used to practice smoking Chesterfields to look-as-smooth-as-Bacall when I was twelve. There was a jagged hole at my hairline in the middle of my forehead. There was a little girl who had a little hole right in the middle of her forehead. And when she was good she was very, very, good. When she was bad... I needed a doctor. Shit. I needed stitches. Dammit I was afraid of doctors.

"Get me to the doctor please, Jordan."

"What's the name of the village doctor, Becker?"

"Erskine." They were hovering outside.

Jordan took charge, "Call him up and see if we can come over." It was two in the morning.

Christ, my head hurt. I started to lose it. A nightmare. Mother, Dad and Billy were coming back. What time did they say? As usual I hadn't listened. Get rid of the evidence.

"Can someone help me clean up?" I was more frightened about being found out than my head. How would I be able to explain the mess? My parents' sacred inner sanctum was sullied. Jordan held my hand while Becker called.

"Can we come over now, doctor? It's an emergency." Becker's tough voice sounded like Mother. She nodded, okay.

As Jordan and I left, he admonished Johnny and Becker, "Please clean up."

He pulled me in the wagon to the Ocean Beach village doctor, full time for the summer season, his office and living quarters over the firehouse.

I hated Dr. Erskine on sight. A balding, fat, sloppy looking man, white coat hastily thrown over a puce and mauve print bathrobe, leered at me from under heavy lidded toad eyes.

"Your name?"

"Allison Abrams."

"The judge's daughter?"

"Yes."

"Please have your friend wait outside." I rolled my eyes at Jordan. He shrugged his shoulders. What could he do?

"Undress, please."

Undress? The second time in one night, "If you haven't noticed doctor, my head is hurt, not my body." He put his paw on my arm. Was I crazy or was this son of a bitch making a pass at me? He started to stroke my back.

"Doctor, look at my head." Trapped, I needed the bastard.

"The cut is clean but deep. I'm going to have to sew you up."

"Will I have a scar?" Vanity, thy name is woman.

"Of course not. Just give me a kiss."

This guy's a dirty old quack. I'll report him to the authorities. Dad was the authorities.

"That man waiting outside looks worried. Did he hit you, dear?" He pawed me again.

"Sew me up or I'll scream."

"Give me a kiss."

"Screw you."

He brought his puckered lips slowly down to me. I held my breath. I could kill you, whack the middle of your eroded head in between those horrible strands of hair that you combed over to hide your baldness. As with Raskolnikov and the pawnbroker, no one would miss this scum. I could push out those toad eyes, "Out vile jelly", the line from *King Lear.* I turned away the kiss grazed my face, murder on my mind, slapped him. Didn't know I had it in me. Nor did he.

The pervert changed his tune. "I'm going to prick you a few times with this needle and thread. You be nice and brave now."

"Ouch. Ouch. That hurts." He was going to sew me up badly. Leave a scar.

Scarface.

"What were you doing with that man in the middle of the night? Hmmm?" Prick. Prick. Prick. Prick. I wasn't in a position to say, 'None of your fucking business'. "Well, my dear, that does it. Nice work if I don't say so myself, I was a surgeon in the army." He put a bandage on my head. "That will be ten dollars. Come back in a week and I'll remove the stitches. Don't get it wet. You'll see, no scar." No scar? Maybe, but I'd never forget this night.

"Let me take you home, Princess." I couldn't tell Jordan about Erskine, knowing he'd go back and punch him out.

"No. No, you can't. I don't know when my parents are coming back. I can get home by myself." Irrational, I wanted Jordan to go away. He wouldn't take no for an answer.

The house was still a shambles when we returned, empty glasses and cigarette filled ashtrays scattered about. I pictured the scene: Johnny started to clean up. Becker, still drunk, "Fuck it, let's go," dragged him out.

Jordan and I tidied up, changed the sheets painstakingly. Mother made their bed like a marine -- you could bounce a dime off it.

"What are we going to do with these bloody sheets?"

"I'll take them to the incinerator."

"Good. She'll never miss them. Does the bed look neat enough?"

"So tight no one can get into it."

Private Jordan got off duty an hour later, the house immaculate again. We rehearsed my story one more time in case Mother and Dad noticed anything. 'I had a terrible nightmare and woke up with my head bleeding, don't know how I did it.' Jordan apologized over and over. I knew he meant it.

Five o'clock in the morning, Jordan tried to kiss me goodnight gently. The Imp insisted, "Get away from him." I wrenched my head around violently to escape his lips, second time in one night. The screen door slammed shut.

Jordan left angry, had the last word, "I know why you like *Gone With The Wind.* You're in love with the wrong man, Scarlett." Oh, God, what had I done? He was right. I was Scarlett in love with Ashley who didn't love her, rejecting Rhett who did. Poor Jordan. He'd taken care of me, a God dammed hero. I'd blown him away as if he were a bad guy, repulsed. Something was terribly wrong.

I swept this revelation under the rug, escaped instead to Fantasy #16: marrying Nick. 'Let me get your parents' permission, baby, I'll ask your father for your hand. If he won't give us their blessing we'll elope. We'll go to Hawaii for our honeymoon. When we come back, I'll rent a larger apartment and we'll move in together. I'm going to be very successful. We'll have a beautiful life together, baby. Just say yes.'

The hurricane changed everything. I'd almost died a virgin, had to make love with Nick before I went back to college. Live sister, life is short. I called him at Famous Music. A switchboard operator connected us. Determined to see him come hell or high water, was going to be in town for a few days after Labor Day, had my 21st birthday, no longer jailbait, legal -- white lie, a few weeks shy, his last chance to see me before I disappeared into the wilds of Northampton. I wouldn't take no for an answer. Nick told me to meet him next Wednesday at two. Hooray.

I sat next to him at the piano -- the best seat in the house, as he played just for me and crooned, "Love Light", his most romantic song. Ever. The stage was set, I ached for him under his spell.

"Like it?"

"Love it," wanted to say, 'I love you.'

Nick put his arm around me, drew me towards him. "You're so enthusiastic." That would have to serve as his compliment of the day. My yearnings for romance remained unfulfilled. Couldn't he have said I was the love of his life? Would he ever know how much time I spent thinking about our visits analyzing everything, searching for hidden meanings?

He pulled me up from the bench, "What are you doing with all those clothes on pretty girl? What *are* these? Let me help you out of them." He started to undress me in broad daylight, nowhere to hide. I felt shy but determined to go through with it, now or never.

"Here are those beautiful breasts that drive me crazy. He kissed me slowly all the while caressing me with practiced hands. Nick removed the rest of my clothes, then his, tossed them. They settled at random as if in slow motion. Tingly, excited, my smooth skin changed to gooseflesh. Sapphire love rippled through my body.

I loved the feeling of being in his arms, surrounded, connected, and filled up with him, in another world, no longer a virgin. We lay in his bed after.

"Was it good for you, baby?"

"Yes, Nick." The best time of my life, nothing else close. He turned away and slept. What now? Do I stay here? Dare I tell him? I love you Nick. How beautiful you are. I feel lonely. Tell me that this was all right. Please wake up and make love to me some more, teach me how. I reached out and touched his 'cock' lightly, watched over him while he dozed, too aroused to sleep. I was hungry and wondered what he had in his icebox. Better not look. What if he woke up and I was eating. I watched and waited. The sapphires finally opened so I could swim in them again.

"Hey, baby. Have a good nap?" He reached over and touched my face, "You have the look of love."

"Really?" Were my feelings that transparent?

"See for yourself. You can always tell." He led me to the bathroom mirror. "It's in your eyes." I'd had it since the day I met him, was he just now noticing? "Let's take a shower, have to get going."

My throat dried out. Meeting Jean. The Imp had its say: "You're not good enough."

"What's the matter, baby? Hey, smile. Let me soap you down." Suds all over, his fingers exploring "Now it's your turn." He handed me the soap. I traced his body with pleasure. The shower water cascaded down our bodies. He entered me. "This is the way I should have taken you in the ocean. Remember?" Of course I remembered, every second, I'd memorized it, made a fantasy track. I was quivering, pressure building. He was waiting. What for? "Ready?"

"Yes." No.

He pulled out. The water washed his seed away.

"We have to make tracks, baby; can't be late for my recording date, doing a demo of "Love Light."" We dressed in haste and tumbled down the stairs, "Where are you going?"

Where was I going? "I don't know." He saw a cab at the end of the street, put two fingers in his mouth whistled, the cabbie blinked his lights.

"Here's some bread." He shoved a ten-dollar bill in my hand, "Don't mind if I take the first one." He climbed in, slammed the door drove off. After all the years of anticipation I crashed, let down, the tightrope between pain and pleasure so thin. Something else was wrong. He hadn't said I love you.

5

Olé!

Senior year was an anticlimax to say the least. I hadn't heard from Jordan after the scary, scarring nightmare of Walpurgis Night. A guilt hangover hovered like a black cloud. I missed that laugh, his jokes, support, and attention -- my friend, confidant, caper mate. I'd cared about him yet turned on him. I re-ran the tape back to where I felt the light switch turn off when he said, 'I love you.' The Imp of the Perverse had won and I'd lost Jordan. Tragic. My fault. Why? What was the matter with me?

I'd distanced myself from Becker. She'd abandoned me in my hour of need, hadn't cleaned up the house, a piss-poor performance and the last straw. It had finally sunk in. I couldn't count on her in a crisis. She was nasty, turned into a meanie when she drank -- a chronic condition. I weathered the loss but knew it was necessary. I was lonely nonetheless.

I stayed faithful to Nick in body, mind and spirit. My college boy dalliances were form without content, stopgaps till I saw him. If a suitor showed interest, I bolted. None of them could live up to him. Plus, I would've felt cheap, could only be with the man I loved.

All I'd managed since September were three lousy dates arranged by secret phone calls and telegrams. For each one, there were four cancellations, ten maybes, and a lot of dashed hopes. Nick was wishy-washy. I'd call, he'd say ring him back in two hours then two hours later, he'd tell me to call back in an hour. I was trapped by his indecision, what he did in between was the great mystery in the sky. Powerless, I wished I could pop a patience pill. I hadn't really expected, though I'd hoped, that Nick would visit me in Northampton. Not his kind of turf.

First had come the fall after-the-Giants-football-game-at-Yankee Stadium date. Nick and I went to the game separately, he with Big Lou the Bayview bouncer who turned out to be his best buddy, I with Dad. The Giants were playing the Pittsburgh Steelers at Yankee Stadium, the most coveted seats in New York -- people killed for those tickets, put them in their wills. I tried to understand what was happening on the field but always seemed to be looking the wrong way. I cheered loudly enough so that Dad knew that I knew what an exalted privilege it was to be sitting in our box freezing my ass off in spite of my twenty-five pound raccoon coat, not understanding the game.

The Giants won led by Y. A. Tuttle and number 16, Frank Gifford, the hunky halfback every girl including me had a crush on. Nick and I couldn't connect at half time, but finally met three calls and one telegram later: "7 stop P.

J. Moriarty's." Our mission was to have a drink at every one of the Irish Blarney Stone bars in Manhattan. There must have been a hundred; we only made it to four. He sent me home in a cab too drunk to go to his apartment. No sex. Horrible hangover. Huge upset. I couldn't, shouldn't drink. Ever.

Nick came to pick me up at seven at our under-the-tree-Christmas-eve date. I led him to our grand piano in the living room. Mother, Dad and Billy were away at parties so the coast was clear. As always the attraction was electric. We never left. I led him to our grand piano in the cozy living room, fire glowing, stockings hung by the fireplace by our quaint Christmas tree.

Nick sat down and did some scales to see if it was in key. He smiled. It was, Mother kept it tuned. I sat next to him, my favorite place in the world. He sang "Magic" his latest composition, which he was about to record. I told him how much I loved it, that he'd broken out of the box. He did an encore, finishing to my enthusiastic applause.

There were magic kisses, and tingles of excitement as Nick lay on top of me under the colored paper cutouts: a green and pink outhouse with a half moon in the window, a few Santa variations -- the extravagant one featured a cotton moustache and beard, lots of paper bells and balls in bright colors, a yellow and white felt Smith banner, a green and white Dartmouth banner for luck. Billy was applying there.

"You have too many clothes on," he said, undressing me. "Take mine off, I have a surprise for you. Hey baby, here's your adorable Christmas present. Take him." I did.

Nick rushed away, fearful that Dad would return. He wished me a happy '60, but didn't ask me out for New Year's. Sorry ending to a topsy-turvy year. Even so, a brand new decade beckoned. I was ready. Hopefully I'd get married, have a career (it would not be acting) have fun, travel, in any order.

I didn't see Nick again until after Nassau during Spring break. I fell in love with the Bahamas from the air when I first saw the water, an underwater rainbow -- turquoise to cobalt, sapphire, navy then amethyst. I went there with Katerine, a kindred spirit, my suite mate and first real friend. She was 5'11 with high cheekbones, svelte, flat chested, straight, chestnut hair down to the middle of her back. She looked exotic, vaguely oriental; everyone asked if we were sisters. It felt like we were, could talk about anything -- she wasn't a virgin either and was the only one who knew about Nick. We'd been inseparable at college since the past September when she moved into my dorm on the quad. We shared wanderlust and men appreciation, both boasting a steady stream of admirers, fortunately, attracted to different types, though I was basically unavailable. Of German extraction, she hailed from Springfield, Illinois, which she called a suburb of Chicago. Who knew that it was two hundred miles away? Who cared? She'd live anywhere but there.

Katerine and I checked into a white two-story guesthouse downtown.

It was the family custom to have a drink at the bar of the best hotel in town, like the Top of the Mark – Mark Hopkins hotel, San Francisco. In this case it was the British Colonial, a grand pink and coral classic on Bay Street. We primped, donned sundresses, and walked there. Privileged WASPy ivy-league college kids on Spring break on their worst behavior were three deep at the boisterous bar getting plastered on tropical rum concoctions. They called it the B.C. On my best Nick behavior, I steered clear of the Trinity seniors on my case. Katerine met a Yalie.

Calypso music was in the air twenty-four hours a day, the first time I'd heard it. Some songs were 'dirty' -- double-entendres, all had a catchy beat. Blind Blake played every afternoon, "My name is Morgan but it ain't J.P." You could hear Peanuts Taylor, a short, radiant bongo player, till five o'clock in the morning if you went 'Over-the-Hill' to the poor black section. "Mama don't raise no corn no corn, very few potatoes, string beans and lima beans but Lord she had tomatoes." Sweet Richard showed me how to do The Limbo. You leaned backward, lowered your body, feet akimbo, knees extended, slowly moved forward under a broom held horizontally by two people. They kept on lowering it. I got way down. Six foot three, Sweet Richard slid magically under a foot high board. How *did* he do it?

We took a boat to uninhabited Hog Island, endless white beach, turquoise water the color of Jordan's eyes -- still ashamed when I thought about him -- conch shells and sand dollars to skin dive for. God forgive me, it was more beautiful than Fire Island. The supermarket heir, Huntington Hartford, later bought the island, developed it and changed the name to Paradise.

I spent my last five dollars on a present for Nick, Courvoisier V.S.O.P., duty free. I arrived at his apartment golden bronze and skinny, having existed on Tang and rum the second week. Dad, 'by accident', had not given me quite enough money to cover expenses. I couldn't complain, had the time of my life snorkeling in paradise.

Nick gave me the body hug. "You smell of the sun, pretty girl." I couldn't wait to show him my tan lines. He did the honors, tore off my clothes. I paraded around nude, brown and white. "I like you thin, stay this way." We rubbed coconut oil all over, made athletic love on a beach towel he put on the floor. I wished I could live with him inside me forever. Still no release, my latest theory: I'd been born premature and whatever I needed to reach orgasm was missing.

Nick dropped the bomb as we dressed. Jordan, he told me, was a big shot in Kennedy's campaign. There was more. Did I know that Jordan had gotten married? Married! If that wasn't shocking enough, his new wife was Jean. Jean the model. Jean, Nick's girlfriend. Jean Hyena. She was out of the picture with Nick, a relief. But she was with *my* Jordan. I was too stunned to react. In my Nick cocoon, I shouldn't have been jealous. But I was.

I headed out to Ocean Beach two weeks after graduation for a little R & R. It was an odd in-between time -- after college, before the future -- a giant question mark in the sky. All I knew for sure was that I was going on a two-month tour of Europe, a present from Dad. I'd made it through with a respectable B average. This time I had the plane ticket and a brand new green passport in a T. Anthony brown leather case. I hadn't forgiven myself for blowing it last summer, trading two months in Paris for three dates with

Nick. What had I been thinking? The Imp assured me that I was an idiot.

I was rafting in the ocean when I spied perfect long legs leading up to a hand holding another.

"Hi, Princess." Jordan and Jean were backlit by the sun, a golden couple in love.

"Have you seen Nick?" asked Jean, perhaps to fill the awkward silence, "He seems lonely lately." You mean now that you're with Jordan. I tried not to hate her. Insecure from the start, I'd spent so much time being jealous I hadn't bothered to get to know the competition. The facts as I knew them: she was divorced from a songwriter; once a model, early thirties at least -- over the hill career-wise, they had a short shelf life. She was certainly older than Jordan. His mother had been a model; maybe that was it. And he'd been on the rebound. What was it about Jean that had captured my two men? Still great looking, always laughing, upbeat, cool, hip, smart enough to have snagged both.

"Yes I have." I could count on one hand the number of times.

"How's your head?" Jordan looked concerned.

"No problem. Everything's cool." Really uncool, my darling Jordan with Nick's ex. Thank God Nick had warned me. Even so I was devastated. And surprised at how much it hurt. We could have been a pair. Now that he was married, I wanted him back. My musings of malcontent were interrupted by a rider, caught it, rising up and thundering down on my orange air mattress. When I landed on the beach, Jordan, still watching, blew me a kiss and flashed the dimple smile.

I forced one back. Nick loved Jean. Jordan loved me. Jordan loves Jean. No one loves me.

Miserable, I told the news to Mother, desperate for sympathy, I should've known better, of course.

"You stupid, stupid girl." She was crocheting, "How could you let him slip through your fingers like that?" She gathered steam and let me have it. "He was handsome, smart, nice, refined. A Harvard man. He had everything."

"Funny thing, Mother, you never liked him before. I guess I didn't love him."

"Love! Don't you know a woman should marry a man who loves her more than she loves him?" It was the only advice she ever gave me.

Katerine and I decided to go to Europe for the summer together. Dad gave me $750. We pored over *Europe On Ten Dollars A Day*, planning our trip -- England, Spain, Italy, Switzerland, France -- down to every peso, pound, franc, lire.

We started our grand tour on a Smith charter BOAC prop plane that cost $300 round trip. It took sixteen squashed hours to fly from Idlewild to London. We got smashed on the inexhaustible supply of baby bottles of scotch. When the captain announced we were passing over the Blarney Stone, we believed him. When we stopped at Shannon to refuel, I bought an off-white Irish knit turtleneck fisherman's sweater. Pounds translated to twenty-two dollars: expensive, but worth every pence. We landed bleary-eyed.

London was sprawling. Avid first time tourists, we saw everything and walked for miles -- kilometers, left no stone unturned. First stop the Elgin Marbles, Phidias' frieze stolen from the Parthenon stranded in the artificial light of the British Museum, a Greek tragedy. The women had terrible taste, dowdy like dowagers and the queen. The men's classic finery was outrageous, outlandish and original: nothing matched but it all went together. I thought of Jordan, 'Think Yiddish, dress British' -- so many things I could have bought him. I found Dad a hand-sewn camel vest, a pipe at Charatan on Bond Street from a sketch he'd made; Billy a red and navy striped scarf. I'd wait till Paris for Mother, couldn't find the right thing for Nick. He had odd taste. I perfected my accent, got it 'quite right' pursed my lips as I froze my face.

We met two gorgeous blonde WASPs -- the originals -- Oxbridge types at "The Grenadier", a pub near Knightsbridge, once the barracks and stables of Wellington's Guards. They bought us pints of ale. Like the rest of the London pubs it closed inconveniently at 9:30. We went to the airport to drink at an after hours bar. I had too much single malt scotch and fell attempting to go up a down escalator, bloodying my left knee. A doctor sewed me up, told me to have the stitches taken out in a week. We were relieved to leave dark and dreary London. A downer. Too much like New York.

We took an overnight train to Pamplona to watch the running of the bulls and the bullfights, following in Hemingway's footsteps, inspired by *The Sun Also Rises*. I'd seen five *corridas* in Mexico City, an *aficionado* at 17. Billy and I'd practiced passes in the foyer, took turns being the matador or the bull.

We pulled into the town July 6th, the day before the start of the Festival of San Fermín, rumpled from a claustrophobic second-class *couchette*. We stashed our luggage in the cell-like room of our hotel, a converted convent, and went straight to bed. The running of the bulls took place at eight the next morning. Miraculously Katerine, an over-sleeper got up in time. Town Hall Square was jammed with men in white, sporting red waistbands and neckerchiefs. The hard-nosed officials wouldn't let us run. No women allowed. I was upset -- we were as good as any guys. We watched from the sidelines scrunched behind a wood barricade, glum then thankful as the men scrambled by -- fear at their heels. A young man fell. Someone reached out, pulled him to safety. Six bulls, eight steers, two oxen thundered by moments later. Pandemonium.

We rested till four, donned white, bought red scarves in stalls on the way to the one-horse town's Plaza del Castillo, formerly a bullring. I asked around, "*Conoce Vd. donde estába Hemingway*?" (Do you know where Hemingway was?) They pointed to Café Iruña, chairs and tables outside French-style. Two attractive American men asked us to join them. After *muchos vinos tintos*, I suddenly remembered I had to have the stitches in my knee removed, asked if there was a doctor in the house. One pointed to the other.

Drew was six feet tall, with sandy reddish hair, tight curls, freckles and blue eyes, Raggedy Andy. He took a small black leather case from his pocket, unzipped it to reveal a tiny kit, something like a Swiss army knife. 'Dr. Drew' washed my knee, sterilized the instruments in vodka and proceeded to 'operate'. The patient lived. He wasn't exactly an M.D. -- going into his fourth year at Johns Hopkins medical school, close enough. We hit it off. A Southern boy from New Orleans taking the grand tour, his last hurrah before becoming a real doctor, also an *aficionado, Death in the Afternoon* his bible, too.

Conveniently Katerine and Jonathan from Chicago also got along. At 6:30, we went to the *corrida* together, sat in *sombra* -- the shady side, boy, girl, boy, girl. The band began to play *pasa dobles* as the *matador de toros* (killer of bulls), Ordóñez, *numero uno* -- the bullfighter Hemingway had fictionalized in *The Sun Also Rises* -- and his *cuadrilla,* team of *torero*s, three b*anderilleros* and two *picador*s entered in shiny *trajes de luz* (suits of light). His was cream satin embroidered in gold, the rest in turquoise, magenta, black with silver thread. Small ponytails, white ruffle shirts, thin black ties, shocking pink stockings, black ballet shoes completed their elaborate costumes. They paraded around the ring and the crowd cheered dazzled by the pageantry.

Dr. Drew took my hand, excitement building, as was the electricity. A trumpet signaled the first part. A black bull roared into the ring like a locomotive, powerful and dangerous. Ordóñez, came out from behind a barrio, held a heavy yellow and fuschia cape. The crowd quieted down as the ritual dance of death between man and bull began. His *verónicas* swirled and swooped like butterflies. After each pass we shouted "*Olé!*" in appreciation. Dr. Drew and I exchanged knowing glances -- we were watching a legend. Ordóñez turned his back on the bull and walked slowly to the barrier, cool, in control.

Two *picadors* astride padded blindfolded horses appeared, medieval-looking in Sancho Panza hats -- bowls with brims, held lances, their job to weaken the bull's neck muscles, lower his head and horns. I shut my eyes buried my head in Dr. Drew's shoulder. A few moments later he whispered it was over, pointed to the *Presidente* in his box waving a white handkerchief to signal the end of the first part.

Three *banderilleros,* colorful paper-decorated barbed sticks in each hand took staccato side steps, arched their backs and planted two *banderillas* each in the bull's massive shoulders. The ballet over, the bull exhausted, end of the second part.

A trumpet signaled part three. Ordóñez entered alone, a sword in his right hand, small red cape, *la muleta,* in the left -- the color of the cape a matter of tradition; bulls are color blind. He took off his hat, a black pillbox with bulbs on both sides, made a grand gesture and dedicated the bull to the crowd. Dr. Drew held me tight. Ordóñez began the *faena,* a series of final passes that led to the kill. He did a sequence of five as he drew the bull closer and closer, Ordóñez the master. Like Hemingway said.

"Olé." "Olé." "Olé." Olé." Olé." An adrenalin rush at every pass. He started another sequence. *"Olé." "Olé." "Olé." Olé." "Olé."*

Ordóñez faced the bull, aimed the sword toward the middle of his shoulder blades, the moment of truth. The crowd hushed, I whispered to Katerine to cross her fingers -- this was it. I held my breath, grabbed Dr. Drew's arm both fearful and fascinated. As the bull charged Ordóñez lunged over his right horn, plunged the sword to the hilt to cut the aorta. Silence. The bull fell dead, a quick and clean death. The crowd went crazy, waved white handkerchiefs to signal to the *Presidente* that Ordóñez deserved a prize. He awarded Ordóñez two ears and a tail for art, superiority and courage. He did a victory lap around the ring, hat raised, picked up flowers, waved. His admirers carried him out on their shoulders. Life and death, pageantry, music, fear, primal emotions and gallons of adrenalin, altogether an extraordinary afternoon. Dr. Drew kissed me: my prize.

We celebrated all night, sang the local song, *"Uno de Enero, dos de Febrero, tres de Marzo, cuatro de Abril, cinco de Mayo, siete de Julio, San Fermín!"* squirted red wine from kidney-shaped leather *botas* into our mouths, missed, watched the fireworks, had our own, necked and dirty danced. At five in the morning Dr. Drew asked if I wanted to go home or back to his room; he had a double bed. The convent or him, was he kidding? Together in a crazy corner of Spain, we liked each other, why stop now? We passed out. In the morning, a Southern gent, he inquired if I wanted to have sex, ready for 'Yes' or 'No'.

I thought about Nick. Was I being unfaithful? So? "Yes."

We squeezed into his shower, kissed, explored -- he had beautiful broad shoulders, long muscles, a swimmer, too. He dried me off, carried me to bed on fire, his hands slow, fingers passionate. We spent the next three days together, a quartet, Katerine and Jonathan an item too. Dr. Drew drawled, couldn't believe how fast I talked, rued that Yankees up North didn't take him seriously because of his Southern accent. I did. Charming. We played, made love, enjoyed each other's company and time together, the North and South at peace in *España,* a dictatorship.

The bullfights over, Drew suggested the four of us go to San Sebastian a beach town nearby to recuperate. We tried to check in as Mr. and Mrs. Drew. The proprietor looked at our passports, no proof we were married -- a strict Catholic country, no dice. Katerine and I took a double room, as did Drew and Jonathan, switched roommates -- ingenious end around. I looked forward to our nights all day. And mornings.

We took each other's addresses, phone numbers, planned to see each other again. Never did. No matter: our time together perfect, no one had looked over my shoulder, cared what I did, with whom, when. Casual sex was not going to send me to hell; it was part of life like sleeping, eating, brushing your teeth. An existential awakening -- I didn't have to be in love to make love. Twenty-one years of enforced Puritanical morality down the drain, chains broken just like that, no hang ups, rules or anxiety. *Olé*!

We had a bad feeling about Madrid. Cold. Formal. Spanish with a lisp, opposite of the relaxing atmosphere of the land of *mañana* -- Mexican Spanish sung slowly. Police were ubiquitous, four different kinds. The *Guardia Civil* was the most menacing, a show of power for Franco, Spain's dictator, his brand of fascism, the Falange. Five red arrows and a yoke over black on billboards, signs and flags all over town threatened swastika-like. Nervous, we decided to go to the Prado then split.

We waited on line to see *Las Meninas* Velasquez's masterpiece, worth every second. I stared at the hoop skirt of the *Infanta*, harked back to the turquoise silk one I'd worn in eighth grade, the lead in Oscar Wilde's "The Birthday of the *Infanta*", an unfortunate style for an undeveloped, tubby body. Mother said I looked like a balloon. My only other acting experience, deflated, drowning in her criticism, I'd remembered my lines -- happy during, mortified after. The *Infanta* didn't look that happy either, the princess a prisoner of fashion tyranny, too.

We took a train to Barcelona, a white city on the side of a mountain that stretched to the Mediterranean. The capitol of Catalonia, their second language Catalan, a strange unpronounceable Romance language with a lot of x's starred Antonio Gaudi, his unfinished masterpiece, the church of *Sagrada Familia,* a sand castle with two spires of spun sugar. His work was astonishing, whimsical, original -- fluid. I'd never seen anything like it. He broke the mold. How did he do it? They said he died alone in beggar's clothes, unrecognized, on mind-altering drugs like Lewis Carroll when he created *Alice in Wonderland.* However he did it, he'd done it.

We discovered *paella,* a delicious concoction of seafood morsels, mussels, fish, chicken, sausage and yellow rice. After serious overeating, we took a postprandial stroll back to the hotel on the *Ramblas,* a bustling promenade filled with street performers and kiosks selling souvenirs, flowers and birds. Men accosted us, tapped us on the shoulder, "*No señor.*" Another then another, we ran away fast, unaware that it was where the *putas* pranced to show their wares. Two women alone, how did *they know* we weren't women of the night?

We took another uncomfortable couchette, arrived the next morning at Nice, a bustling city that rose on a mountain from the sea. We picked up our white Renault Dauphine.

Katerine was disappointed, not enough cylinders whatever that meant. It would have to do. We separated, planned to meet at three to go to the *plage.* I set out to buy a bikini, lots of boutiques selling them clustered around the tangled streets. I took a #42 pushing #44, their biggest size, French women cut small, typically #36. When I found a bottom that fit, the top wouldn't. After four fresh shopkeepers with attitude -- tsk tsk tsk you're an *enorme Americane* – finally found a shop that sold tops and bottoms separately, snagged a #44 top, #42 bottom, white ruffles piped with black. I kept it on under my sundress, met Katerine in the lobby of the Negresco, the old world palace Becker had recommended for drinks.

"Let's take a swim." We crossed the crowded Promenade des Anglais. It hurt to walk barefoot, the pebbles like jagged marbles. Two great minds, Katerine's bikini was lavender and white gingham check; a true size 38, she had no problem. I took my dress off self-consciously as I stripped away puritanism of the body, nothing wrong with showing it. 56.7 kilos. 125 pounds -- you converted kilos to pounds by multiplying by 2.2. Fighting weight. I shut my eyes. If I couldn't see them they couldn't see me. The bright blue Mediterranean beckoned, couldn't get to it, too painful.

We found a little bistro and ate our first *Salade Niçoise.* Scrumptious. Katerine, a cook, asked me to ask the waiter how to make it. He replied to my halting French in broken English, "Whatever eze in ze refrigerator from ze day before." His version was potatoes, string beans, lettuce, tomatoes, tuna, onion, hardboiled eggs, anchovies, capers pimento. "You add ze vinaigrette." Katerine nodded as he talked. She'd remember. I took notes, my small yellow pad ever ready, would have to start from scratch, never had a leftover in my life.

On the Riviera, our maiden voyage, destination Juan-les-Pins between Nice and Cannes. I read the seductive signs: Antibes, Grasses, Vallauris. The dramatic Grand Corniche wound in and around white cliffs, blue sea beneath. A good driver in the city frightened, slow and uncertain in wide-open spaces, I was thankful to be the designated navigator.

Juan-les-Pins was a small town, just the right size. We checked into a dollhouse. Our concierge recommended *Les Pirates,* a private beach club -- we'd have to pay a few francs to get in. Rows of chaises stationed like sardines faced the sea over a sandy beach, brownish, nothing to boast about. The attendant motioned us to take two empties. The women had the best bodies I'd ever seen, slim, great legs, perfect boobs -- most topless. Shocked, I wondered what proper etiquette was. Pretend you weren't looking? I'd had my bikini only one day, now this. The men wore small, revealing bathing suits leaving little to the imagination. Yes, I stared.

I couldn't wait a second longer for my first swim in the Mediterranean. I dove in, the water perfect, refreshing, so clear I could see my toes. I swam underwater fantasized that Nick was swimming with me. Where was he? Did he ever think of me? I prayed the bikini top would stay put -- moot to worry in monokini land -- elated. Upon my belated return, Katerine sat next to an interesting looking man with grey curly hair. "Ali, meet Alain. Help!" She was bad at languages.

"*Enchantee.*" I dried off, did five minutes of translation, enough to keep them going, my tan fading, not enough beach time, assumed the prone position for serious sunbathing. Seven chaises down out of the corner of my eye I spied a blonde Adonis, and spent the next hour sneaking sidelong glances. He didn't know I was alive. His indifference fueled my ardor as the Imp egged me on. 'Do something. Change his mind.' I asked Alain, *"Savez-vous ce gars- là?"* (Do you know that guy?) I pointed discreetly.

"*Oui.*"

"What's his name?"

"Jean-Pierre. J. P. (The French had double names.) Do you want to meet him?," heavy, French accent. Would I like to sleep with him tonight, a better question.

"*Oui.*"

Katerine nodded approval. Alain walked over to Jean-Pierre. I shut my eyes, sucked my stomach in. Katerine alerted me they were coming over. J. P. didn't speak English. We shook hands as my hands shook. The smallest blue bikini, tall, slender I loved how his lips pouted when he spoke, my tongue was hanging out, salivating like a bitch in heat. Shame on me.

After a few minutes, J. P. said goodbye, kissed me on one cheek then the other. Alain shrugged his shoulders. "*C'est la vie,*" he'd done his best. Probably liked thin French women. I'd blown my chance. *Enorme.* As a consolation prize Alain invited us dancing at the local club, *Whiskey a Go Go,* we'd meet at the door, nine.

I had the perfect dress: light blue and white gingham dirndl, lace, spaghetti straps, *très* Bardot -- her style the rage on two continents. The D. J. was stuck on one song, "*Chérie je t'aime chérie je t'adore... Mustapha Mustapha.*" Everyone sang.

Men sidled over, asked me to dance, offered to buy me a drink, couldn't be bothered, smitten with J. P. who never showed. Alain walked us home at three in the morning, a party town.

At the beach by two, everyone in the same chaises, like lemmings, Alain came bounding over. J. P. stayed still. I took a swim, thought about him, toweled off, glanced to see if he'd noticed me. Katerine, cool, nothing got *her* flustered, told me to relax, we were going gambling at the Monte Carlo Casino in Monaco.

"We?"

"Alain, J.P., you, me, Alain's car." All arranged, done deal, I noticed that J.P. hadn't asked me.

We wore the same dresses from the night before. Alain and Katerine communicated in sign language and laughter in front. I sat in the back with J. P., white dinner jacket, a blonde James Bond. For the forty minutes it took to drive thirty kilometers -- you multiplied ks by six to get miles -- on the Grand Corniche to Monte Carlo. I tried to talk to J. P. And tried. I couldn't believe it, finally had what I wanted, was miserable. There but not there, handsome outside, empty inside. A stiff. Attracted yet uncomfortable, I thought of Jordan in *his* white jacket, our movie star kiss. I would've had a good time with him.

We felt like royalty as we arrived at the glamorous Belle Époque casino. The gambling tables -- craps, roulette, blackjack, baccarat were crowded, beautiful women all dolled up, suave men, jackets and ties. J. P. and I watched in silence as Alain and Katerine played roulette. I didn't like the odds, wanted to play blackjack, an ace at cards, motioned with my finger for J. P. to follow me through the crowd to the blackjack table, not surprised he didn't want to play. I bought chips. The minimum bet was twenty francs -- four dollars, steep. Very. J. P. stood behind me. At least he was polite.

I stuck on nineteen. The dealer went over. Next round I doubled down on two tens, got an eight and a jack. The house held on seventeen. Another winner. I played one last time. Black jack. Voilà. I stood up, cashed in my chips, flushed with success and 200 *francs,* a fortune, forty bucks. J. P. was indifferent. Lucky in cards unlucky in love.

We stopped at *the* Hôtel du Cap Eden-Roc for lunch. Sara and Gerald Murphy had rented it for the summer of 1923, fellow expats Fitzgerald, Hemingway, their *ami* Picasso had come to visit. Fitzgerald immortalized it as the *Hôtel des Etrangers* in *Tender Is the Night.* After the Lost Generation, the Riviera was found now famous, like Woolcott Gibbs' *Season in the Sun* had shone the beacon on Fire Island.

The Hotel had the most beautiful pool on the planet filled with salt water, extending to the horizon, vanishing to the sky *and* heated. Blasted out of beige basalt, cut into the edge of the cliffs along the rugged Cap d'Antibes coast overlooking the glossy, glimmering Cannes Bay. I swam dreaming. The turquoise of the water, light blue sky, navy blue of the bay a brilliant backdrop for a movie starring Esther 'Ali' Williams doing water ballet. I went through my repertoire. Then I did laps. I didn't want to leave, ever. Katerine finally coaxed me out of the pool -- we had to get on the road.

We overate our way down the Italian Riviera, a plate of pasta -- thick, thin, flat, corkscrews, pellets, shells, ears -- at the beginning of every meal except breakfast. Italians were hot compared to the cool, contained French. Different energy. They talked with their hands, something Mother equated with bad manners. I spoke Spanish, fellow romance language, *ensalada mixta* became *insalata mista.* Close but no cigar, sometimes they got it, more times not.

Florence was a medieval stage set. We made a beeline to see *David,* saved him till I'd seen the rest of Michelangelo's marble masterpieces. His hands, that body, those lips, the most beautiful I'd ever see. If he could only come to life, we would live happily ever after. Katerine had to drag me away.

All roads finally led to Rome. We never got anywhere without getting lost, two or three hours late, scared to death by the traffic. Crazy Romans drove around at breakneck speed on every kind of contraption, two, three and four wheels, on the curb and off. The men made a career out of following us in spite of the hastily learned, devastating warnings my cousin taught us that had absolutely no effect whatsoever, *"Va via subito."* and *"Poussa via, cafone."* (Get going fast. Get going bumpkin.)

Too hot to be trotting around sightseeing and dreaming of water, we arrived at the tourist clogged Trevi Fountain. Should I go in --Anita Ekberg in taffeta – as in Fellini's *La Dolce Vita*? No. I turned my back in my drip-dry camp shirt, black dirndl skirt, tossed a coin over my shoulder and wished I'd get married to Nick. Overwhelmed by Rome, hounded by men, we left as fast as our slow car would go.

After three weeks in Italy none of my clothes fit must have gained ten pasta pounds, bread the other culprit -- my stomach stuck out and I felt gigantic. Why was everything I liked fattening? Discouraged by my lack of self-control, I had to go on a diet immediately or buy a sack.

The car had morning sickness, floored during the ascent to the Alps could barely climb. Katerine cursed, complained constantly about its pathetic power missed her VW beetle. The mountains were 'neat' her favorite adjective. I felt hemmed in, never liked Heidi. We took the train from Visp to Zermatt admired the Matterhorn, the White Tower. Couldn't get *me* up there, hated the cold, the concept, eager to get to Paris, a city girl.

Finally! The smell of fresh bread intoxicating, discovery at every turn, a destination on every street, I wanted to stay forever, kicked myself for not going last summer. *Idiote.* We settled into our hotel, Pas de Calais, Rue des Saint-Pères, Rive Gauche, sixth *arrondisement* in striking distance of Deux Magots, the fabled rendezvous of the literary and intellectual élite -- Jean-Paul Sartre and Simone de Beauvoir regulars, Hemingway's haunt as well. A brisk eight-minute walk, I sped up my usual snail. We found an empty outside table at the corner of the café under the white and green canopy. Lucky. No one sat inside. I asked the *garçon* what a *croque monsieur* was, translated for Katerine, ordered one *pour elle et une croque madame pour moi* -- toasted ham and cheese for her, same, fried egg on top for me.

"*Cherie*, that's a dammed good idea." American, mid-thirties, attractive, black hair, lively brown eyes, solo at the next table, looked up over his *International Herald Tribune,* made the perfect sign, thumb and forefinger in a circle, three other fingers straight in the air. After talking cross tables for ten minutes he invited us to join him.

Peter Gilman was an ex-newspaper reporter and Navy flier, bestselling author. *Diamond Head,* his potboiler about Hawaii had just been made into a movie starring Charlton Heston. Katerine was all smiles she could talk again. I found exactly what I wanted, a cool expat writer who knew James Jones, William Styron and James Baldwin.

Peter took charge, introduced us to *his* Paris. Self-assured, wry, he played to me while we talked and walked, had demi-tasse café conversations at home base, Deux Magots. He chain smoked Gauloises, strong and smelly, Katerine and I Chesterfields, in expat heaven, *la vie en rose.*

Peter took my hand as we ascended the dramatic Daru staircase at the Louvre. His felt clammy. I wiggled out by gesturing to pay better attention to the astonishing Hellenistic "Winged Victory of Samothrace" eight-foot marble goddess flying on high. How I loved angels. The pictures I pored over for Dr. Phyllis Williams Lehmann's Greek Art History 201 didn't do her justice. It was a killer course so tough I almost failed, my first C-. Who could memorize every stone on the Acropolis, the Temple of Zeus at Olympia, and the Temple of Apollo at Delphi for the mid-term exam? I was never going to be an archeologist. According to the professor the Nike's right arm was raised round her mouth to deliver the shout of victory. She would know. Her husband Karl had unearthed the Goddess's missing right hand on a dig in 1950. On their return trip Dr. Lehmann identified both the tip of her ring finger and thumb in a storage drawer at the Kunsthistorisches Museum, Vienna, now at rest in a glass box below the statue -- victory for posterity.

I read the floor plans like Sherlock Holmes looking for a clue to the whereabouts of Michelangelo's unfinished slaves, dragged Peter and Katerine to the basement where we finally found them. I wanted to touch the "Dying Slave", a sensuous seven foot six and a half inch nude hunk sleeping one hand behind his head, at peace. The "Rebellious Slave" had a coarser body the muscles contorted, in combat, at war. Michelangelo visualized the slaves imprisoned in huge blocks of marble -- only by carefully removing the excess stone could he set them free. The master had, indeed.

Peter took us to the *marché aux puces* -- flea market, hadn't picked a present for Mother yet, getting desperate, what if she didn't like it, the question that hung over my head like a noose. We walked in and out of stalls looked at French *tchotchkes.*

"*Cherie,* look what we have here," he said as he picked up a sleek black vase shaped like a champagne flute with a silver base. "This is a vintage Bakelite solitaire made in the USA in the '30s or '40s. Perfect example of Art Deco," Peter was proud of his discovery.

I picked it up uncertain, Mother didn't have anything like it. "Katerine do you think this is Mother?"

"How much?" asked Katerine. Forty-five dollars, a king's ransom, which they both assured me was a steal, worth so much more. I bought it, shrugged off Peter's congratulatory hug.

He showered me with attention but the more he showed his affections, the more I began to distance myself. The Imp was on my case to dump Peter, "too old". "You can do better". "Not good enough for you." Paris was my love of the moment no room in my heart for another how I rationalized it.

Katerine was awed -- her first author. She hung on his every word, positioned herself close whenever possible. Peter began to respond, his little lectures and *bon mots* now directed to Katerine. One night as he walked us home from Café Flore, next door to Deux Magots, they held hands. I had a full-fledged jealousy attack as it hit me I'd lost him. Suddenly the most important thing in my life was to reclaim Peter, needed a plan. Why not stay in Paris? With Katerine out of the picture I could win him back -- she had to go back and re-do senior year.

Some envious, unattractive classmates in our house had ratted on her the past October invoking the Smith Honor System. Her crime? She had a car. Though she'd parked her Beetle off campus, car privileges were off limits to seniors till spring term. The student honor court of that uptight learning prison without soul found Katerine guilty, her punishment -- she'd have to leave, repeat the year. Katerine had driven home to Springfield tail between her legs, licked her wounds, accepted her sentence, another year stuck in Siberia, two months in Europe to ease the pain.

The concierge pulled switches behind the counter of our cramped hotel lobby as I called Dad, person to person, to his office. I gushed, "So beautiful here, I'm happy, happy, happy." Time for the pitch, I crossed my fingers, touched my *figa.* "Dad I want to stay. I could get a job." I threw that in to convince him, uncertain if it was possible.

"No." Emphatic verging on tyrannical, I was shocked at his tone. "You *must* come home. Your mother's going into the hospital for a hysterectomy." He sounded worried. "She's scheduled it for the day you arrive. You *must* be here." No big deal, an ordinary operation they took out your plumbing. She was fifty, strong, healthy; it wasn't life threatening. Why was Dad so insistent?

"What can I do for her? Let me stay in Paris, please," I pleaded, knew that Mother wouldn't let me help her, my return an exercise in futility.

"You'll be on that plane. Understand? It's your duty to take care of your mother." Could I stay without money? What would I live on? Teach English? My grammar was bad. I'd starve. The image of a tattered little girl begging for bread arose, *très* "Les Misérables."

"Yes, Dad." I hung up, hung my head, my hopes dashed, Paris bubble smashed.

Peter hired a car and chauffeur to drive us to the airport. We sipped champagne and exchanged phone numbers -- he might be coming to New York sometime. He kissed Katerine goodbye on the lips, gave me the typical French -- one on each cheek. I flew home, the Winged Victory's wings clipped.

6

Mais Non

Paris interruptus I landed with a crash, having flown too close to the sun. The thrill of traveling and living abroad, fun and freedom done, New York dirty, ugly hot. I'd pulled the Monopoly Chance card, 'Go back three spaces.' In my blue room, feeling blue, I flashed on Jordan who'd observed that 'it wasn't my color'.

Dad and I drove up Broadway in the Buick to the Columbia Presbyterian Medical Center, a small city on the very upper west side. Mother lay in a flower-filled hospital room, light blue quilted bed jacket over her hospital gown, ever chic. I gave her a careful kiss, held one hand behind my back with her present.

"You shouldn't have bothered to come back, that was your *father's* idea. I don't need you," she snapped, combative right off the bat. I sat down next to her, put the package on the floor.

I told her about the trip, sharing some of the not incriminating highlights, ended with Peter, the bestselling author. I presented my gift to Mother with a flourish. "Here's a little something from Paris." I'd taken pains to decorate the package to match the vase, black shiny paper with a silver bow, a long stem red rose *très* art deco. She admired the wrapping, carefully opened it. Her face contorted in a look I'd seen many times before. Disdain. She hated it on sight and nothing would ever change her opinion. I felt like she'd punched me in the gut.

She turned it over, tapped it, sneered, "What is this made of, *plastic*?"

"Bakelite, mother."

"Plastic is plastic." I'd committed the greatest sin: a lapse in taste. She laid it on the bed as if touching it might give her an allergic reaction.

"It would look great on the window sill," still hopeful, Pollyanna.

"No, put *that* in the drawer." A command. She pointed, I picked it up, carefully lowered the corpse next to her Kleenex tissue packs. "Put the rose in there," she growled, gesturing in distaste at a hideous floral arrangement sent by a client of Dad. I fought tears in the car, Dad silent. I shouldn't have listened to Peter and Katerine.

I felt trapped as I unpacked, dependent on Dad for money, under their thumb. After four years at college and a summer in Europe, felt like I'd never left. What was I going to do with the rest of my life? No career had beckoned, I hadn't paid attention to the future and now it was here. Time to get a job. No other option. What? Rich woman. Poor woman. Beggar woman, thief, doctor -- nope, lawyer -- no way, Indian chief. I lost the button game.

Billy was gone, a freshman at Dartmouth. Mother had hired a decorator to convert his bedroom to a family den.

Lonely, I called Nick. His fancy answering service, a woman with an upper class English accent informed me Mr. Rose was out of town. Brit speak secretaries were the latest business rage.

"Till when?" They didn't know. I left a message I was back, my number. He'd never call, didn't know why I bothered.

I sorted through a stack of old telephone messages from my time in Europe, the names and numbers of potential *beaux* written in Mother's cramped hand on her "Don't Forget" pad. Peter was still on my mind. He'd probably already found another candidate at Deux Magots. I called Freddy back. I'd met him the past February at Princeton -- 6' 3", hunky, super WASP from Newport. We'd almost had a fling but I'd stayed true to Nick. Then. Now, Peter in Paris, Nick who knows where, Freddy would more than do. We made a date, something to look forward to -- we'd go to El Morocco with his friend King.

I spent a few days at MoMA, the Met, caught up on some movies, joined the 92nd YMCA -- they had a big pool. Not used to so much time on my hands, out of the city rhythm without a daily plan, I escaped back into bookworm mode took on the rest of Camus' *oeuvre,* all the time fretting about what I was going to do in life. No small consideration.

Desperate for company, I phoned Becker, a back slide but even her self-centeredness was better than being alone. She'd been in Europe like everyone else, returned from Italy a week before me. She boasted about the Italian count she'd fallen for -- the real thing, his family's crest on his gold pinky ring, something about the Papal guard -- never once asked me about *my* trip. She filled me in on the Fire Islanders. Jordan was working feverishly on the Kennedy campaign. The election was going to be close. Very. We'd missed the Twist, a new dance craze from a song sung by Chubby Checker. Everyone was doing it. I made a date to go to her apartment, brave the West Side, her brother Scooter could teach us. His lesson was simple: you took a towel and pretended you were drying off your fanny.

Mother came home from the hospital. A tough bird, she was fine physically, hated being a patient not allowed to lift anything, robbed of her favorite pastime, shopping. The more vulnerable she was, the meaner. She ordered Alberta, our rotund gold-toothed Jamaican maid, and me around. Her chore of choice was to dispatch me to Gristedes, the overpriced grocery store around the corner for items she'd forgotten in the delivery order; or down to the Madison Avenue Delicatessen at 86th, for the best lox and bagels on the Upper East Side and the worst waiters. Sammy the waiter told Dad what *not to order* in an abusive voice.

When Mother's friend Helen came by to visit, Mother shooed me out of the house, "I don't want you spoiling my date" -- she didn't share her friends. Out of her clutches for a few blessed hours, I took a bus forty blocks down to Liberty

Records where I listened to Nick's new album, "Love Light" in a soundproof leather booth. A breakout sound, his voice curled around the lyrics. I shut my eyes, pretended I was sitting next to him on the piano bench as he sang to me. Where *was* he? Back in the blue room, I played it full blast, singing along. Dad burst in, hands over his ears.

"The music's too god dammed loud! I can't hear myself talk on the phone," at the top of *his* voice.

"You can't barge in like that, Dad. Please knock," I yelled back.

"What is that?"

"Nick's new album." He turned around slammed the door. A stand off.

Although I'd managed to walk off the pasta in Paris, a rudderless ship without a daily destination or schedule, feeling empty, lonely, no Nick or Katerine, worried about 'the problem' -- what to do with my life, started to binge. One morning Mother cornered me.

"Did you eat the coffee cake?" *J'accuse.* "There was none left for your father's breakfast." She looked me up and down. "Your stomach's sticking out like a balloon. It's disgraceful."

I trudged down to the Madison Avenue Deli to replace the purloined goods, bought a pecan coffee ring for Dad, six chocolate donuts which I polished off – inhaled by the time I spotted our green awning. I got Dad's home intact miraculously, barricaded my door and slept.

Finally the night of my hot date with hunky Freddy arrived. We were going on the town to El Morocco with his best friend from Princeton, Rex, called, King, whom I'd met before. King had a connection. Alberta answered the bell. I heard Dad usher them into the den. Running late, behind my bedroom door, I put on the backless dress from Paris, hoping to recreate the movie star audition look.

I took three giant steps across the hall into the new den for a belated grand entrance infused with adrenaline.

King whistled. "Love the dress you almost have on." King had a big personality, nattily dressed like many short men -- bowtie, pink shirt, black velvet jacket. Freddy a study in contrast, white bread to King's pumpernickel, wore the old-money uniform -- well frayed navy blazer, grey flannels, crisp white shirt rep tie. Dad flashed me the 'You're late again' look. Freddy and King made room for me between them on the couch. I sat with pleasure sandwiched by suitors -- swains. Dad was enthroned in the black Eames chair, Mother's first concession to modern comfort. The shelves of the new white glass and brass bar behind him were filled with crystal Steuben glasses, bottles of booze, and a brass ice bucket. Mother had arranged olives, peanuts, celery and radishes on a wicker chest that served as a coffee table.

She made her entrance in a long blue velvet hostess gown and lit the white taper candle proffering a plate of cheese and crackers. Freddy and King jumped up. "I didn't know you had such an attractive mother." Score one for silver-tongued King.

"Please sit down Mrs. Abrams, let me help." Score two. She wouldn't think of it.

Freddy ate everything, said nothing. Dad poured drinks and held court. We talked about the election. King, articulate and informed, was thrilled to be voting for Kennedy, Mother and Dad on the same train.

"I'm supporting Nixon, sir," Freddy quietly announced. Nuclear blast. Dad hated Nixon.

"Mrs. Abrams, did I notice a grand piano on the way in?" King interrupted.

"Why do you ask?" (awsk?)

"Mind if I play?" Great save. We filed into the living room. Dad claimed the black tweed couch on the far side removed from the scene. Mother gave King the royal treatment, opened the piano bench to show him her sheet music. He admired her Broadway musical collection picked a few favorites, placed them on the lectern. Mother sidled down next to him, insisted on turning pages. She could have stood. The thought flickered through my mind she was flirting. No. Couldn't be.

King, the star of last year's Princeton Triangle show sang in a strong tenor voice. He knew Sinatra's repertoire by heart, crooned, "I was a stranger in the city...."

Freddy and I leaned against the wall behind them facing Dad who couldn't see him caressing my naked back. I got chills, a bad boy.

Dad trapped us at the front door on the way out and warned Freddy, "Have her home by 10:30." Not again. Was he serious? How embarrassing.

Freddy was diplomatic. "We're going to El Morocco, sir. I expect that we'll be later than that." Dad moved the curfew to midnight.

"12:30" I said, as we walked out the door, safety in numbers.

We cabbed to a four-story townhouse with a royal aura – *the* New York nightclub frequented by café society. I'd seen celebrity's pictures in the papers shot against bold zebra stripes by Jerome Zerbe. Like the other hangouts of the rich and famous – 21, the Stork Club and the Colony – El Morocco had begun its life as a Prohibition speakeasy.

A velvet rope was overseen by an imperial -- white tie and tails, distinguished looking maître d' named Angelo. He stopped us in our tracks, gave us the onceover. King led the charge. "We're guests of Mr. Perona," he explained, referring to the club's owner. "My dad is his physician."

Angelo's piercing blue eyes relaxed as he smiled, cool defrosting to charming a chameleon. The velvet rope parted. Amen. "Welcome." He ushered us to the right into *the inner sanctum* where Mr. Perona sat in the head booth, the king of the jungle surrounded by zebras and peacocks. He embraced King, told him how much he admired his Dad, welcomed Freddy and me warmly.

"Seat them by the dance floor," he told Angelo.

It was the size of a postage stamp. We sat down at our table, white card in the middle, "Cover charge $20." Whoops. Our waiter removed it with a grand gesture, winked, courtesy of Perona who'd waived it for us. King ordered a bottle of Dom Pérignon brut. I took out a Chesterfield, Freddy jumped to attention to light it with the blue and white striped El Morocco matches. The musicians started a rumba.

King swayed in his seat, then stood and put his arms out to mimic Gene Kelly. "Gotta dance," he beckoned. Freddy nodded approval -- he would've if he could've. I'd never danced with King before, but ballet, modern, plus Viola Wolff dancing school had prepared me.

King knew all the steps and moves, a great leader. By the time we got to the foxtrot and samba, we were in sync, a team. The band struck up a lindy while King twirled me around with fancy footsteps and arm combinations I didn't know existed, his rhythm so contagious I didn't miss a beat. Everyone cleared the floor to watch, and applauded as we finished. Flushed with success, we nodded to our new fans on the way back to Freddy. A dapper older gentleman with a Douglas Fairbanks moustache sprang from his table took my hand and kissed it. His wife looked away. King saluted the codger: "Isn't she gorgeous?" Though I was flattered by King's flirtation, I liked Freddy more, attracted to his strong silence.

Cinderella arrived back from the ball way after one. Dad waited on the living room couch, coiled and ready to strike. Freddy tried to leave but not before he received a tongue lashing from His Worship. Frustration was the operative word in our budding relationship. We had no place to play. His first year med school cubicle came with a roommate; my parent's apartment off limits. I got creative and volunteered to shut down the Fire Island house for the winter. Still recuperating, Mother gave the go-ahead. She made a list of instructions on the red lettered "Don't Forget" pad: turn off gas and water; empty out icebox; take garbage to dump.

A quick check of my wallet revealed I didn't have enough money for the trip, not wanting to touch my nest egg, $387.56 in my savings account garnered from graduations and birthdays and gathering quarterly interest on my bank card. I'd have to ask Dad -- he'd doled out the occasional twenty to cover bare essentials, carfare and movies since I'd been back. I avoided the bound-to-be-horrendous confrontation with him till the last minute. He had 'poor boy syndrome.'

Grandfather Isaac had opened up two pharmacies, one in Williamsburg, Brooklyn, the other in Patchogue. Dad's only memory was going fishing. After he'd died, when Dad was eight, the family's fortune slowly faded: prosperous to precarious. Dad had worked his way through City College, St. John's night law school, graduated into the Depression in '31 and opened a labor law practice. The labor movement as young as Dad, he could barely make ends meet working day and night. These days his office flourished, yet it was difficult for him to part with the money he'd fought so hard for. Old habits never died. It was equally hard to stay sympathetic when I was put in the position of having to beg. Though my reasons were legitimate -- mostly, I had to steel my nerves before asking, knocked discreetly on their bedroom door the night before the trip.

"Come in."

Dad -- voluminous Brooks Brothers blue boxers, undershirt, long black socks, leather slippers had his head down in his cedar walk-in closet, the top drawer pulled out of a tall chest. The closet smelled woodsy looked like a haberdashery: shoes lined up like soldiers, jackets and pants sorted by color. The small change he dumped from his pockets nightly overflowed into a bronze bowl on the top of his bureau. He sorted pennies, nickels, dimes and quarters into piles, meticulously placed each coin into beige paper packets from the bank. King Solomon's treasury.

I summoned all my courage, gripped my *figa*, "I need some money to go to Fire Island tomorrow."

"Don't you have any left from what I gave you the other day?"

"Four dollars, but I need twenty more for the train, taxi, boat round trip, and to eat." Good at math, I'd done my homework, written it out, and added up the list of expenses to the penny. I wasn't sure if I could count on Freddy to pay, our first trip. "Want to see?" I waved the paper in front of him.

"No." I had him. Dad picked up his gold money clip, a hundred dollar bill locked inside a tiny glass case on top -- he'd never be penniless, peeled off two tens. Slowly. "Do a good job out there."

"Yes, Dad. Thanks." I bolted from the room and began to breathe again.

On a glorious late September Indian summer Friday, Freddy and I drove to Bay Shore along the Southern State Parkway in his black Benz 220 SL, top down. He looked handsome in jeans, penny loafers without socks, of course, navy and crimson trimmed tennis sweater tied around his neck. As he smoked Marlboros, he exhaled out of the side of his mouth. Sexy. We parked, boarded the Fire Island Maid. Freddy paid, no problem.

I loved showing him the sights on the ride over. A sailor, he pointed out the type, class and dimensions of the sailboats in a monotone. I unlocked our wagon. "How cool." Freddy pulled our bags along happy with his job. I relaxed he liked the island. We were going to have a good time. He put both bags in my bedroom, left so I could put my bathing suit on in private.

"Hello beach, hello ocean, I'm back." Freddy put his arms around me. Sloped down shoulders, developed arms, smooth chest -- so big he made me feel small, no easy task -- my own *David.* "Let's take a swim." I dropped the red striped cover-my-thighs towel, the ocean finally warm, heating up since June, dove in. Freddy followed. Good dive. We tantalized each other. He touched my nipples. I touched his. He liked that. So did I. We rushed home, showered off the sand, jumped into my bed. So much foreplay in the water, it was over too soon. He apologized next time would be better. And it was. He'd been on the wrestling varsity, showed me some holds, his arm circled my waist while I was on my knees, first position. We rolled around as I tried to escape. He pinned me. I lost then again I won. Athletic lovemaking, a lot of sweat, he never said a word.

We took a break from bed to go to Maguire's on the bay where we each devoured a five-pound lobster. On Sunday following Mother's list to a tee we turned off the gas and water, emptied out the icebox, packed it into a carton from Clegg's to take back to the city, wagoned the garbage to the dump, and rode back on the ferry, connected and content.

I overslept Monday, exhausted. They ganged up at dinner that night fearful I was 'sleeping my life away.' The pressure was on. 'Get a job.' They were right but what?

The prestigious place to work for an art history major was the Museum of Modern Art. Dad knew someone through his client, Nelson Rockefeller and got me an interview. I thumbed through my art history notes and books and refreshed my memory on Magritte, Matisse, Dali, Picasso and Pollack.

I took the Fifth Avenue bus down to 53rd Street all dressed up, black suit, white Peter Pan collar shirt, circle pin, string of pearls. I waited in a stark white room, held the newly minted resumé I'd typed hunt-and-peck style on my silver Olivetti with two carbon papers for copies.

"How fast can you type, Miss Abrams? I don't see it on your c.v."

"I'm not sure."

"Would you care to take a typing test?"

"Of course."

She seated me in a white cubicle in front of a black typewriter, handed me a few blank papers, two typed sheets to copy. I rolled the paper in as my stomach rolled over, felt like I was at the start of a swimming race. On your mark, get set. She pushed the stopwatch told me to begin. Go. I typed my heart out, adrenaline pumping, slow. While Miss Williams reviewed it, I paged through the cartoons of *The New Yorker* prayed for a miracle. She shook her head no -- they were looking for fifty-five words a minute, clean. Seventeen with several strikeovers didn't cut it. I failed, disgraced, demeaned, tried not to take it personally, did. No one else would hire me without typing. Haunted by the horrible experience in Dad's office, I'd refused to learn, the Imp back in action, "You're better than a secretary!"

Freddy and I saw each other once a week, taken with each other, at least our bodies. He called Monday nights to confirm our next date, a taciturn New Englander, he hung up after long awkward silences, mission accomplished. King filled in the spaces, called often to chat about movies, art, opera, Broadway, books. He came on most of our dates. I knew he liked me, but kept him at arm's length. Between the two of them I had a perfect guy.

Around this time Mother decided to send me to a shrink. We were shopping at Bloomingdale's, Mother's drug of choice, on the escalator between the mezzanine and second floor. She turned around looked down at me.

"Helen's kids are seeing a psychiatrist. I've made you an appointment with him"

"Can you please turn back around so we can talk about this safely?" I'd heard some talk about Dr. Sigmund Freud and analysis, words like 'ego', 'id'. You laid down on a couch had your head shrunk by a Jewish doctor who'd gone to med school then had his head shrunk. I didn't know anyone who'd ever done it and was surprised that Tina and Jane were going. It couldn't kill me.

I showed up at Dr. Blatt's office, Mother's insidious punishments, painful putdowns and endless criticism on my mind. He motioned for me to sit down across from a desk almost as cluttered as Dad's. I kept looking at the couch, worn brown leather, wondered what secrets had been revealed there. He got down to business. "Why are you here?"

"My mother thought it was a good idea."

"Why?" Was that the only word in his vocabulary?

"I sleep too late." We weren't exactly off to a great start. He changed course.

"Tell me about your life as if you were writing your autobiography." The flood gates opened, a litany of loneliness: the young years at school, the best student, no friends; camp, the best athlete, no friends; high school and college, popular with boys, no friends except Katerine; no 'Mrs.', no prospects, no job -- hopeless. I was still going strong when he signaled me to stop, our session over. I didn't mention the Imp.

"I'll take you on." I hadn't realized this was an interview. "Come twice a week same time as today. You can stay in the chair, I'm not a strict Freudian." Not crazy enough for the couch -- good or bad sign? "You suffer from low self esteem. See you Thursday." Odd turn of events, I'd expected to have my head shrunk, instead I'd have to inflate it.

First impression: Musty, dreary office, paunchy, unattractive he had a brush mustache, the kind that men who are losing their hair seemed to favor – I hated facial hair. Minus.

Dad got me a job in display at Saks Fifth Avenue. He knew Henry Callahan, the silver-haired head of display from Fire Island who knew Lester Gaba. A miserable $53 a week, at least I was working. My job as the fashion coordinator was to accessorize the clothes on mannequins in the windows, the only woman in a department of twenty-five queens. Our office was one flight down from 'Main' in the basement, a room in which to dress the dozens of dummies, Saks' silent saleswomen. I wore basic black -- was there any other color? They called me 'the beatnik' because I didn't wear lipstick and wore my hair long. First stop for me was the salon on the ground floor where Mr. Fred created a beehive, the latest style. A lot of teasing, hairspray, bobby pins and time, I worried if backcombing was good for my hair. Who cared? Fashion was fashion.

"I must have the right purple for this Norell." My boss, Mr. Eastman, a nervous Nellie, chewed his lip, squinted at the sequined sheath. He executed Callahan's designs for the Fifth Avenue banks of windows planned months ahead of time to showcase special collections, designers and events. The concept of window dressing: seduce a shopper with pizazz and they'll come in and buy something basic.

"Do you want it lighter, darker or in between?" I worried.

"I'll know it when I see it."

"I've already dyed five pairs." White satin pumps, size six, the mannequin's size, five different purples, a treacherous color. My eyes lied, couldn't remember if it was red purple or blue purple.

"Don't bother me with details." It did bother me, didn't know what to do. Terry saved me. Southern with navy eyes and straight black hair, my ally.

"If I weren't queer, I'd want to be your boyfriend." Ah, the conditional -- I would have wanted him, a man with women's sensibilities. We struck up a friendship.

"You need a swatch." He turned the dress I was trying to match inside out. "Now let me look. Aha. This is perfect, darling." He took a tiny scissors and snipped a small piece from the 'waist' beside the seam, held it between two fingers, raised it over his head, triumphant. "Now you can match this and no one will ever know." My heroine.

As I sifted through a tray of fake diamond earrings and tried to decide the right pair for a dinner dress, Terry burst into the basement, "Darling, you must come up to the fifth floor, I've found a dress that's absolutely you -- too divine for words."

We took the employees elevator together. It was glorious. "It may be me, but it costs two hundred dollars."

"You need a sugar daddy to spoil you rotten, girl." Not an option so far, Nick the exception I seemed to like guys my age who could barely support themselves let alone me. "The sable must look like it's floating in the wind. Careful, it's worth twenty thousand." Mr. Callahan lisped, affected, anxious as I held it while Terry and Derek, another designer, tied invisible wires to the coat, attached them to the wall.

"Don't worry, I won't let anything happen, can't afford to, it's worth three times my yearly salary." Mr. Eastman did not laugh.

"I must have sixteen-button gloves, not Audrey Hepburn eight." We were doing windows to celebrate the formal opening night of the opera. I rushed to the glove department, signed out two pairs of white kid sixteen buttons, arrived back in the window, breathless.

"What took you so long?" No matter what I did was wrong.

"What am I going to do Terry, Mr. Eastman hates me?"

"Not your fault, he hates women." We sat at Jiffy's around the corner, getting smashed on their monster martinis, "You're going to have to quit."

"My Dad won't let me."

"Talk to him about it. Tell him the truth: you're being persecuted."

"Bad timing. Dad's getting the labor vote out for Kennedy immersed in the campaign." So was the rest of the country. JFK and Nixon was all anyone talked about. "I'll have to do it after the election."

I proudly voted for John Fitzgerald Kennedy the first November Tuesday. A squeaker, wanted to share the victory with Jordan, called, heard Jean's voice and hung up. Three long weeks later I unveiled my unfair working conditions to Dad, the workingman's hero. Perhaps my plight was not of Dickensian proportions, still a case of exploitation. I brought it up at the dinner table as Dad stood to carve seconds from the leg of lamb. Mother rang her little silver bell. Alberta in black uniform, white apron and starched lace hat, waddled through the pantry door, passed roast potatoes and peas, her smile showcasing one gold front tooth. I guided the lazy Susan toward me for the mint jelly. Dad heard me out. "How long have you been working there?"

"Three months January first."

"I want you to work there at least six months. Better for your resumé. Then you can give two weeks notice." Though Eastman was in the wrong, I'd have to do three more month's time -- so much for workers' rights.

Christmas was complicated, fraught with peril, packed with pressure from relatives, family, boyfriends, girlfriends and lack thereof. An emotional roller coaster of expectations and memories collided in the name of a tradition once holy, now a buying spree, stirred up anxiety, no one happy.

In retail, 'the season', which seemed to start earlier each year, was big business. For the display department at Saks it meant a Cecil B. De Mille -- Callahan production. The Sunday after Thanksgiving, our stalwart twenty-six teetered up on ladders and scurried down to the basement from six in the morning till ten at night, placing thousands of tiny lights and greenery all over the ceiling of the main floor, cascading down the pillars. Winter wonderland. Hell.

Billy came home from Dartmouth and repossessed his room. He put his foot down, they had to entertain in the living room until he left. We each had our own social circles never saw each other.

I answered the phone on the first ring, home after work, sore feet up on my antique pine desk.

"*Cherie. Ça va?*" Peter Gilman's distinctive voice. "I'm coming to New York, going to the MacDowell colony with a new book for a couple of months in early January. When I see you, I'll tell you everything." Elation. "Beautiful, can I crash with you?" Shocked.

"No. Of course not," I snapped, *merci* to the Imp, 'Crude. He doesn't know you well enough to ask.' I got a grip, softened my tone, it was Peter. "I live at home with my parents." How could he have known?

"Really." He paused. "Why?" He had me.

The answer, afraid to live alone, was none of his business. "Not enough bread."

"I'll find a place to flop. Call you when I get in. *À la prochaine, cherie.*" A roller coaster ride, first I wanted to see him then turned off.

Peter sat on a barstool at the Oak Bar in the Plaza Hotel, the same frayed black corduroy jacket, black shirt, and jeans he'd worn in Paris. His blow lunch tie seemed off, his shoes unfortunate, crepe on the bottom, Hush Puppies. His beat Bohemian look that was so perfect for Paris, seemed dowdy and dirty in contrast to the other men – crisp, starched, sharp, well tailored, elegant. The chicest bar in New York was a bad choice. He didn't fit in. I should have suggested someplace downtown. The Village was more his speed. Off my game.

"C*herie,* you look beautiful." He gave me the two-cheek kiss. "This is their loaner tie." He picked it up, looked at it in disgust. "Hideous. They wouldn't let me in without one."

We caught up. He told me about his new novel. I passed on telling him about my job, knowing that fashion and the silly behind-the-scenes minutiae and manipulations weren't his long suit. He swiveled on his stool, stared out the window that overlooked Central Park. "Like to take a ride, *cherie*?" He pointed to a row of hansom cabs and horses lined up for hire.

"Of course." Strictly for tourists, I'd never ridden in a hansom cab. I picked a white horse and carriage with a red interior like a fairy tale. The driver tipped his top hat. We cuddled under furry blankets that shielded us from the crisp air. Peter took my hand, the moment I'd been dreaming of for months.

"You're *la plus belle femme* in Paris and New York," He tried to kiss me.

I resisted, blurted out, "What about Katerine?"

"Oh that. Just to get you jealous." It had worked. "It's always been you. You're the one, *Cherie,* je *t'aime.*" He shoved his tongue down my throat. The Imp went to town, 'Dump him right now!' A light switch went off, click. I pushed him away, moved to the far side revolted, wished I could push an eject button and never see him again. I spent the rest of the ride plotting my escape. For once I welcomed Dad's curfew, the perfect way to wiggle out.

"Sorry Peter gotta go, have to be home by ten," I said believing my own lie. He pulled me closer, not getting the hint. This time I shoved. "Please put me in a taxi," frantic, desperate to get out of his clutches. He didn't know it had to be lit up on top, and hailed the wrong one. "Taxi." Available, thank God. As Peter opened the door, I rushed inside. He started to climb in. The Imp was right on the ball, 'Say anything to get rid of him'. I put my hand up to stop the vermin, my voice loud and anxious, "No! Don't bother."

"Why?" He backed down. I tried to pull the door closed. He kept it open.

"You're going downtown." How could I explain I was repulsed?

"*Cherie,* what's wrong?" Peter, bewildered, reluctantly let me go, stood out in the cold. I sped uptown realizing I'd just cut him out of my life with a knife, no anesthesia -- cruel, heartless bitch. In the following days, he called and called, but I wouldn't see him. Wrong, I was righteous, told myself he'd used poor Katerine. I swept the incident under the rug ashamed, neglected to tell Dr. Blatt. First round K.O. for the Imp.

As the season sped by, wooed by both Freddy and King we remained a trio, wowed by Freddy in bed, attracted to King's smarts and vitality. Freddy asked me out for New Year's Eve. As I stocked shelves with Saks' red Christmas boxes and other bah humbug drudgery, I looked forward to our date, thinking that for once I'd beaten my New Year's Eve curse.

Freddy took me to his sister's bohemian flat in Greenwich Village on the big night. Swathed in a swank black dress with sequins, my hair in a beehive courtesy of Saks, I realized to my horror that I was overdressed, a serious fashion gaffe. Everyone else wore work shirts and jeans, even Freddy once he took off his Chesterfield coat. Downtown dressed down. The only saving grace was King, nattily attired as usual, his date Missy also gussied up. I couldn't shake an outsider feeling and was ticked off at Freddy for not telling me the dress code.

King ignored Missy and put the moves on me -- forbidden fruit. To make matters worse, Freddy flirted with a stunning six-foot black model, Luna. Consumed by jealousy, I drank too much, mixed eggnog and scotch followed by wine. Lethal. Freddy called a limo -- you couldn't get cabs on New Year's, paid him a shocking $50 to drive me home where I barfed up the party, didn't remember most of it the next day.

Noisy football games hammered my hung over head at our Bloody Mary New Year's Day party. Everyone was rooting for some team. Loudly. I took stock at halftime when I could hear myself think. On balance I was a lucky girl. I'd had the time of my life in Europe. My first resolution was to live in Paris. My inability to type hatred thereof and distaste at being a secretary and therefore getting a job had crippled me and my future. I made a resolution to bite the bullet and go to typing school. It couldn't kill me.

I hadn't seen Nick since spring -- he was out on tour or in L.A. I missed my sapphires. In his stead I'd become involved with two friends, sleeping with one and having fun with the other. One plus one equals none. I knew it was a losing equation, not sure how it would end. I didn't like Dr. Blatt. Mother was difficult. Dad distant. I made a resolution to get my own pad. Last but not least, I was going to lose the eight pounds that had crept on.

7

Triple Play

I sang the post holiday blues, Christmas lights dimmed, short grey days, streets full of slush, Freddy away skiing. One day as we changed the Fifth Avenue windows to resort wear for the snowbirds and vacationers heading south, I heard persistent knocking. I peeked under the halfway drawn shades. There was my old friend Alan Gold waving at me, having miraculously recognized my calves as he walked by. We made sign language through the glass, planned to meet after work.

Alan, handsome in a rugged way, was part of the Jewish upper middle class crowd that lived on Park Avenue between 79th, and 96th. Another Christmas Jew, he dressed 'shoe'... chic...Ivy. His parents, like mine, had tiptoed past the 'No Jews allowed' co-op restriction, made it into a mostly WASP building. I'd met Alan when I was thirteen and he fourteen at Miss Viola Wolff's, a dance school for the privileged children of Upper East Side Jews.

At Jiffy's, I complained about my plight and the crazy boss who had it in for me. Alan was sympathetic, talked about his job in advertising at Grey, an account executive in training 'on the fast track'. Alan was a great dancer, wanted to go to the new Peppermint Lounge. *Pourquois pas*? Freddy hadn't asked me to go steady yet. No pin or ring.

I spent a week practicing the Twist. We discussed the dress code at great length, wanted to look right but didn't know anyone who'd been there to ask. According to Igor Cassini's gossip column, "a mixed bag." We guessed dressy. I settled on a black off the shoulder dress and rhinestone belt to emphasize my small waist -- I'd been dieting.

Alan looked handsome: black suit, open shirt, red tie pocketed in case required. We had drinks in the den, the obligatory interview with Dad and Mom who knew him from when.

Our doorman Patrick, a robust, red-cheeked Irishman who took extra good care of us because Dad was counsel to his union 32B, blew and blew his silver whistle to snag a cab. Park at night was Siberia East. After a forever five minutes, one came by. Alan tipped Patrick for his trouble. We stopped at West 45th Street in front of a big Peppermint Lounge sign emblazoned on a canopy. A brute of a bouncer guarded the rope behind which a group of drab downtowners lined up. He motioned to us, unhooked it and waved us in.

"How did we get in so easily?" I was surprised.

"We dressed right. He took us ahead of those *schlubs*," our strategy had paid off. Alan bought us J & B's at the bar. We drifted to the dance floor at the back. Joey Dee and the Starlighters played on a small stage, "Let's twist again..." We twisted together apart, the first time I'd ever danced without touching my partner, sweated up a storm -- sorry, Mother, ladies 'perspire'. A blast.

"I'm starving." Alan nodded in agreement. "Let's go to P.J. Clarke's." Everyone went there to have 'the Cadillac of burgers', for some the last stop in their nightly rounds, others, the first. It was a New York institution. We cabbed to 55th and Third, navigated past the long mahogany bar three deep with serious drinkers. It was *the* quintessential no frills c. 1900 Irish saloon, sawdust on the floor, stamped tin ceiling. Owner Dan Lavezzo dared defy New York's drive to modernize.

In a small, crowded room off the bar past the jukebox, Frankie, short and slightly slimy, guarded entry to the fabled back room, keeping the well-heeled swells of all ages waiting. I took Alan's hand, cut through the line and led him to Frankie. Rumor had it he had a checkered past, a sometime pimp who matched up rich dowagers with young studs; I liked him, always took time to schmooze and smile, intrigued, could it be true?

"Hi Ali." Frankie planted a kiss on my cheek. "Where've you been, beautiful?"

"The Peppermint Lounge."

"And?"

"The place is tacky, but Joey Dee's fabulous." I began to twist. Show off.

"So I've heard." Word travelled fast. "Need a deuce? Let me see." He stuck his head into the back room. "You're in luck, table twenty-two just paid their check. Come this way please. Who's your handsome beau?" He was nosy. His job.

"Meet Alan Gold, rising star of Grey Advertising."

Frankie led us to our table. Alan wrote out our order on a pad with a pencil, the menu in chalk on the wall: Two cheeseburgers, $2.64 each, Fries $.87, Irish coffee. $2.86.

Alan, a cool customer, got me going in the role of seducer. I began to touch and brush up against him, asked a million questions, a 'good little talker, you can charm a snake,' as Mother never failed to point out, left-handed compliment from a snake. In Europe I'd noticed that while I couldn't bargain, I could keep up a conversation on any subject except the stock market. Business was a bore.

I was eager to learn about advertising. Alan explained that the account executive was the business manager, known as "the suit." The art director, usually Italian, and the copywriter, usually Jewish were "the creatives." My juices were flowing, my interest piqued by Alan and a possible new career.

He switched the conversation to the Knicks, a diehard fan. I told him I'd love to go to a game crossed my fingers, praying my nose wouldn't grow. He was thrilled that the Mets were coming, "the first new National League baseball team expansion in fifty years." I was a softball player, big hitter and fair fielder, couldn't run. He hoped to get tickets for the opening game. "Wouldn't that be exciting." This time I meant it.

I cornered him for a goodnight kiss at the front door. I'd always had to stave off passes, now I made one the tables turned. The ice finally melted, a hard won kiss, sensual once he got started. We began to date, regulars at the Peppermint Lounge. Our necking at the front door intensified, no place to go, the usual.

We got a break in March. Mother and Dad gave Alberta two weeks off, flew down to Las Brisas, a new five star luxury hotel in Acapulco. Hurray. After twisting the night away at the Peppermint Lounge, I invited Alan up.

On April first I told the boys in display I was leaving, "As much as I love you all, this department is prejudiced against straights." Terry hugged me, cried, he'd miss me, happy I was flying the coop.

"Sorry, Mr. Eastman, I quit." I shut my eyes fearful he might slap me.

"You never *could* get me what I needed," he snarled. "No loss." Sticks and stones ... Finally out of his clutches.

Dad kept up the pressure to get another job -- it bothered him I was out of work. Me too. Broke, on the dole again, bought the Sunday Times Employment section on Saturday at the candy store, a day ahead to get an edge. I wrote the Smith alumni office. Without typing there was nothing. *Nada. Rien.* One day on the crowded Madison Avenue bus during rush hour I had to stand, and looked up at the ads to pass time: "I dreamed I went to a party in my Maidenform bra," a woman in a white bra and black dressy skirt was surrounded by fully dressed revelers, shocking, riveting.

An ad for the Speedwriting Institute arrested my attention, 'u t kn rt 120 wds pr mnt n gt gd jb'. (You too can write 120 words per minute and get a good job.) I could learn to speedwrite using English letters, not have to learn Pitman stenography, a language of scribbles. Dad was happy to pay for a six-week course especially since typing was included in the curriculum. I signed up.

Speedwriting was a breeze, typing a disaster. No letters on the keys. You were supposed to look up at a chart in front of the room, follow it with your fingers. The Imp in charge, my attitude was bad, 'Why should you have to learn to type to get a job?'

asdf, asdf asdf, asdf, shit

jkl; jkl;, jkl; jkl; fuck you

qwertyuiop to hell with this

u r n a fx, u r n a fx, u r n a fx

My days disastrous, depressed, distressed at my learning disability, I escaped into the night. No commitment from Freddy, King still in attendance, our perennial triple play, I justified seeing Alan, too. In different social circles, neither knew about the other, my secret safe.

Mother woke me up one Saturday at eleven with a tirade, "Your room looks like a hurricane hit. You're living like a slob, burning a candle at both ends. Your father doesn't like it."

"I'll clean up. Now let me get back to sleep."

She sat down on the end of my bed. "There's another matter I want to discuss." Now what? I braced, ready for the worst. "I don't know what you see in Freddy. He's a lemon, moony, a hick." Attacking my 'David'. "King is peppy, on the ball. Sophisticated. He told me how much he likes you on the phone last week. You've picked the wrong one, stupid girl."

I exploded, on the defensive, The Imp righteous about my wrongness. "It's none of your business. How dare you put Freddy down?" Then 'on the phone last week' soaked in. They were having private conversations, he was cultivating her -- Mother *was* flirting with him. I could just hear her. 'Yes, King, 'of course, King', you're so smart, King.' Bitch!

"Lower your voice. You don't want the neighbors to hear." They couldn't, ours the only apartment on the floor. "Keep your room neat while you still live in this house," an order from the sergeant or off with my head.

"Yes Mother." I wished a million times I was attracted to King. Freddy may not have been Mr. Excitement, but sexually he was hardly a hick. She hadn't mentioned Alan. He sucked up to her like King, a guarantee of success you'd think but I never really knew. Mother's put down of Freddy made him even more attractive. It flashed through my mind that her vile flirtation with King, her daughter's suitor was just like what Georgiana had done to my aunts. I didn't bring it up, what was the point?

The next Sunday Mother and Dad out for the afternoon, I made Freddy brunch in a tight red sweater, wearing my pointy new Maidenform bra. Ah, the power of advertising. After lox and bagels and Bloody Marys, we started to play around on the black living room couch. He whispered, "Why don't you sit on my lap?" Great idea. I tore off my underpants, stuffed them under a cushion picked up my full skirt sat on him, looked into his doe eyes. He turned me around, lifted me up and down. Up and down.

I heard the key turn in the lock. "Holy shit!" Stuck.

"Stay calm," he instructed, "act natural."

"What if they...?"

"Don't worry, they can't see anything. You're sitting on my lap. That's all."

Dad was alone, "Ali?"

"Hi Dad, Freddy and I are in here." And he's in me.

He put his scarf away in the hall closet, took in the scene from the foyer. I reminded myself to keep breathing. And smiling.

"I came home early to do some work," he said. "Your mother stayed at the Colemans; the girls are singing."

"Good." Bad. Adrenalin pumping, gripped by fear, the air sucked out of the room.

"Hello, Mr. Abrams." Cool as a cucumber.

"Sorry, Freddy, I don't have time to socialize," Dad apologized.

"Bye sir," cheery. Dad turned, headed down the hall to his room. I heard the door shut waited to make sure before disengaging. Freddy wanted to keep going.

"Are you crazy?" My well-behaved WASP had a wild streak, danger man. "It could have been a catastrophe." He zipped up. "You better go." Mr. Innocent's halo never left his head.

"Did you want to get caught?" I wondered if Dr. Blatt was shocked, the obvious answer -- a revenge fuck -- never left my lips, nor did I share the shame. I was a bad, bad, girl.

"I didn't think he'd be back so soon." I changed the subject, "Why does Dad treat me like a little girl?"

"Have you shown any signs you're a grown up?" No answer. This brought up his favorite theme, independence. "Move out of their apartment get your own, your mother infantilizes you. She's managing your life, a puppeteer, strangling you while you dangle from the strings."

The Imp invaded. 'You don't know how to cook, clean, do laundry, you'd be lost without your Mother.' Stuck, I didn't fight back.

"Why don't you get a roommate?"

"I don't have any friends."

"What about Katerine?"

"Still at Smith."

"Why not after she graduates?" Great idea. "How's typing class going?" Elephant memory.

"Not well." Those damn covered keys. "I could type faster if only I could see the letters." You had to type eighty-five words a minute to graduate; I wasn't close.

Isabel and I shared our woes at lunch in the school cafeteria, "I've been here three months, can't pass the typing test."

"I've been here four, can't pass the speedwriting test," complained Isabel, "just can't get the hang of it." Her dream was to go to Japan, get a job as a secretary with an American company.

I had the answer. "This is made in heaven, Isabel, I'll take yours if you take mine."

We beat the system, breathed a collective sigh of relief when we both passed, well worth a morality gap to get on with our lives.

I answered a New York Times ad: 'Book secy' with confidence. Gary B. Jenkins had a one-man office -- a closet on Madison Avenue and 55th. He explained that his niche was creating small ads for nonfiction books in the Sunday Times Book Review.

"Miss Abrams, can you type eighty-five words a minute?"

Piece of cake, "Yes, sir." I typed ninety-five clean, easy, I could look at the keys.

"This job comes with a big opportunity to grow. $70 a week, take it or leave it." I took it. I needed a job and this was a possible entrée into advertising.

I typed eight hours a day, a robot on automatic pilot, stuck in the dead letters department like "Bartleby the Scrivener."

My breasts hurt like hell. I learned that I was pregnant under an assumed name, a surreptitious lunch break visit via subway to get a legal rabbit test for pregnancy at Margaret Sanger's Greenwich Village clinic. She coined the term *birth control*, established Planned Parenthood, American birth control activist, sex educator, nurse, saint.

"Mrs. Marlon," I could dream couldn't I, Smith or Doe too obvious, "we're happy to tell you that you're pregnant." R.I.P. Mr. Rabbit. I knew it anyway; had missed two periods. The sixty four thousand dollar question was who was the father, Freddy or Alan? I couldn't take the chance of picking the wrong groom for a shotgun wedding: Dad would shoot *me* if he found out. I had to have an abortion, was scared to death with good reason.

I'd grown up in the shadow of a family tragedy. Mother had a beautiful, older sister referred to as 'the pretty one.' Mother never got over being number two in her mother's affections, jealous of her sister, reluctant recipient of her hand me downs. Adele was married to a promising state senator with whom she had a young son. My uncle suffered a sudden stroke at thirty-five, became paralyzed and bound to a wheelchair. A week later my aunt discovered she was pregnant, and worried about how she could take care of an invalid, a five year old *and* a new baby. Grandmother and Mother talked her into 'taking care of it'. Adele died on the table, the abortionist drunk. Grandmother died of a broken heart months later her favorite daughter lost, her fault -- a double-edged sword. I definitely couldn't tell Mother.

I unearthed a torn slip of paper with a telephone number I'd kept squirrelled away in my passport for the rainy day that had just arrived, passed on by a friend who'd had one, and lived to tell about it. He did his thing somewhere in Baltimore for five hundred dollars. I'd heard there was a doctor in Pennsylvania with a clinic and a long waiting list, but I didn't have the name or the time. Puerto Rico was a last resort, a thousand dollars -- far more than the $347 my savings account held. I'd laughingly referred to this as my 'abortion money,' the joke on me.

I thought about telling Freddy, still wishing and hoping for a ring, but feared an unwanted pregnancy might tarnish the rose. Alan was good for the balance and insisted on accompanying me. My instincts were right; he was a mensch.

I waited two of the longest weeks of my life for an appointment, prayed for a doctor who was sober. I planned to ask for a personal day off, but when Mr. Jenkins hollered at me for a typographical error the day before, I quit. Maybe not the smartest move, could have been hormones, needed a 'Get out of jail free.' I'd worry about Dad's reaction later. A dead end was a dead end.

I said goodbye to Mother trying hard not to cry, Aunt Adele's death hanging over my head, my darkest hour.

"You're such a moody girl, Georgiana" as in grandma, her deceased rival for Dad's favor, a put down lurking around every corner, life with her like navigating a minefield. "Have you fallen off the roof?" a euphemism for getting my period. Rather the opposite. I told her that Alan and I were going to the championship lacrosse match between Maryland and Johns Hopkins. She barely nodded. I needed a hug, wished again she were a normal mother so I could confide in her. She didn't *do* sympathy.

I wrote her a letter that I hid in deep drawer. "To be opened only if I don't make it."

"Dear Mother:

I have passed like Aunt Adele. The difference is that unlike your mother who I never met who loved Adele, you've never been on my side and don't hug or love me.

Your daughter, Ali."

I left out 'love', hurt, hurting, haunted.

Alan and I waited an endless hour in a deserted parking lot in a forlorn corner of Baltimore. A sedan pulled up and flashed its lights cloak and dagger fashion. A man in a trench coat drove me an hour and a half away with two other 'patients.' Alan was not allowed to come. At my impending doom, it was time to pull out my existential philosophy. Instead I cried. The trench coat warned if I kept it up they'd turn around and take me back. I cried more in the makeshift operating room, "Please, please. You're hurting me." They didn't give me enough gas, would have been a boy. I asked.

Contrary to my expectations, I lived. I cried again when they returned me to Alan, who cried too, from relief. He'd waited four hours in fear. He proposed to me in bed that night in a tacky motel room. Click. I turned off, The Imp emphatic, "You don't love him." I told Alan I'd think about it. I didn't want to hurt his feelings, but there was no chance. I never saw him again. My loss. Great guy.

On Monday I went to our family doctor for a clean bill of health and a diaphragm, made him swear not to turn me in, the illegality of my act as terrifying as the act itself. I didn't tell Dr. Blatt about the ordeal, didn't trust him, too intimate, ashamed of my crime and the reasons behind it.

Freddy invited me home to Newport to meet his mother, the long awaited next step imminent -- I'd made the right decision not to tell him. A mansion. Old money. Lots. His mother was a dour dowager of few words -- the branch hadn't fallen far from the tree. I wanted her to like me, but couldn't get a conversation going. I overate the best angel cake ever courtesy of their maid, Annie, two pieces at the dinner table, one sneak midnight raid. Sugar air, on Cloud #9, I ascended to WASP heaven.

A few weeks later Freddy invited me to a party in advance. Odd. Burned before, I asked about the dress code. To my astonishment he said formal, King would pick me up. I knew better than to ask questions. Mother and I went shopping for a dress, scoured Bendel's, Bergdorf's and Bonwit's, found a long black chiffon sheath, rhinestone spaghetti straps at Bloomies. Mother charged it.

"Take good care; you're so rough on clothes."

Tied to her purse strings, "Yes, Mother." I had to get another job.

King, dapper as ever, white dinner jacket, red carnation, escorted me to River House, the Art Deco apartment house on Beekman Place, the swankiest address in town. I'd played on their private tennis courts -- hallowed ground, all white required, no Jews, Catholics or Negroes allowed. Didn't mention my last name, safe as long as no one asked.

I pestered King to tell me what was going on. Mum was the word. We were fashionably late, entered the grand glass lobby through rococo iron gates. The garden overlooked the East River -- the view of New York views, Freddy hadn't spared the horses. The party in full swing, a hundred guests danced to Lester Lanin's band playing Glenn Miller's, "Pennsylvania *6 5000.*"

"You guys are late." Freddy held hands with Luna the black model from New Year's Eve swathed in a Norrell silver sequin sheath, shimmering, shining, stunning, all six feet of her. "We've been waiting on you to make the announcement." My stomach dropped ten floors. I quickly downed a flute of champagne from a silver tray proffered by a waiter in a monkey suit.

The band played a fanfare. Freddy stepped in front of the bandstand, still holding her hand, "I'm a lucky man, the lovely Luna has accepted my marriage proposal, I want to announce our engagement." They kissed.

Shock waves traveled through the stunned crowd. Crossing the color line? A Negro? The Civil War may have been 100 years ago but nothing had changed in their world. Oh dear, my dear, it just wasn't done. King led a restrained toast, "To Freddy and Luna. Hip, hip, hooray." We hoorayed twice more, wished I could faint. No such luck. My emotions ranged from jealousy -- why wasn't it me -- to anger and betrayal. When was the last time I'd slept with Freddy? A month ago, that rat had been two-timing me. Despair struck, my hopes dashed, our triangle smashed. I didn't want King without Freddy. Three minus two equals one.

Did I think I was going to get away with it? Three different guys, sleeping with two, loving the third and Nick still under my skin. A triple play and I was out.

August 5, 1962. Marilyn died. I cried.

8

PJ Party

I'd been seeing Dr. Blatt twice a week for a few years, except for the interminable month of August when all shrinks took off, a conspiracy. I stayed with him, stuck between Scylla and Charybdis. I needed help but couldn't stand him. He droned, a monotone. I could have shouted "Fire", and his response would be, "How does that make you feel?" I couldn't stop staring at the tufts of hair sprouting from his nose over that untrimmed mustache. No connection. Train wreck. What did an ugly geezer know about my problems -- still single, almost an old maid, everyone else married, Jody, my suitemate from Smith on her second kid -- no knight on the horizon to rescue this damsel in distress.

I failed at free association, regurgitated and recycled the same old high anxiety and low self-esteem, no insights into the whys and wherefores, embarrassed to tell anyone that I was seeing a shrink in the first place. Who could I discuss it with? Definitely not Mother, positively not Dad, who was against the idea, anyway. Nothing was wrong with *his* daughter. The Imp ruled the roost.

Dr. Blatt informed me he was going to modify my treatment plan and start me on pill therapy: tranquilizers. They would calm me down. I followed the doctor's orders, a pill-popper from way back -- sexy 'dexies' as in dextatrim to lose weight. I'd never been a good sleeper, punched the pillow all night. He added sleeping pills a month later.

Giving the devil his due, we made some progress in the real estate department. I signed my declaration of independence, and took an apartment with Katerine. Our pad was a big one bedroom on the second floor of an ugly white brick Charles M. Greenthal building on a singularly stark block between First and Sutton, the view of First Avenue even uglier. Dad got it through one of his connections. I envisioned an airy aerie, all white Matisse room, modern verging on futuristic. But Mother showed up with movers who carried in a traditional couch like the one in the den but brown. She said it was soothing and tasteful. I thought it was drab and depressing. I had to cancel an order for a white sectional from Roche Bobois. Katerine was furious but there was nothing we could do. *Fait accompli.*

Dr. Blatt hadn't helped in my quest for an orgasm, his advice, "Masturbate." No way José, I wanted the real thing. He kept harping on it, a broken record. "It will free you." I ignored him, certain the right guy would give it to me. From time to time I worried if he were the wrong shrink. Dad was supposed to pay the bill once a month, and didn't, which got me into another set of discussions with Dr. Blatt. "Why is your father delinquent in paying the bill?" Here we go again. "Is this his way of showing disapproval?"

"I don't want to discuss it."

"I believe he has difficulty paying all his bills." What do you think, that's news? "Tell me what you know about how he grew up." His father's early demise plus the Great Depression - what did it matter, how could it help? He couldn't change Dad, could barely help me. Dead end.

I sputtered on with Nick, the impossible dream and eternal thorn in my side. He was getting very, very famous. Surrounded by his voice on the radio, jukebox, even on TV, when I couldn't stand it a second longer, I'd find him. Nick never initiated the call. If he was in between romances, broken up from another in a series of thin beautiful blondes, models or actresses that I'd read about in the tabloids, we'd see each other.

He'd moved up in the world, now in a two bedroom on Sutton Place around the corner, the Steinway, stage center, stacked with music, a bigger bed still in earth tones. When I got to his apartment (God forbid he'd ever pick me up), we had nothing to talk about. Our serial one-night stands were bittersweet. He sang his latest song we listened to demos or cuts from a new album, and made love. Damn those sapphires, I'd fall for him all over again. Always a little bit in love, the embers just needing fanning. Our silent deal: I wouldn't stay overnight; he gave me money to take a cab rather than walk me around the corner; never called the next day. I beat myself up for having gone to see him in the first place, reopening wounds I had a terrible time closing -- a sucker for punishment.

I didn't tell Dr. Blatt, knowing he'd say I was a fool. Right Imp? I did say I still had insomnia. He upped the ante, gave me a stronger prescription. I knew I'd become addicted. Sleep was sleep, I wasn't going to rock that boat. Were the pills helping? No.

I applied for a job in the *Sunday Times Help Wanted* section: 'exec secretary, fashion advertising agency', passed the typing test, sailed through the interview in a black suit, crisp white blouse, faux red flower on my lapel -- conservative chic. Mr. Little asked me to wait, upon his return took me to meet my potential new boss, a partner in Eastman, Neville and Stone, an agency of thirty. We walked to Morton Stone's corner office. A big bear of a man arose from his chair jacketless, striped shirt spanning a big belly, ready to pop at any moment, a shirttail out. He chain smoked Camels, as he finished one he used the butt to light the next. I watched a drop of white spittle form on his lower lip. He peppered me with questions. Antagonistic. I held it together, managing to remain polite.

"Why do you think you're qualified to work here?"

"Because I'm smart, a hard worker, and know fashion." The standard interview question, I'd practiced, could beat my own drum. If I didn't, who else would? Let's have a cheer for Ali.

Fatso was satisfied. "Any questions?" 'Why are you such a slob?' Nice try Imp. I shook my head, no.

A day later Mr. Little called to announce they were happy to have me on board. I only wished my boss could have been natty Mr. Neville, much more to my liking. Nothing was perfect.

E N & S was on Madison Avenue and 39th, a five-minute walk to their clients: Helen Harper sportswear, William Winkler fabrics, M.C. Schrank sleepwear. Their showrooms were at 1407 Broadway, a giant bilious green building, the epicenter of the New York garment manufacturing industry aka rag trade. Made in the U.S.A.

Stone was an Abuser with a capital "A", Bad Boss with a capital "B." He criticized me at every turn, nitpicked, "Look at this typo. Do it over." "There's a smudge on the carbon copy." A master of malevolence, he could always find something wrong, never once praised me if I'd done something right. I took it on the jaw without punching back, on familiar ground, accustomed to Mother's put downs, bloomed in the muck lotus-like, determined to make it work whatever the cost.

There was lots of action creating, producing and placing print ads, a team effort. I discovered I could wear many hats, the miracle of 39th Street. I learned how to budget first, a mathematical equation: x amount of dollars equaled x amount of print ads: 'space' plus production. Many 'space' variables – four-color, black-and-white, one-column, full-page national or local, full-page-color with bleed, the most expensive. The circulation of the magazine determined the rates – the higher, the more expensive. The fashion 'books' were *Seventeen, Glamour, Mademoiselle, Harper's Bazaar, Vogue* and the *New York Times Sunday Magazine* -- considered "the Bible" the place to be 'seen' and see what others were up to. You decided which to use depending on the client's profile -- *Vogue,* a high fashion audience; *Seventeen,* the youth market. The agency made 17.65% by placing the ad. I loved figuring out how far I could stretch the client's dollars, like doing a double acrostic.

Production included the costs of a photographer, model, retouching, typesetting and engraving. The agency took a 20% mark up. The insertion date -- day the ad would run, and the closing date – when the finished 'plate' was due at the publication, ruled the production schedule. Always a race to make it, the occasional late night -- advertising was a pressure cooker. In the thick of it, in Seventh Avenue heaven, I dove in headfirst.

I looked at 'tear sheets' of their old ads. Ugly models. An oxymoron, didn't know there was such a thing, decided to fix it. I gathered fashion magazines from the last six months, tearing out ads with good-looking men and women models, marched into the art director's office. Seymour had a cleft chin and Superman jaw, could have been a model himself. I asked him to identify my finds. He knew a few, told me to call Ford and Stewart model agencies for the rest.

"Introduce yourself to the booker and ask her to send you the latest head sheets." He dug into a pile, found one, three pages of stamp size pictures of models, two columns, stapled together, arranged alphabetically alongside their stats: age, size, weight, hair color, eye color, rate.

"If you see someone you like, ask for her head shot." He rummaged around a bigger stack found a black and white glossy picture of the legend, Suzy Parker.

"This is a head shot," he explained.

"Have you worked with her?" He nodded. I was impressed, the most famous model in the world.

"You're going to be the booker's new best friend." Lesson over. I enjoyed learning the tricks of the trade from a pro, followed his instructions to the tee and so became the agency's first casting director.

My first M.C. Schrank ad, full color page in August *Seventeen,* featured four pairs of pajamas, juniors. Seymour said he wanted it to look like a pajama party. I arranged for 'go sees.' The bookers sent the models I'd picked out, plus their recommendations, twenty of them, a 'cattle call'. I took Polaroids, made notes on a yellow legal pad on my clipboard as the models tried on the PJ's one by one in the executive suite converted for casting. The rest waited outside. They looked different without makeup, scrawny, plain Janes. I narrowed it down to eight, had three favorites needed four, scurried to Seymour's office. Help! He sipped coffee from a paper cup, Pall Mall in hand, as he took his time scrutinizing the Polaroids then referred back to the headshots, serious business. I slowed down, stared at his perfect profile, began to wonder if he was available, whether it was kosher to date in the workplace. He agreed with the three. We chose the fourth together, another blonde, part of the same corn fed Midwest cheerleading team. Go girls.

"Book them for two hours each." Seymour gave me the time, date, address -- he'd hired the photographer a month in advance. The striped PJ reminded me of our Venetian gondolier, my experience accessorizing at Saks kicked in -- it needed a boater to top it off. Seymour told me the drill. I could 'borrow' merchandise in exchange for a credit in the ad good for them, too. I headed to the millinery market, hundreds of hat showrooms clustered on West 38th, hunted, found the perfect flat straw hat, 'Hat by Madcaps', size eight type face.

I was nervous at the shoot, like a two-hour final. Had I done it right? Remembered every detail? More than a grand: $750 for the photographer, four models at $45 per hour – $360. Astronomical. Seymour introduced me to Hal the photographer as the new 'stylist'. My ears pricked up. Stone showed up to take charge of Tom, the client. If Tom had comments – he *was* footing the bill - Stone would pass them on to Seymour who'd talk to Hal, the chain of command.

Chubby Checker's "Come on baby, let's do the Twist" blasted. Hal's' assistant ran around setting up lights. Since it wasn't a beauty shot, the models in the dressing room had to make themselves up. I supervised 'hair', put Holly's in bunches, barrettes in one, a ponytail, another. On the set, I 'pinned' the clothes in the back, instant tailoring no one would see, it was 2D. I brought out the *pièce de résistance* from a round hatbox, placed it on Holly's head at a rakish angle. Everyone nodded in approval. "Ready for a PJ Party?" camped Hal, as he began to shoot. My job was to make sure that the 'merch' stayed perfect. If there was the slightest glitch, fold or wrinkle, I took my shoes off, tiptoed onto the set and fixed it. Chubby Checker still ruled. A long two hours -- exhausting, exhilarating.

Seymour called me -- the 8 by 10 'chromes' from the shoot had arrived by messenger. I rushed to his office, couldn't wait to see the fruits of so much labor. We scrutinized them one by one over a light box. How did the models look? How was the merch? We agreed when we saw 'the one'. Stone's job as account executive was to sell it to Schrank. The day he was scheduled to go Stone never appeared, caught a case of what Seymour called "the vapors", apparently the scared-y cat's M.O. every time he was up at bat. I'd have to pinch hit.

"Watch your back!" And front. At 39th and Broadway, the most congested crosswalk in the world, a man pushed a rack of plastic-covered merchandise hung on wire hangers, narrowly missed hitting me. My insides were aflutter, Seymour's 'Knock 'em dead, kid,' rolling around in my head.

At Schrank's pajama-filled showroom, head of advertising, Miss Norma Rambach, kept me waiting for ten anxious minutes. "Come in." No nonsense, tough cookie, late fifties, married to her job, "What do you have?"

"The chromes from the *Seventeen* shoot." She didn't ask for Stone, I didn't have to tell. Seymour had stacked a deck of three, placed the best shot last. I laid them on her light box. She pored over them.

"Which do *you* like?" she asked.

I took a deep breath pointed to 'the one', "It's fresh and the merch looks great." It did. "So much energy, it will jump off the page," easy to sell something I liked. She looked at 'the one', back at the other two, placed it on top.

"I'll sign off on this. Tell Stone he's got a winner." Home run.

9

Grouper

Summer was "icumen in." No one could live in New York without leaving, at least on weekends, the just rewards for a hard week's work. If you didn't you'd die from the sweltering heat and humidity, stuck knowing there was a beach and relief nearby. The problem was that Ocean Beach was finished for me: no friends, boyfriends, or potentials. My memories stung like the beach flies of a sticky August day.

Dr. Blatt had another real estate recommendation, 'take your *own* summer place. Look in the *Village Voice*.' Seek and ye shall find. I answered a stamp size ad under "Summer Shares":

Full share, on bay,

Mem. – Labor,

Ocean Ridge, F.I.

Ocean Ridge? I'd never heard of it. No one else had either, had to be out east. I met with the house organizer, Caroline. She was tall and gawky, wore glasses, a typical Bryn Mawr pseudo intellectual, in other words a drip. Awkward interview, had to pry out the skinny, she answered my questions in a drone: east of the Pines, you took the ferry from Patchogue, there'd be six other girls, the house was charming, Entitled to a bed every weekend. I passed muster, wrote a check for $450, a fortune but worth it to be away from the manger.

Reggie and I sat next to each other on a cracked, cramped seat in the grimy smoking car, a dark cloud hovering over a crowd of commuters puffing away -- the joys of the Long Island Railroad.

"Tickets please."

"Two to Patchogue."

"$1.90. Change at Jamaica. Change at Babylon."

Reggie had it. A sport.

"Do you think we can get away with this? I'm only paying for one share in the house and I didn't ask them if I could bring out a date."

"Sweetheart, you worry too much," said Reggie. "The girls are going to love us. How can they resist?" He was tall, pale skin, brown hair, bedroom blue eyes, round horn rim glasses, clean cut, a not so meek Clark Kent, they'd certainly love him. We'd been dating exclusively, every weekend and two nights a week, for six months.

We met at the EN&S Christmas party, he was in telecommunications -- somehow involving pay TV systems which I didn't understand, why would anyway want to pay? He'd grown up in Bronxville, the richest per capita enclave in the United States. His father, the high school principal, was poor according to their stratospheric standards. Reggie did very well. His red XKE

Jaguar, the most beautiful car ever, was in the shop as usual, why we had to take the train in the first place. The introductory ad in the *New Yorker* was unforgettable, the XKE parked in a jungle, "A different breed of cat." He was planning to trade it in for a Porsche, German engineering beat British style.

I'd fallen for Reggie. He liked to do exciting things, ran with a fast jet set crowd, knew how to have fun in style. He took me skiing at Sugarbush. I looked hot in my tight, stretch ski pants on the coolest slopes in the East, yet couldn't learn to ski for the life of me. After my morning lesson we took a ski lift to the top. Soon bored by the slowness of my sorry snowplow turns, Reggie waved goodbye and left me stranded, not that I could blame him. I saw a compound fracture or face disfigurement in my future took off my skis and walked down. The frozen form of water was scary.

I guess I loved him, didn't have a clue how he felt -- he'd never said anything, which I supposed kept me interested, an old hand at WASP love -- no sentimental indulgences. I hadn't brought up Nick.

Reggie lit our cigarettes, my worries not allayed, "What if something goes wrong? I'll lose my share and won't have a place to go for the summer."

"Nothing's going to go happen, loveliness, I promise."

"Jamaica. Change at Jamaica." The crowd surged across the platform to another overcrowded, dilapidated train. We changed at Babylon and a few stops later arrived at Patchogue, a way station on the way to the ferry and a new part of Fire Island.

"Taxi!" "Taxi!" The station bustled with a corps of beefy men vying for our fares. We had to wait until our cab was filled to the gills with as many people and their bags as the driver could pack in. The proverbial question hung over our heads: would we make the ferry? It didn't always wait, for some reason at war with the L.I.R.R.

We pulled up to a huge scow with a belly for produce and people, a row of seats on each side of an open top deck -- not nearly enough to accommodate all the passengers. Unlucky ones would have to sit on the floor. We boarded, stowed our luggage below, hustled, captured two seats. A young crowd ate, drank beer, smoked cigarettes hung out -- party, party. I remembered taking the Friday Daddy boat to Ocean Beach after work in Dad's office, the witchboard a world and time away. How far I'd come... assistant account executive. Great job if not great pay. All was well in the world.

Finally the ferry docked. The island looked different at this end. No welcoming wagons, it was narrow and uninhabited. I could see the ocean dunes from the bay, wooden boardwalks traveled in different directions. Reggie picked up my suitcase, we took a left turn, followed what we hoped was the right one. We entered Ocean Ridge, no scrub pine trees, barely two hundred feet from bay to ocean, sparsely settled compared to Ocean Beach; dotted with modest new Monopoly houses interrupted by poison ivy and sand. The exceptions were notable: a "Bucky" as in a Buckminster Fuller geodesic dome, a cantilevered handkerchief, and a few other outrageous experiments in modern architecture. We ended up at the ocean. Two A-frames later I realized our mistake.

"We have to backtrack."

"Sweetheart, that's fine except next time please don't pack so many clothes." I'd done it again.

At the bay, behind tall weeds was a small fisherman's shack. We knocked.

"Is this the Wilson house?"

"Yes."

"I'm Ali, your roommate."

A short, overweight, decidedly unattractive woman with straight black hair and a big behind opened the door as she gave us the once over.

"Where is *he* staying?" She emphasized the word 'he', looked askance at Reggie.

"Reggie is my date, he's staying with me," I said, emphatically. The other reason for taking my own share was so I could sleep with my boyfriend, the ongoing morality play with Dad in its second act: keeping up virginal pretenses. Were they kidding? Just my luck, in a country running rampant with "free love," these girls were total prudes. Make love not war was the national anthem and my mantra.

Lynn didn't ask us to come in. We stood awkward, until Reggie took over. "Let's see what your house looks like, loveliness."

Adorable. A gingerbread house, dark amber wainscoted wood walls, low roof with eaves, red and white checked calico curtains. The kitchen was part of the living room, separated from the living quarters by a bar with three stools. There were two small bedrooms with two beds each, one john, no phone, electricity, or heat. I spied a row of five kerosene lamps, our light brigade. The refrigerator worked on gas, as did the hot water and the globe in the bathroom. We'd stepped back into the olden days. As Yogi Berra said, "Déjà vu all over again." I remembered our first Fire Island houses.

The back deck was on the bay in the kind of bulrushes that Moses must have been hidden in. A honeymoon cottage perfect for one, maybe two couples. The question was, where were seven girls going to sleep, not to mention one guy? Then I noticed a sleeping loft for one and two convertible couches. We put our bags down and tried to make small talk with Lynn. No go.

"Where are the other girls?"

"At the beach, I suspect."

"Let's go find them Reggie." Any excuse to escape from the deep freeze.

An enormous stretch of virgin beach sand swallowed up the few other brave souls huddled against the high dunes for protection from the wind of the crisp Memorial Day weekend weather. We ran to the ocean, touched it with our toes. Brrr.

"I love it here Reggie, this is the way Ocean Beach used to be."

"I don't mind roughing it like this, sweetheart, I was a good boy scout, but what are we going to do about food?" His priority.

"Where are we going to sleep?" Mine.

"Lynn is uptight, but I'll warm her up."

"What if the others are worse?"

"I told you, stop worrying. Come on, let's see this joint." We walked eastwards on the beach feeling like pioneers. The houses stopped abruptly as did Ocean Ridge, the dunes rose high, unspoiled. Reggie tackled then kissed me. "Too bad it's so cold, sweetheart, or you know what."

We sat down and looked at the ocean, isolated from the rest of the world. "This is what it must have looked like when my father came here as a kid."

"I thought the only one who came before us was Robinson Crusoe."

"Did you know that Melville finished Billy Budd on the island?" I asked, proud of the literary heritage.

"I'm not surprised. This must be what Australia's going to be like."

"Australia?"

"Sweetheart, I've been meaning to tell you." Reggie cleared his throat, "I'm moving to Australia. Teleprompter has hired me to look into Pay TV there. It's the opportunity of a lifetime. Your friend Reggie's going to make a fortune."

"Are you joking?" I knew he wasn't. "With the salary they're offering me, plus the incentive plan, I'd move to Timbuktu."

"I hate to sound trite, but what about us?"

"You know I'm crazy about you, sweetheart, but at this point in my career I have to make some sacrifices."

"How long will you be there?" The conversation sounded like something out of a Grade B movie. The magic spell was broken, replaced by despair. One moment I was in heaven, the next in hell.

"As long as it takes," he was dead serious, our relationship dead in the water.

"What does *that* mean?" Dripping in sarcasm.

"Don't try and tie me down, sweetheart."

"Are you talking about a week, month?"

"I don't know ... at least a year." He may as well have said 'forever.'

"When are you leaving?"

"Wednesday."

"You're kidding!" Shocked. "Why didn't you tell me?"

"Because I knew you'd take it like this."

"Am I supposed to wait?"

"Absolutely not."

How could he drop me like this? "When were you planning to tell me … on the way to the airport? Don't you care about me?" I was inconsolable.

"Of course I do, sweetheart, you're great in the sack. Let's go back to the house, I'm hungry." It was a left-handed compliment.

We walked back in silence. I focused on keeping a stiff upper lip, staying cool, wasn't going to cry in front of him if it killed me. What difference would it make, anyway, it was a done deal.

The living room reminded me of the small car in the circus that a host of huge people somehow squeeze into. Six girls were putting away provisions from hefty looking cartons. Lynn growled at me, "We picked up the food while you were gone. Jane ordered it from the Patchogue A & P, Monday and they delivered it on the 4:30. We only have enough for seven.

"Let me help you. I'm Ali. This is Reggie." Unfriendly faces, I shook each hand, "Remember me, Caroline?" She was the one who'd interviewed me, faint smile. They looked like the girls at Smith who never had dates on Saturday nights -

the ones who never talked to me because I did. Without a second thought I categorized them all as losers. How did I get myself into this one?

Where *was* Katerine now that I needed her? She had the knack of being popular with women in spite of being attractive, a personality trait that had eluded me. Flying, in Mexico. Determined to spring away from Springfield, she'd become the first Smithie stewardess, a career that was too *déclassé* for the rest. She didn't care. She had wings. Katerine had an alternate share so would be here next weekend -- too late.

"Let me help, too." Reggie joined in. "Sorry, ladies. If there's not enough food, allow me to buy some more. Whatever you need."

So nice to have a man around the house, Reggie was a charmer, all right. How could he be leaving? What was I going to do?

The chill barely thawed through dinner, no one seemed to be able to get a conversation going.

"Where is your guest going to sleep tonight," queried Caroline.

"We'll sleep on the pull out couch."

"Against the rules. You have to sleep in your own bed." Lynn, the loser's arms were crossed in defiance, the big honcho of the group. Reggie and I exchanged looks.

"Is there any place to dance?" Reggie changed the subject.

"The casino."

"Anyone care to accompany us to trip the light fantastic?" Six turndowns.

We climbed the stairs of an oversized, weather beaten shack on the ocean ten minutes from the house. The Casino or 'Caz' had a bar, jukebox, deck. No gambling. The seedy room was in contrast to the attractive crowd. The joint was jumping, the only game in town for two singles communities, Ocean Ridge and Davis Park. The canteen below sold hot dogs and soda pop.

Everyone bundled up for cold weather, no heat, the night air was chilly. The dance floor was packed. "Under the Boardwalk" by The Drifters played and played and played. We picked our way through to the bar.

"White wine for the lady."

"No white wine."

"I have a better idea." Reggie led me outside to the deck.

We huddled together in a secluded corner and he pulled a skinny looking cigarette out of his pocket with a flourish. "Ta da. This is your house present. Enjoy it sweetheart, there's more where that comes from."

"What is this?"

"It's not what you see -- it's what you get."

"Tell me Reggie."

"It's a joint made of the wicked weed, also known as grass or marijuana." He said the word with relish, 'mary ju wan ah'. "The real name is Cannabis."

I peppered him with questions, suddenly nervous, "Is this harmful?"

"Sweetheart, it's safe, promise. You're going to love it."

"Why?"

"Because it makes you feel so good."

"What do you mean?"

"It makes you feel different. Enough gabbing, am I going to light this or not? Trust Uncle Reggie, this stuff is the best. I wouldn't give anything bad to someone I love." Someone he loves? He'd waited till he was leaving to sort of tell me.

He rambled on.

"The only thing is don't tell the judge I gave it to you on account of it aint so legal." The Bronxville preppy sometimes talked like a gangster for fun. He moved out of the wind and took out a lighter.

"You inhale it like a cigarette," he said inserting it between his lips to demonstrate. "Hold it in your lungs as long as possible before you exhale."

"Promise to take care of me if anything happens?"

"Sweetheart, this is a present, remember?"

"Mind if I ask one more question?"

"What?"

"Is it habit forming?"

"You mean like a junkie? Get outta here. This is really good stuff. I'm lighting up." He took a long drag and held it in. I'd remember later he hadn't said no.

My turn. Smoking from the same cigarette was pretty unsanitary if you asked me, I followed instructions, inhaled deeply, held it, exhaled.

"That's a good girl."

I must have done something wrong because I had a coughing spasm, felt like my lungs were going to explode.

"I'm dying."

"No, you're not. Try again."

"Can't I miss a round?"

"No."

We continued the ritual until there was nothing left except the stub. Reggie waved it at me. "See this sweetheart? This is a roach. Save it. There's at least one more hit left."

"Now what happens?"

"Patience, my dear, patience," he said with a W.C. Fields accent.

Suddenly giggly, I rode a champagne bubble, like Glenda the Good Witch in the "Wizard of Oz", heard the Beatles, "I want to hold your hand…" Crazy about the fab four, I'd seen them on the Ed Sullivan Show, Paul the cutest.

Back inside, I threw my arms around Reggie's neck, "Let's dance."

"Sweetheart, calm down. People will see us."

"So what?"

"This is a public place."

"Don't you love this song? 'I want to hold your hand. I want to hold your hand." I pressed my body into his.

"Sweetheart, this is no time for a body lock, we're supposed to be dancing, not doing it."

"I can't help it." I was feeling aroused.

"You don't have to broadcast it."

"Mr Postman look and see..." Half the room was doing The Stomp. I joined the line. "I could dance all night."

"I know, sweetheart, but Reggie wants to take a midnight stroll home to beddy bye and a little bed dancing."

"Did you really mean it when you said, I love you?"

"I said that?"

"You're so cold and WASPy."

"That's why you love me." He had a point.

"Why don't you take me with you to Australia?"

"Sweetheart, don't spoil the evening."

"Don't leave me Reggie." I started to cry, my emotions plummeting from the top of the Empire State Building to the ninth circle of hell. I heard the strains of Nick's "Love Light," couldn't believe my ears and began to bawl.

"What's the matter?"

I blabbed on about Nick -- pot was a truth serum.

"Stop crying. You know how much I hate it. I'm not leaving you; I'm going off to make my fortune. You need another artist, not a businessman. There's a big difference. Now come on, give us that dazzling smile."

"What's there to smile about?"

"I'm still here.

I was in a blue funk with a case of Holly Golightly's 'mean reds,' sitting on the white beach in a black bikini -- proper mourning attire. Reggie had gone off into the sunset like some goddam cowboy at the end of a western, leaving the heroine tearful because she knows she'll never lay eyes on him again. 'Keep smiling, sweetheart.' Why did everyone always tell me to keep smiling? What was I, a clown laughing on the outside crying on the inside? I missed that sonofabitch even if he was a bastard for leaving me.

To make matters worse, that weekend had really messed me up with the girls who gave me the cold shoulder. They hadn't forgiven me for 'bringing an extra guest' and 'not asking beforehand.' There were a lot of rules in a grouper house. Last weekend I'd compounded the felony. I'd come out alone, missing Reggie like crazy, encountered stony silence from the girls -- the outcast of the island, fled to the beach where I let myself be consoled by a strolling musician. Tall, curly auburn hair, freckles, and an infectious smile, Danny Arnold was a composer who'd just lost fifty pounds on some kind of a cuckoo vegetarian diet. As we walked along the water's edge, we discussed music, classical, jazz, folk, and bebop. His knowledge was encyclopedic, astonishing. Danny was a beatnik his conversation peppered with lots of 'like man' this and that. He invited me to his house on the bay in Davis Park to go kayaking. He was charming, entertaining, why not? I was on the pill. I spent the night.

The next morning he walked me back to Ocean Ridge. Upon my return, the girls were even cooler. Caroline pulled me aside, "Did you sleep with Danny Arnold?"

"What business is it of yours?"

"Someone saw the two of you on the beach together."

"So?"

"Housemates don't go out with men who other members of the house are dating."

"What do you mean?" This couldn't be a rule.

"Lynn went out a few weeks ago with Danny and she's crazy about him. That means hands off to the rest of the house."

"How was I supposed to know?"

It seems that after this famous date he never called back. In their eyes I'd committed a house crime. Was it really my problem? I wrestled with the morality and decided I was clean. Though I had no plans to see Danny again, I wasn't going to apologize on principle. Those girls. Bad news.

Katerine finally made it out. We neared the volleyball court. "Let's get into the game." my rallying cry.

"Do they let women play?"

"They will when they see how fabulous we are." I was a great server, Katerine, a spiker all five feet eleven inches of her, had the longest legs I'd ever seen, a natural advantage. We laid down our beach towels and waited to challenge the winners.

The game over, the defeated swiftly abandoned positions and ran into the water. I tied up my bikini and got ready to play, hoped that the string would hold. My St. Tropez treasure a tad too daring for active sports -- too late to change. I strode onto the court, Katerine behind me.

A guy in sweats shouted, "Take the two empty positions. One of you front middle, the other back right. Boy girl boy girl. We'll zee for rotation." We got into place, volleyed for serve and won.

I was in the server's position. They weren't ready for my sky ball into the sun, "One nothing." There was spirited play after my next serve and two tall hunks on the other side made mincemeat of us.

"Eight to one, switch sides."

I studied them so they didn't see, wondered if Katerine had noticed. How could she help it? Both were at least six two, one dark and Semitic, the other blond, my fatal weakness. One set and the other spiked. We couldn't overcome their teamwork and talent. The game ended a depressing fifteen to one. At least we didn't get bageled.

"I'm going to drown my sorrows in the water. Coming Katerine?"

She'd struck up a conversation with a stranger. Drove me crazy. I'd tried in vain to teach her New York manners, "Don't talk to people you don't know and even then be careful." Her Midwestern open upbringing as strong as my native mistrust, she wasn't going to budge. I dove in and cooled down in the refreshing water, floated on my back, feeling better than I had since Reggie left. I should exercise more. Too bad they didn't have tennis courts. I swam the horizon, turned around, back-stroked to the shore.

"I thought you'd never return." The blond from the game was next to me, "You're a rather good server."

I dove underwater to compose myself, surfaced. "Thanks."

"I usually don't give compliments or have to chase people half way to Europe to give them." I took the bait, hooked.

"We're facing South America." The water was calm, I wasn't. I stared into his light blue eyes. He had a slight English accent or was it an affectation? English public school? Oxbridge? Smart and sexy, God did I want to touch him, feel his beautiful muscular body against me.

"What's a nice guy like you doing in a crazy place like this?" He'd set the tone; I'd keep it, wasn't so certain about 'nice'. I ducked a wave.

"In general, I'm summering here, specifically I'm attempting..." he paused wickedly, "to meet you. My name is

Eric London. *Et tu mademoiselle...* or is it *madame*?" He swam closer. Clever. Did I speak French? Was I married?

"*Je m'apelle Ali.*" My accent was perfect.

"Indienne?"

"*Pas de tous ... Je suis Americaine.*" Like Jean Seberg in *Breathless* the newcomer on my best movies list. "*Et tu brute*?"

"I'm English and Swedish with some French, a dab of German ... you might call me an amalgam *con molto brio.*"

"*Hablas muchas lenguas, tambien puedas hablar el español?"* I rolled it off rolled my r's. Something about him triggered my competitive juices.

"*Oyez. Oyez.*" Street Spanish. "It helps me get along with the Puerto Ricans in my neighborhood," he sneered, "Spanish not one of my favorites."

"Obviously you haven't read the *Siglo de Oro* or any of the mystical poets, San Juan de la Cruz and Santa Teresa de la Barca, nor the pre-Spanish Civil war generation: Juan Ramon Jimenez, Ortega y Gasset and Miguel de Unamuno." Five years of Spanish literature courses kicked in, "but my favorite is Federico Garcia Lorca." I considered reciting one of his poems then thought better of it. Overkill.

"She's got a modicum of intelligence to boot. Sorry, *señorita,* didn't mean to insult the Spanish language. Of course I've read the existentialists, in English. Perhaps you'd like to accompany me home to the *barrio* ... you'd make a beautiful translator." He swam closer, wouldn't let the fish off the line, reeled me in. Every time he was on the verge of being pedantic or sarcastic, became seductive again. He had me coming and going. We drifted out too far, swam back. "Where do you live?"

"Near Columbia, of course. I'm at I School. You know, International Studies?" Testing me again…had I heard of it? If not I was a common peasant.

"Do you know Milo, he's there, too?" Competing for the cool award, I played the name game.

"Of course. He's my best friend." Small world.

"You must be the Eric he used to talk about."

"How, may I ask, do you know Milo? Don't tell me, what's you last name, Ali?"

"Abrams."

"You had a big romance with Milo when he was at Amherst, met him on the train going back to Northampton after Thanksgiving vacation freshman year."

"Right." Unfortunately, Milo left me when I wouldn't sleep with him. Eric had quite the memory. Our first round ended in a draw.

"Milo always had perfect taste. Would you care to take a sunbath on my blanket? I assure you that the sun rays are at their zenith there."

Eric had properly assessed my sun addiction. Stay cool and don't sound too eager. "I'm going to ride this one in."

I missed it. Shitpissfuck, my friend Sissy's favorite swear word. He didn't. We walked over to Eric's sunspot. I admired his body again, the black nylon racing suit left nothing and everything to my imagination. I felt like pinching myself to see if I was dreaming, gorgeous and articulate, several foreign languages. I'd forgotten to ask where he'd gone to college, no doubt Ivy. What was wrong with him? Nothing. Perhaps a bit pompous, but so what?

Katerine sat on their blanket talking to the dark spiker. Nice work Katerine. Each of us assessed our choices of partners. Had we chosen the right one? If you believed the old opposites attract syndrome, and I definitely did, we had. Max was slender, gangly, curly black hair and old-fashioned silver rimmed glasses over a slightly beaked nose and an intellectual face. An architect -- perfect for Katerine, who'd fallen in love with New York Jews the same way I went for WASPs. Eric and Max had met at Yale. After they'd graduated, Max continued to Yale Architecture, Eric on to Columbia. Max was thirty-one, Eric twenty-eight, or 'pushing 30' as he described it. They weren't interested in what we did.

"As much as I adore the company, I'm starting to catch a chill," I shivered.

"My compliments to the most beautiful goose flesh I've ever seen. May I offer to warm you up?"

"Thanks but I need a hot shower. Katerine, why don't we invite these gentlemen over for a drink?"

Max gave Katerine an affirmative squeeze. Eric, on the other hand, had a surprise. "I accept," he said, "with reservations, for as it turns out, I have a previous commitment... unless I can bring her along."

He was going to be Big Trouble, but I couldn't say no: don't bring another her to our house of hers, really a house of 'mys': 'my towel', 'my tea bag' 'my man.' "Of course," hoping I sounded mildly enthusiastic.

"Where's thy castle, my lady?"

"It's serf's quarters but it hath a sunset fit for a king." I gave him directions. Katerine and I hurried back along the boardwalks.

"Isn't Eric gorgeous?" I was in lust.

"Did you notice Max's hands?"

"No."

"Long fingers. Tapered... you can tell so much. I'm sure he's a genius," her priority.

"Have you ever seen shoulders like that?" I gave myself permission to focus on his body, knowing he was overeducated. "What about him bringing another woman over?"

"Pretty ballsy. Frankly, he scares me some." Katerine got insecure when it came to fast talkers. "You'll have to play it very cool if you're interested in this one."

The thought had already crossed my mind. "What are we going to tell the girls?"

"Nothing. We'll pretend they just dropped by without asking."

"What are you going to wear?"

"I only brought a pair of jeans." Katerine traveled light.

"What should I wear?"

"Something white I suspect. You've got two suitcases full."

They arrived late just as the girls were sitting down to dinner.

"*Bon soir.*" Eric shook my hand, "This is my friend Bunny." A brunette barracuda if I ever saw one, short shorts to show off perfect legs, squeezed out a smile.

"Hi Katerine." Max gave her a shy peck on the cheek -- he liked her. "We brought you a house present." She accepted the offering, a bottle of Côtes du Rhône, perfect red table wine, blue and white calico bow. She gave him a hug. He laughed nervously, delighted. Upset, I led the group onto the back deck just as the flaming orange ball set, streaking the sky with amethyst.

"Impressive. Did you arrange it just for us?" asked Eric.

"Yes, my liege." I tried to hide my disappointment, had to share him with *that* girl, whatever her name was, who clung to him like a parasite. He enjoyed the moment. Why was I always attracted to difficult men? Radar. Set me loose blindfolded and I'd find the most impossible man. Eric *had* come after me in the water unlike Nick who I'd chased and never had a chance with. Maybe things would be different with Eric but whatchamacallit wouldn't let him loose.

Katerine pulled me aside, wanted to talk privately. We moved into the darkness. "Max invited me to dinner. I'm going." Needless to say Eric hadn't asked me. They left too soon. I barely managed a smile then proceeded to polish off half of Katerine's present. Nothing worse than drinking good wine while feeling bad.

The next morning she appeared, glowing, "Max is neat. This could be it."

I drummed up some enthusiasm to cool down my jealousy attack. "Great," tried to sound casual, "What was going on with Eric and *that* girl?"

"I don't think he likes her all that much."

"How do you know?"

"He kept asking me questions when she wasn't around which wasn't that often."

"What did he want to know?"

"Where we live in New York. What you do. What kind of a family you come from."

"What did you say?"

"I told him he'd have to ask you."

"You mean to tell me you didn't say I was a nice, normal Jewish girl?"

"Are you?"

"Many moons ago." I worried about 'normal.'

"Have to hurry, just came back to get my bathing suit, going to meet Max on the beach." Katerine was always in a rush, the hare to my tortoise.

"Did she stay overnight?"

"Don't know."

"How come?"

"We went to bed early. Eric's door was closed this morning."

"How's their house?"

"No great shakes."

"Why don't you come to the beach, we'll see Eric, I'm sure." I pulled on a white one piece, more secure, a tad see through when wet, what the hell.

I saw Eric playing volleyball and froze. Lit by stark sunlight -- nothing subtle about the beach, I didn't want Eric to think I was chasing him but he noticed, and motioned me over. I waited for the next game, consumed by jealousy and insecurity. Finally they finished off their opponents. Our turn.

"Shall we spot you ten points," Eric taunted.

"No thanks, we can beat you without your generous offer, I had spinach for breakfast," didn't ask what he'd eaten with whom.

"Aha! I hear the sweet sound of aggressive competition. So be it."

They killed us. Max put his arms around Katerine, claimed a victory kiss. The rest of the players scattered, Eric and I stood by the court awkwardly, "You're so competitive, brown-skinned girl. Let me give you a consolation hug."

"No thanks." I backed away.

"Do I detect frostbite?"

"Of course not," I snapped back.

"Let's see that beautiful smile." I stuck out my tongue.

"My, my. I can't help it if I'm fatally attractive to women. You didn't come into my life until yesterday afternoon: twelve thirty six to be precise. And I, sought-after man that I am, had a previous commitment, which I honored as a gentleman, I might add."

I pondered that. If I had another date, I'd have broken it, managed to see Eric even if it meant 'shooting someone down.' I was ashamed of myself, but only for a second. Eric hedged his bets and brought her over to me -- a lot of nerve, not particularly gentlemanly in my book. The Imp hung tough: 'Do *anything* to get him, the end justifies the means.' I let it slide, dove into the water. Eric followed.

"Can I offer you a ride back to New York tonight?" he tried to make amends. "Why don't we have a bite if you don't have plans?" I nodded yes, kept swimming, jealousy stuck in my craw.

Sunday night dinner in his neighborhood, Broadway and 113th, was as romantic as you can get in a brightly lit Chinese restaurant, taking into account how much I hated Chinese food. At age seven, the day after our traditional Sunday dinner of Chinese take-out on the maid's day off, I came down with measles and blamed the food. Ditto ten years later when I got the trots after eating Chinese in Mexico City. I had to be the only Jew in New York City, if not the world, who didn't like all those unidentifiable slimy things drowning in mystery sauce. When you put one from Column A: #27, with three from column B: #16, #46 #54 on one plate, mixed them up, it always tasted the same -- disgusting. The inevitable followed: upset stomach and headache. That's how the fortune cookie crumbled, my bad fortune. Years later I found out I was allergic to MSG. The smell would always revolt me.

I gamely used the chopsticks and praised Eric's superb knowledge of the cuisine. We exchanged family pedigrees, resumes, IQs. He claimed genius; I implied it. We compared sports prowess. He didn't play tennis; I was a champion. I didn't play soccer; he'd played on the Yale team. I agreed that it was depressing that it wasn't a full-fledged Varsity. Now he played for Columbia. Of course I'd watch him come the season.

He drove me home and didn't come up for a drink. I was surprised, disappointed, had rehearsed my response to the sexual assault that didn't come all night. Eric invited me out for the weekend. I accepted in a flash, Katerine off flying, it would be just the three of us.

"Do you always travel so light?" Sarcasm his weapon.

"You heap strong man gottum big muscles good wagon."

"I don't know why you need all this stuff. I like you in your bikini."

I could barely talk, let alone walk down the boardwalk, all I wanted to do was touch those strong shoulders. I looked down at the shiny poison ivy in full red bloom, thought better about tackling him. Their house was in the middle row, indistinguishable from the others except for its color, dark green, hence its name, 'The Green House.' We walked up the ramp to a front deck into the living room. White bread. No charm. Katerine was right, 'no great shakes.' At least there were only two of them sharing one house.

"Welcome to our Hobby house." Max sat reading in his black bathing suit, his Le Corbusier round black frame glasses perched on his nose.

"What's a Hobby house?"

"I'll let old man Max do the honors."

The architect held forth, "There's a great guy from Patchogue named Hobby Miller who designed and built most of the houses out here, multiple dwellings just for groupers. This is his small version, room for just four. The big one has four bedrooms and fits eight. The bar fronting the open kitchen is standard, as are front and back decks. No frills, functional, they work."

Eric piped in, "We've renamed Ocean Ridge 'Hobbytown,' or if you prefer, 'Hobbyville.'

Max held up a perfectly rolled joint, "Can I offer you some smoke? I just bought an ounce for five bucks. It's something else."

"How many times do I have to tell you -- *fantastique* or *molto bene*."

"*Fantastique*, you affected fart." Max lit up.

"We love each other, we really do," Eric put his arm around him. We each took a few tokes.

"This grass is really great," he giggled. "I'm going to the Caz..."

"No thanks." Exit Max. We were alone.

"Shall we take a shower? No bathtub, Hobby houses being what they are, a dip in the great Atlantic?" asked Eric.

No contest. "Last one in's a rotten egg." We rushed to the beach, three minutes away.

The silver moon path beckoned. "Come in. Come in. Come play with me." Eric shed his shirt, tore off his wheat jeans, no underpants. I tried not to look. Did. Wow.

"Come on slow poke." He pulled off my clothes, drew me close, kissed me slowly, his tongue explored my mouth. I felt his hardness. The water was warm, Caribbean calm -- a big bath tub. "Meet you in South America," he taunted and swam away.

"I'll be in Caracas before you've reached Cuba." I kept up. A tie, he turned, swam towards the shore, shallow water so we could stand.

"Eric wants you." He entered me. Two pieces of seaweed entwined.

"This hurts a trifle."

"The water is washing away your natural juices. I'm going to have you on the beach." He carried me out, spread his big shirt and lay down on his back. I slid onto him.

"Come on ride me. That's right. Ride." He held my breasts and pushed me back and forth, back and forth. So excited I could barely stand it. Out of control, feeling strange, I stopped. "Keep going."

I began to shudder as I caught fire, exploding, the reverberations travelled down to my toes. Fireworks. "Ooh."

"That's a good girl," he coddled me like a baby, "Now come again." A long-buried primal feeling deep within ignited -- first tension, then a feeling like I was going to die if I wasn't released. "Ready to come together? Tell me when."

"Oh, God, now, Eric, now." A second of limbo followed by an intense explosion.

I felt his waves blend with mine. The most profound physical experience of my life, I groaned with pleasure on top of Eric and the world, started to cry.

"What's the matter, did I hurt you?"

"No." Speechless, I'd given up. *I want to marry you...spend the rest of my life in bed, your sex slave,* what I didn't say.

"Did you like it in the water?"

"I prefer the beach," the understatement of my life.

"Let's take a dip to wash off."

Katerine and I were invited separately to move in together with Eric and Max on weekends. We were both delighted, as were the girls from the bay house. For the past month, we'd enjoyed the pluperfect arrangement, alternated cooking with clean up detail. If Katerine and Max did breakfast, it was our turn for dinner.

"Hey you guys, come up for daylight. There's a wonderful example going on outside." Max spoke through Hobby's paper-thin walls.

"What are we having for breakfast?" asked Eric, and began to suck my nipple.

"*Huevos rancheros.* Five minutes. Get up Ali, it's one of my goodies." Katerine loved to cook, something always boiling, baking or frying. She tended to be experimental, her ratio of success reasonably high. Speaking of high, we were so stoned by the time we ate -- ravenous, as if we hadn't eaten in three weeks, anything tasted spectacular.

Eric dashed to the shower.

"Hey," I chided. "Leave some hot water for me." Eric was shower happy.

"Come in, we can save together." I obliged. "You know what I'm going to make for dinner tonight?"

"What? Could you pass me the soap, Mr. God?"

"Mongrel god. Eric's Special Spaghetti." I soaped his beautiful shoulders and back. "Do you know how? I didn't think that cooking ran in your race."

"Sure it does you prejudiced bigot. At least it isn't Jewish chicken soup again which is the only thing you know how to cook."

"You forgot about my bluefish." Dr. Blatt suggested I try my hand at cooking. I'd bought the *James Beard Fish Cookbook* and had big success with of all things -- the lowly, dark, oily bluefish, elevated to haute cuisine. You stuffed them with fresh parsley, dill, lemon, and onion, put more lemon slices on top, doused with red or white wine to cut their dark taste, baked then broiled them. Good and healthy.

"We got lucky last weekend," the blues were running, we ran into a fisherman with a big catch, who could spare some extras, "but we can't count on it." Practical.

"If I had a fishing pole, I'd catch one. Dad taught me how to surf cast."

"When *am* I going to meet him?"

"Soon." I guarded my privacy now that I had my own apartment, in no hurry to have Mother and Dad meet, greet and charcoal grill him. I had to keep Mother away, didn't trust her. She'd for sure flirt with him. Eric began to bug me, piqued by Dad's fame. I didn't kid myself that he wanted to meet Dad to ask for my hand. Back to the menu, "What kind of sauce?"

"Marinara plus Eric's famous garlic bread."

"How thinning."

"You don't have to worry about your weight."

"Not true, I've gained at least five pounds since I met you."

"Let me soap down that delicious beef on the hoof."

"If you're serious about the spaghetti, I'll go to the store and get the ingredients." I hated the mile-long walk.

"I have everything except that miserable excuse for tomatoes they sell in town. See if you can score some locals."

I threw my arms around his neck and kissed him, "You're so adorable."

"I prefer to be thought of as devastating or debonair... adorable describes children or these..." Eric tweaked my nipples. "What's this outburst about, young lady?"

"You just said 'that miserable excuse for tomatoes'."

"I remember what I say. I'm not senile yet, though I'm sure it's imminent."

"I once had an argument about tomatoes," pronounced it 'toe mah toe,' the Bostonian way Mother had drilled in which bothered other guys. Eric took it in stride, had his own affectations. I launched into a story about a French woman I'd met on a classical bus trip from Athens on the way to the Temple of Apollo at Delphi, the tomatoes merely an excuse to share a mystical experience. I recounted that after three hours crisscrossing the valley of Phocis, taking hairy hairpin turns, we slowly climbed the southwestern spur, finally arriving at the top of Mount Parnassus. The second I'd stepped down from our chariot, a white and black beaten up tour bus, surrounded by sky and that brilliant Greek light, I had a special feeling, spellbound by the ruins -- the remains of another day. I was Queen of the Mountain, a goddess, surveying my domain. A grey green plain of olive trees sloped down to meet a shock of turquoise -- the Gulf of Corinth in the distance. A moment of profound peace etched indelibly in my memory, I felt the magic again.

"Are we discussing your Greek Art History course or tomatoes?" Eric butted in. I was stunned into silence, my crystal reverie shattered into shards, "It's important when you tell a story, and obviously you're one of those people who shouldn't, to have a beginning, middle and end. That was totally illogical.

You rambled around the Cape of Good Hope and never came back."

"Sorry." I felt bad when he nipped at my heels. I continued, chastened, but wasn't going to let him stop me, "The point is that French woman on the bus argued that American tomatoes were substandard, '*comme les merdes*' (like shit) compared to French, we put so much effort into growing them big they've lost their taste, '*Pas de bon gout*'. Bigger was not better. She was so offensive that I wound up defending America on general principle even though she was right, the *merde*."

The hot water ran out. "When it comes to taste you can't fault the frogs." Eric toweled me off.

"When it comes to impertinence you can't match them."

"Another case of prejudiced bigotry."

"I love France, just hate the French, Jackie and Jack's trip to Paris showed those snobs." I loved how she spoke French and dressed chic. Hooray U.S.A. It had been almost nine months since he was shot. Poor Jackie. Poor us, the bubble burst, hope and Camelot gone, we'd never get over it. I began to make the bed, Eric a neatnik.

"I'm concerned about the country being run by that imperious Texan, Lyndon Johnson and our position in Vietnam. I'm going to have to figure out a way to stay in school for the rest of my life to avoid the draft the way this war is escalating."

"My brother Billy worries, too." I slipped on my black bikini, tied the yellow pareu.

Eric dropped his voice, "Know how Max got out?"

"How?"

"Pretended he was a homo."

"They believed him?"

"He walked into the induction center holding hands with one of his flaming interior designer friends, winked at the sergeant, put his hand on the doctor's knee."

"I didn't know Max had it in him." I put my hair in bunches.

"My dear girl, if you were faced with being drafted, you'd get desperate, too." Eric slipped on his black, nylon racing suit, khaki shorts fresh white tee.

"It's our duty to defend our country."

"From whom," he countered. I shrugged my shoulders, stumped. "The guys going over don't know either, if you figure it out let me know. We're not fighting an enemy like the Japs or Nazis, democracy at stake, black and white issues that pulled the country together. This is grey, and it's tearing us apart."

"Breakfast's ready." Katerine called from the kitchen, sound travelled straight through the wall.

"Coming." Before I had a chance to tell Eric I agreed, if I were a guy I'd be a draft dodger, too, he dropped his voice, "Don't discuss politics with me again unless you're better informed. Max is a goddam hero for bailing out. Your brother better watch out." He relaxed, "You manage to look adorable even when you're all wet." You were saying about the tomatoes..."

"I'll walk a mile for a tomato," and fireworks with you.

A mighty cauldron of water boiled. Another pot containing chopped garlic, onions, green peppers, olive oil, and local tomatoes cooked on low, Eric's Special Spaghetti in progress. He dipped the wooden spoon into the sauce and tasted. "Everything's ready."

"To eat?"

"To go to the sixish, I'll cook the pasta when we get back, only takes a few minutes, I want it *al dente.*"

"What's a sixish?" Katerine looked over Eric's shoulder, checked out his sauce. He gave her a taste and she nodded approval. "I haven't been to one."

"That's because you're always flying to some exotic place like Houston or Mexico City."

"Someone has to support us." Katerine's American Airlines stewardess routes and wages minor, her fringe benefits major, she could fly almost anywhere in the world for twenty-five dollars *round trip,* our bar overstocked with mini bottles of booze, flight leftovers.

Eric cleared his throat, "*Sixish, sixae, sixa, sixam, sixa, sixae, sixarum sixis sixas sixis.*"

"That's first declension, female."

"We know you guys speak seventeen languages between you,"

"Eighteen."

"Sorry, Eric, eighteen, but what's a sixish?" Katerine was still on it.

"A local weekly Saturday night happening around seven. You take a glass, fill it with your libation of choice, follow your nose and the other locals in the direction everyone seems to be going until you arrive at a place that has ice, mixers and sounds..."

I interrupted, "And all the people that you just saw five minutes ago on the beach, all talked out, nothing more to say."

"And there you have it." Eric had to have the last word.

"It's an impromptu cocktail party, better stoned, speaking of which I happen to have some fantastic new Columbian. Take two puffs each, no more, very strong." Max proffered a perfectly rolled joint.

We strolled to Davis Park, the grouper community to the west, the houses older, smaller, crowded together; narrow boardwalks threaded over overgrown patches of poison ivy. We followed the trail of tinkling ice cubes, stopped at a two-story house. The upper deck overflowed, the walk outside overcrowded. One hundred stoned souls, a 'happening.' I knew more people than I realized, not all on my A-list, like my ex- housemates who cold-shouldered me.

"What do I do now that I've finished my drink," queried Katerine.

"Repent that you didn't nurse it, elbow your way into the house, beg or borrow a libation, if they turn you down, improvise and have another hit."

I felt claustrophobic, too crowded. Max looked uncomfortable, too. "I'm getting the urge for Eric's spaghetti."

"Can't we stay? Right back...want to walk around a bit." Katerine, an inveterate explorer, took off. Max lit up another joint which we lost track of, others coming from different directions. Share and share alike, don't Bogart, a community high in progress. I got separated from Eric.

"Hey, like how ya doing?" It was Danny Arnold, the hip musician. "Like you haven't been around."

"I've been hanging out in Ocean Ridge... good talking to you," cut him off, didn't want to have to introduce Eric to a one-night stand.

I loved going to parties, played a game - how many attractive men could I talk to or make eye contact with -- capture -- but only the ones who didn't want me. Katerine was right -- I was a flirt, bad boys my specialty. It took one to know one but she liked good guys. I'd often been accused of looking over one man's shoulder for another. Tonight was different. I was 'with' Eric, tied by an invisible string. Suddenly I felt paranoid. Where was he, didn't trust him, too good looking and he knew it.

I wove in and out of the crowd desperate to find him. Everyone's smiles seemed frozen on their faces, men's lewd, women's threatening. Christ I was stoned must have had five hits, hell ten. Overindulgent, suffocating, no air outside, how long had Eric been gone? Could have been five minutes or fifty, on grass time. I imagined the worst scenario -- he'd met someone else. Nowhere to go, I headed to the Casino, and spied Eric talking to Bunny on the deck where Reggie had first turned me on two months ago. Crazy, jealous, I raced up the stairs, steamed over and slid my arm into his to take possession.

"You remember Bunny don't you?" Short shorts again.

"I'm sorry, did we meet?" my turn to be a bitch. She deserved it.

"I guess I'll get going. So nice to see you again, do call when you have a chance." She smiled, kissed Eric on the mouth and slithered away.

"We get separated one minute and what do you do?" Righteous.

"What *was* I doing?" On the offense, "Catching up with an ex girlfriend who I haven't seen since we met."

"What did you talk about?" Attitude.

"Is this an interrogation?" An army brat, his father a general, he didn't like to be questioned, like his dad I supposed. I repeated the question, a broken record. "Quit it. You don't own me and I'm not a criminal. Jealousy doesn't suit you. I told her that I was sorry I hadn't seen her because I was with a nice girl who then burst into the conversation and acted like hell. You deserve to be spanked. Come to think of it I might enjoy that. As a matter of fact, so might you."

Suddenly it was my fault. "Sorry." I took a deep breath. He had said, 'I'm with...' On the other hand what was he doing with her at the Caz? I wasn't sorry, another red warning flag, which I chose to ignore, ineluctably turned on by the adrenalin rush.

"Don't let it happen again... I hate possessive women."

The munchies set in, "I'm starving."

Katerine and Max were in their bedroom with the door closed. The water in the cauldron had almost disappeared; the sauce in the pan burnt, black char on the bottom. Eric announced in a loud voice, "Don't worry folks, I have the situation in hand. Might I suggest a little peanut butter and jelly on garlic bread to hold everyone until then." Ominous silence.

10

Erosion

"Are you guys decent? My friends are here." Max called through the wall while Eric and I languished in bed, my favorite place.

"More like indecent exposure," I giggled.

"Coming." Eric stroked my breasts. "*Quel fromage.* There goes our Saturday morning you know what."

I traced those shoulders, "You mean *dommage.*"

"Don't correct me," he snapped, "I *know* the difference, said it on purpose. You didn't get it." I brushed it under the rug bit my lip. He let up, "We better meet Max's guests before we're accused of indecent etiquette."

"I wish I cared," I sighed.

"Know what you mean."

Our domestic situation had disintegrated. No one doubted that Max was a genius when it came to architecture, but he'd proven temperamental and selfish in day-to-day living. Our disagreements were ridiculous, invariably about little things like last Friday's incident. Eric's avocado had ripened for a week on the windowsill. Katerine and Max came early, made guacamole scarfed it all down in a stoner haze. Eric maintained that he was the rightful owner, since he'd bought it, and they should've shared. Both sides threw the book, stony silence all weekend, no communication between 'them' and 'us' last week. My best and only friend stood by her man, right or wrong, and was not speaking to me. Dr. Blatt was on vacation -- August was August. Dreadful. No one to talk to. The weekend before Labor Day, Katerine was flying so Max had invited friends not to be outnumbered.

A small army greeted us. A dark man with intense eyes and no front teeth dandled a two-year old girl. "This is Joe Antamoro," the famous geometric abstract expressionist; "his wife, Helene Silver," tough looking blonde, art critic and historian, the avant-garde power couple; "Henry Geldzahler," a fattish squat man who had a striking resemblance to Tweedledee (or was it Tweedledum?), *the* modern art historian and critic and first curator of twentieth century art at the Met, later New York City Commissioner of Cultural Affairs. I'd read up on Geldzahler in *Women's Wear Daily,* the fashion 'bible.' His name was dropped at Thursday night openings at the Jewish Museum and MoMA which I attended religiously, an art rat. While most curators and critics kept their distance from artists, he hung out with his favorites, Willem de Kooning, Jasper Johns, Larry Rivers, Andy Warhol and David Hockney, *the* stars of the art scene.

No one said a word. Had Max told them to deep freeze us, too unimportant to talk to or were they shy? I gave them the benefit of the doubt. We retreated to the bedroom. Eric lugged out a new coffee table book on astrology, a present from a publishing friend hot off the press.

I glanced at it, fascinated, “Let’s take it to the beach.”

“Too heavy.”

“You big heap strong man.”

“Okay speedy. Hurry up. What are you doing? Why do you start something just when we’re trying to go.” Trying to make up my mind, the problem *du jour* which pareu went best with my bikini. ‘Eenie meenie minie mo.’

We plunked down in the usual place. Call it squatter’s rights, territorial compulsion, once the initial geographic decision where to put down the towel was made, people returned like lemmings for the rest of the season sometimes forever; how you could always find family or friends.

I read out loud, ‘There are twelve signs of the zodiac. Each has its own properties and ways it relates to other signs. The day, hour and year you are born determines your sign, and natal chart.’

“How do you know what sign you are?”

I flipped a few pages, “Here’s a chart. When were you born?”

“Let’s see, as I remember it was a stellar day, January 1, ‘36.”

“You’re a Capricorn. The goat. Cardinal earth. Other famous people born on your birthday include Lorenzo the Magnificent, Barry Goldwater, Paul Revere, Alfred Stieglitz, J. Edgar Hoover, E.M. Forster and Ouida, whoever that is or was, and last, certainly not least J.D. Salinger. What a writer.” I devoured his books, Holden, Franny and Zooey old friends.

"Like it so far. What are you, why are you such a fruitcake, Zania?" He'd taken to calling me that when I got 'overwrought,' meaning that I changed my mind or plans from one second to the next.

"Libra. Sounds like freedom -- *libre*, or book -- *libro*. Cardinal air the scales. Look who's born on *my* birthday! F. Scott Fitzgerald." Astrological oneupsmanship, "Sophisticated, God, I'm sophisticated," I vamped, like Daisy Buchanan languishing on a white sofa, white dress, long string of pearls. "My favorite writer."

"You just said that about Salinger."

"I can have two."

"Zelda Fitzgerald should have been born on your birthday, another nut. I'm going to play volleyball."

I continued to read what I now thought of as the book of revelations between dips in the August ocean -- warm, murky, oily. Holy moly. My misery had company. Indecision was a Libra trait. Then, too, 'You can usually be found wherever there are gay social activities.' A social animal, I loved parties and people -- the other side of that coin -- hated to be alone. 'You enjoy social success through your pleasant disposition and cheerful outlook,' right so far. Still skeptical, I read Eric's zodiac. 'You tend to be too severe in your judgments and rather cool and calculating in your affections. You have a solid reasoning ability.' True. We were opposites: I was up in the air, and he was down to earth.

I splashed him, "You're a pessimist and I'm an optimist.

"I thought you were an optometrist." He tried to duck me. "You don't believe that hogwash do you?"

"So far it rings true."

"I brought the book out here as a joke, you can't tell me the day you're born has anything to do with who you are. Prove it."

"I can't. That's just what it says about your sign -- you have to see it to believe it. No leaps of faith."

"So what?" Belligerent.

"Let's drop the subject before we have an argument."

"What's wrong with that?"

"Libras are peacemakers. Mediators, like Dad," another Libra. I'd looked everyone up -- Mother was a Scorpio who ate her young with a tail that stung, figured. Billy and Katerine were both Aries, Cardinal fire signs, action central. On the money. I was so angry with Max I hadn't bothered to look him up. Nick was a Taurus -- fixed earth, he'd never change. We shared Venus, as our planet -- love of beauty. Libra was a cardinal sign, which meant leader. Then I noticed 'm' as in masculine. A steel hand in a velvet glove, why I kept butting heads with Billy, another cardinal, who kept accusing me of being too strong and not feminine enough. I was and wasn't, hooked on astrology, couldn't wait to learn more.

"How are you going to solve the war between Max and Katerine and us?"

I sighed, resigned, "Can't, I am *not* liking either of them. I want to and suspect Katerine feels the same. All we can do is hope there's a truce for Labor Day."

We sat down at the bar to have a drink and a joint with Max and guests. Joe was in charge of the baby. Completely. Gaa gaa and goo gooing the while, he fed, washed, changed her diapers. Helene, Max and Henry talked nonstop. Fortified by the joint, I tried to climb into the conversation with Helene, alone for the moment. "How do you know Max?"

"He and Joe go back." No further comment.

"I enjoy your art criticism." She nodded.

I tried again, "Where did you go to school?"

"Sarah Lawrence after I left Smith."

A wedge in, "I'm a Smithie too."

"Dreadful place, had to transfer, academic without the intellectual." Massive put down, my back up, I agreed with her about academia -- it rhymed with anemia. I'd been far more stimulated at Fieldston, fearful of making waves with Mother and Dad, I'd stayed, memorized and spit it back didn't have to think, just remember. Two different systems, one inspired creativity -- what was your idea, the other cut and dried, what was their idea? Or as Einstein said, "Education is not the learning of facts but the training of the mind to think."

"What are you two gabbing about?" Henry Tweedledee rescued me from the calamitous conversation, sat next to his big bud Helene while Joe played with the baby on the couch. So far she hadn't touched her; Dad was Mom. Was that their deal?

"Not much." Helene looked bored, had made mincemeat out of me. I hadn't mentioned advertising, ashamed in front of the high brows.

"What does your handsome boyfriend do?" inquired Henry.

"I School." He gave Eric a smoldering look as he moved across the room to sit with Max, Joe and the baby. Eric didn't catch it. Want him Henry? Over my dead body.

I finally figured out something to say, "You really ought to see our beach, it's one of the most beautiful in the world,"

"Can't compare with Greece." Henry shook his head. The old 'everything's better on the other side of the pond' attitude sounded snotty.

Helene smirked, "Nothing does. The light." They were stealing my lines. I looked at Tweedledee's pasty skin, her permanent scowl, and gave up.

"Let's go to the sixish." Desperate.

"Great idea, Zania." He'd had it, too.

We paused to watch the sunset over the bay as the golden fireball sank behind the mainland, one last flicker, the flame extinguished. "Do you mind that Henry's after you?"

"What do you mean?"

"Don't you notice how he looks at you?"

"You're imagining things. What can he do to me? Ah's bigger than he is."

We did the sixish, the Caz, came home late, drunk and stoned.

After brunch, Bloody Marys and Alka Seltzer on the rocks, our hangover ritual marred by the presence of the odd family and Henry who'd slept on the couches, we escaped to the beach. The ocean was lake like. I stood on my head underwater.

"What are you doing?" asked Eric.

"Curing my hangover, an old trick I learned in the orient. I'm starting to feel sad, next weekend's Labor Day."

"What's the problem?"

"Our apartment lease is up September first." I dove under. Together for two months on weekends, some nights during the week, I wanted to live with him full time, how to broach the subject? I surfaced.

"Do you want to move in together? Is that what you're hemming and hawing about?"

"Well..."

"Fine. We'll find a cheap apartment in the village, split the rent, I have to do some studying, big exam Monday. See you back at the ranch." Done deal, matter of fact, Capricornish or was it Capricornian?

I spent the rest of the afternoon daydreaming, sex every night, and every morning. Dad would die, living in sin -- he could never know.

There was a flurry of activity upon my return, they were packing up, the baby crying, "Where's Eric?" No response. Stone faces, our bedroom door closed. I breezed in, Eric lay face down on the bed.

"Shut the door," terrible voice, something wrong.

"What happened?"

"Don't want to talk."

"Tell me."

"Shut up and leave me alone."

Not taking 'no' for an answer, I put my arms around him. He wrested free. I heard the front door slam. "They've gone."

"I could've killed Henry."

"What?"

"You heard me. I'm taking a walk." He slammed out of the house. Run after him? No, leave him be, he had to come back sometime. I cleaned up, packed, thought about how much I hated being alone, remembered being lonely even as a little girl. Billy didn't mind. He'd take his toys and invent a whole fantasyland. I'd look at a doll and all I saw was a doll that wasn't real, couldn't talk or keep me company. Instead I dove into fantasyland by reading every fairy tale ever written about becoming a princess or queen.

I remembered a lonesome Friday night I'd spent in our apartment last year. Katerine was off flying. I'd rattled around -- no good movies on television, didn't have a book I felt like reading, the apartment clean. Johnny Mathis on the stereo singing "Heavenly, that's how I feel..." made me feel worse. You weren't supposed to call men ever, which killed me. Even if I could've, believe me I wanted to, it was doubly uncool at night, an advertisement that I didn't have a date. I dialed a gal from work who'd said she was looking forward to spending the night at home.

"Melanie. It's Ali. Thank God you're home."

"Hi."

"Remember what you said about an evening alone?"

"Yes."

"What are you doing?"

"Having a wonderful time."

"What does that mean?"

"I don't know, catching up on stuff I never have a chance to do: sewing, cleaning out my pocketbook, doing laundry, plucking my eyebrows. You know." I didn't.

Eric burst into the living room.

"What happened?"

"I sat down at the bar to study, no one around," in his Speedo, "all of a sudden someone kissed my shoulder and grabbed my cock. Henry! I picked him up by the neck and started to squeeze, I wanted to kill that faggot. He screamed, Max rushed in and pulled me away. Henry started to cry. I ran to the bedroom."

"He couldn't resist you."

"Don't say stupid things, hear me? This is the last time we'll *ever* mention this. Clear?"

"Right." Sometimes he was scary, the thought of him strangling Henry or worse. I held him tight.

Friday Labor Day weekend, with the afternoon off from work, Eric and I drove out early with plenty of time to get to the Moses victory party at six in Ocean Beach from Ocean Ridge. Mother had threatened in her iron voice, 'Don't be late.'

"Help!" I called from the bedroom.

Eric bounded in. "What's the matter?" He looked at the bed strewn with my clothes, "The room's a mess."

"Which top do you like better, the poor boy or the peasant blouse?" I'd already decided on the bottom, a white Laura Ashley lace slip.

"I thought something serious had happened."

"Which one hides the five million pounds I've put on better?"

"Speaking of which, when did you polish off the whole Skippy jar? I was looking forward to a peanut butter and jelly sandwich."

Caught. "Sorry." Ashamed. Grass was the culprit, being stoned eliminated what little appetite control I had, turned me into a ravenous glutton, a midnight icebox raider. Pig. Pig. Pig. Eric was so regulated, no excesses.

"The one you're wearing. What's the difference? They're both white. Step on it speedy or we'll miss the beach taxi. You haven't told me if I look all right." Eric preened.

"They're going to love you." He was preppy perfection: blue Brooks Brother's shirt, white pants, blue and white seersucker jacket slung jauntily over his shoulder.

"You look very Point O' Woods."

"What's that supposed to mean?"

"That's the all-WASP community near Ocean Beach that has an iron fence around it to keep out Jews and Catholics."

"Are your parents going to mind that you're bringing home a mongrel WASP rather than a nice Jewish boy?"

"Of course not, Dad defines liberal. Billy and I've trained them. They're used to me going out with any thing-but-Jewish boys, Billy with only-not-Jewish girls."

Eric looked at his watch, irritated, "We're going to miss it." He had a point. We raced down to the beach in front of the Casino where a red jeep was parked, *White Cap Taxi* neatly lettered in white on the door.

"You the party that's going to Ocean Beach? Thought you were going to be no shows."

"Sorry," said Eric, giving me a nasty glance.

"That'll be nine bucks each, one way, payable in advance." A fortune.

The driver looked surprised when we paid separately. Going Dutch was our deal, I had a job, he was at school.

We took off westwards, the beach aglow in magic six o'clock light. I watched the swimmers, jealous. I shouldn't have worn the poor boy, a walking advertisement for boobs. I dreamed I went to my parent's party in my Maidenform bra.

"Does visiting your family always make you this uptight or are you nervous about bringing me along?" Both.

"I'm just excited."

"What's so special?"

"It's a victory celebration, Fire Island is saved. They beat Robert Moses."

"Sounds like he's a villain." Eric twirled an imaginary mustache.

"That bastard's tried to ruin Fire Island for forty years by razing all the houses to make another one of his roads. The sonofabitch almost succeeded."

"Why don't you be a good girl, calm down, collect your thoughts. You really shouldn't swear so much, it's not ladylike." Eric's linguistic demands -- no run-ons, exaggerations, swearing or side trips -- rattled me. "Start at the beginning, Zania."

I took a deep breath. "Dune erosion is The Big Problem. Almost every year Fire Island gets the shit kicked out of it by hurricanes and nor'easters."

"Beaten up, battered… go on."

"Dunes are the island's first line of defense. Waves cause most of the damage not the wind. More and more people have built houses on the ocean dunes. Laying the foundation destroys the dune grass that holds it together, the sand anchored by its tough roots, sounding the death knell -- *sayonara* dune. That's why Fire Island got hit so hard two years ago in that surprise hurricane, March, '62. Almost a hundred oceanfront houses were swept away, the dunes worn down too low to protect them from the water -- the *hubris* of living on the dunes.

"Governor Rockefeller appointed a temporary commission to deal with the aftermath of this major catastrophe, put his boy, Robert Moses on it. Moses decided the only way to solve Fire Island's erosion problem once and for all was to demolish all the houses! He'd build a four-lane highway, connecting Fire Island to the mainland on both ends by bridges -- a thirty one mile ocean boulevard for the masses at the expense of the 'elite' home owners."

Eric whistled. "That megalomaniac."

"The law required a hearing to be held at Jones Beach a mere legal technicality. Moses didn't count on the Fire Islanders who unbeknownst to him, had banded together and formed the 'Citizens Committee for a Fire Island National Seashore'. At Dad's insistence all homeowners transferred their voting residences from Manhattan to the incorporated village of Ocean Beach. It was on July 21st, fifteen hundred strong registered voters showed up.

"A showdown?"

"Yes. Moses attempted to adjourn the meeting and stop them from testifying like an authoritarian dictator. It was a zoo. Everyone yelled and screamed at everyone else, half the people were outside listening on loud speakers. Charles Collingwood, the CBS correspondent, took the floor, quoted a 1937 letter to the *New York Times* from radio commentator Elmer Davis, 'Moses would save Fire Island the way Hitler is saving the Sudetenland -- to the distress of many of the inhabitants.'

"Brilliant."

"Unexpected. Moses was so enraged he stalked out to a background chorus of boos, hisses and catcalls. The quote made headlines the next day in all the papers. 'Go down Moses.' 'Moses called Hitler.'"

"Then what happened?"

"A *deus ex machina.* Moses had so much power that the road was almost a *fait accompli* in spite of the Jones Beach hearing. But then Rockefeller asked him to resign as head of the New York State Council of Parks. The official reason -- Moses, at seventy, was three years past the mandatory retirement age. Also, he'd accepted the chairmanship of the upcoming World's Fair in Flushing Meadows and was seen as overburdened.

To get even -- no one fired Robert Moses, the sovereign prince, he not only resigned from the Council of Parks, but also from the four other state posts he held including the Long Island State Park Commission. Rather than call his bluff, Rocky accepted. The noose was off our necks. With no one left to champion his highway, the islanders and politicians have begun a push for legislation to protect Fire Island by making it part of the National Seashore."

"*Quel* saga. Good girl, articulate for once," he said, the usual edge to his voice.

"My timing wasn't bad either." We stopped at the foot of the oh-so-familiar walk.

"You'll pick us up at ten to take us back?" asked Eric.

"Yep. Me or another driver." He roared off. We climbed up the stairs to my old, secret Nick-watching aerie, down onto Ocean Breeze Walk. I could see the initials 'AA L BC' carved inside a heart in the cement: Allison Abrams Loves Bar Cohen, a reminder of puppy love at age fourteen. In daylight there were ghosts.

"Much wider here than in Ocean Ridge," Eric commented. "I can't see the bay and the walks are concrete. The houses are on top of each other, seems a tad overcrowded." Why did he always make me feel defensive? We climbed the ramp to the house. Mother greeted us.

"You never mentioned your Mother was so young and attractive," smooth verging on oily. She beamed.

"Your father's on the deck, the speeches start in five minutes, there's a brush and comb on your dresser."

I got the hint. "Excuse me Eric, I'll be right back."

I worked to get the kinks and curls out. Damn mirror; fatty, fatty two by four… I had to go on a diet. I gave my hair a few more futile strokes.

Billy and a beautiful blond were canoodling on the chartreuse couch, oblivious to the party. Eric talked to a dark, attractive woman I didn't know. Goddammit he was at it again, an incorrigible, compulsive flirt in full seduction mode. He was getting my goat, ruining a triumphant evening, triggering jealousy setting off my insecurities. It took me two seconds to get to him.

"I want you to meet my brother." I pulled him out of her clutches. "Can't I ever leave you alone?"

"I was just standing there when Joan started to talk to me."

"Please don't embarrass me in front of my family."

"Are you going to pull that jealous act again? What was I doing?" Mr. Innocence.

'Flirting, as usual' did not leave my mouth. "Billy, this is Eric London."

"How're you doing," delivered with the offhand coolness verging on antagonism that he reserved for any man I was with, our sibling rivalry in full force. Category #11: Who had the most attractive partner? He introduced Kirsten, a knock-out who had Billy wrapped around her little finger. Draw.

"Nice to meet you, Kirsten."

"Kirsten... do I detect a Danish accent?"

"*Ja.*" The conversation ended at the beginning.

"Please excuse us, we're going to see Dad." Billy hustled the Danish pastry out.

Had I detected yet another flirtation? "Coming Eric?"

Dad was surrounded on the overcrowded deck. We wedged in. "I've heard so much about you, sir, understand you're to be congratulated on the Fire Island National Seashore issue." Ah, Eric, another smart move.

"Thank you. Senator Javits, this is my daughter, Ali."

"And her friend..."

"Eric London, Dad."

Eric seemed super snowed by the high-powered politico, "Senator you are our savior."

"There are many champions here," Javits, fast on the draw, diplomatically deflected the glory back to Dad, "Without Mike's support and vision the islanders wouldn't have banded together in the first place." 'Jake' adored Dad, who was shy, eyes cast down, uncomfortable in the limelight. I beamed, basked in the reflected glow, never prouder.

Our moment over, we drifted out of frame into the sidelines, bumped into Meggy with her father, the ex-mayor of Ocean Beach, married with one child. So far.

Dad rang Mother's silver dinner bell, interrupted our small talk, "Could we please have your attention?" In a few minutes everyone quieted down, "I'd like to welcome you, Senators, Representatives, Members of the Citizens Committee for a Fire Island National Seashore, my family, friends..."

Mother was nowhere to be seen, in hiding when Dad spoke publicly -- afraid he'd make a mistake and embarrass her. He never had. Billy nuzzled Kirsten.

"We're here tonight to give Representative Delaney a mandate to take this National Seashore Bill to Congress to save us from the erosion that we can no longer protect ourselves against and forever foil the ruthless plans of Robert Moses..." Everyone booed. Dad speaking made me nervous too. I needed a drink and told Eric I'd be right back. Mother crocheted on the couch in hearing distance. I sat down next to her.

"Eric is so handsome and articulate. Very refined." She gushed. "Where have you been hiding him?" Keeping him out of your clutches. "Any news?"

"What do you mean?" I knew what she meant -- marriage plans.

"No, Mother. Not yet."

"We need your support to take the bill all the way to the President. Ladies and Gentlemen, I give you Representative

Delaney, the man who can do it." Delaney gave an eloquent speech about keeping Fire Island carless. Everyone clapped.

"They're winding up." Mother went to join Dad now that it was safe. My audience with her over, I went to get a drink from Ernest, the bald butler who served us comfort food during the hurricane, holding down the dry sink bar.

"How y'all doing, Miz Ali."

"Great. I'd love a J & B on the rocks." I watched him deftly make it, "Thanks, Ernest. You still in charge of the Butler's Ball?"

"Yes, ma'am. Trina and me made it hop again this year, two great dancing bands. Sorry y'all missed it."

"Me, too Ernest, I'm at the other end of the island past Cherry Grove and The Pines." No one in Ocean Beach had heard of Ocean Ridge.

"Good enough. I don't see no ring. You got yourself married yet?"

"Not exactly but I have a boyfriend."

"That be good news, keep me posted." I took a few swigs, back to the deck, fortified. Something was wrong. Billy stood, arms crossed over his chest, antagonistic. I couldn't see whom he faced, my view blocked by a woman with a large-brimmed straw hat. I snaked around to get a better view. He was right in front of Eric, who postured like a bull, Joan the dark mystery woman at his side, way too close.

Billy's face was contorted with controlled rage. "What are you doing hitting on this woman? I came over to talk and you're writing her number down on a cocktail napkin." He took one step forward. "You *are* my sister's date."

"Yes."

"Prove it."

"I'm not married to her," sneered Eric, "I can talk to anyone I like."

"You *are* her escort." Billy didn't like his attitude and Eric didn't like the scrutiny, a pissing match. Billy moved a step forward. Eric stood up straighter, stiffened, scowled, menacing. The mood was ugly. I was stricken and afraid. Eric was a loose cannon, and I'd never seen Billy so steamed. Would they fight? People started to move away as if from the plague, my worst nightmare.

Out of nowhere came a familiar voice. "Let's calm down guys, this is a party." Jordan! I couldn't believe my eyes -- my old flame -- well, the flame I'd extinguished many times. He stepped in between the two antagonists -- inconveniently, my brother and boyfriend -- with authority, forcing them apart.

Billy dropped his guard immediately, "This guy's supposed to be Ali's boyfriend and he's all over this woman," My brother defended my honor.

Eric spit. "I've had enough." Joan shrank back. I moved forward.

"Is he your date?" Jordan looked into my eyes.

"Yes."

Eric snapped. "I've had it. No one tells me what to do." He turned around in a fury and stalked out, no apology or goodbye.

"Eric," I cried.

"Let the asshole go." Billy blocked me from going after him, would've tackled me rather than let me follow.

Jordan put his arm around me. "Come here Princess, it's been a long time."

My future had just walked out of my life, shamed in front of my family, hell the whole world. I was stunned by conflicting emotions. Mother and Dad missed it but they'd hear, and I didn't want to be around. I pleaded to Jordan, "Get me out of here."

He jumped into his usual save-the-day role assuring Billy he'd deliver me back later, "Let's go 'downtown'." He flashed the dimpled smile, took my hand, and led me away. "Who was that arrogant bastard? Bad news. What a jerk." I couldn't argue with his assessment, didn't want to admit that up till fifteen minutes ago I was moving in with him.

I came to my senses by Midway. "What are you doing here alone? Where's Jean?"

He looked downcast.

"Don't tell me you two got divorced." He nodded no.

"Jean died of a heart attack two months ago."

"My God!" I felt terrible. Poor Jordan. I was jealous of her but never would have wished this.

"I thought you would've heard."

"No. I'm out of the loop in Ocean Ridge." Our positions reversed, I hugged him, realized how he'd extended himself to help me. "I'm so sorry."

They'd been happy in D.C. She collapsed on the floor one night. He couldn't resuscitate her; she was only thirty-three. His friend Sean invited him out for Labor Day weekend. He'd arrived at Dad's political party late, only to find

Billy and Eric in a confrontation. His tragedy far eclipsed mine. I repeated how sorry I was, my envy of Jean and 'them' so shallow.

Ever handsome, charming, and upbeat, I put my arm through Jordan's. We passed what had been Sis Norris, now The Sandpiper. "I'll beat you on the bowling machine," Jordan rallied. The new owner had made no apparent changes to the old joint, jammed, the Beatles blasting, "It's been a hard day's night…" It had.

"I can't handle this crowd. Let's go to the playground." We passed Bayview, a line spilled out onto the sidewalk. "Do you ever hear from Nick?" speaking of ghosts.

"From time to time." I didn't want to say I was the one who called him. We dropped the subject, mutually uncomfortable. We perched in the swings behind the Community House overlooking the bay, the mainland in the distance, the moon a lemon slice. "Let's smoke." Jordan took a few tokes, an old hand. We played catch up. He'd had some pieces published and was working on a novel. Devastated by the loss of his hero, JFK, he was now volunteering for Bobby Kennedy. With Jean gone, he was moving back to New York to be an editor at Simon and Schuster -- publishing, like advertising, a revolving door. I told him about my job, proud.

Jordan was thrilled I'd found a career, encouraging, "You're smart and beautiful, go get 'em Princess." He kissed me. Same knee jerk reaction, the light switch turned off, the Imp back in play: 'Get rid of him, you'll get stuck,' I pushed him away.

He was horrified, not the first time I'd burned him. "Same old Ali, wasting your time on losers, rejecting the good guys." He had a point. "You should see a shrink."

"I *am* seeing a shrink," I protested -- not too much.

He assessed my many years of no progress with Dr. Blatt in one second, "He's no good. You're still up to your old tricks." He was right. "I know someone who can help you. I'll get his number. Hope you wake up, Scarlett."

I wanted to apologize for rejecting him again, but before the words came out of my mouth, he'd disappeared into the night. What *was* wrong with me?

11

Diamond Tiara

I always thought of Labor Day as a *tabula rasa* -- fresh slate. This one was in spades. Eric packed up my clothes from the Green House and dumped them with the doorman at my building. He left no note and never called. I bit the bullet, and my fingers not to call him. Couldn't. Didn't. A cad. Katerine snuck out of our apartment with all her belongings while I was at work one day. I heard she'd moved in with Max. I loved and missed her. What could I do? Nothing. She'd picked him over me. What would I have done? Kept both.

I couldn't face Dr. Blatt. How do you fire your shrink? I called him one evening while I was high, a state that erased fear and fortified my nerve and blurted out that I wasn't coming back. When he asked 'Why?' I lied and told him Dad had refused to pay anymore.

I may have been feeling a new lease on life, but our apartment lease was up. Fearful of living alone, I moved back in with Mother and Dad -- the worst case scenario -- felt like

I was on death row. To make matters worse I was a blimp, couldn't fit into any of my clothes, needed a tent. There she goes into the drugstore, stepping on the scale … she's the Fat Lady. Pasta, garlic bread, guacamole, peanut butter, donuts, chocolate chip cookies, William Greenburg Jr. brownies -- three months of binging had taken its toll.

Mother pulled me aside, "Your father thinks you need to lose a few pounds."

"Can't he tell me himself?"

A Mack truck desperate to dump its load, I remembered a chance meeting in front of the Altschuler tennis courts a few years ago with a tall, pleasant man who talked me up, gave me his card: Dr. Robert Atkins, weight loss specialist. Bob was gracious enough to squeeze me in right away, his waiting room filled to the gills with people fatter than me. A nurse ushered me into a spacious, comfortable office that housed a huge library of medical books and Bob, formal in a white coat. We talked for a few minutes, I'd packed it on over the summer omitted the cause: grass. The medical scale loomed, I took my shoes and jacket off as I got on for the moment of truth, shut my eyes as he fiddled with the weights, saw in disgust that I was up thirty-five pounds. The Imp went to town. 'How could you let yourself go like that?' I hated myself.

Bob got it, "Don't worry, it will come right off." easy for him to say. I took notes on a yellow pad in the hot seat. His plan seemed radical: eggs and bacon, steak, lettuce, pickles. No carbs. No fruit. Eight glasses of water a day. I could add some vegetables after the initial weight loss. He explained how healthy it was, good for your heart and cholesterol, seemed to know what he was doing, handed me a mimeographed stack of recipes in case I wanted to cook -- fat chance. I glanced over them. The cheesecake looked easy. "Delicious," he declared. "The secret is to substitute ricotta for cream cheese." Bob calculated it would take four months. I'd have to come to see him once a week for a weigh in. I could do it. I had to. The best part: he didn't charge me.

Stone had it in for me, made me retype any document that had even one error, hostility masquerading as efficiency. No matter that I tried to hide the mistake with Correcto tape, his eagle eyes found it. Seymour called it jealousy -- I'd produced two successful location trips for Helen Harper, a sweater manufacturer. The ads were full color pages in *Glamour, Mademoiselle* and *Seventeen*.

I hired a private plane to fly us round trip for the day to Bar Harbor, Maine, then a boat to Seal Island for the first 'shoot.' 'Us' was Seymour, Dennis the photographer, his amusing rep Donald Munson, Tom (the client), part American Indian Gail Hire (the talent). I dressed her in a Helen Harper tweedy lavender fisherman's turtleneck, purple pants, and positioned her next to a craggy fisherman in yellow oilskins, a study in contrast. 'Something wonderful happened in Seal Island ... when you wear a Helen Harper.' I didn't write the headline but Seymour and Donald, dueling for my attention, made it come true.

We rented a sleek van for the next shoot, drove to an Amish town in Pennsylvania called Bird in Hand. The ad was supposed to have been an Amish couple but at the last minute 'The husband' refused to be in the picture -- against his religion. 'The wife' gave up the faith for five hundred dollars, and posed on her odd, horse drawn cart in a drab bonnet and homespun dress beside the model in a red Helen Harper sweater. The headline: 'Something wonderful happened in Bird in Hand.'

Seymour and Donald continued to compete, I chose Donald. We smoked a joint, toured the rolling hills of picturesque Lancaster County sampled 'shoo-fly pie' from a roadside stand -- filled with molasses, dense, and doughy, inedible even though I was high. I bought a red, green and yellow Pennsylvania Dutch hex sign touted to have the power to protect the owner from harm. I could get lucky.

Stone began to torture me more if possible. As with Terry from Saks before him, I had an ally in Seymour who implored me to start looking for another job -- he'd give me a reference. This time my savior was a hot-blooded male who offered an incentive plan. We could date once we were no longer working together. Inspired, I wrote my resume, realizing I'd accomplished a lot in three years. Judy Wald, owner of an advertising employment agency had the perfect fit. Two men who'd worked at Doyle Dane Bernbach, Marty Stein, a suit and Aldo Gaetano an art director had opened a new fashion advertising boutique. The partners interviewed me together.

They offered me my dream job: account executive, fashion coordinator and casting director. The hex sign's magical powers worked even from the floor in my blue room. Some day soon I'd have my own digs again and give it pride of place on a wall, hang it high. The low, it was hardly a dream salary --

$9,500 a year, one third of what a guy would get. Unfair wages. Trapped. Wanted the job. Nothing I could do. No women's union. Too bad Dad couldn't organize then represent us.

I barely made it through the obligatory last two weeks -- Stone vicious, Seymour victorious.

S & G was in the smashing, unsurpassed Chrysler building, whose Art Deco crown never ceased to take my breath away, I got to work on time at nine my first day, a miracle. There was a roll top desk with a typewriter in my office, the window looked out on a spire and a piece of the sky. I signed a million papers. Sue the accountant informed me I was entitled to health insurance that covered some psychiatry. Hooray.

My client was Crompton Richmond, a manufacturer of cotton corduroy, velvet and velveteen, milled in Greensboro, North Carolina. Their clients were 'cutters' of women's, men's, children's clothes, both high and low end manufacturers -- Ann Klein to Lee jeans. They billed $500,000, all print. HUGE.

Ellen Boyle was head of the fashion department, a big part of my job to keep her happy. Marty Stein, attractive articulate was the mouth. Gaetano, quiet with a Yul Brynner-style shaven head, took me to meet Ellen for lunch at the Algonquin Hotel. Compulsively early, we waited for her in the cozy front parlor on the order of a gentleman's club, none of the chairs or couches matched. My thoughts were on the *New Yorker's* famed round table, I could almost hear Dorothy Parker drop her drop-dead line, "Men seldom make passes at girls who wear glasses."

Ellen, trim with freckles she powdered to hide, was of Irish extraction and lived in WASPy Bronxville. We discovered that her son attended the school where the father of my still absent beau (not-a-word-from-Australia-yet) Reggie, was principal. Small world. She immediately ordered a "very dry Beefeater martini, extra olives." Mine was Dewar's on the rocks, I'd switched from the heavier J & B. By the time the food arrived, we'd had another round on an empty stomach -- five breadsticks didn't count. And I was smashed. Ellen ordered yet another as I attempted to say no. She wouldn't have it, insisting on a drinking partner. I held it together till she left. Barely.

Meanwhile back at the office, Marty sized up my condition -- slurring words, singing songs, high as a kite. He sent me home in a taxi, the first of our weekly drunken lunches, or as I called them. "Ellen half days." I couldn't hold booze; she had a wooden leg.

True to his word, Jordan got me the number of a shrink. I liked Dr. Goodman immediately. He was attractive, his office comfy. I settled into a chair and relaxed, Jordan wouldn't steer me wrong.

"Why are you here?"

"My friend Jordan knows one of your patients, thinks you can help me."

"What's bothering you?" What wasn't? I launched into the latest version of my life highlighting the themes: no girlfriends, no boyfriends, overweight, not married, back living at home, a failure with Dr. Blatt, and hooked on a million pills.

He frowned, "Which ones, why, are you still on them?" I named the names, uncertain about the reasons, had just refilled Blatt's prescriptions.

"You don't need them."

"Dr. Blatt said I did." The only time I'd ever challenge him.

"No, they're harmful." I couldn't just stop taking them cold turkey though. He explained that I needed to withdraw slowly. I might get the shakes or sweats. He'd oversee the process. "Why do you think you have no women friends?" He changed topics, kept me on my toes.

"I don't have a flying clue."

"Could it be that they're jealous and always have been?" Never thought of that. "You're a beautiful woman with low self esteem. I'll be happy to take you on as my patient. Our time is up." Pandora's box had opened and out flew hope. We arranged for Tuesdays and Thursdays at twelve lunch hour convenient. I happily wrote a check, would've paid a million, insurance would reimburse eighty percent. I'd pay the rest myself and never again have to worry about Dad's late payments. I skipped out the door.

Since we were no longer co-workers, Seymour called and asked me out, "Anywhere you'd like." He wanted me to do the picking and planning he'd pay. Fine.

Elaine's it was. I'd bumped into Donald Ward aka Red, my favorite waiter from Goldie's who'd opened a joint on Second Avenue between 88th and 89th a year ago, 'I had to stop by.' Would I ever.

I treated myself to a new hairdresser, Monsieur Marc on West 56th, a reward for progress with Atkins -- minus fifteen pounds, and the big date with Seymour. He tried to talk me into bangs, *fringe* as he called them. 'Hair' was plural in French -- "Zey are *parfait* for your face." Fearful of change I gave him a hard time. Monsieur Marc gave up, threw his hands in the air disgusted. I gave in. He spent ten minutes on 'zee fringe airs,' cut them right below my eyebrows. "*Voila* zee bob."

Three long crosstown blocks over and one down brought me to the far eastern wilds of the Upper East Side, an unknown planet: downtrodden. Seymour looked snappy, standing in front of a chrome yellow canopy, a bright splash of color on the drab avenue.

"Wow!" he said.

We noticed a white Christmas Carousel horse in the far right window. Someone had a sense of humor -- welcome to the merry-go-round. The hypnotic sounds of Brubeck's *Take Five*, Paul Desmond on sax cool background music for a hot place, instantly intoxicated, the energy as electric as PJ Clarke's. At the end of the crowded bar on the left was an abstract red, white and blue Paris Review poster by Jack Youngerman; on the right a line of round tables covered by blue and white checked tablecloths filled by a blur of mostly men. An overhead shelf ran along the side, displaying a few books and posters. The décor was funky, Italianish. First impression: party, party.

"Hello precious, you finally made it," Donald was enthused. We air kissed.

"How are you?" I was relieved to see him, in safe hands.

"Perfect as usual. Who's this divine man?"

"Seymour, the best art director in fashion advertising." Donald left us dangling in mid air, stranded. The bartender looked familiar. Ray Lindie.

"Hey Ray, how's your racing? I'd met him in the Great South Bay taking swimming and racing lessons from lifeguard Bob Fenton, age seven.

"I can still beat you, Ali." He winked. He could.

A very long five minutes later, Donald materialized, and motioned for us to follow. He led us to Elaine, an august presence at the end of the bar: 350 pounds, white ruffle collar over a floral dress, oversized reading glasses, the fat lady in a Fellini movie. Donald introduced us in obeisance. Though they were partners, clearly her majesty was in command.

"Ali's a Fire Islander, friends with Barbara and Sarah." He referred to the Gardiners, my childhood buddies from the literary dynasty. Barbara must have backed him. My credentials established, I gushed, a pleasure to meet the latter day Gertrude Stein. Elaine nodded.

Donald led us down the line. I pointed to an empty table on the right, but he pranced past an open arch to another empty against the wall. Everyone gave us the once-over. Who were we? Elio, pronounced 'el e oh,' a tall, wry Italian, introduced himself as our waiter, took our drink orders, suggested the veal chop in a thick Northern Italian accent, hand over his heart. "On my life you won't be sorry." A whopping seven fifty, Seymour said it sounded good. In business.

Seymour came on strong, made it clear he liked me. The Imp butted in: 'I could do better.' My head swiveled as I checked out the other tables, drank my Dewars, on the lookout. Elaine scooped me up by the scruff of my neck, left Seymour behind and fed me to the wolves at Table #4 where she kept her pets: Jack Richardson, Ben Gazzara, Gay Talese, Vlad Kristov.

I squeezed in stimulated by a table of talkers. Elaine held court -- her trump cards infallible street smarts, fearlessness and a big mouth. She volubly passed judgment on each poor sucker who walked by, gave them lip and made them wait, maltreating them if she didn't want their business; gathered them into her ample bosom if she approved. She let her stable of writers and artists run tabs if they had 'the shorts,' supporting them in times of need.

I sat next to Ben Gazzara, who'd played Brick in "Cat on a Hot Tin Roof" -- and swooned. He flirted in the lowest, sexiest voice ever. Married, according to the screen magazines, to actress Janice Rule. Shame. Gay Talese, a dapper Italian don and literary legend was engrossed in conversation with Vlad, a painter whose work I knew and admired as much as his high cheekbones and bright blue turned up Slavic eyes. Blond, he'd dated a succession of beautiful brunettes, lately China Machado the Eurasian Dior model. I'd missed Jack Richardson's off-Broadway play, "The Prodigal." He'd won an Obie and a Drama Desk award. His long face and demeanor reminded me of Don Quixote, the knight of the sorrowful countenance. Jack gave me the skinny on fat Elaine. He'd promised her that if she got large enough tables he'd supply the writers. He'd delivered. Jack pointed to the poster overhead, his present. "There is nothing which has yet been contrived by man, by which so much happiness is produced as by a good tavern or inn." Boswell.

Jack slid off a turquoise and silver ring on his right pinky and placed it on my right index finger. Persian. Someone had given it to him with the caveat he must pass it on. I solemnly promised to keep the covenant, gave it back to him for his son, decades later, middle of the night, Kinko's.

Elio interrupted, dinner was waiting. I returned reluctantly. Seymour, a Taurus (the bull) had been doing a slow burn, steam coming out of his nostrils. When he saw his target, he charged, telling me off in no uncertain terms. "About time. I was giving you five more minutes." Rightly so, I'd abandoned him. What had gotten into me? Under Elaine's spell I'd allowed myself to be seduced, no excuse for bad manners. Seymour silently fumed, a downer drowning my up. I dove into the veal, three inches thick, tender, tasty, the best I'd ever have, and focused on a getaway to the table of tables.

The ladies room was narrow, its two oblique stalls smelled of pot. What I wouldn't give for a toke to chill me out, relieve the pressure of being on display. It made me fearless. I combed my hair, loved the bangs. Monsieur Marc was right. "Hello Princess, don't you look gorgeous." I imagined I was wearing a diamond tiara, and that Jordan had complimented me.

Back with Seymour, Vlad table hopped over and parked his vodka, saving the day -- night. Table-hopping I'd later learn was the M.O. of the denizens of Elaine's. It turned out that Seymour and Vlad knew each other from the art world --

Seymour had shown at Kennedy, a classy gallery that represented American artists, Vlad at Pace, equally distinguished. I hadn't known Seymour's secret -- a talented painter moonlighting as art director. We got drunk, they talked shop: Andy Warhol's Campbell's soup cans and garish silkscreen portraits, the explosion of Pop Art. The Princess liked being in the company of two attractive artists vying for her favors.

Donald stopped by. "May I steal Ali for a few?" Seymour assented -- I wasn't leaving him alone this time.

We passed the bar without interacting with the crowd. The blue-collar locals' bar bordered the most exclusive 'club' in town: saloon to the right, salon on the left, an invisible fence that no one ever crossed. Donald deposited a dollar's worth of quarters in the Wurlitzer jukebox, pushed B 26, 'Take Five' four times. He led me out the door, around the corner to 88th street, whereupon he proffered me a joint in an empty alley.

"I just heard Lyndon Johnson signed a bill creating the Fire Island National Seashore. We're safe from Robert Moses now thanks to your Dad's efforts. I may even vote for LBJ."

"Congratulations to us all." Month old news, I enjoyed his take, proud of Dad.

The empty table next to us was now filled by a small man, black-rimmed glasses, a typical Jewish looking nerd. Woody Allen did standup comedy in the Borscht belt, wrote his own material. Funny, he didn't look funny. "Just ignore him," advised Vlad. "Elaine lets him keep his privacy." So we played 'let's pretend Woody isn't here.'

Seymour and Vlad continued to discuss "The Silver Factory," Andy's' oversize tin foil and silver-painted warehouse. Vlad described a party there, the wildest of his life and he'd lived hard. Drag queens, playwrights, Bohemians, street people, Hollywood types, and wealthy Waspy patrons comingled, careened and caroused. Pills popping, drugs abounding and booze flowing. Warhol's creation, a midtown Elaine's East 47th, fifth floor.

Seymour called it a night. After conferring with Elaine, Elio handed him our bill, Vlad warned him to check it carefully. "There are sometimes irregularities." Vlad whispered in my ear, "You should come back, the night is still young." It was 12:30 on a work night. He slipped me the telephone number of one of the two pay phones side by side on the wall across from Table #4. I waited to say good night to Elaine, overheard Donald tell her that Table #14, in Siberia, the far side of paradise, back of the room, out of sight, there but not there, had complained about the service.

"Give the creep the check," she snapped, one tough broad. I recoiled at the mix -- acid and acuity. I gave her a peck on the cheek, she dismissed me from court, a curtsy came to mind, but I refrained.

"Come back precious," cajoled Donald, posturing like a peacock as we said the long goodbye. Of course I'd come back, I'd taken a big bite of the apple, had the night of nights and knew it, why not tomorrow? I might be able to drag along some friends. It wasn't cool to go alone, dammit.

We walked back to safe and staid Park Avenue. Seymour didn't kiss me good night, due to my erratic behavior I had no doubt we were going to be Platonic. I wondered whether to circle back, Vlad was so attractive, Elaine's a magnet. I had an early appointment at work. Saved.

I couldn't wait to see Dr. Goodman, my new chief confessor, distressed about flip flopping with Seymour and the sudden obsession over Vlad. He asked me to describe the process. "It's as if an Imp of the Perverse takes over and I become another person, do the wrong thing." This was the first time I'd articulated the Imp.

"You hear it then act against your better judgment." I blanked out.

"Ali?" His voice jolted me back.

"What did you say again?"

"A negative voice in your head -- internal dictator like Hitler runs you."

"How do you know?"

"No one else is there." I got it. "You'll learn to distinguish between the voice of reason and the destructive Imp of the Perverse, well named at that." I lost what he was saying again. Dr. Goodman changed the subject.

"Is Seymour a good guy?"

"Yes. Solid. Predictable."

"What about Vlad ?"

"Not sure."

"You know."

"Smooth operator."

"Why you like him."

"What do you mean?"

"It's all connected. When you don't love yourself, it feels bad to feel good. If someone loves you you reject him. Rejection is a more comfortable position." He'd hit a nerve. I stopped breathing.

"What are you thinking about?"

"Jordan, the man who sent me here, called me Scarlett because she scorned Rhett who loved her, yet was in love with Ashley who didn't." I told him the light switch went off when Jordan first told me he loved me, flashed on the many times I'd turned on him, still chasing Nick, the ultimate Mr. Unavailable, hung my head.

"We'll talk about this more." We would, again and again. I told him about the diamond tiara, being a princess. "How did it feel to be desired by those men at Elaine's, a chocolate cake everyone wanted a piece of?"

"Great."

"Because you're rich and famous?" I shook my head, no.

"Why then?"

"I'm bright and beautiful, at ease with a table of heavy hitters," shut my eyes as I said it, not a piece of cake. "I can talk with the best of them and I belong."

Three months later I'd lost thirty pounds, triumphant I'd made it. Atkins beamed as we reviewed my progress, a sometime rocky road, the low point when I 'plateaued' and had to cut portions. I followed a strict regimen of a two and a half ounce can of tuna for lunch, hidden away in the presentation room at S & G, almost starved, but lost four pounds the next week. Bob said maintenance would be tough. I had to weigh myself every day, if I gained more than three pounds, go back on phase one of his diet, meat, water and whipped cream. I walked out of his office light hearted, thin, if not skinny. Christmas parties next week, time to celebrate: size #8/10!

I skipped the four "Bs," headed straight to Ohrbach's, a boutique-like department store on 34th that advertised 'high fashion at low prices.' Now that I was spending my own money, I'd have to economize -- in style.

There was big publicity for the big day that Orhbach's launched their knock offs of the season's French designer clothes, one quarter the price of the originals. I wasn't willing to brave the crowds. On my maiden voyage two days later spied the perfect faux Chanel -- white jacket with red and blue braid trim and gold buttons. They were out of my size, dammit. A Mini winked at me -- super short black jersey dress with a white leather pointed collar, heard that Mary Quant, the hot London designer had named it after the Mini Cooper, the diminutive British car. I grabbed it and high tailed to the pantyhose section, stockings would not do. A package was open for inspection, 'Black opaque, Marks and Spencer', another British brand. I stuck a fist inside, thicker than stockings, ballet tights with feet. In a big open mirrored dressing room, with my own hook to hang hopefuls, I tried on a small. Encased like a sausage, I went to medium. The pantyhose made the Mini.

I ran back to the rack, got another pair in tan, wondered if they ran, bought a second black one in case. Expensive.

$6.50 reduced to $3.25, probably cost a pound in London. I thanked the lord, the queen and Ohrbachs' buyer. Goodbye girdles and garter belts, I'd burn them. Freedom.

Shoes had to be in the right proportion, the shorter the skirt the lower the heel. At least that's what I'd read in WWD. Baker's down the street had wide sizes, cheap prices. I narrowed it down to patent leather pumps with a little grosgrain bow in front, a French Louis heel or short black suede boots. Unsure which way to go, I took both.

The *Seventeen* magazine bash was sought after. 'Space reps' invited their favorite fashion women clients, agencies and advertisers to be wined and dined. Redhead Barry asked me to the gala aboard a private yacht, we'd circle around New York and the Statue of Liberty drink champagne. I couldn't wait to inaugurate my Mini. Wouldn't you know there was another aboard, worn by a blonde, hers even shorter than mine. In the fast moving fashion world you could only stay ahead of the curve a mini minute.

Stan Richardson, attractive and tall, wore a gold wedding ring yet talked me up. His family's company made well-tailored suits for women in sumptuous fabrics, the American Chanel: a classic box suit jacket paired with a straight skirt. I talked up S & G. He'd seen our ads, was impressed -- a potential client. Stan was going away for the holidays but promised to get in touch, have a drink, and talk business -- monkey business more like it.

I kept noticing the gal in the other Mini on the starboard side working the room – boat. We sized each other up. I made the first move. Becky was from Philly, a producer of TV commercials at DDB (Doyle, Dane Bernbach). I was jealous. Her agency was at the top of the creativity quake. The warhorses -- agencies like BBDO (Batten Barton Durstine & Osborn) and B & B (Benton and Bowles) who played it safe -- were at the bottom.

Salt and pepper, we became new best friends. Becky would say or do anything, the more outrageous the better. She got away with it by batting her big blues. We teamed up for the season, our mission to meet every important/talented/interesting V.I.P. in the business at the Christmas parties. A small industry, scuttlebutt rampant, we knew about the bigwigs and recognized their work in magazines, TV, and radio. The top guys competed like crazy for accounts, billing and recognition. Cut throat.

The best parties were all on the same day, the Thursday before Christmas. Becky had it all mapped out. Papert, Koenig, Lois, PKL was in the Seagram Building, a stark, bronze modernist shrine designed by Mies van der Rohe with interiors by Philip Johnson that had arisen on Park Avenue in '57 to forever change the landscape. Other glass boxes would follow, none would surpass. George Lois' colorful Esquire covers punctuated the stark white walls. A thug-like boxer Sonny Liston in a Santa hat, the December '63 issue pulled a punch. Magazine images once staid illustrations now jumped off the page. Lois led the charge. We shook hands with the big guy with big ideas -- one of the best in the business. He didn't have time for us no matter how cute we were. We moved on.

At the DDB office party on West 43rd, Becky introduced me to Helmut Krone, the art director who'd designed the mold breaking ad campaigns for the Volkswagon Beetle, 'Lemon' and 'Think Small'. Notorious for being turtle slow as he fretted over the right typeface, he ignored the freaked out 'suits' buzzing around his office. Clients were *their* problem, damn the deadline. A quiet man, like most artists, he didn't say much, but when he did cut to the chase. I treasured his measured words.

The mega-star copywriter Mary Wells turned heads in a flamboyant hat and the mandatory suit for a corporate exec. Hers was a Chanel. She ignored us -- small potatoes.

Howard Zieff, a jolly apple-cheeked photographer invited us to join him, happy to hang out. He'd shot Bill Bernbach's print campaign, "You don't have to be Jewish to love Levy's." An American Indian, Chinese man, choirboy, Italian mama, and Buster Keaton chomped on sandwiches in large subway posters all over town, putting a tiny Brooklyn bakery Levy's on the map, the apotheosis of rye.

We'd done it, had no dates after, "Let's go to Elaine's." I knew the ropes, could get us in, we had to eat to get a table.

Donald greeted us, "Hello precious." I kissed Elaine, introduced Becky who she seemed to like, thank God, pretty girls were valuable commodities for her 'boys.' She awarded us Table #2.

Nicola, a Napolitano, slight with a mischievous smile, waited on us, and flirted shamelessly. We ordered veal chops. Vlad sauntered by and invited us over to Table #4.

"Of course." We sat down at the big table. Elaine hunkered down next to me, sneered, hands on her hips in defiance, "My boobs are bigger than yours." It came out of nowhere -- her mood swings scary unpredictable. I hadn't realized we were in competition. I should have left, kept on drinking to allay my dread. As I swam in the shark tank while she eyed her next meal, I felt controlled by her approval or lack thereof. She pulled the strings, who'd sit with whom, who'd get the brass ring.

Much later that night, Elaine changed her tune, threw me a crumb, "You should have your own talk show." Push me-pull me. She was passive aggressive, unpredictable. I wanted desperately for her to like me, suspected she never would, wasn't one of the boys. Worse, I was a girl with big boobs and a brain. Threat? No, she had bigger fish to fry. So I hoped.

Nicola grabbed me on the way back from the ladies, "Go home with Vlad, he's great in bed." Speechless. What nerve! Becky left at some point, trashed. Donald and I went around the corner for a toke. Upon our return I couldn't stop looking at Vlad. As outrageous as it was, Nicola had planted the idea.

In the wee small hours flying, too drunk to go home, Elaine put me under Vlad's protection. I sort of remember getting into a cab with him, taking a long ride downtown. The wood and string sculptures in his walkup loft looked like wings. Beautiful. Ethereal. Too stoned for sex we went to sleep.

In the morning he was slow and sensual, knew how to kiss, touch. After we showered, had a cup of coffee, he started to make calls about his trip to St. Maartin for Christmas, felt unaccountably lonely as I overheard his plans. He was leaving and I was going nowhere. Fear crept in -- had I made a mistake? His phone rang at noon, early for a night owl. He shrugged and took the call. His face grew dark, "Yes Elaine, yes, Elaine, yes Elaine," he looked at me oddly. My parents had called her, frantic that I was missing and now the police were out looking for me. He didn't tell her I was there but told me I should get home. He, of course, was shocked that I was still living with my parents. I said goodbye, mortified, raced home to face Mother and Dad's wrath.

"Where have you been?" "How could you not come home?" "Why didn't you call?" No good answers, total disaster, Dr. Goodman out of town.

I holed up in my room, desperate to escape. I opened the travel section of the Times, spotted a super cheap flight and hotel package -- $250 for a week in a Dutch island somewhere in the Caribbean. I phoned a travel agent and booked it, limped through Christmas morning, took a plane late that day. Unsure where I was headed, anything was better than my blue room. Aruba the ugliest island in the world, was flat, no foliage -- they'd razed all the trees for paper. No wonder they practically gave the tickets away. At least I could play tennis on clay. I put on my whites, met a tennis player from Amsterdam, spent the rest of my time with Hans on the court, in bed or in the water.

Happy New Year in Dutch was "*Gelukkig Nieuwjaar.*" Unpronounceable. We had a fine time on a yacht gambling off shore. For a brief moment I thought of Jordan and wondered whom he was with, surprised when I felt a pang of jealousy. What was his sign? Maybe we weren't astrologically compatible -- remembered I rejected him because he loved me. I wondered where Nick was, which stratosphere.

Dr. Goodman and I had a Big Talk. I told him the Vlad story, confessed I was a wreck, "He's back and I haven't heard from him."

"You went home with a man at 3:30 in the morning who didn't ask you out or buy you dinner at a place where the owner isn't nice to you, knowing that your parents were going to worry and there would be hell to pay. Another one night stand. All you show men is a sex-starved little girl, relaxed in bed and anxious the rest of the time, not a mature, capable, intelligent woman, the kind that men marry. You scare them away."

"Don't say that."

"What do you want me to say? Everything's all right? You're responsible for your life and no one else. You don't listen or learn, want your recovery handed to you on a silver platter. You're lazy. If we're going to continue, you have to meet me half way. I can't do it for you." Was he quitting on me?

"What are you saying?"

"I want you to lay off men."

"What do you mean?"

"Just what I said. No sex until you can stop self-victimizing, waiting for calls that don't come from men you've fantasized relationships with. If you took longer to go to bed, you wouldn't feel so insecure. You'd know he really liked you and didn't just want sex. When you sleep with a man the same night you meet him, you have nothing to say to each other in the morning. You could wait forever, and he'll never call you again, unless he wants to get laid. Men want what they can't get, and after they get it, don't want it."

What would I do without men? What would I do without Dr. Goodman? A moment to decide, "Okay, you win. No men."

"On the contrary, you win." He threw another curve, "Time to move out from your parents' apartment." He was right. He wasn't done.

"Buy a vibrator." Were all shrinks in cahoots? This time I'd listen. What the hell, I might enjoy it.

Luckily an old high school friend needed a house sitter he could trust for his million-dollar modern art collection. Within two weeks I moved into a floor-through on 72nd between Park and Lexington. I didn't like the Warhol electric chair, but adored the Jim Dine bathrobe and the molded plastic Tom Wesselman nude that lit up when you plugged it in.

I found a drug store on the far West Side, wore sunglasses, snuck in and bought an electric contraption. A home companion not nearly as good as a man. Quantity replaced quality.

I threw myself into work, had a half a million dollars to play with, squeezed every last print ad out of the Crompton budget. Aldo, the Italian art director and Hope Bloom, the brainy cool (yes, Jewish) copywriter worked on a new campaign that would feature Crompton's cutter's garments on location. She'd later have her own agency built on brainstorming, write brainy books.

Ads were usually shot the safe way in studios, the lighting controlled, no elements to battle, the fashion showed off better. They rolled giant bolts of paper, different colors called no seam behind the model. A live setting would give Crompton an edge. They signed off on the idea. I'd produce seventy ads on location. And away we went.

Ellen loved Italian food, hated the snobbery of the five star French restaurants: Le Pavillion, La Côte Basque, La Caravelle, Lutèce or Le Grenouille. She preferred to leave them and their cream sauces to the Kennedys and Rockefellers. She adored Orsini's with its *dolce vita* on West 56th Street, a favorite hangout of movie stars and society people, more about the ritual than the food. The waiters wore formal attire, the walls red velvet. Muted crystal chandeliers and candlelight defined the decadent darkness perfect for a discreet rendezvous, in our case, a drunken business lunch. Outrageous prices -- $8.50 for ossobuco risotto -- didn't bother us a bit, armed as we were with expense accounts and American Express credit cards. Matinee idol handsome Armando Orsini kissed our hands, *"Bellas signorinas."*

We talked mostly about the affair she was having with the married president of Crompton. Holidays were a particularly sensitive time as she envisioned her lover together with his family in Connecticut. I would never go out with a married man. It was up to me to envision locations, cast, produce, style and sometimes write the ads. I brought up my crazy-like-a-fox ideas as she worked on her second martini and let her guard down.

"Let's shoot an ad at Elaine's, we can run it in the *Sunday Times Magazine*," I suggested one lunch. She bit. Next challenge was to get Elaine's permission. I did so after I quoted the paper's enormous circulation. No fool, she knew free publicity when she saw it. The full-page four-color ad featured a male model in a moss-green velveteen Bill Blass suit cozying up to Elaine, "Crompton is when you don't have to wait an hour for a table at Elaine's." I wrote it. Actually, it wrote itself.

Michael Aaron, our downstairs neighbor, owned Sherry Lehman, the finest wine store in New York. I approached him with a similar proposal -- the ad would run in the *New Yorker* his upscale audience. Antonio, a distinguished looking model wearing a flocked velvet jacket, inspected a bottle of Château Lafitte Rothschild, the best French wine according to Michael, the expert. He had mined it from the store's stellar wine cellar, born in Prohibition -- the former repository of The 21 Club's speakeasy booze.

True to his word, Stan Richardson, scion of the suit manufacturing family, called. I could earn a few Brownie points or even better, a bonus, if I could bring in a blue chip account, up the ante in the ad game, become a player rather than just a paid employee. We arranged to meet at Bemelman's Bar at The Carlyle, the tony hotel where President Kennedy had stayed after snubbing the Waldorf. Whimsical illustrations by Ludwig Bemelmans adorned the intimate, discreetly low-lit amber room. I was late. Stan sat hidden in a banquette where no one could see, a half-finished drink in front of him. Another Christmas Jew, he was married to -- what else, a *shiksa,* the trend, lived the suburban life in the sticks -- WASPy Darien, Connecticut. He had two kids and a Porsche, ran Richardson with his sister's husband. Two scotches later, homemade French potato chips for dinner, I was too smashed to broach business.

We began to meet weekly at the Carlyle with similar results. We sometimes listened to Hungarian war refugee

George Feyer tickle the ivories in the Café Carlyle. I never saw Stan sober, suspected he was an alcoholic although I'd never met one before, and worried every time he drove home. Convinced he had a death wish, I lent him *The Possessed* by Dostoevsky, which questioned whether man had the right to kill himself. Three months later he made a pass, "It would be neat if you came with me to Montreal for a hockey game." We'd fly home the next day. An attractive married man whose account I wanted, what would Mary Wells do? I didn't dare bring it up with Dr. Goodman. Of course he'd say, no. Becky thought I should go for it and tell him I wanted my own room. Great advice.

Montreal was beautiful, especially the old French quarter. We dined at the *magnifique* Le Paris and stayed at the businessman's favorite, Bonaventure Hotel. The Canadiens killed the Rangers in hockey and he didn't get me my own room, though he'd promised -- there was some screw up at the desk. I was screwed. No business was discussed and sex was tainted -- he was married and drunk. Lose lose.

On the awkward flight home he made plans for me to meet his partner for drinks at Trader Vic's, the latest 'in' place relocated underground in the Plaza from the Savoy Hilton, its old haven across the street, demolished to make way for the new GM building. Nothing lasted in New York. The 40-foot outrigger canoe Marlon Brando had manned in *Mutiny on the Bounty* was at the bottom of the stairs, authentic wood and stone carvings, bamboo, tikis -- a subterranean Polynesian paradise.

We drank Scorpions, a killer concoction that came with a gardenia on top. One was wonderful, two a knockout punch.

Jake turned on the charm, more conventionally handsome than Stan. I flirted back, knowing this wasn't the first time the competitive adrenaline seeking brother's-in-law had set their sights on the same woman. Married guys who acted single by day went home to their lawns, dogs, wives and 2.3 children by night, I knew exactly how Ellen felt after he left. Lonely.

The next hung over day they invited S and G to pitch their account. Marty, a silver- tongued straight shooter praised me. How did I do it? He should only know. Then he shot me down -- the client wanted 'principals' only to attend the first meeting. Richardson had cut me out. I was shocked, hadn't seen it coming. Betrayed. I walked out of Marty's office tail between my legs. In one second, triumph turned to defeat. Was it that I was a woman? Not part of the boys' club? Of course. Richardson could dress women but didn't want to do business with them. Stan had used me then tossed me away. I consoled myself that at least I'd get the account if they chose us. They did. I didn't -- not allowed access to Stan or Jake. No bonus, either.

The Possessed was still in his glove compartment, most likely unread, when Stan was found dead two years later, his Porsche wrapped around a telephone pole. Marty and I represented S & G at his funeral. As we paid our respects to his widow, I was fearful of eye contact a neon scarlet "A" blinking on my chest. I mourned secretly, shamed. Adulteress. Forgive me Lord and Stan's wife for I have sinned. Never again. As for you Stan, sorry you chose to go. Your right I suppose.

Mother called mid-March to invite me for dinner, back from a triumphant trip to Buenos Aires where Dad's relatives had treated them royally. They had a present for me. When I arrived on time at seven, she could barely wait to give it to me, but Dad arrived at 7:40, late as usual. He'd barely taken off his coat, hung up his hat when she thrust a big package wrapped with used Christmas paper, red and green bells at me. I opened the Bonwit Teller box, white with violets. As I took out the medium brown soft fur, Mother explained that nutria was an Argentine water rat warm as toast for my first fur coat.

I modeled it for them. Strange, the arms were four inches too short and I couldn't close the gold buttons. On automatic compliment pilot, I oohed and ahhed and made a big deal about it. "I don't deserve it," was how I ended my saccharine monologue. Mother didn't argue. "I can wear it with my black kid eight button gloves," I said. That would make up for the short sleeves. Mother folded it back into the box. I thanked them profusely for such a thoughtful, expensive gift. Who said I couldn't act?

I thought about it again on the way home, too small was too small. She hadn't asked me what I wanted. Didn't she remember that I hated brown? Always had. The style was boxy, the worst possible look for someone with broad shoulders and a big bust, made me look square. Oddly enough the nutria turned out to be a great gift.

My next session with Dr. Goodman was a dilly. I told him about the fur coat, overcome with guilt for being an ingrate. He asked such quick questions I didn't have time to think.

"Describe your mother."

"Small."

"How tall?"

"5' 2 ½. Size 6. Trim.

"What's her favorite color?"

"Brown."

"How would she look in the new fur coat she bought you?"

"Great."

"Are you telling me that your fashionable Mother with perfect taste bought you a coat that fits her, in her color and her style? Remember the Parisian dress that was two sizes too small? She's following the same pattern, not giving you a present, she's dressing herself."

I stopped breathing. He offered me the option of the couch. I took it. I couldn't look him in the eye.

"What's the first memory of your mother?"

"Jumping up and down on my bed in my bedroom when I was four or five, I touch the right side of my head in front of my ear, look at my finger see blood, must have hit my head on the edge of the windowsill. I look in the mirror in the bathroom, part my hair, a wound is bleeding, deathly afraid to tell Mother, she'll punish me for doing something wrong. She catches me dabbing at it with toilet paper. I cower. 'What have you done you stupid girl?'

"Is she still angry with you?"

What a question. I thought about it, whispered, "Yes." Tentative. Oh my God. "Always."

"Are you angry at her?" I fingered the dent above my right ear. "Of course not," hesitated, "I was when she and Dad stopped me from seeing Nick Rose." I'd filled him in on that trauma our first session still pissed off.

"Fear of your mother is an abnormal reaction. All of your problems spring from your relationship with her. It's toxic." The Enola Gay had dropped the atomic bomb. The Imp went nuclear, "How dare he suggest something's wrong with Mother." The voice of reason cut through the mushroom cloud, "He's right."

I raced back to work managing to drum the conversation out of my head with a Crompton casting call. Over the next days Dr. Goodman's comments kept sneaking back into my mind. I tried on the nutria again and again. Dr. G was right: it was Mother's size not mine. 'Abnormal reaction' was stuck in my head. Fear was *not* what most Mother's make their children feel. Love is.

I had to pull myself out of the doldrums, a rough patch, called Nick. His English answering service assured me he was out of town until further notice.

The next week I was invited to one of Jonathan Michaels's parties, a glorified mixer. His list was legendary -- Upper East Siders, socialites, Ivy Leaguers -- he knew everyone. You paid a nominal fee to go to a glamorous apartment or a cool restaurant and meet someone glamorous or cool. 'He' was standing at the top of the 25-foot high landing of a duplex in the Hotel des Artistes. We locked eyes. I watched him hurry down to meet me, excited. Andy had gone to Brown, a playwright. Another 'Indian,' he looked like me -- black hair and brown eyes -- or was it Dad? Sparks flew. I suggested Elaine's for our first date, she granted us

Table #2. I asked him up to see my art collection afterward. Against doctor's orders, I attempted to seduce him. Andy, a nice Jewish boy, retreated.

Dr. Goodman was adamant. "You can't come on like that, I know there's a good girl buried in that thick sexpot armor. Get to know Andy. Practice what it's like to have him desire you, make him prove he cares, pick when you're going to grant him your favors."

"It's a free society. You're too old-fashioned, the country is 'making love not war' and no one cares about the consequences."

"You're not cool enough to have a one night stand," Dr. Goodman countered. "You've spent painful days and tortured weeks waiting for phone calls from men that you've slept with the first night and never heard from again. Remember Vlad? He listed the others. Dr. Steel Trap Mind never forgot a thing. "You get emotionally attached to a man just because he puts his penis inside you when all it is for him is getting off. You're lucky Andy is a gentleman. What else do you know about him? Is he relationship material? I bet you don't know the answer. All you see is his outside. Andy is handsome but what about inside? Wait and see. Find out."

I resigned myself to follow the rules no matter that I didn't like or believe in them. Eight weeks into the relationship Andy had passed all the tests, with Dr. Goodman's permission, I finally allowed him to take me to bed in Peony, a guest cottage, more like a shack, on the ocean at the Cape. The challenge of waiting was compiled by fears I'd never have an orgasm again naturally since I'd overused my vibrator. It had shorted out with an electrical flash one particularly lonely night, a sign from God?

We made beautiful love in our cottage by the sea, charmed by our queen size, four poster, fluffy pillows, wainscoting, early American floral wallpaper and each other. The vibrator had not done me in. I was crazy about him, certain he reciprocated. We became an item.

Andy rented a fisherman's shack in Chilmark on Martha's Vineyard for the summer. He spent his early mornings writing, and worked from eleven to five at Poole's Fish Market in Menemsha. I told Dr. Goodman I wanted to suspend our sessions -- the insurance had run out. It was a white lie. The insurance had actually finished a month ago. I'd been paying since but now needed the money to commute to see Andy on weekends. Dr. Goodman asked if this had anything to do with our conversations about Mother, in our last session he'd likened my troubles and thorny relationship with her to that with Elaine, both put me in the victim position. I said no. He left the door open for the future.

Getting to the Vineyard weekends was expensive and iffy. The island's notorious fog put the flight in a small plane from La Guardia at risk. If I couldn't land on the island, I had to take a three-hour ferry ride from Wood's Hole to Vineyard Haven. Or I could ride a Greyhound bus for six hours, followed by that same forever ferry ride. Andy would pick me up in 'Alfalfa,' his midnight blue Alpha Romeo convertible. With the top down he'd drive us to Chilmark where we'd swim at Zack's Cliffs. Distracted at work, I waited for the weekend all week fantasizing about being a couple. Content to lead his life, I lost mine.

We went to Barbados for the Christmas holidays to visit his friend, Max Eastman, a lefty revolutionary who had switched to the right and become an influential editor at conservative *Reader's Digest.* A big bear with a shock of white hair, he had a speaking disability, his mind as sharp as a tack. His wife Yvette, married before to writer Theodor Dreiser, was kooky in a delightful way. Our romantic guest cottage sat on a white crescent beach next to the elegant Sandy Lane Hotel where Mom and Dad had vacationed over the years.

I overate at the extravagant buffets of the luxury hotels on the Platinum coast. We played word games; Max astounded us with his winning word "simoom", a hot dry North African wind, or so he told us. Without a dictionary, we had to trust him, gave him the points. When I got back to New York I discovered he was right. Andy and I swung in a hammock and made love by night; swam, snorkeled and played tennis by day. Paradise.

Three days before New Year's Eve, while skin diving for white sand dollars under the turquoise water of the Caribbean, Andy came up for air, took off his mask, beckoned me over.

"What's up?"

"This isn't working for me. I'm done." A bolt out of the blue, oh my God, did he really say that?

Shock waves rippled through my body, "What's wrong?"

"You're sucking my soul like Miriam in D. H. Lawrence's *Sons and Lovers,* he pronounced. He went on, I went out. "Forsaking your own identity, no life of your own, too needy… two different people in and out of bed." I only heard snippets of what he was saying, my head separated from my body.

"Offered a screenwriting job… moving to LA …" He'd decided, that was it. I should have paid attention to the signs -- I'd had to beg him to go to Barbados -- didn't want me to come, I'd talked him into it. He'd decided before we left. Andy's Virgo traits -- I looked him up -- logical, articulate, down-to-earth communicator, so endearing before now turned against me as he shut me out without sentimentality. Over was over, a done deal.

I'd been dumped, not good enough, what man could ever love me? I swam out a mile where I considered drowning myself but was too good a swimmer. Why did falling in love make me lose myself? Even Mother had commented, 'You're a different person when you're around men.' I supposed she meant I cozied up to them, was not myself, but rather a persona I thought they wanted me to be, acting as if they were the center of the universe.

I crawled back to Dr. Goodman, distraught.

"Exactly what did Andy say?"

"I was my own person in bed, confident and secure, but the rest of the time I sucked his soul."

"Could Andy be right?"

I hesitated. "Maybe." I steeled myself to ask the burning question, "Why?"

"Because your mother stole yours."

"What are you talking about," I gasped.

"She didn't do it on purpose; her mother stole hers." He was sympathetic, "Unfortunately, your mother can't love you or anyone else. She didn't get love so she can't give it. You've suffered the consequences."

"I don't understand." I felt my eyebrows knit together in a scowl of puzzlement.

"It's complicated. If a child doesn't get what I'll call unconditional love from her mother when she's very young, she takes it to heart, develops a defense mechanism to cope with rejection, takes a 180 degree dive: nothing's wrong with the mother she needs for survival, it's her fault she can't get love. To keep up this fiction she freezes -- buries her feelings. They contradict the truth. A toxic thought process -- what I call the voice, you call the Imp -- self-put-down-artist-in-residence replaces them." The Imp jumped to Mother's defense, "Liar. How dare he say that? Don't listen to this bullshit." I brushed it off intrigued.

"Frozen or buried feelings give birth to a black hole. The subsequent M.O. is that one runs on empty attempting to fill up a bottomless pit with booze, work or drugs, which all sound different but are really the same." He changed pronouns, brought it home, "You use food, a penis or Andy." I hadn't told him about pot. "You've heard the old joke, "At the moment of impact his life flashed before my eyes." I hadn't.

"You've suffered an identity loss and consequent low self-esteem except when you're in the water or bed, the only places you seem to have confidence as Andy noticed. Why is that?"

"I took a deep breath. I'd never thought of it before. "Sex is the only time - besides being in the water I ever feel happy. One hundred percent pure physical pleasure. Endless thrills. Filled. I can touch someone, be held, connected, feel something, out of my mind into my body in an existential state of the perfect now, no past or future."

"Invariably it heads south. You wait by the phone for the call that doesn't come, fixated on a one-night stand or a lovesick relationship in pain. As we've talked about before, you worship at the altar of rejection, need to feel bad to feel good, attracted to bad boys like Eric, who reinforce your negative image. The other side of the coin is you reject good guys like Jordan who love you for who you are -- too uncomfortable. Feeling good makes you feel bad. Another symptom of this syndrome is feeling empty -- loneliness. It drives you."

My entire belief system crashed around me, mile high waves with hurricane winds. I felt seasick, come for consolation -- poor me Andy had left me, a victim again. Instead, Mother was a soul thief and I had a black hole. It felt like the end of the world. I sat up from the couch, looked him in straight in the eye, "It's hard to believe that horrendous scenario."

"Don't despair. There's good news, you're not alone, I've treated others like you: it's an illness and there's a cure."

"Really?" A ray of hope shone on the bleak horizon.

"I can help you. You've had a slip with Andy that's cost six months, now you have to get to work." The Imp went to town, desperate, "This is preposterous. Get up and leave right now." The voice of reason broke through again, "He's right.' I knew it was one of those moments, a turning point, how I handled it would determine the rest of my life. I shut my eyes and crossed my heart. "All right Dr. Goodman I'm in." The Imp protested, "Wrong, wrong, wrong." I tattled on him to Dr. Goodman.

"What are you going to tell the Imp?"

"If you pardon the expression, fuck off."
"No men again, dig out the vibrator." I didn't object.

12

The Glass House

Fire Island shares avail.
Glass house. Davis Park area
Call eves TR 6 - 5343. Ed

I awakened the morning after the interview-party-to-get-a-share-in-the-Glass-House in my own bed hung over but triumphant. I'd managed to snag a share without sleeping with Ed, the guy in charge, prepared to lose the house rather than have sex with him. I looked in the mirror and imagined my diamond tiara sparkling the way it had that night at Elaine's. After I shared that moment with Dr. Goodman he'd suggested I put on the tiara when I felt proud of myself.

On the train ride to Patchogue I hid behind enormous black sunglasses, a straight black fall of real Italian hair, read the Friday *Times* on Saturday to catch up on all the movie reviews. The stale air of the Long Island Railroad was nauseating. I felt too ill to renew acquaintances with the people who nodded my way on the ferry ride to Davis Park, too apprehensive to get my usual hit from the sight and smell of the Great South Bay. Would I like the house? Was it the same one I'd fallen in love with years ago with Eric while exploring the beach?

"Taxi." No way was I going to walk all the way to Bayberry, a mile east of Ocean Ridge, my two suitcases filled with rocks.

"Hop in. We can't go until I fill up the jeep," said the driver who introduced himself as Fred.

Three other passengers hopped in. Fred drove us on a sand path that wound around the wooden walks of Ocean Ridge, abruptly cut through scrub pine and holly. We arrived at Bayberry Dunes a narrow sand spit that sloped up high ocean dunes, the boardwalks a triumph over poison ivy. Mr. Miller must have been working overtime as there were Hobby houses everywhere. Some spectacular modern homes dotted the stark landscape, one of them a cantilevered 'Japanese House' where we left off the trio. We arrived at the Glass House a minute later.

"Close as I can get you."

It *was* the same one. Hooray! I paid Fred, hugged him, feasted my eyes on a symphony of glass and wood, squares and rectangles suspended in space on the dunes. Spectacular. Mine. I started to lug my bags up the boardwalk.

"Hey, need some help?"

I turned to locate the voice. There were two octagonal fort-like houses, mama and baby surrounded by a stockade next to the Glass House.

"Here I am. Up here." A man waved from the top deck of mama. "Hang in, I'll come down." I waited. "What's *your* name," he asked.

"Ali. Who are *you*?"

"Tony," he said. "Have a hit." He handed me the joint he'd been working on. I took a toke handed it back.

"Take another. There's plenty more."

"Thanks." I took another.

"Where are you headed?"

"The Glass House."

"Guesting?"

"I have a share."

"Cool. We're neighbors." He carried my bags up the boardwalk. As we pushed through pine brush, I was surprised to see a small two story house hidden on the left, the guesthouse that Ed described, 'Sal lives in the Glass House. You'll sleep in the guesthouse. No electricity but gas lights in the johns, candles and kerosene lamps in the four bedrooms.'

"Thanks."

He dropped my bags. "Come by later." I watched him wend his way back to his house. Portly not handsome -- certainly not for me but interesting -- a gentleman.

Clothes and suitcases in every room, I left my bags outside, walked up to the main house. Sal greeted me at the door. A Gauguin look alike he had shiny black hair, full moustache, aquiline nose, about 5' 5". When I'd met him at Ed's party, I hadn't realized he was so short -- on a barstool, his presence large.

The kitchen was cooking heaven. Butcher board counters abounded, two spotless stainless steel sinks shone. A stairway led upstairs. "Mind if I take a look?"

"Yours, too."

I climbed the stairs to the glass living room, Sal followed. Three views, the beach and ocean left; Tony's houses and the dunes center; Bayberry, the Great South Bay and the mainland to the right. Breathtaking. An enormous built-in wooden couch with matching square chairs, caramel leather cushions glass coffee table in between. The architect-owner Ed Knoll had done the modernists proud. Less *was* more, the view the decoration.

I slid the glass door open to an enormous deck that jutted out over the dunes. Strong, harsh light illuminated the scrub pines, glimmering dunes and glistening ocean, calm and flat, bay-like.

Sal's laidback tour -- he hadn't said a word yet, continued up the stairs. His dressing room/bath had an oversized sunken tub. A king size bed was built into the only wooden wall of the bedroom, the other three glass; pale sea foam sheets and pillowcases matched the drapes. You could pull them together if you wanted privacy at night -- from seagulls and sandpipers? I imagined what it would be like lit by starlight.

"This yours?"

"Uh huh."

"Wow." Sweet dreams and great sex. I promised myself I'd get my chance in that bed.

"More."

I followed him as he climbed to the top of the house, a moon deck with a 360 view, "So this is heaven."

"Fynurgic."

"What?" I thought I'd heard wrong. He repeated the same word.

"Right." This was the first time I'd noticed Sal's quirky vocabulary of made up words with specific private meanings. A film editor in advertising, he worked on thirty or sixty second spots, listened to sound tracks sped up, run backward or forward all day. Strangely, I sort of understood what he meant. I liked Sal, the little king of the glass house.

"Find a room?"

"There seem to be clothes in all of them."

"Pick any empty bed except for the room with two mattresses together on the floor. That's Ed, Katinka and Finnstick's."

"Finnstick?"

"See that dog on the beach? It's Katinka's dog. Finn for Finnish, stick -- he's a retriever," one of the rare times he explained.

"Got it." A private path led from the house down to the beach. The dunes towered forty feet high covered by beach grass, beach plums and wild roses. Sea gulls circled above squawking, sandpipers skittered. A few brave souls were sun bathing, one bare-breasted woman wore Rudi Gernreich's black topless bathing suit, two years old and still shocking.

Sal and I walked east. There was a special feeling about Bayberry -- endless white beach, no signs of life, the land uninhabited, a last outpost -- my island primeval. I thought about Indians gathering seashells for wampum, just the purple part, and pirates, 'wreckers' building bonfires to attract ships, attacking. There could be buried treasure where I was standing.

"Hello ocean I'm back." I put my toes in the water. Brrr. Freezing. Hard to believe I used to get in every Memorial Day. On the way back, we spied Al with my housemates in front of the Glass House. I was introduced but felt left out, they all knew each other, same feeling I'd had the first day at camp or at school, should have brought a date. Help.

"Hi Mom. I'm lonely. Can I come home?"

"Sure, dear. Just take a beach taxi. We'll pay. I made your favorite lamb stew for dinner." Knee jerk reaction, I caught myself on the fantasy express calling for comfort that had never existed in real life. Mother always packed or pulled a punch. The voice of reason, a recent entry to my psyche, pointed out that this was an opportunity to make some new friends. "I could do it."

"Do you like to cook," asked one of the girls. I came back down to earth.

"I make a *great* omelet..." Reality check: I hated the art and act. Shopping was exhausting, bored by chopping, I ate along the way full before I served. Instead I bought whole cooked chickens from the deli, or went out to eat, a chronic feast or famine situation. I associated being in the kitchen with being upset. Mother had kept me out of *her* domain, denied me the pleasure of cooking, allowed me just the drudgery of cleaning up. The voice of reason suggested I should go to cooking school. The Imp retorted, "You've got to be kidding."

"We're having a major meal tonight."

"I'd love to help."

"Sure. Delighted. Later." Scotty was in shape, California, blonde, yoga teacher. "Which room are you in?"

"Not sure."

"You'll have to bunk with Bobby, it's the last free bed. Don't worry, he's harmless."

Why had I paid five hundred bucks to share a room with a strange man? If I hadn't been out so late last night I would've gotten up earlier, made the first boat and could've had my choice of rooms and roommates. The Imp was a poisonous spoiler. I cut off his head put on my happy head, forgot 'if', along with 'would've', 'could've', 'should've'.

Mighty were the dinner preparations, chopping, cleaning, marinating, a co-creation and major production. We were going to be twelve. Everyone had a course or chore assigned. Bobby, my roommate-to-be, and I had to unbeard and clean at least a million mussels. He was funny, knew his musical comedy and could sing any tune or show, including intros. We tried to stump each other. One person began, the other had to finish, tell where it came from, who'd sung it.

Within an hour in between songs we became friends. An advertising copywriter at BBDO, "they play it safe but the paychecks keep on coming." He knew Sal "from the business," but never heard of S & G and didn't know from fashion. Bobby told me his life story -- a blimp once, he'd lost a hundred pounds. His parents owned the Shubert Theatre in New Haven hence his encyclopedic knowledge of shows. We compared diets: Dr. Atkins, a winner; Metrecal, a canned diet drink that tasted like chalk a loser; Slenderella's slimming machines an ineffective rip off. The Park Avenue Starvation Special was a dangerous diet of five hundred calories a day and an injection of pregnant women's placenta three times a week. I'd lost fifteen pounds fast on that one. I'd also fainted.

"What worries me the most is pot," I confided. "All I have to do is look at a joint and I gain five pounds. I'll eat anything. Anything. And too much." I remembered last night's munchie attack and groaned. Confronted with calamity, the usual nothing in the icebox, I'd improvised and made an open sandwich of sliced onion with a leftover packet of hot Chinese mustard on a Saltine. I'd finished off the box.

"That's why me don't smoke," he was emphatic.

"I couldn't give it up for anything," truer than I wanted to believe. I never smoked at work but… every night. It made me feel happy and relaxed, which were precious commodities in short supply without it. "Do you know what fynurgic or something like that means?" He shook his head.

"Do you know any of the other people in the house?"

Bobby lifted up his shoulders, hands, eyebrows looked up at the ceiling.

"What about the house next door?"

"Which one?"

"The one that looks like an octagon."

"You mean Tony's house?"

"Right."

"I met him once, big deal in the music business, some kind of a producer or a promoter, rock 'n' roll all the way." Nothing wrong with that in my book.

When everything was prepped, Sal, who'd been in absentia, graced us in the kitchen, "Coming to the sixish?"

My fall was secured by a turquoise beaded headband, an authentic black and white squash blossom American Indian necklace around my neck over my Irish knit turtleneck (it got chilly at night), and white bell bottoms, scored from the Army Navy store. Finally fashion had come my way, hip to dress ethnic, eclectic, look like an Indian. I traded my circle pin in for hoop earrings. Bye, bye, Ivy.

We left the house en masse, glasses and joints in hand. Tony the pied piper of Bayberry playing gourds strung around his neck led his troupe of strolling musicians -- a man with a recorder and a drummer on bongo -- down the boardwalk. We picked up more people as we puffed on joints, sipped drinks and wended our way to wherever. Forty or fifty people milled around a Hobby House near the bay. Everyone knew Sal.

"Hi Sal. We took the Grey House this year."

"Did you hear that Bob Dylan took the beach house two down from yours?"

He nodded, would respect Dylan's privacy, leave him in peace. Sal stayed aloof -- we had the killer house, people would expect invitations if he didn't keep his distance. Groups of housemates stood together like a bunch of unsharpened pencils, rubber bands around them, everyone in their twenties en route to never growing up. A portable radio blared, "Seventy seven W A Beatle C." Sex, drugs and rock 'n roll forever.

Where was Sal? So short I couldn't see him, Bobby had vanished. The Imp and I wrestled as I pushed back against my new kid on the block paranoia. “You’re wrong. I’m going to have fun.” There was no payoff in pessimism.

“What’s the matter?”

“Oh, Tony, I’m…”

“Not used to being ignored, and don’t know anyone to talk to.”

“How did you guess?

“Because this community is tight like a fraternity house.”

“I’ve failed, no one’s asked me to pledge.”

“How’d you like to get pinned?”

“No one ever asked me before.” Half-hearted response, wasn’t sure I wanted to play his game, men still off limits. Something about him was seductive.

“Really (reeel eeee),” he milked the word, “a hot chick like you?”

“What’s the name of the fraternity?”

“Do you always answer a question with a question?”

“A lawyer’s trick I got from my Dad.”

“You’ve had time enough...what’s the answer? Or do you want me to repeat the question?”

“Well…”

“Indecisive, too, I see.”

How did he know me so quickly? Was I transparent? Throughout this brief interchange I’d stared into his eyes trying to discover their color, one moment green sea glass, the next amber. Whichever, he was interesting, sensitive and perceptive.

“Yes.”

"Does that mean yes, you'll get pinned or yes, you're indecisive."

"You know what I mean."

Tony took my hand, maneuvered me out of the crowd led me to the end of the walk and the bay where we could watch the setting sun. He kissed me slowly on the lips.

"We're pinned. Got it?"

"Yes, Tony." His eyes were gray green with yellow sparklers that reflected the sunset.

"Now I have to get my guests and date back home otherwise my dinner is going to be ruined." He looked to see how I took this piece of information, immediately quelled my jealousy attack, "She's an old friend and I don't want to hurt her feelings."

Sal and my housemates were leaving the disbanding sixish. Bobby waved.

"Don't forget our deal. Hang with us any time. Hey, what's your New York number?" Tony had a pen and small pad in leather, organized.

I caught up with Sal. "Have the Grillicsteins? Grillics and grunyons?" No idea what he meant but I felt welcome.

Dinner at ten by candlelight was an event to rival a King Henry the Eighth banquet. Sal came downstairs and motioned us to come up. "The eating factor," was all he said.

"I think that means dinner, don't you?"

A long polished amber wood refectory table lined with benches and throne like chairs at each end stood mid level between the kitchen and living room. I'd volunteered for table setting -- twelve pewter water glasses, crystal wine glasses, white Arabia plates, carafes of red and white wine at each end. Glass candlesticks with white candles and a dozen votives flickered, illuminating pale pink wild roses in small bud vases, a triumphant find at the risk of poison ivy. I'd added white clamshells as ashtrays, looked gorgeous if I had to say so myself. Sal and Ed sat on the thrones. I was between Bobby and Ned, a tall, attractive friend of Sal's who was just visiting like in Monopoly.

"A toast." Everyone raised glasses.

Sal first, "Here's to the Glass House, great summer, the last eight." Short, sweet, and slightly odd.

Ed next. "I'd like to drink to Sal for putting us all together, to Katinka, Finnstick and the summer of '66."

"Bobby stood, "Here's to the chef and dinner production crew. May we eat, drink, and be merry all summer."

"Your turn, Ali."

"To the most beautiful house I've ever seen and getting to know you all."

Bobby began to sing 'Getting To Know You', from *The King and I.* Ned from Nebraska joined in, as did the rest of the table. The ice was broken.

During seconds, I remembered to ask, "Sal, what did your toast mean? Something about eight years."

"The Krill Factor."

"What?"

"Bayberry's dead." Sal drew his finger across his throat."

"I don't understand."

Ed explained, "When Fire Island was made part of the National Seashore two years ago, Bayberry wasn't on the map, so it didn't make it, now considered to be a condemned community. Homeowners had to choose between half the estimated value of their houses immediately or the use of their houses for the next ten years, no remuneration, at which point the feds will take possession. Ed Knoll chose the latter."

"You mean it's all over for Bayberry in eight years?"

Sal quietly added, "Mounties."

"Sal means that federal troopers will live here," elucidated Ed.

I pictured a Mountie on his horse, red jacket and hat, dogs panting by his side on the beach in front of the Glass House singing a Sigmund Romberg song. Out of the corner of my eye I noticed Scotty starting to clear, my cue. The unwritten rule in housemanship was that when you don't cook, you clean. Bobby and I did the dishes, a convenient excuse for the continuation of our musical comedy song-a-thon. Ned, a 6'4" tall drink of water, hailed from some obscure state like Idaho or Nebraska, wore a WASP uniform. Madras Bermudas, button down shirt, red blazer, loafers without socks were as anachronistic as his crew cut Everyone else had long hair, jeans, tee shirts, barefeet. Hip was in, preppy out.

Ned suggested, "Let's do *Music Man.*" After we finished 'Seventy Six Trombones' and 'Marian the Librarian', he decided to sing Robert Preston's patter song, 'River City.' A booming baritone, he started over and over, stuck after the first three lines, couldn't remember the rest for his life.

"Sorry, folks, I've blown it. Anyone know the rest?" The party had moved up to the living room where after dinner joints, coffee and brandy were in progress. No one replied.

"Looks like Ned got hung up in River City," cracked Bobby.

"Ned, it will come to you, I promise." I tried to soothe him.

"I know the song backwards and forwards, performed it in summer stock," swore Ned.

"Tomorrow or in the middle of the night you'll have a blinding flash," Bobby rolled his eyes signaling for us to move upstairs. "I, for one, need a brandy as a reward for dishpan hands."

The door to the house slid open, a new arrival. A short, mustachioed, English-looking man appeared.

"It's Miles," Bobby whispered, "He's a *schnorrer,*" an after dinner regular, he came in like a dog for the leftovers. Sal indulged him.

"You guys must be finishing up."

"Make him a plate." The word came down from on high.

"Sure thing Sal," mumbled Bobby, unwrapping dishes he'd just put in the fridge. Ned and I went to the deck, brandies in hand.

"What do you do in real life, Ali? Don't tell me, you're independently wealthy and don't have to work."

"Whatever gave you that impression?"

"You're a rich bitch playgirl type. Jet setter."

"You're wrong. I work hard." Did I ever.

"Executive secretary?"

"No. Executive."

"No prissy old maid look? Horn rimmed glasses? You're joshing me, not the type."

"That's an insult," I exploded. "I happen to be an account executive, fashion coordinator, and casting director."

I defended my turf vehemently secretly fearing that I was losing it. I'd been worried about my next career move; the way S & G had treated me on the Richardson account rankled. The reality was clear: I was at a dead end. They weren't going to let me advance to Go.

"Don't be that way, beautiful." He tried to put his arm around me. I pushed him away. "Relax. They don't grow women with ambition like that in Nebraska. You should be married with a few kids."

"The next thing you'll do is to accuse me of being a dyke."

"I wouldn't be making a pass at you if I thought that, would I?"

"Thanks for the vote of confidence. Now why don't you go back to River City or where ever you come from and leave me alone?"

Ned skulked back into the house. I burst into stoned tears. Provincial asshole, what right did he have to say all that men's roles versus women's stuff then put moves on me? What would Dr. Goodman say? "What do you expect when you come on so strong. Drinking too much. Laughing too hard. You look like you're an easy lay out for a good time. You should project calmness, give the impression you'd be a good wife and mother -- that's what men want, who they marry." I was getting it finally, at least in theory.

I imagined Billy's take, "I only like sweet young vapid, soulless models who spend all their time looking beautiful and adoring me, don't threaten, try to run the show, or dominate. You're much too strong willed.'

What about Dad? "You're not married, no grandchildren."

I was half flower child, half businesswoman, total rebel, straddling two generations, blowin' in the wind. Maybe Dad hadn't noticed. Dr. Goodman had, "You've never said a word about your father."

"What's there to talk about?"

"Hey there, you with the stars in your eyes," sang Bobby from *The Pajama Game.*

"Are you talking to me?" I replied with the line from the song.

"Come on in," said Bobby. "Ned just remembered the rest of 'River City'."

Everyone drifted off to bed leaving Sal and me alone as we drank brandy and smoked a last joint.

"Would you like to take a walk?"

A euphemism for another four-letter word, I liked Sal, didn't want to screw up the summer by making it with him, wanted to be friends. "No thanks, I'm tired."

Bob and I slept in the same room in our 'harmless' separate beds. My diamond tiara sparkled. In heaven.

13

A Piece of Cake

"This is the best trip to the beach I've ever had, wish it would go on forever." Tony and I sat in a luxurious black stretch limo, partitioned off from the driver and the world by tinted windows. We drank champagne from frosted flutes, smoked one of Tony's milder joints, and listened to the latest Beatles album, *Revolver*, an advance copy from England, on his earphones knocked out by 'Good Day Sunshine' and 'Eleanor Rigby'. He asked if I preferred the Stones' latest 'Paint It, Black.' No contest. Why did men go for the Stones? I liked but didn't love them, too gritty compared to the Beatles whose words I could remember and music was melodic. A gracious host, Tony deferred.

"We'll be there...."

"What?" He motioned for me to take off my headphones, put the rear speakers on with the Beach Boys latest, 'Good Vibrations.'

"We'll be at Fort Bliss," his house, "in a half hour."

"So fast?"

"Ten minutes to the dock, ten by water taxi, ten by beach taxi."

"You know what I like about you the best?"

"What?"

"Your style."

He brushed off the compliment. "If the weather's good Sunday night we'll fly back by seaplane. Primo."

I was and wasn't looking forward to spending the weekend. When Tony called on Monday and asked me out, unsure of my next step due to the lack of chemistry and my deal with Dr. Goodman, I put him off till my next session.

"Why not have a practice relationship," Dr. Goodman surprised me by saying. "It's been six months. Make sure you have your own room, it'll give you the upper hand."

"What if Tony doesn't want me to come if he can't sleep with me?"

"You'll find out ahead of time that all he wants is sex. If you feel uncomfortable, go back to your house."

Dr. Goodman told me to practice. All right I would. When Tony called for an answer, I asked, "Do you have room for me?" I meant a room for me.

"No problem." I hoped he understood.

He picked me up in the stretch where I now lounged in comfort. "Who are you? Tell me everything."

"I'm from the Grand Concourse and Little Italy, via Brooklyn. Jewish mother, Italian father. I'm a Wike. Half Wop. Half Kike." A mixed bag, two different religions and cultures wrestled for territory on the map of his face, "To neeee. A lot of my friends are crazy mixed up combos." Jordan was half WASP half Jew. Where was he? "Two different types breed an exotic variation," certainly true about Jordan.

"You have the whole weekend to figure me out. No secrets. I've been separated from my wife for two years, in the process of getting a divorce. She lives in Woodstock with my three kids. I have them summers. They arrived with their nanny this morning and know you're coming. The rest of the guests will be here tomorrow on the ten o'clock ferry. Tonight's family."

I gave Tony a hand with the groceries: ten food cartons, three soft drink cartons, two cases of wine, a carton of hard stuff. People tended to overbuy on the isolated island. 'In case' psychology ruled: in case we stay until Monday; in case there are extra guests. Tony had bought enough food in case we stayed for the rest of the summer.

"Planning a party?"

"You never know. No such thing as too much." After we put everything away, Tony asked if I wanted to take a swim.

"Where can I change?"

"I put your bags in the bedroom to the left of the master bedroom, downstairs." An upside down octagon, the living room commanded the top floor and views, bedrooms and baths below. I breathed a sigh of relief, changed into a black bikini, "I'm going in your pool, Tony," the first I'd seen on Fire Island.

"Deep end towards the Glass House." I did a few laps. Salt water. Sweet.

"You didn't tell me you were related to a fish."

"Lots of things you don't know."

"I'm hip, looking forward to finding out."

"Dad. Dad." Tony's kids scampered into the water. Their nanny took a break, went to the house. He introduced me. They were ten, eight and five. Adorable.

The evening was uneventful, never bored by Tony. Not turned on either. He didn't make a pass, just a goodnight kiss. So far so good, I relaxed.

"Morning. Sleep well?" Tony knocked, outside the door.

"Mmm."

"Breakfast's ready."

I put on my white bikini, turquoise and white pareu, ran upstairs.

Fort Bliss was the opposite of the Glass House, or Grass House, as we fondly referred to it -- dark window seats with plump pillows, French provincial.

"Is this spread just for us?"

"You're not one of those coffee and juice only people are you?"

"Of course not. I love to eat. Can't you tell?"

Tony deftly plunged the coffee down into the glass pot, captured the bagels from the toaster oven -- he had his own generator -- at the perfect golden brown moment, put a fresh red Western bandana in a straw basket, arranged the bagels, covered them, tied the ends. "Breakfast's ready kids."

We devoured prosciutto and melon, lox and bagels, Italian bread with provolone, scrambled eggs with green peppers, tomatoes and onions, Italian sausage and kippers. "You're going to have to roll me to the beach."

"Another Bloody Mary? More coffee?"

"Have you ever thought about opening up a restaurant?"

"Of course. After we go gold again, platinum better." Three of Tony's gold records hung prominently in the living room in glass cases. He *was* a big deal in the music business.

"Tony, we're here." A couple trooped in.

"Welcome to Fort Bliss. Just in time for breakfast. This is Ali, she's slumming from the Glass House." He introduced, a light skinned black man in a Hawaiian shirt and his sweet, shy, smiley blonde girlfriend Lizbeth.

"What's shaking?" asked Garfield.

"I figure we take the Sailfish out on the bay."

"Yeah man, far out, I was thinking that myself, brought a few poles and reels for some serious fishing."

"Right on. There's squid in the fridge unless you're doing a lure routine. We haven't forgotten you girls. There's sun bathing by the pool or on the beach, water volleyball later, I brought a net." Tony defined host. He'd anticipated everyone's weekend fantasies, indulged us with the perfect equipment.

"Can we go sailing, too, Dad?"

"Natch."

"Can I go fishing with you, Garfield?"

"You got it Jolie." The kids were included. "As for you, brown skinned girl, I have something special which I shall soon reveal."

"What, Tony?"

"Later." I hated waiting, positioned the chaise by the pool at the precise angle to ensure maximum sun exposure, picked up my homework, a week's worth of back copies of

Women's Wear Daily, and carefully held the paper down so as not to block the sun.

"You need a periscope," Tony interrupted my train of thought. "Aren't you afraid you're going to ruin your eyes?"

"No, I like the challenge."

"What's happening in the fashion world?"

"More Mini skirts, psychedelic prints, boxy shapes and what's my surprise?"

"A piece of cake."

"Do you mean that literally or figuratively?"

"Both."

"Thanks for shedding so much light on the subject."

"I don't mean to tease you but sometimes you act so naive. It's hash baked into a fruitcake." Ugh, those gummy pieces of plastic, "We did it last weekend. Far out."

"It's not LSD is it?" I felt suspicious, heard of some cases where people who'd done LSD landed in the hospital.

"No, it's exactly what I said, hash."

"How much time does it take to work?"

"An hour," so much for instant gratification.

"How long does it last?"

"Depends on your metabolism. Two or three hours, tops four."

"Any weird side effects?"

"Garfield and I jammed like crazy."

"Do you really think I should try it?" Why was I making Tony the decision maker?

"Doesn't matter. Don't care if you do or don't," what a salesman, the ball back in my court, "You'll enjoy it, beautiful flower child." I was a play toy to him. He'd never asked about my job. "You've smoked hash, haven't you?"

"Once in Torremolinos. They didn't have grass." I'd fainted, vowed never to do it again. In spite of the red flag warning that there could be stormy seas ahead, I listened to the Imp who assured me that there was nothing to lose.

"I'll try it."

"Come to the kitchen."

Tony unwrapped a large round fruitcake from silver foil, one fourth gone, sliced a slender piece, put it on a blue and white striped plate, and gave me a silver fork and red bandana napkin. We sat on the bar stools. "What time is it?" I asked, for some reason wanting to keep track.

"Ten fifteen."

"Let them eat cake." I ate slowly, small pieces. What would happen? How would it make me feel? I ran down the other drugs I'd tried.

Mescaline: A winner. Acapulco. I rolled down a grassy hill, took off my clothes, swam in a pool au naturel.

Peyote: The Vineyard. Disgusting. Couldn't keep it down long enough to get high.

Poppers. Del Ray Beach, Florida, nothing else to do there but flirt with lifeguards. I'd fainted, never again.

LSD: No way. I was chicken. What if I had a bad trip?

Cocaine: Twice. Disastrous results both times -- diarrhea of the mouth, no sleep, sick after.

Hard drugs: No interest.

Pills: Uppers and downers, on one diet or another, during exams, with Dr. Blatt, a pill popper. Thorazine. Seconal.

Dexamil. Dr. Goodman didn't believe in them. I didn't sneak. Once in a blue moon I talked him into some Valium for the occasional bout of insomnia, yellows, five milligrams.

"Where should I wait," I had a strange sense of anticipation, wanted to be in the right place.

"Let's hang at the pool." Perfect. Water was safe.

"What time is it?"

"Ten forty five." Bored, nothing was happening, time not on my side.

"What time is it now?"

"Eleven fifteen."

I didn't feel any different, too big a breakfast, maybe I hadn't eaten enough cake. Disappointed, I excused myself, snuck upstairs to the kitchen, cut a hefty piece, wolfed it down, rewrapped the cake careful to hide my gluttony; slunk down to the pool. I dove in at the deep end and swam to the bottom -- rough, like coarse sand paper, pushed off. Ouch. My toe throbbed. I surfaced.

"Did you hurt yourself?" Tony sounded alarmed.

"Why?"

"There's blood in the water. Let's have a look."

"No." Defensive.

"Swim to the other end. Try the steps."

A jellyfish, no coordination or motor control, "Can't."

"Hang in." Tony had to help me out. I sat down on the chaise my right big toenail dislodged, and watched the blood flow.

"Take me back to that red river valley. Pretty, pretty red. Better red than dead?"

"Wait here. I'll be right back, going to get the first aid kit."

"Going, going, gone?"

"Don't move. Nothing serious. You've almost lost your big toenail."

"Okay, get lost. We're a lost generation. Lost in the stars."

"I've stopped the bleeding and taped the nail. How do you feel?"

"Ask me how do I feel. Funny."

"It's the hash. Go with it."

"Another piece. We want more. Ate it. One it. Two it. Three it. Four it. Five it. Six it. Seven it. Eight it."

"I see."

"I see said the blind man. Sun too bright. Put out light."

"Sure. Let's go up to the living room. Put your hand on my shoulder."

"Put your head on my shoulder."

"Why don't you lie down on these pillows? You can look out the window and watch the ocean. I'll be back."

So long for a while. Bye bye love. Be happy go Lucky, go Lucky Strike today. Terrible taste. Fillings. Metallic. Metal mouth. Hate dentists. Nightmares. Teeth fall out. Crumble. Dry mouth. Drink me. Open icebox door, door, door. Coffee tea or milk? Nice glass of mother's milk? Premature. See you later incubator. Breast fed year. Sucked thumb. Overbite. Space. Braces. Silver smile. Retainer. Bad taste. Won't go away. Eat. Leftovers. Peanut butter? Cookies? Nothing helps. Eat more. Drink more. Can you stop this? Can you top this? Come down. Calm down. Second piece. Sloppy seconds. Second place. Who's on first? Yogi Berra. Yogis lie down on nails in mouth.

"How ya doing? Laying out I see. You look nice and cozy. Where's everyone. What's happening? You all right?"

"Who you?"

"Garfield. Remember?"

"Me iron jaw. Hurt toe. Locked jaw."

"Do you mean lockjaw? Step on a rusty nail?"

"No. Cake."

"I made the cake. Scored a hundred dollars worth of hash and brought it to Tony last weekend as a house present. Everyone did it. We laid out like crazy."

"Nuts, mental, cuckoo, cuckoo."

"Let me give you a kiss to make it better, sexy." Bad breath, wash out mouth wash.

"Poor baby." Hand on shoulder.

"No. No. Let me go. Go away. Don't touch merchandise."

"Chill, I got an old lady. Man Tony has one crazy chick on his hands. Want some advice? Stay cool."

Mirror, mirror on the wall, who's the sexiest of them all? Oh Marilyn, poor Marilyn, someone's hung you in the closet and I'm feeling so sad. Done in. Whodunit? Paid with your life. Happy birthday, Mr. President. Poor Kennedy.

"How's it going?"

"Do something, Tony. Bad trip. Want to come down. Head won't stop. I want to get off."

"Don't worry, it can't last, promise."

"Nails in mouth three hours."

"A joint will mellow you out. Take a hit."

"Don't leave, scared."

"Take another toke."

"Antidote? Need antidope. 'The lady is a dope.' Overate. Feel rotten. Glutton."

"Put on my headphones, chill and I'll be back in a little while."

Tapping me? Some new guy, when you see a guy… "What's shaking sister?"

"Sick. Tripping. Wasted."

"Can I help?" Enemy? Touch me? Go away. "*Va via subito. Poussa via cafone.*"

"I don't speak Italian can tell there's no welcome mat here. Jeez, I was only trying to help. Man you're uptight." Good riddance to bad rubbish. Alone. Decadent. Decadenzia. Inside out. Wasted. Drugged out. What time? Howdy Doody time.

"We're going to have dinner now. Want to join us?"

"No, no, Nanette." Need air. Bad vibes. The party's over.

Dr. Goodman's words penetrated the fog, 'If you're in trouble go to the Glass House.' I did the zombie.

"Hungry? Join us," Sal nice.

"Stoned. Sick. Tony's hash cake bad trip, see you next fall."

"You're fucked up. Shame nice girl like you rich, good family. Tony's a bad guy, why?"

"Whirly birds."

"Lie down. My room's safe."

He led me to his bed. I crashed.

Two enormous blue lips appeared on the horizon laughed crazily, threatened, "I'll huff and I'll puff and I'll blow your house down." The lips morphed into a Magritte rose with a teardrop that changed to a drop of blood. The petals started to bleed. Torrents. I began to drown in the bloody waves. I started to cry. Would I ever come down?

I crept to the hall in the dark, spied Sal, Bob and two girls downstairs. I sat on the landing, overheard my parents talking. "She's a stupid, stupid girl," Mother snarled as she crocheted. "I do everything, clean up after her take her shopping buy her beautiful clothes. She's the pretty one," she cursed, cackled like the Wicked Witch of the West in *The Wizard of Oz,* "too popular, changes men as often as tee shirts." Her ball of yarn unraveled, slithered across the floor turned into a green-eyed monster, attacked me. I shuddered in fear fended her off.

Dad's bent rod snapped. He lost me. I backstroked away. He was angry, "She *was* such a good little girl, so proud of her then, a handful now, don't approve of her behavior, have to keep my eye on her," his right eye turned green, "I don't want all those men to touch her," so did the left. Dad cast out again.

Jealousy was crawling all over me. I tossed and turned finally in the world's greatest bed, stoned and alone at the bottom of the barrel. I'd fallen from grace onto my face. Splat.

14

Dear Mr. Mayor

Dad called me at the office Monday morning the day after. Marsha, the secretary told him I'd called in sick. She called me. He reached me at home.

"What's the matter?"

"Terrible cramps." Terrible liar.

"I have something to discuss with you Allison."

"Yes, Dad." He never called me that unless something was wrong. A feeling of dread overtook me. I braced myself. Had he heard? Did someone rat me out? Oh, God, what was I going to tell him? Why *had I* done it?

"Mayor Lindsay and his family are coming for the weekend in two weeks."

"Wonderful news. What an honor. Great." I relaxed. I'd play the perfect political daughter no problem.

"I want you to bring a date. And Allison..." Oh, oh, still using my formal name. What now? Fearful again.

"Yes?"

"Promise me something." The formal voice.

"What Dad?" He doesn't want me to get drunk. Fair.

"Don't flirt with the mayor."

I was stunned, crushed. Why would he think that? Tears welled up, I put the phone on the table, dug for a Kleenex, wiped them away, picked it back up.

"Did you hear me, Allison?" Stern.

"Yes, I promise," choked it out.

"All right then, goodbye."

The weekend had knocked me for a loop this finished me off. I dialed Dr. Goodman, got his answering service. "The doctor is with a patient. Do you care to leave a message?" I gave my name, hung up.

Dr. Goodman called back, "What's wrong?"

"Don't know where to start."

"Are you in danger or can this wait till our appointment tomorrow?"

Was I suicidal? No. I'd never kill myself, albeit bottomed out. Color it black. "I can wait." I didn't go to work the next day either, paralyzed, suspended in space.

"I'm crazy Dr. Goodman."

"Don't say that, too much negativity. You're supposed to be putting up a fight instead the Imp is walking all over you. What happened?" I told him about my lost-as-in-loser weekend, Dad's cautionary call. "Your bad trip may end up by being good for you."

"What do you mean?"

"It dredged the truth up from your subconscious. You've had a double whammy, both of your parents are jealous, different reasons, you've suffered the consequences and must face that they're imperfect, human."

I jumped in, "Can you believe that Dad asked me to bring a date made me promise not to flirt with the mayor. As if I would. What does he think of me?" His silence my cue to answer the question myself.

"I'm a bad girl."

"'Don't flirt with the mayor' is the tip of the iceberg. The charade is over; you were Daddy's good little girl, the light of his life. When you grew up changed from chubby to sexy and men started to pursue you, he became jealous, as you realized on your 'trip.' Every time a suitor made a pass at his beautiful daughter, a knife in his back. He came down hard and you paid him back in spades. Now he's afraid of what you're going to do next."

A tempest of Shakespearean proportions boiled in the cauldron of my mind, a million mixed up emotions vied for attention, the top three, guilt, shame and despair, "Is there anything I can do to fix it?"

"Start to mend fences. Take a date like he asked. Is there someone who would make your father proud?"

"Tony, but I'm not sure… remember I told you that Mother and Dad once forbade me to see Nick because he was a dope addict and wasn't?"

"Yes."

"Tony *is* a doper."

"Why would you bring him? Revenge for seven years ago? Your father tried to protect you from a singer who most likely had a bad reputation with women, granted a mistake but you've been the big loser ever since, at odds with him. Rebelling didn't get you anywhere unless you think that making sex your priority has been fulfilling. Time to bury the hatchet and quit being a bad girl."

"Okay, dumb idea, I just don't know anyone else to ask." The Pathetique.

"Call your father and tell him the truth, there's no one. Sound sorry."

"He won't believe me."

"Come from your heart."

Dr. Goodman cleared his throat again, more bad news. What was left? "Quit smoking marijuana, it doesn't agree with you, exacerbates your bad decisions."

"I won't." Defiant, Custer's last stand.

"You can for a while," the indefinite future.

"No, I can't." No sex, no pot, no fun or escape. It would be a hard day's night … and day.

"We will not be able to continue our sessions if you don't." I was cornered, nodded my head yes, reluctant. Hell, I was going into the trenches without armor.

I climbed the grueling five flights to the apartment that I was housesitting for a friend -- more like a modern art museum for his multi-million art collection. The only things I owned, my clothes. I opened the Medeco, two more locks dazed, a deer in headlights. I sat on the fuchsia and chrome couch and reviewed the session. I flashed on 'doing it' with Freddy in front of him, hung my head ashamed, Daddy's big bad girl, indeed. I had to get unstuck, stop the record going round and round in the same groove. I was at the bottom of dark, dangerous water, weighted down by a sinker, a distant ray of light glimmering. I took a deep breath, snipped it pushed off, started to stroke towards the surface. A survivor.

I told Dad the no date news, promised him not to flirt with John -- on a first name basis with the mayor. Lindsey had awarded Dad a plaque with the New York City seal for settling the hospital strike. The family was proud witness to this honor. John squeezed my hand as we stood lined up for the official photo. I was incredulous. He couldn't be coming on -- the mayor! In front of Dad! I got the message, pretended I didn't. I'd have to keep him at bay, had given my word. I breathed a sigh of relief, the honest communication hadn't killed me.

After a few days of the vapors I returned to S & G retroactively angry that they hadn't given me the Richardson bonus; nor had I received a raise in over a year. It was time to move on, the unwritten law -- needed to land another job first. I called Becky made plans to give her my grass -- if I had it, I'd smoke it -- asked if she could get me into DDB. The advertising business was a merry-go-round, everyone rode from one agency to another, lied about their salaries to up the ante. If anyone could swing it, Becky could. When the going gets tough, the tough get going.

She came through, got me an interview with Fred Butler, the head of personnel. He gave me a hard time, wanted to discuss the job over a drink, all over me, smarmy. The first woman account executive at DDB, a 'suit,' I'd be 'on' Burlington Industries, a fabric manufacturer based in Greensboro, North Carolina and the Cameo account, *The Little Something* and *The Little Nothing* their brands. Stockings and pantyhose billed millions of dollars in TV, print and radio. Fred assured me there'd be room for creativity in promotion. I fended him off determined to get a job on merit, no nookie. I hounded him, called twice a day for a week until he gave up and offered $12,000 a year, a third of what men made, still a big raise. I wondered if I'd like big agency business cut off from the fun of casting, styling and producing, put my worries aside, grabbed the brass ring, my star rising. Giddy up.

I called Dad, proud. So was he, "Good girl." What a feeling. The diamond tiara sparkled, light radiated out like the Columbia pictures logo.

Stein and Gaetano were not happy campers, but wouldn't hold a grudge -- it *was* DDB where they'd started. I couldn't leave them in the lurch, said I'd stay till I wrapped the rest of the ads. I informed Ed I'd start the week after Labor Day, in the driver's seat, called the shots, a valuable sought after commodity -- I knew fashion *and* business.

On martini three at our farewell Orsini lunch, Ellen cried into her cups, Crompton would miss me. We'd had a great run.

My next session with Dr. Goodman was a doozy. I wanted to talk more about Dad, pulled my resentments out of the bag, "He's always working, never had time for me," stuck in my craw.

"From what I gather, his mother...."

"Georgiana."

"Came to New York from Argentina for an arranged marriage with your grandfather."

"Isaac." Dr. Goodman was climbing Dad's family tree. I welcomed his insights.

"After his dad died, only eight, his protector gone, he shut down in self-defense, love deprived, smothered by his mother and four emotional older sisters. He filled his black hole with work, work and more work, fishing, the one place he can be alone." I saw Dad in a new light. "When your aunt introduced them he fell for your mother, hook, line and sinker. Strong. Independent, big personality, dominating..."

The parallels were remarkable, "Great gams, small."

"He married his mother. They fought to dominate your poor Dad, a wounded warrior." No wonder Mother had despised Georgiana -- she was competition. "Your mother runs him. He runs away to work." Dad was on the lam. I got it.

"What now?"

"Forgive him for not having time for you or your brother, accept him the way he is -- work is his life and he'll never change. Eliminate his anxiety, don't flirt with the mayor or anyone else when you're around him, it's like pouring salt in a wound." Ouch.

Tomorrow was the big day, the Lindsay family finally coming to our new home in Seaview, next door to Ocean Beach, a world away. There was a food store, ferry service, no 'downtown.' The houses closest to Ocean Beach were old-fashioned, the eastern end, modern. Our low slung, Bauhaus style glass house was grey, white trim, 'Sans Souci, East' -- still no pun on Abrams -- third house from the beach. I couldn't fault the location or amenities: sun deck, flower garden and birdbath, five lots on each side, a tennis court or a swimming pool someday, room for both. Topsoil, gardens and flowers, grass, Jewish upper middle class, Seaview was a summer Scarsdale. I missed our funky house felt trapped in a rich ghetto, not my cup of tea but my opinion didn't count.

The grouper takeover had driven Mother and Dad out, their exodus inevitable, as Ocean Beach metamorphosed into Coney Island. Fishermen's shacks meant for four swelled to twelve on weekends, reflectors and gold chains rampant at the beach by day, makeup and hair grease by night. Mother referred to them variously as 'the element,' lower class, 'Bridge and Tunnel', 'BBQ' (Brooklyn, Bronx, Queens). She summed it up, "Not our kind, dear."

When they first told me of the move I asked Mother if Dad was going to mind giving up being a judge, "He served the Ocean Beach community long enough, it's time for him to get into Seaview politics, they need him more, have already asked him to go on their board."

They were out at a round of Friday night parties. I stood in the immaculate white kitchen afraid to touch the pristine counters and appliances, wished we could go out for dinner instead of cooking, never my forte. Billy lounged on the white leather couch in the white living room, his girlfriend

Casey, Rapunzel locks framing her Ford Model face, set the oval Saarinen pedestal table, six tulip chairs neatly tucked in. They were staying at the Greene's -- separate bedrooms, farmed out by mother, not enough room for us all to sleep in the four-bedroom house. I'd moved to the maid's room in the back, John and Mary would stay in mine, their daughter in Billy's.

Time to preheat the broiler for the steak. I'd never seen an electric stove, and was bewildered by its mysterious buttons, afraid to push the wrong one. Casey came to help. If our conversations so far had not revealed an intellectual giant, she certainly was a looker: perfect features, blue eyes, that blonde mane. I could see how well she'd photograph.

"I'm pretty sure I know what to do. There was one like this in Eileen's house, (as in Eileen Ford, the owner of the model agency) in West Hampton last weekend. Here, I'll do it."

"How do you like it out there?" An edge crept into my question. According to Women's Wear Daily, 'the Hamptons' were 'in' and Fire Island was 'out'. I should have taken a house in Southampton when I had a chance instead of insisting on that damn Glass House.

"Cool. Eileen didn't want me to go to the beach and overexpose my skin, we played tennis and hung out at the pool, went dancing at Alan Patricof's super psychedelic disco L'Oursin in Southampton. Everyone was there. Bobb Goldsteinn's "Lightworks" are amazing -- films, lights, slides and sounds come at you from every direction," later to be called The Joshua Light Show. 99.9 % pure unadulterated envy.

"I'm starving. Let's cook that steak." 'Let's' for Billy, meant you and Casey cook the steak while I wait until it's ready in the living room watching the baseball game on TV.

"Got it Casey." I put the steak on the coils of the broiler under the oven and joined Billy in the living room where the Mets were losing again.

"Do you smell something funny?" Billy was alarmed. Smoke! We raced into the kitchen, opened the broiler, "Fire!"

"Get out of the way." Billy pushed me aside, grabbed two dishtowels one in each hand that caught fire as he attempted to get the steak. He tossed them into the sink, turned on the faucet, wrapped wet towels around his hands. "Let's put the flames out. Hurry."

I filled a glass with water, threw it on the coils. Nothing happened. Casey emptied another glass. No help. Billy seized the fire extinguisher and sprayed gobs of foam until the fire finally died.

There was only a brief moment of relief before anxiety engulfed me. "Mother! She can't see the kitchen this way." Casey and I scrubbed and sprayed until everything looked white and shiny again and the kitchen would pass inspection.

Billy said, "Can we eat now, I'm starved?" I was hungry, too. Casey lost her appetite -- that particular affliction unfortunately had never possessed me. "Anyone care for charcoal broiled steak?" Billy's joke was not funny.

Knocked out by stress, the sea air, and scotch, dead to the world the next morning, Mother's rage-struck face was three inches away from my head, her voice deafening, "What have you done to my oven? Something's wrong, it doesn't work, you know I have to cook for the mayor today. How dare you do this to me!" She started to cry, shook me, hysterical, "You broke my stove you miserable daughter, stupid, stupid girl. Get out of the house. Get out." She pinched my arm.

I was guilty, no defense, didn't know how I'd done it but I'd done it. I pulled on a bathing suit, grabbed my grey sweatshirt, ran out of the house. I walked to the beach in darkness, hadn't told Mother what happened hoping to get away with it. As punishment I was banished from the kingdom, better, I supposed, than the furious spankings she used to give me.

It was five o' clock on my Mickey Mouse watch, the fucking middle of the night. I wandered the beach. What was I supposed to do, go visiting? 'Hi, I realize it's a tad early but I wanted to say hello.' Where would I go? Who did I know anymore? Only Mother and Dad's friends, those goddamn groupers had chased everyone away. I could go over to Becker's parent's house, 'Hi Mr. and Mrs. Becker. I know I haven't talked to her in years but I'm stranded because my mother threw me out of the house.'

I arrived at the desolate beach, took off my sweatshirt sat down, put it back on, cold. If I'd brought a beach towel I could've taken a nap. I was definitely not a morning person, needed my beauty sleep. The sunrise transformed the ocean from black to gold, purple to blue.

"Hi, Ali." It was Meggy. Hadn't seen much of her after some stupid childhood argument, cool in spite of our many connections -- Christmas Jews, Upper East Side, private schools, Smith, our Dads. "What are you doing on the beach so early?"

"Why are *you* the early bird," the old dodge a tricky question with a question trick.

"It's the nicest time of day. I can escape from my husband and kids for a few moments of blissful privacy."

"Kids?" I thought it was kid.

"Brett, Jr. is four and Samantha's two. You should meet them, they're wonderful."

"You working?"

"No. Full time housewife's fine with me. What's with you?"

"Am I pinned, engaged, or going to be married? None of the above, not even close." I didn't think to tell her about my career.

"Like being single?" No. I hated it.

"I just haven't met the right man, not easy to find someone I can be in love with and still be friends." Dr. Goodman had rehearsed me, unmarried at twenty-seven, you needed a good answer. I paid lip service to his clever line in the beginning, now it had sunk in. I specialized in meeting the wrong men who couldn't love, rejected nice guys who could. I suddenly realized I'd done the same thing with Meggy, she'd been too nice, wasted my time with nasty Becker instead. Katerine was still M.I.A.

"I see. They say you've been summering at the other end of the island." No secrets on the beach.

"Bayberry Dunes."

"Where's that? I've never heard of it. How do you like it there?"

"The Eastern most community, it's finished."

"What do you mean?"

"Condemned, not part of the National Seashore, don't think I'll go back next season." If ever, decadent, doomed, dammed, over was over.

"You still haven't told me why you're up so early."

I explained what had brought on Mother's wrath.

"You must have shorted the stove by putting the steak on the electric coils *under* the oven which are used for heating, rather than in the broiler which is the same compartment as the oven -- you just flip the switch," easy for her, a Phi Beta Kappa. "I see you're not big on home ec. I'm sure someone can fix it. Want to come by?" Great offer, too awkward, they weren't invited to tonight's party.

"No thanks Meggy. Can you stay a few? I'm dying to hear some hot or cold gossip." She nodded, yes. "Is Sean still hanging around with young girls?" Jordan's friend had tendencies.

"Infants," she shrugged her shoulders, "Do you ever see Nick Rose?"

"Not since he got married." He'd eloped two months ago, married a singer he met at Peter Lawford's infamous as in Marilyn-had-a-tryst-with-JFK-there Santa Monica beach house My heart broken, no more hope, the sapphires gone forever, extinguished. I'd never get over it. Couldn't talk about it.

"So famous."

"No kidding." Tried to sound casual.

"By the by, what your mother did is disgusting and doesn't surprise me, she's known as the bitch of the beach. Frankly, I've always been afraid of her." She dropped the bomb politely, "Pardon my saying it but you have the world's scariest mother, have to go now, you know where we live. Always home, exciting life we lead, so long." Kind. Practical. Honest. No nonsense. I could see the rest of her life as a straight line while mine curved into a question mark.

I sunk into the sand, stuck. Meggy's condemnations circled like sharks, 'Bitch of the beach.' 'World's scariest mother.' She was afraid of her too. The Imp put Meggy down, 'What does she know?' I put my hands over my ears to drown him out, tossed off my sweatshirt and dove in. Who would throw their daughter out of the house at five in the morning? Something snapped, a wake up call. Oh my God, Dr. Goodman was right, Mother *was* 'toxic.' Where had my head been? Upside down, buried under the sand like an ostrich. Out of the corner of my eye I saw Casey beckoning, caught a wave back in.

"Your mother wants you to know that everything's under control and you can come back for breakfast." Safe to return. No, it wasn't. Ever. "Something wrong?" What wasn't?

Mother took me aside to inform me in no uncertain terms that someone had to come all the way from the mainland to fix the stove. It had cost one hundred and thirty five dollars. I'd not heard the end of it. For the rest of the day she gave me a wide berth as if I had the plague.

We met the mayor's wife Mary -- we should call her Mare, and kids at the Zeeline dock They'd taken the 10:30 ferry. The mayor would arrive by helicopter on the beach at 2:30. We ate a buffet lunch on our deck -- white chaises, grey wrought iron chairs, white umbrella, and wood buckets full of deer proof orange zinnias and marigolds. I delved into the *Salade Niçoise* and overate Greenberg's brownies and *schnecken*, small Jewish sweet buns that looked like snails, the translation from German. The stove fixed, everything was going according to schedule except for overcast weather and the daunting realization that my mother was the scariest mother alive.

Mare was regular, unpretentious, enthralled by Fire Island. She complimented Mother on the house, decorating, and food. A perfect politician's wife, she had the knack of making everyone feel comfortable under any circumstances. Except for me.

"Wait till John sees this place. We've heard so much about your beach."

"They say it's one of the ten most beautiful in the world. We've travelled three continents, but never matched it." Another politician's wife, Mother made a provocative statement, opened the door for comparisons. As I studied her face it morphed into the grotesque mask top right of Picasso's *Desmoiselles d'Avignon* I'd always hated. The frightening image faded.

Billy picked up the gauntlet and ran with it. "I like the Greek islands; Rhodes was glorious. I want to go to Tahiti and Bali." He'd get there.

"I prefer the *Costa Smeralda* in Sardinia." For a twenty year old, Casey sure had been around. Women's Wear kept showing pictures of all the B.P.s (Beautiful People) frolicking there in the 'Eye' column. I tried to contain my jealousy again. "We shot the collections there last year. Makena Beach in Maui is truly exotic." Triple threat: gorgeous, thin and well travelled.

"Acapulco was beautiful before they overbuilt it," I stuck in my two cents. "My favorite is still Sandy Lane in Barbados, that crescent beach, turquoise water, the skin diving." And Andy, my lost love.

As always, Dad listened quietly. When everyone finished their comments he added, "The most beautiful beach of all was Veradero in Cuba: the whitest sand, the finest fishing, the nightclubs, dancing, cigars...bah, I'll never forgive Fidel." Another loss in the same league as the Dodgers' betrayal. Dad had to have friends smuggle in his beloved Upmanns, Montecristos and Macanudos from Switzerland.

I studied Dad, so handsome. 'You couldn't get your father by being good so you decided to get him by being bad.' I smothered an impulse to hug him moved next to him. "I'm sorry about Castro, too."

Bad timing, Dad stood up, "Time to meet John. Let's go." I couldn't rush the process, no instant gratification.

They'd cordoned off the beach area at the end of our walk to create a helicopter landing. Six security guards in khaki with Walkie Talkies and guns converged on us. Mare and Dad handled them. We made a small encampment of colorful striped beach towels and waited. The mayor's family was used to the drill, but I could feel the tension in the rest of us. With a half hour more to wait, Dad left to surf cast. The Walkie Talkies started to crackle. He sprinted back and planted his pole in its sheath, as a helicopter appeared overhead, alit on the beach. After the blades stopped whirring, Dad stepped over the rope.

The door opened, the mayor waved, descending from Mt. Olympus, a tennis racquet in his free hand. Five star entry.

Mayor Lindsay kissed Mare and his kids first, then Mother, shook hands with Billy, winked at me. I stared down at the sand. So what if he was one of the most gorgeous men I'd ever seen in my life: tall, blonde, patrician, Yalie -- just my type. I was going to be on my best behavior if it killed me. This was a test.

"This place looks great from the sky, even better down here," he took a practice swing with his racquet. "No chance of sun I'm afraid, the cloud cover's too thick. We still on for tennis?" They were.

After Mother's house tour he changed into whites ready for the doubles match on one of the coveted three clay courts, four blocks away, a little politics, some fun -- the Mayor and the president of the Seaview Tennis Court against Billy and the president of the Seaview Association.

"Service." John served first, an ecstatic look of concentration on his face. He lost the first point, second and the third. Love forty, Billy shot a look at Dad, we're beating the mayor, what now? I couldn't see Dad's face.

Had to hand it to him, Billy, the world's most competitive human being threw the game perfectly, no one would've guessed in a million years. As the set continued, Billy controlled the ball and the score as he alternated beautiful strokes with brilliant misses for all the world to see -- an erratic player with great potential, imperfect execution. The final score was the Mayor and his partner 6-4, 6-2, straight sets.

Life Game Rule Number One: In politics sometimes one loses to win.

Life Conclusion Number Two: Billy had come a long way.

Back at the house Dad kept 'the gang' on schedule, "Time to get ready for the cocktail party. People are invited for five." He sounded casual. I knew they'd been working on the invitation list for weeks, orchestrating the entertainment and the people to suit the mayor's dual needs. On one hand, he needed economic support -- heavy hitters from the rich Jewish community; on the other, he liked show business. There'd be both.

I put on my fall and new clingy white cotton collarless jumpsuit, left the buttons open in a deep V-neck, black and white Indian necklace. Mother had insisted we shop together, my hippy Bayberry clothes -- jeans and tee shirts, were a no-no.

'People get dressed up these days in Seaview.' After disappointments at the four B's we scored at Paraphernalia, the far out new Madison Avenue boutique that looked like an art gallery with its minimalist interior and tractor seats, a continuous 'happening' frequented by Julie Christie and Twiggy, the superstars of the moment. I grudgingly squeezed into white shoes that hurt, tied on a white suede braided headband. Off to the races.

"Well hello darlin', don't you look gorgeous."

"Hi, Goldie." I stared at the woman he was escorting. Ethel Merman! He introduced us. Miss Merman looked like a birthday cake: canary yellow organza dress, pink, blue, and yellow ribbons festooning her hair.

What do you say to a legend? "Can I get you a drink?"

"Just clear the way to the piano for us honey, we've got some big singing to do... tell me, it's in key isn't it?"

"I hope so, we borrowed it from Charles Strouse down the street," our charming neighbor was the composer of *Bye, Bye Birdie,* the first rock musical. If it wasn't, he was to blame.

"This is my daughter, Steve. Ali, this is Congressman Solarz," my only moment with Dad.

The party overflowed from the living room onto the deck, the island's elite dressed to the nines, tent dresses unfortunate for big boobs, I'd look pregnant. There were Puccis, caftans, minis, bright papier-mache necklaces, dangly earrings, frosted nails, toes -- mine platinum, yes, Mother, they matched; men in sports jackets and ties. Sadly everyone wore shoes. I moved through the crowd nostalgic for the old days, craziness subdued. Three waiters circulated with silver platters of hot and cold *hors d'oeuvres,* two manned bars, indoor and outdoor. Billy had strung lights on the deck for after sunset. Dad propelled John, who towered over him, through the crowd, Mutt and Jeff from the comic strips. Equals.

"Hello baby," the sapphires, hair to shoulders, white tracksuit, sneakers.

I picked my heart up from the deck, "Nick, what are you doing here?"

He cocked his head, "John found out we were visiting the island for the weekend and asked me to sing. Your parents can't still be holding a grudge. I'm married..." He checked me out, looked up and down, "You've missed your calling Valentine, should have been an Indian in the movies." Ah,

Nick, the angels smile down on you, world famous heartthrob and star I knew you'd be. Where was Sandy Taylor? Talking to the mayor, I recognized her from pictures. Nick marched me over, the introductions proceeded; his bride, a voluptuous brunette not unlike me, was a famous singer in her own right. I smiled, hoped to project a semblance of sweetness, sore and a bad loser.

"Quiet, everyone, please." Dad hushed the boisterous crowd and bailed me out of my abyss. "We have a lot of firsts tonight: we're honored to have New York City's first family with us on their first trip to Fire Island, John's in his first term, we hope you'll get to know him on a first hand basis." Everyone clapped. "We have a few surprises in store…let's have a big hand for the first lady of Broadway, Miss Ethel Merman, who'll be accompanied by our own Goldie."

"There's no business like..." her voice had to be carrying to the mainland. No one could belt out a song like Merman. She sang a few more of the mayor's favorites. John applauded and took over as master of ceremonies.

"I'd like to give my thanks to Mike for being such a good friend. Without him as my right arm and ally, the city would still be out on strike. Give him a hand." Everyone clapped. "I have a surprise, please welcome Nick Rose who tells me he started his career here."

Nick sat down at the piano, "You're my funny..." He'd remembered. I missed the thought of him, fantasizing for seven years about those sapphires. Why hadn't it worked with us? My insecurity? Bad timing? No, I'd confused high voltage chemistry, magnetic attraction and electricity with love -- nothing in common -- an impossible dream. Sandy stood next to him as he sang to me, *déjà vu*, wondered if he was thinking about Jean, too. Would never know.

"Miz Ali. Miz Ali. There's a telephone call for you." Gold tooth Alberta, black uniform, white apron and cap, interrupted my reveries.

"Can you take a number? I'll call back."

"He insists it's urgent."

"Who is it?"

"Mr. Sal." Right in the middle of my song, more bad timing.

"Excuse me. Pardon me." I pushed my way through the crowd to Mother and Dad's bedroom, shut the door picked up the white phone that lay on the bed, "Hi Sal. Where are you?"

"Pay phone. Bayberry."

"What's the matter?"

"Tony. Thought you should know. Total Krill Factor. Dead. O.D.'d yesterday. Found in his apartment."

"Sorry, your time is up, please deposit five cents for the next five minutes..."

"Sal? Sal?"

"No more coins."

"What's your number? I'll call you."

"Don't know. Rimskis. Korskoffs."

"Please deposit five cents for the next five minutes." Click. Dial tone.

Tony dead? Had he been mainlining? The Imp interrupted, "If you'd asked him to the party it might not have happened." I rushed to mother's bathroom, dabbed water on my face, toweled off, combed my fall, flushed the Imp down the toilet.

Knock. Knock. "Anyone there?"

"Out in a minute." Mourn later.

Charles Strouse accompanied Sandy singing a medley of his songs. I drifted, unable to connect.

"Hi, Allison." The mayor. "How'd you like to take a walk on the beach?" Holy shit the mayor was coming on, Dad's worst fears come true, what was I going to do? "The party is winding down..." He was insistent. I glanced around furtively, paranoid Dad would see us, nowhere in sight thank God, took a deep breath, "No thanks, Mr. Mayor…" Formal was better.

"John."

"John." You're incredibly handsome but I promised Dad. Think up a good reason. "Sorry," very, "but Mother asked me to help hostess," I gestured at the deck, "still plenty of people left . . . another time." My tiara sparkled.

He rebounded from his bad shot.

"I'm building a brain trust. Mike says you're smart as a tack. If you're interested in volunteering, please call." He handed me his personal card. Ten minutes later he pulled me aside again, "Speaking of the brain trust, I'd like you to meet the man in charge, my right hand, the *very late* Jordan Kaplan." What a night, first Nick, now Jordan. He embodied the height of fashion in a dashing navy Nehru jacket, crisp white collarless shirt, and white bellbottoms. His hair long, its sides pulled back into a ponytail, the rest falling free to his shoulders. The mayor slid away

"You look gorgeous, Princess." So did he -- those glittering turquoise eyes, that dimple smile, tonight reserved, cool verging on frosty. I didn't dare ask why he was so late -- not my business -- maybe he didn't want to see me.

I plowed through the snow, "I have a crazy question."

"Shoot."

"What sign are you?"

"Libra. October first."

"You?

"October first, too. Our birthdays are the same!" I should've known: dimple, dapper, diplomatic airhead. In spite of the amazing coincidence, we walked on eggshells -- he didn't trust me. Why should he? "Let's take a walk." The aggressor, I knew the answer, took a shot anyway crossed my fingers.

He shook his head, "I told John I'd tag along to a few more parties." He turned on his barefoot heels. For the first time he rejected *me,* the turns of the worm complete. I didn't blame him but the same birthday was surely a sign. I pictured Peter O'Toole in "Lawrence of Arabia," riding into the desert to find a lost Arab boy, coming back lips parched, sun blazing, the boy behind him on the camel, triumphant, Maurice Jarre musical flourish, 'Nothing is written.' Yogi Berra's version, 'It aint over till it's over.'

Goldie played, 'The party's over...' The last of the guests said their goodbyes. 'The gang' -- Mother, Dad, the Lindsays, Billy, Casey, Nick and Sandy, Jordan, regrouped, onto the next party. I made my excuses, stayed home spent, the strangest day of my life, what hadn't happened?

I woke up the next morning in a sweat, couldn't shake a crazy dream: I stood naked in the Seaview living room next to Katerine who was dressed. I had a man's body and a penis. What did it mean? Lesbian? I had enough worries. Tony was dead, Nick married, Jordan had blown me off. The house was deserted, empty coffee cups and the *Sunday Times* strewn all over the living room. Early. Ten. Where was everyone? I looked at the neat schedule of events taped to the mirror over Dad's dresser. Gloria must have typed it.

'9:30 A.M. Brunch at home of Congressman Stephen Solarz.'

Mother had let me sleep, a convenient way to get me out of the way. I washed my hair, would let the sun dry it, sucked down a cup of coffee, and retrieved my favorite sections, *Arts & Leisure, Weddings, Style, Book Section.* Someone had started the crossword puzzle in the *Magazine.* Damn. I sat on a deck chaise, distracted, half reading half dealing with my disturbing dream. I flipped to the obituaries, "Anthony Melvin di Angelo, music producer, 33, died yesterday of a heart attack." They'd covered up the drugs. What a waste. Those poor kids. The Imp voiced Mother's standard sarcastic response to my problematic *beaux,* "You sure know how to pick 'em." Fuck off Imp. Have you no respect for the dead?

I glanced into Mother's full-length mirror on the way to get a beach towel from her cupboard, stopped, stared, surprised. I could see my cheekbones and hipbones, a good girl, no binging. Of course I'd starved for the weekend. My hair had dried curly. Braids, bunches or a ponytail like Jordan?

No. I'd stop trying to be someone else, leave it natural, untamed. Jordan was right -- I looked gorgeous.

The light at the beach was dazzling. I picked up a piece of cobalt sea glass, stuck it into the bikini top, laid down my towel, and faced the sun. A shadow blocked it, the metaphor of my life, Mother. "I let you oversleep." As if she'd done me a colossal favor. She set down her blue beach chair, laid out a blue and white striped towel with tar spots.

"I have something special for you." I dug the treasure out from between my boobs, peace offering -- her favorite color. She glanced at it, shook her head, no, just like the Bakelite vase.

"You didn't brush your hair." Her face metamorphosed into the mask from *Les Demoiselles d'Avignon* again. I stifled an impulse to scream, 'No I didn't.' Barely. Why did I keep forgetting I'd never be able to please her? Run, Ali, run. Can't climb Mount Everest barefoot. I spied Dad setting up for surfcasting, perfect excuse to leave.

I watched while he baited three hooks with squid, delicious morsels to entice stripers -- striped bass, a succulent white fish that ate only other white fish. I'd assisted Dad in the squid cleaning ritual a million times, disgusting looking and feeling. The process was worse -- you ran them under cold water, peeled off the purplish part, pulled out the intestine, sliced the remains into strips stored in an old Vita herring jar stored in the ice box, now in one of the plethora of pockets in his worn khaki fishing bag.

He bought squid from George Stretch's fish store 'downtown' by the bay beach. Haven and hangout of the island's anglers -- they'd catch up with the latest in fish tales, lures, lore and learn where and when 'the fish were running.' Stretch had a crystal ball. The 'weigh in' on his official fish scale kept fisherman known to exaggerate with their hands honest. He recorded the weight, length, bait or lure, size of pole, kind of reel, date, time of day of their catch in ink in his grand ledger for posterity. It *was* written.

Dad finished threading, now or never, "I didn't flirt with John," although he tried, "was upset you brought it up," to put it mildly.

"I asked you not so much on your account as his. Do you remember the City Hall ceremony?" Dad had noticed, Dr. Goodman right. "I saw how he looked at you. I wanted to protect you from his notorious womanizing. Mare is a great gal. I've seen too many political careers ruined by extracurricular activities." Double trouble for Dad -- horrified at the Mayor, terrified I'd respond. Two loose cannons. "Sorry if you misunderstood," enough said, he cast out. The line arched over the water and landed beyond the breakers.

"The mayor asked if I'd join his brain trust -- thanks for giving him the good word. Sounds like fun, I'm thinking about it. What do you recommend?"

"Please do." Dad reeled in slowly and smoothly to simulate the movement of a live fish and fool the striper into taking the bait. "You're a smart girl, have a good head on your shoulders, can be of great help." Wow, a big time compliment and it would please him.

"I was very proud of you this weekend, Dad. I love you." I kissed him on the cheek. "Catch a big one." We'd just had our first talk, easier than I thought. Easy? Hell, it had taken me forever to dig out from the silence of the fifties.

The ocean shimmered, seductive. Tiara firmly in place, I dove in did a back dolphin, went into a tuck, put my arms around my bent knees, touched my head to them, shut my eyes, submerged. The water cradled me. I surfaced, swam east towards the Hamptons, wished I was there.

15

Miss Liberty

August around the corner, I could hardly wait to see Dr. Goodman before he abdicated his throne feeling rocky, concerned about the tumultuous events of the weekend, penis dream front and center, my burning question, "Am I becoming a lesbian?"

"No, not at all, it's an excellent sign of improvement, extremely positive, turning point -- if you have your own penis you don't need to use them to fill you up. Understand?"

Yes and no, my fears allayed, continued down the list, "What about Mother? She threw me out of the house in the middle of the night." I told him the story.

"When will you get that she's not on your side?" He cleared his throat, something was up, fasten your seat belt. "As you've told me, your mother's older sister was 'the pretty one,' she was the ugly duckling -- jealous and angry. She transferred that jealousy and anger to you, another pretty one." He paused to see how I was taking this. Satisfied, he continued, "With your mother in the picture you're going to keep hurting yourself like you did last weekend. She's toxic and is never going to change. You can. You're going to have to cut the unhealthy cords that bind you to failure and doom you to unhappiness."

"And?"

"Divorce her." I couldn't believe my ears. The Imp went nuts, 'That's crazy, don't listen.'

"I don't want to hurt her."

"You have to save your own life. There's no other way. Don't worry about her, she's a tough bird and has your father."

In shock, "What would I have to do?"

"Write her a letter, explain your reasons for leaving and don't send it. Use it for reference when you feel you're losing your resolve. Disappear. Don't call or confront her. If she calls you -- and she will to get you back, cut it short. Don't react or interact, give her a wedge in, you're busy." I sighed, mourning the loss of something I'd never had, Mother's love.

"Are you sure?" I felt shaky. Rocked. Still in shock.

"It's not the end of your life, it's the beginning -- your future. You can do it. You're strong. Look how well you did with dear Mr. Mayor." All I'd done was say no. On second thought, it *was* a big deal. "Your talk with your father is very promising. It must have felt good." Did it ever. "Keep it up." I loved having someone on my side, rooting for me.

Next on the list, "Nick Rose still makes me shiver and I'm sad I lost him."

"You never had him, showered him with unrequited love. His marriage is the period at the end of your sentence. Kiss him goodbye." I shut my eyes and imagined a kiss.

"I want another chance with Jordan, we're meant to be together and I blew it." Last but somehow the most important.

"Join the mayor's think tank. Take a back seat, don't pursue. If Jordan still loves you and I believe he does, he'll come around. Keep your eyes on the prize -- a healthy relationship. By truly loving yourself you can find true love." I wrote this in bold black Pentel capital letters on a yellow pad, stood it sideways on my night table -- first thing I saw in the morning, last at night. My incentive plan, mantra, goal.

He prescribed "good reflections" to repeat in front of the mirror, tiara on, twice a day: 'I'm beautiful.' 'I'm a winner and I'm winning.' 'Who's better than you?' Evidently the brain makes new synapses when you say something out loud whether you believe it or not. I would do my homework, had nothing to lose and *everything* to gain.

The last, "I'm upset about poor Tony."

"Don't give him another thought, bad company. Bayberry's not healthy for you, don't go back."

The Imp resisted, recoiled, 'What will you have left?' I blurted out, "Mother *and* Fire Island?"

"If you don't let go of the old, there's no place for the new." He had a point. Right as rain, the Imp wrong, I put a stick of dynamite, lit it and exploded him. "I'm proud of your progress. You've made significant strides, have stayed off men, pot and overeating. Congratulations. Come September I'm cutting you down to one session a week." Music to my ears, I loved Dr. Goodman.

The brain trust met at City Hall on Wednesday, seven p.m. An ordinary no frills ordinance office twenty-five straight chairs in a double semi circle, an easel in front shouldered a 24" by 36" blank paper pad. I took a side seat, curious and nervous. Jordan opened the meeting on time, "For the newbies," he acknowledged me briefly, "this will run two hours. The mayor may or may not drop by." He established the ground rules: "When you get that earth shaking idea, raise your hand politely, wait till I call on you, tell us your breakthrough in twenty five words or less, I'll write it down," he pointed to the pad. "The key concept, ladies and gentlemen?" He shook his head, wagged his index finger back and forth, a principal warning his students, "No criticism or critiques, you're welcome to amplify, implement." He smiled, that darling dimple sold it, "Ideas need to fly, not have their wings clipped. We'll refine into concepts after." Brainstorming without fear, brilliant.

Jordan wrote the topic for the night on the pad: "How to revitalize and restore Central Park." He gave a brief history. Frederic Law Olmsted and Calvert Vaux's grand design, the lungs of the city -- great escape from skyscrapers -- had fallen from grace. Dirty and littered with cigarette butts, ill kempt with worn out grass, dangerous at night --it was a dump. The Mayor, an avid cyclist, had recently initiated a weekend ban on cars, which was just the beginning.

After ten minutes I got the hang of it, raised my hand calmly, "Turn the water back on in the Bethesda fountain. It's been dry for decades and the poor Angel of the Waters is parched." It would take a decade and a half before she was hydrated. I managed to maintain my cool, 'added on' a few times, stimulated.

As I waved a half-hearted good-bye, Jordan called out and asked me to join the group for drinks around the corner. The local Irish pub where we adjourned bulged at the seams with 'pols' and lawyers and stank of stale beer. Jordan's girlfriend, Molly, one of the brainiacs sat next to him at the bar. She had freckled white skin and the smarts of the auld country stamped on her face. What had I expected? I gave them a wide berth. Like MacArthur, I would return next week at same time and the same station.

I reported the highlights to Dad the next morning. I'd forgotten how smart and savvy he was when he was not being my father. His comments were cogent and relevant. He must have felt the same because he asked me for lunch at the Brass Rail in his lobby after my next City Hall session. We'd found high ground, had a date. "See you next Thursday, I love you."

Dr. Goodman was encouraged by my budding relationship with Dad, but in the same breath urged me to hold fast, and stay away from Mother who, as predicted, tried to entice me back with shopping offers. "Keep your conversations down to three minutes, and have an excuse ready to cut her off." Yes, Dad. No, Mother.

My 'Mission Impossible' assignment which I chose to accept was: shake my bad habits, reactionary behavior to Mother and make 'the museum' a home, three categories: food, clothing and shelter, a trifecta. The first order of business was to brush off the Imp's, 'housework's beneath you' spiel. I imagined sweeping him into a dustpan. I hired Agnes the maid

-- me -- to straighten up, bought a saucy apron. I found a place for everything and kept everything in place. Clean, I love you clean! I bought bunches of daisies from the new Korean florist on the corner to celebrate, wrote a card, 'To Ali, love me,' arranged them in vases, renewed them every two weeks, eternal spring an indulgence I deserved.

Rule 1: Neatness counts. Keep guest ready. If someone wants to drop by it can only take a half an hour to clean up. I posted this on the fridge with a gold star magnet.

Taking laundry home to mother was not an option under the circumstances. I faced sky-high piles in front of a colorful heap of towels and underwear paralyzed by the Imp's refrain, 'waste of time, waste of time,' pictured it clean, my existential refrain, 'you are not your laundry,' flushed the Imp down the toilet. I hauled four bags down, took a cab across to the Laundromat, finished last week's Times Puzzle and Double Acrostic in time for Sunday's answers. Ah, the sweet smell of success and clean clothes, sang a round of the Hallelujah Chorus, amen.

Rule 2: No mounds allowed. Do laundry once a week.

Rule 2A: Have own washer and dryer in next apartment.

The last of the unholy trinity was food, couldn't live on crackers alone. I made a shopping list. The problem was execution. If not bewitched, I was bothered and bewildered by shopping -- too many decisions, hard to plan ahead -- how did I know what I'd want to eat for a whole week? In the aisles and arms of D'Agostino's quality super market, intrigued by their ad, 'Please don't kiss the butcher,' I duked it out through two anxious hours of indecision, even asked surprised shoppers their opinion. Exhausted, I paid a delivery boy to carry eight cartons up the daunting five flights, and literally kissed him. I stayed on Atkins, cooked eggs and bacon, made tuna fish, nothing too ambitious. My staple was the $3.50 roasted chicken from David's around the corner. I could devour half, guilt free and delicious. The concept of cooking school came to mind, hovered then disappeared into the stratosphere.

Rule 3: Never leave fridge or cupboard bare. David's and D'Agostino's deliver. Keep Planter's dry roasted peanuts out for guests. Skippy crunchy peanut butter is off limits. (I'd eat the whole thing.)

On girl's night out at Elaine's, Becky saved the day. "Hire a maid to do the dirty work -- dust, vacuum and clean -- every working girl deserves one. I'll give you my girl Grace." Saving grace. We sang a round of "Everybody Ought To Have A Maid," from Sondheim's *A Funny Thing Happened On The Way To The Forum.*

Rule 4: Never be home when the maid comes. Nerve racking.

Rule 5: Take out garbage every two days, max! No free dinners for critters.

I got an A in Homemaking 101. My pad looked like a million bucks, passed *my* white glove test.

For the first time ever I didn't need a man around, relegated dating to the back burner, a love affair with myself in progress. A new project at DDB dropped in my lap, gift from the gods: write the liner notes for a Brigitte Bardot LP to be cut from the sound track of her upcoming TV special made in France, sponsored by my client, Burlington Cameo.

The writers wouldn't accept the assignment -- a promotional giveaway was beneath them, not the sacred three: TV, print or radio, nonetheless a great opportunity for me. Inspired by Bardot's breathy, sexy voice -- reminded me of Marilyn's -- trumpet fanfare: da, da, da, da, da da, I conquered my writing block. I took track four's crooner, songwriter Sacha Distel's "The Good Life" to heart, and finished the liner notes. I picked the cover photograph, went to the mastering at the studio, proofread the copy, made sure the label read, 'promotional copy, not for sale.' In other words, I produced an LP. One day a messenger brought me the finished album, my baby. *Special Bardot.* The client loved it, gave me high marks at the agency. I bought a gold star, hung it from my 18-inch, 18k Tiffany chain.

Wednesday night was the centerpiece of my week, including the carousing after. I got to know and like Jordan's girlfriend, Molly. She was an entertainment lawyer, fast on her feet, quick with a quip. They looked happy together. I let him go. Completely. Happy to have *them* for friends.

On a chilly November Wednesday, Molly was absent. Jordan slipped beside me at the bar after, "Can I buy you a drink Princess?" I'd given up ever hearing those magic words again. My stomach flip-flopped -- that dimple, those Paul Newman eyes, good spirits, the whole package.

"Sure." Where's Molly?" She had the cold going around, would be back next week *but* they'd parted ways amicably -- a lot of smarts but not enough spark between them. I prayed he couldn't hear the thumping of my heart.

"Let's get out of this dump. Pick a place, Princess."

"Oak Bar? Bemelmans? Trader Vic's?" I didn't mention Elaine's, not private enough, I wanted him all to myself.

We had a Libra indecision contest as we stood outside in the cold, "I like them all."

"Bemelmans." Most romantic.

"Your wish is my command," he removed his black Astrakhan hat, bowed with a flourish, dramatic, Dr. Zhivago. I curtsied, Lara, regal in my great coat trimmed with fur, long black boots, and fox Cossack hat -- a pre revolutionary Russian winter the latest fashion.

We snuggled to keep warm on the way uptown in a Checker, talked about future think tank topics: "Free Philharmonic concerts in the park," "How to bring Hollywood to New York." We enthused about John – "a good friend to the arts".

"Feh!" interrupted Max our vocal Jewish cabbie, as he glared through the rearview mirror, and turned around to verbally assault us at red lights. "That *schlemiel* is the worst thing that ever happened to this city. Nothing works, everyone's on strike. He doesn't know the system. At least Mayor Wagner," Lindsay's predecessor, "got deals done. Okay, under the table, so what? This *nudnik* doesn't know from labor."

"Talk to her father. He's the fixer." Jordan pulled me closer.

"Sure. Sure." Nothing would shut up Max or the other cabbies who would forever crucify our saint.

We nestled at a cozy table at the Carlyle. Jordan ordered a bottle of bubbly, *Cristal* brut, lifted his flute, "Here's to us, Princess." We clinked glasses. As he kissed me, I could feel myself surrender, then doubt as the Imp tried to rain on my parade, "you can do better,'" "you could get stuck with him." I put up an umbrella, relaxed into the kiss and pinched myself -- my prince had waited.

I felt safe with Jordan, bared my soul, shared my battles against the Imp, villain of my life, what Dr. Goodman called intimacy -- nothing to do with taking off my clothes. We postponed sex indefinitely and reverted back to old-fashioned values till we were both sure secure I wouldn't hurt him again. The wheel had come full cycle, *I was* a born again virgin.

We dated like teenagers held hands, necked, ate popcorn at the movies, danced at the chic Le Club where Jordan was a member, bumped into Michael Caine on the mini dance floor in my Mini, his Bond Street blazer almost concealing his big bum. We got all decked out for a Thursday night art opening at MoMA, went to Elaine's after. She flirted shamelessly with Jordan, competed with me, another Mother. No problem. No contest. We saw *Cabaret,* marveled at Bob Fosse's outstanding, outrageous, verging on vulgar choreography and Joel Grey's bizarre, unforgettable M.C. A pleasure to go on the town together a couple, 'Life is a cabaret…'

Dr. Goodman added more homework: repeat three times, in front of the mirror, 'It's safe to be with Jordan.' 'I deserve his love.'

As the months rolled by, I felt more and more certain of us, savored every second of his company, comfortable around him, like family -- except for Mother. One night there were no Imp interruptions as he kissed me good night. I felt a brand new feeling that suffused every pore, glowed like candlelight, and lit up my heart. It had to be love. Jordan, in tune with my every mood through invisible antennas, felt it too.

"Princess, are you ready for us?" Was I ever.

We registered as Mr. and Mrs. Kaplan at The Plaza. Our sumptuous 16th floor suite had a splendid Northern view of Central Park. Jordan ordered champagne and chocolate. We smoked a joint -- it had been a long, long time, took separate showers. I slipped on a white satin Jean Harlow nightgown and a satin and lace negligee. Jordan set the stage, lowered the lights and lit a candle. I began to get nervous -- maybe he wouldn't like my body, Jean was longer and thinner -- oops, I booted the Imp out of my head.

Jordan kissed me, repeating how much he loved his beautiful Princess, a melody. He entered me, "Open your eyes look at me."

"I see you Jordan," wanted to memorize the moment -- not sport sex, a stray cock to fill me up -- his heart, mind *and* body connected to mine, in love for the first time. I felt secure in his smooth, strong arms, surrounded by his beautiful body -- a perfect fit, turned on by his soul. I shuddered with pleasure as he told me his plans in advance, "I'm going to tongue your ear, tweak your nipples, devour those beautiful breasts." He wanted to know what excited me. I told him shyly I liked to be on top. He rolled us over, coaxed me, "Princess, you're almost there." He knew when, I obliged. We came together.

The next morning Jordan caressed my breast, "Morning Princess. Sleep well?"

I pushed his hand away, realized what I'd done horrified, "Help, I'm having an Imp attack."

He jumped out of bed pulled on his black jockeys, put his tie across one eye pirate-like to improvise an eye patch, began to brandish an imaginary sword. "Avast you varmint. Don't you dare mess with this beauty's head or I'll have you drawn and quartered, make you walk the plank and keel haul you." He had an imaginary duel, ran the Imp thru and thru, kicked then stomped on him. "Now die blackguard."

So light on his feet, funny, out tumbled, "Oh, Jordan my Captain, I love you." by accident. There are no accidents.

"Aha, my lovely wench, allow me to reward you for your favor." He kissed me. "Perhaps you should reward me…" We went back to bed.

Under Dr. Goodman's auspices I moved in with him the next month, kept my old phone number, didn't tell Mother and Dad. Jordan sold his novel, *War Games,* a political thriller, for a good chunk of change -- movie rights, too, more than enough to decorate his new brownstone on East 64th, the prettiest block in town, in style. He quit Simon and Schuster, worked on a new novel, hunt and pecked away on his trusty Smith Corona electric portable. He liked to cook or we went out, thrilled to play house, the Imp banished from our magic kingdom.

After the promo fountain dried up at DDB, I discovered that the business of big business was not a pleasure. There were too many numbers and the buys and contracts of television were a nightmare. Far from the fashion world, no shoots, casting, or styling -- nothing creative, used to having my hand in the pies while they were being made, not just selling them,

I was bored. Jordan and I talked about it as we took a bubble bath toe to toe in his claw foot tub.

"I signed on to be a suit, now I'm stuck. I might be able to learn but my heart isn't in it. Most of these guys went to business school. I love DDB but hate my job, what would you do?"

Jordan turned on the hot water added pine-scented bubble bath, whistled, 'I'm forever blowing bubbles,' "Write. You have your own voice and talent." He would know. "Become a copywriter. If not at DDB then somewhere else. I'll buy you an IBM Selectric," the latest, it had a ball instead of a typewriter ribbon. "We can make the second bedroom into your office. All you need is a portfolio. The Bardot LP is a start. Take some of the Crompton ads you wrote, tear some ads you don't like out of the *New Yorker, Times Mag.*, the women's pubs, and do them better. Write a 'spec campaign,' board a TV commercial."

"How come you know so much, smarty pants?" I splashed him.

"Dan, my friend from Simon and Schuster, great guy, I'll introduce you, was an assistant editor and had trouble making ends meet. Over six months I watched him put together a portfolio and get a job as a copywriter at Young and Rubicam. He works on his novel early morning, writes jingles by day, brings home the bacon at night. That boy is poor no more. He says the ad biz is wide open -- they're looking for talent. A 'book,' plus a TV reel is the currency, how you show your wares and sell yourself. Andy locks one away -- worth sixty grand, keeps tweaking it, speaking of which..." Jordan tweaked my nipples -- electricity bolts shot through me.

Lucky, lucky me -- just what the doctor had ordered, bright shiny spirit, best friend, cheering section and the world's greatest lover -- I would know.

"Fabu idea." I'd taken to overusing the shortened version of "fabulous." "Do you really think I can?"

"Of course. You can have anything you set your sights on, Princess… you got me back." Two writers, why not? Jordan gave me a soapy kiss, put his fingers inside me, "Hmmm. Mmmm. You're all wet," pulled me onto him whistled, 'Pretty bubbles in the air.'

What was the perfect food to lick off each other's bodies? This was the salacious question we pondered roaming the super market aisles on a sexy, shopping safari. Jordan picked Reddi-wip whipped cream spray in an instant. I finally chose Hershey Chocolate Syrup -- we could have sundaes. I realized at the check out counter that Jordan and I had become the best pronouns in the English language -- 'we' and 'us.' He wanted to please me as much as I wanted to please him, a two way street, mutual admiration society. Food for thought. I wasn't using Jordan to fill me up nor exchange his life for mine -- our relationship a co-creation acquired through hard work -- had no role model. Sometimes 'he' -- watching the basketball game, other times 'me' -- shopping for shoes. Always coexistence without resistance, a balancing act where the bottom line was love. Yes, he could lap up my cream.

One early spring day Jordan asked me to get dressed up for a surprise on Thursday (New Yorkers' Saturday night). Did I still have 'the little black Paris dress'? Of course, would never give it away, just needed shortening. *Merci Monsieur* Feraud.

Jordan looked dashing in a white dinner jacket as we cabbed to our mystery destination, a window table at the Rainbow Room. We ordered dinner, danced in between courses, couldn't keep our hands off each other, "Heaven, I'm in heaven..." Fred and Ginger.

"Curious why we're here tonight?" Jordan flashed a mischievous dimple smile.

"You want to prove that we can have a good time here?" I remembered our date there after that movie star fiasco, years ago. "The prettiest place in New York, why?" Mum was the word.

"Ready for dessert?" Jordan danced me back to my Art Deco throne overlooking night in the city, twinkling lights, stars -- magic. Our waiter ceremoniously lit a sparkler, served our chocolate *soufflé* atop a white doily, adorned by a gardenia on a silver platter. After the shooting stars stopped, I noticed a ring nested on the soft petals of the intoxicating flower. My heart fluttered. Time stopped.

Jordan knelt down nimbly before me, "Will you marry me Princess? I want us to last forever."

"Yes, Jordan. Yes!" My prince arose, took the dazzling diamond from the gardenia, slid it on my wedding finger. The ring and glass slipper fit, the sweetest kiss of my life, we were going to live happily ever after. He cued the bandleader who announced our engagement, Jordan and Ali were going to be Mr. and Mrs. The orchestra played George Gershwin's last song, our first, 'Our Love Is Here To Stay.' The other dancers gave way for our duet on top of the world.

At home that starry night, we took a break from steamy sex to plan our wedding. After deliberations, 'Libra – ating,' we decided on June. Why wait? We'd known each other forever. On the beach where else? Formal -- we both loved to dress up.

The next day, I called Dad and asked if Jordan and I could drop by for an after dinner brandy. We sat close on the red couch in the den. I turned my ring around.

"Cigar?" I breathed a sigh of relief. Dad liked Jordan, could tell by the fat Upmann he offered, the best Cuban smuggled in somehow.

"Thank you, Mr. Abrams, I'd love one."

"Mike."

Dad smelled the cigar, gave it a few twirls, used the cutter to puncture the end, lit a match, spun it slowly to warm it up, finally ready for ignition. "Let me do it." I lit another match, circled the end as Dad puffed till the glow was even, repeated the ritual for Jordan.

"Brandy?" Dad tipped over the gallon Courvoisier V.S.O.P. bottle, an iron cannon on wheels its cradle, pushed the magic button, poured Napoleon's favorite into four thin-skinned Steuben crystal brandy snifters.

Jordan looked at me, 'Now?' I nodded. He stood, struck a formal pose and asked Dad permission for my hand. He spoke eloquently, from the heart. He was successful, a good provider, would take care of me. Delighted, Dad gave us his blessing, a weight off his chest, his daughter in trusted hands. Mother put on the charm. I couldn't tell if she approved. Probably not, she liked men she could control, and Jordan wasn't her pawn, albeit Harvard and handsome. I flew in Wonder Woman's invisible airplane, shielded, what she thought didn't matter. Finally.

Everyone congratulated everyone. Mother oohed and aahed at the ring, 2.3 carats set in gold, a diamond from my best friend. Dad toasted, "To my lovely daughter Ali, and esteemed Jordan, welcome to the family. *Salud, amor pesetas y el tiempo para gozarles.*" Health, love, money and the time to enjoy them -- the Spanish toast covered everything in the right order.

With formalities finished, the nuptial negotiations began. It went without saying that they'd be delighted to give us a wedding, what were our wishes? June. The beach. Formal. Mother reluctantly accepted there'd be no fancy New York club or hotel, grumbled, two and a half months was barely enough time. Dad handled Mother, "You can do it." They'd book Goldie's for the reception, enough room for seventy-five guests, give or take. The big scramble would be places to stay, a decent hotel, hell any hotel was hard to come by. Flynn's in Ocean Bay Park would barely do. We'd have to farm out like at the Lindsay party. Couldn't gamble on good weather, we'd need a tent in case it rained,

Jordan took my hand, his kind turquoise eyes shining. It was real. We were going to have our dream wedding. We could do anything together.

On the way out we visited my blue room, great opportunity to round up strays. I touched my trusty, portable Olivetti in its grey green metal case on my desk, started to open it, Jordan shook his head no I should take him up on the Selectric. I found the teddy bear he'd won at the Fireman's Ball deep in my crammed closet, a keeper; left my cherished, comfy blue and white cheerleading saddle shoes size 8 ½ C for posterity --

how could I throw them out? I took the hex sign from the floor, knew the perfect spot to hang it.

We waited for a cab, Teddy on top of the overstuffed carton under the canapé. I held onto Jordan, would never let him go again, proudly introduced my fiancé to Jim the doorman. It was official.

"Miss Ali doesn't travel light." Jim was a long time victim of my over packing.

"That's the understatement of the year," quipped Jordan.

"Can't you teach her?"

"I never fight lost causes."

As we cuddled in the cab, secure -- we were engaged. I asked, "Why did you trust me after so many rejections?"

"You left me in peace with Molly and got along with her. I knew then you'd beaten your demons."

"Why were you so late to the party for the mayor?"

"I was at Sean's, afraid to see you, but I'd promised John." I knew it.

"Why do you love me?"

"You're smart, fun, beautiful, can't cook, follow my lead, laugh at my jokes, great in bed, and you can't beat me in Scrabble."

"Yes I can."

"And you, Princess?"

"Have a few hours? You're funny, brilliant, sexy, drop dead gorgeous, a nice guy and against all odds, you love me."

Billy sent a telegram from Oxford, ten heartfelt words: 'Great guy Jordan lucky man stop Congratulations Home June 10 Love'

Mother and I went shopping for my wedding gown both on our best behavior, the most time we'd spent together in months. We found 'them' at my alma mater Saks with the help of old display pal Derek. The great debate was trendy lace Mini or long, strapless lace confection. Derek lobbied for the Mini -- super chic, better for the beach. Mother disagreed, the strapless showed off my best assets -- swan neck, sloped swimmer's shoulders. The Mini was too much -- or little -- she didn't say legs were not my strong point. Her no nonsense made sense. Honest, practical to the bone. I heard her, agreed, and chose to be an old fashioned girl.

I'd wear a pearl choker with grandmother Etta's cameo in the middle -- something old; the dress something new. Mother would finally lend me her real diamond and pearl drops -- something borrowed; a garter something blue. We traipsed to the wedding accessory district on west 36th and found a real fake diamond tiara fit for a Princess.

The engraved wedding invitation read, 'Formal and bare feet, Sunday June 26, at 6 P.M., the beach at F Street, Seaview, reception to follow at Goldie's.'

Katerine RSVP'd from Katmandu in a quick long distance phone call -- more than three minutes cost a fortune. She'd stand by me as maid of honor. We caught up quickly. She'd lived with Max for a few years, managed his architecture office. When he put the moves on another brunette she'd fled to far-flung Nepal, got a job working for the Tom Dooley Intermed Foundation. As she waxed poetic about the great cause, "the Dalai Lama asked Dooley to provide medical care to escaping refugees from Tibet..." time was up. I marveled at what an adventurer she was, couldn't wait for her to meet my Jordan.

Two weeks and counting, the phone rang in my home office -- had kept the same line for years in different locations thanks to the magnificent but mysterious wires of Bell Telephone. Jordan was writing away, door closed with "Pet Sounds," the latest and greatest Beach Boys blasting.

"Sweetheart, it's Reggie. I'm back in town. I thought about you a lot while I was in Australia."

"Funny, you didn't write." I cracked, hostile.

"Let's grab drinks tonight, you free?" I wasn't. Jordan and I were going to the movies. The Imp egged me on, "Tell Jordan you're having cocktails with an old friend from out of town. He won't mind." He didn't.

We arranged to meet at the white and gold Café Pierre at the Pierre, a grande dame old world hotel on Fifth Avenue. Reggie looked drop dead gorgeous. Long brown locks, tanned, horn rims, Clark Kent. I felt regal as we entered the Versailles-like lounge with its chintz, damask and candelabras, and guilty -- Jordan would love it. We sat at a corner table, candlelight and champagne.

"Sweetheart, I missed you."

"You could have dropped me a line, a postcard with a kangaroo -- they surely have mail in Australia. I waited and waited to hear from you. Gave up. I thought I'd never see you again." I pouted in the victim position again. Snivel. Snivel.

I missed you so much I came back to ask you something important." Reggie took my hand, "Allison, will you marry me?"

I was shocked. Out of nowhere. "Too late Reggie, too late." Timing was everything.

"Say yes, sweetheart. You know how good we are together." Hadn't that been my line before he left?

"Reggie..." I wanted to run away, direct confrontation not my long suit.

"Spit it out, sweetheart."

"Reggie, I'm getting married next week. Haven't you heard?"

"Who's this guy and what's the story? Do I have a chance?" Forceful.

"What is this the second degree?"

"I'm just trying to figure out my competition." He paused, took a puff of his cigar, "Why don't we elope? I've struck it rich in Pay TV have started my own cable company. We can travel anywhere you want, sweetheart, in style. I'll pamper you." The Imp was gleeful. "Great opportunity. You won't be a princess, you'll be a queen jet-setting around the globe."

"Reggie, I'm very flattered that you asked me but..."

"Why don't you sleep on it?" I agreed. The Imp hit it out of the ballpark.

I tossed and turned in bed with Jordan, kept harking back to the Sugarbush skiing disaster. Reggie had taken me to the top of the slope when I'd never skied before and expected me to ski down, abandoned me at the crest when I couldn't, ruining the sport for me forever. I rummaged through old prescription bottles in a cardboard box in deep closet, hadn't popped a pill in years, but tonight needed to knock myself out.

I cabbed uptown to see Dr. Goodman at lunch break from DDB, my last week there. Ali Abrams Kaplan or Ali Kaplan, hadn't decided yet, would start in a month as a copywriter on Clairol, at Foot Cone & Belding, a hot account thanks to genius writer Shirley Polyakoff, and her line of lines, "Does she… or doesn't she…? Only her hairdresser knows for sure." The pay wasn't that great, a foot in the door, on the first rung. Up to me to perform, show them my stuff. I was psyched.

The Imp and I duked it out in the Checker, room for us both and more. I reran the Sugarbush disaster.

The Imp butted in, 'Reggie took you on that fabulous trip. How many guys have done that for you?'

"It was my fault -- I wasn't a fast enough learner."

The voice of reason interrupted my musings, 'It wasn't your fault. He was selfish.' Beat. Got it. I should have said, 'No, I can't ski down this perpendicular mountain after one lesson barely learning the snow plough on a baby slope. No thank you, you're a sadist to suggest it.'

The Imp snapped, 'He was looking for a companion to share his sport in love with you. This was his way of showing it.'

"He disappeared for three years without a word."

'Making his fortune. A guy's gotta do what a guy's gotta do.' The Imp rebutted.

"I'm retroactively angry at him."

'Give the poor guy a chance.'

The voice of reason cut through again, 'He's not a worthwhile candidate. Despite all the dash and flash he's a cold fish. Stick with Jordan. He's the winner.'

When I saw Dr. Goodman, I confessed I'd been a tad tempted by Reggie, had worked it through and bested the Imp, was sticking with Plan A. Jordan and I, happily ever after.

"Congratulations. I've been waiting for this, you've made great progress but can't move forward without three things: forgiveness, thankfulness, and an open heart. Find compassion and wash away negative emotions before they become cancer of the soul and hurt you. Be grateful every day." He cleared his throat, "Our work is over."

I'd had a feeling that this might be our last session but the reality of losing my sounding board, confidante and conscience -- hell savior, made me uneasy. I took a deep breath, realized I was excited at the prospect of being out into the world on my own two wide feet. I was teary as we said goodbye.

"You've found yourself and will have a fine future with Jordan. Let's see that smile." Dr. Goodman was the best investment I'd ever made.

On the way back, "Cabbie, could you stop at the next payphone and wait a sec while I make a quick call? I'll make it worth your while."

"Yeah, yeah lady but don't gab too long."

I told Reggie 'no' with a quarter in the phone booth by Bloomingdale's. I added that he was right, I should be with an artist --Jordan was a writer.

Dr. Goodman's 'wash away' sparked an idea. I decided to borrow a page from the Jewish New Year's holiday Yom Kippur, the Day of Atonement. I'd wash away all the old things I didn't want to bring into my new life -- float them out to sea to start over clean. I wrote my list on a legal pad, dressed in a nautical theme, crisp white camp shirt and navy blazer, ready for my deep cleansing caper. I told Jordan I had some errands to do and breezed out the door. I descended into the dingy depths of the Lexington Avenue subway, my destination: Bowling Green, the southernmost tip of Manhattan. I climbed out into the strong sunlight, crossed the street to the Whitehall Ferry Terminal, went through the turnstile and paid a nickel for the five mile twenty-five minute trip on the Staten Island ferry, the greatest bargain in town.

A *basso profundo* horn blared as we embarked. I stood at the open bow, smelled the salty sea air and watched the dramatic Manhattan skyline looming in our wake, a picture postcard from my enchanted isle. The Hudson, East River and Atlantic's waters converged, the harbor bustled with energy. The Queen Elizabeth, the grandest, most glamorous ocean luxury liner, pride of the Cunard Line, two signature stacks of red and black steamed into her berth on the East River. I faced the Statue of Liberty, awed as ever, by her green patina, the color of hope, her light a freedom magnet. I put my hands together in prayer bowed to begin the ceremony.

I tore off a slip of paper from my list, read out loud, "Anger at Mother. I forgive you." difficult to spit out, still raw -- it would get easier, balled it up tossed her overboard.

"Bye, bye resentment of Dad." optimistic, our relationship building, cast it into the deep, he'd taught me well.

"Toodleoo Freddy and King, hope we can be friends again, not a trio, a sextet -- everyone married." Easy.

"Alan Gold, please forgive me for not being able to love you back. I apologize poor Peter Gilman, I was possessed by demons, hope you'll forgive my bad behavior one day." I dropped them with love into the water.

"*Ciao,* Eric. Good and bad. *Grazie.* I forgive you. Kicked him out.

Adios Andy. Stopped soul sucking." I batted him out to sea.

"Bad timing Reggie. Still won't ski." I lobbed him overboard.

"Farewell sapphires, beautiful Nick." I hesitated, he'd always have part of my heart, let him go gently into the blue with a kiss.

"Hello Becker. Finally with Jordan, let's twist again." I let her fly.

"Goodbye jealousy. Don't dare darken my door." The destructive byproduct of insecurity had invaded the romantic domain for the last time. I cast it away.

"*Va via* victim, never again." I threw as hard as I could.

Last, but not least: "Good riddance Imp," I heaved, but the Imp wasn't so easy to drown.

"You think you can get rid of me just like that?" The Imp taunted.

"Yes I can. I'm done with you mister misery." I encased him in cement -- wasn't taking any chances -- dropped him overboard, mob style execution. "Don't take it personally, just business."

I felt lighter, bowed my head in reverence, thankful, sent a mental telegram to Georgiana hopefully in heaven: 'Sea change grandma stop Free from your legacy Hooray love Ali.' I smiled, raised my arms in victory in front of Miss Liberty just like the twelve-year old swimmer on the bay dock, gold medal pinned to her flat chest, the winner.

We got married at twilight. The weather was splendid, no need for the tent. Goldie played his jazzy version of the traditional Mendelsohn Wedding March on the little piano the guys carried down to the beach. I held a bouquet of white roses and Dad's arm as he proudly walked me down the steps onto the sand. The guests were assembled in front of a glorious floral arch festooned with white peonies, phlox, lilies of the valley and roses. Meggy's son held my train. Her daughter, the flower girl, scattered rose petals. Adorable. My four aunts, emotional, had their handkerchiefs out. I passed Mother who looked chic and happy. Billy gave me the V for victory sign. Katerine stood tall, beamed. As Dad gave me away, I saw a tear in his eye. Jordan, my knight in white tux smiled the dimple and squeezed my hand.

Lili, our interfaith minister, officiated as we exchanged vows and faced the ocean and our future together.

"I do."

My tiara sparkled in the storybook sunset.

Epilogue

I surface dived into a back dolphin, floated on my back lost in water thoughts, reflecting on the changed currents of my life. I remembered when water was the only safe place. So lucky the tide had turned.

I spied Jordan waving from the beach and caught the next wave in.

Thank yous are in order

I learned how to say thank you in lots of languages including Filipino -- *salamat*, because they *are* the words of words. Over the many years of *Water Baby's* life, 1980 to the present, in deep drawer from '87 - '12, there are many who deserve it.

Dmitri Nabokov (R.I.P.) was the first, calling me an 'upper East Side Erica Jong', my idol, and doing some early editing. After Nick Delbanco pronounced I had a 'voice', he let *Water Baby* into his Bennington Summer Writer's Workshop and has been around cheerfully ever since.

Enter my great friend and fabu editor Debra Scott to help change a rusty memoir to fiction. I'm grateful to psychologist Dr. Robert Botinelli for his brilliant expertise. Earth angel Paula Botinelli was my first reader, cheerleader along with Benny Granelli, Miriam Chavez and Susan Calhoun Moss. *Gracias.* Doreen Mole West Fishtein had the patience of Job and the wisdom of Solomon, as I wrote and rewrote. *Merci bien mon amie.* Marjorie Sudrow has forever stood by in the wings *avec amour* from Paris. Walter Bernard shared Fausta Kingue, divine designer, and has always given a helping hand albeit with a softball glove. I'm grateful for all the tips from talented writer Tom Clavin.

I'd like to send special love and thanks to the Big Apple Yan Xin Qigong group, Lei Zhong, George Pace Yang, Charlie Gong, Mir and Santi and their families.

My pal Russell Mercier took a beautiful cover photograph on a perfect day at the beach. As I took the last lap, the talented Jessica Strauss punctuated perfectly. Last definitely not least, I thank my brother Peter Israelson with love, a lifesaver indeed.

To each I send a bouquet of brilliant Gerbera daisies.

About the Author

Susan Israelson was born and raised in Manhattan and is a graduate of Smith College. She was a fashion coordinator, stylist and a Madison Avenue advertising copywriter. She is the co-author of *Lovesick, the Marilyn Syndrome.* She writes poetry, the occasional tagline, paints, plays tennis and lives between East Hampton, San Miguel de Allende and Paris.

Made in the USA
Middletown, DE
28 August 2017